In the gathering room were mounted deer heads, snowy egrets, snakeskins . . . and everywhere, birds of prey. . . .

The DeLandes stared at Montgomery and me, all gathered around the Grande Dame DeLande. She was still a striking woman, black-eyed and pale-skinned, long silver hair entwined with a strand of pearls. The rumors of this dark-eyed siren were numerous, most of them shadowy and twisted. One, that the Grande Dame had cuckolded Monsieur DeLande by sleeping with one of her own sons and had conceived a child. And laughed about it to his face. . . .

Into the silence Montgomery spoke. "Nicolette Dazincourt DeLande. My wife." The room was silent for a long moment. Then one brother began clapping, slowly and distinctly. Taking my hand, he bent his lips to my fingertips and said gently, "Miles Justin. The peacemaker." A second brother, still seated, nodded. "Andreu. The Eldest." Another tilted his head. "Richard." Shorter and heavier than the rest of the brothers, he had eyes that were cold and unreadable.

Marcus, however, stepped up to me and pulled me into his arms, kissing me on the lips, hard. His eyes were on Montgomery over my head, and he laughed low, like a growl as he released me. "Welcome home, little sister." Montgomery stiffened beside me, and one of the sisters hissed. . . .

BETRAYAL

GWEN HUNTER

POCKET STAR BOOKS

New York   London   Toronto   Sydney   Tokyo   Singapore

This book is a work of fiction. Names, characters, places and incidents are products of the author's imagination or are used fictitiously. Any resemblance to actual events or locales or persons, living or dead, is entirely coincidental.

An *Original* Publication of POCKET BOOKS

A Pocket Star Book published by
POCKET BOOKS, a division of Simon & Schuster Inc.
1230 Avenue of the Americas, New York, NY 10020

ISBN: 0-671-89153-7

First Pocket Books printing August 1994

10 9 8 7 6 5 4 3 2 1

POCKET STAR BOOKS and colophon are registered
trademarks of Simon & Schuster Inc.

Stepback art by Joanie Schwarz

Printed in the U.S.A.

To Bobbie Joyce Hennigan Prater Turner, my mother. For showing me what true strength is. For showing me how to survive in an unfair world with dignity and courage and faith in God. For standing by me all these years. For being my biggest fan. I love you.

Acknowledgments

My thanks to all the following:

Ronald A. Rossitto, First Assistant District Attorney, Calcasieu Parish, 14th Judicial District, Lake Charles, La., for advice on legal procedures in Louisiana.

Isom Lowman, M.D., for medical advice on rape exams, and Guy Kahler, M.D., for medical terminology.

Scott Pfaff, Curator of Herpetology, and Zerry Pollock, at RiverBanks Zoological Park, Columbia, S.C., for information on cottonmouths, and the breeding habits of alligators.

Betty Louise Cryer, of Westlake, La., for advice on dolls, and for letting me use both her and two of her dolls in the novel. The dolls are stunning. Her studio is in Westlake. My thanks for letting me place her in New Orleans.

Irv Eisenberg, of Bonsai Unlimited in New Orleans, for advice on bonsai, and permission to use his name in the book.

Any errors in legal, medical, or technical matters should be credited to my poor understanding rather than to these excellent individuals.

My thanks also to:

Mrs. Erine Bergeron Wheeler, of Westlake, La., for her time, her willingness to share her French accent, the stove key, and the recipe for homemade soap. Thanks for the bar of soap!

ACKNOWLEDGMENTS

Judy Thibodeaux Feagin, of Westlake, La., for sharing her French accent, and for making me welcome in her home.

Bruce R. Simms, president of Van's, for permission to use the restaurant in the novel. Great Onion Rings and Fried Oyster Po'Boy!

Hoyle Byrd, Jr., and Peter Thomas, owners of Petunias, for permission to use the restaurant in the novel. My thanks to Hoyle, R. Rip Naquin, and Jay Loomis for making my visit so delightful. The *pain perdu* was out of this world!

Kathern Hege, of Hege Jewelers in Rock Hill, S.C., for advice on diamonds.

Mike Prater, for advice on stocks, for being my computer specialist, for help with classic cars, and for getting me through the tightest deadlines. I couldn't have done it without you!

Bob Prater, my father, for advice on the Basin, and the bayou, and for catching that small thing about the .38.

Rod Hunter, my husband, for the information on the 1930 Cord L-29 Cabriolet. And for eating four months' worth of cold suppers.

Sgt. Gary Leveille, of the Charlotte Police Department, for advice on weapons.

Jack "Mad Dog" Hunter, for advice on weapons. Thanks for the SIG. It worked.

Kenn Cruse, of Cruse Vineyards, Chester, S.C., for permission to use his wine in the book.

Vera Duhon, of Lake Charles, La., for the proper spelling of coon-ass.

Ronnie McWaters, for teaching me to talk "Yankee."

Margie and Jim Crump, of Mobile, Ala., for making us welcome in your home.

Jane Chelius, my editor, for making this book so much stronger, and for telling me about cats and medications.

Jeff Gerecke, of JCA Literary Agency, for believing in me. And for loving the game so much.

BETRAYAL

PROLOGUE

My name is Nicolette Dazincourt DeLande, and I have committed murder.

How do you synopsize a life, I wonder, cut it back and down, hacking into it like an untamed wisteria, rampant with lavender blooms, tendrils all coiled around and choking. How do you trim and clip the lush foliage of a life, making it docile and compliant, conformed to a foreign shape and structure. What kind of life is that . . . colorless and staid, to fit a mold of another's making. Yet . . .

Do you have any idea what a southern girl is taught to do? Not a big-city girl, but a girl from Cajun country, a girl from the swamps, south and west of New Orleans, just off the Atchafalaya River. My daddy was a veterinarian, and not a rich one either. So by the time I was twelve I was equally proficient with Daddy's shotgun and Mama's old zigzag Singer. I could embroider, run a trotline—a catfish line—gig for frogs, crochet an afghan, spin-cast for bass, and handle the vet clinic in a pinch. I could splint a dog's broken leg, weigh him and dose him with morphine to hold him till

Daddy got back, make X rays, birth puppies, kittens, or pigs, perform the Heimlich maneuver or CPR on a choking or electrocuted pet, put a damaged one to sleep, calm the owners, collect the fee, and send them away satisfied. I could play the flute, which I hated, draw, write bad poetry, speak passable French, sing in the church choir, and cuss fluently, albeit under my breath and never out loud. I could do all that. And it was a damn good thing.

I met Montgomery Beauregard DeLande when I was still a gawky teenager, climbing trees and playing Tarzan and Jane and army. He was tall and redheaded, with blue eyes and a lanky frame that captivated all the girls in Moisson. He had a knife scar over his right eye and another that marked his collarbone. That scar peeked out, along with a tuft of curly red chest hair, whenever he was playing softball, or working with Henri Thibodeaux bent over the hood of a restored antique Ford. And he had a smile that would light up a dark room better than the finest crystal chandelier.

Montgomery was an older man. Twenty-two if he was a day. He was one of the DeLande boys from Vacherie, a town halfway to New Orleans. And God knows I would have given my soul to have him just look at me once. I almost did. I may have.

CHAPTER

1

Life never was easy in south Louisiana, except for those wealthy enough to make the choices and purchases that changed the life-style. My daddy wasn't one of the lucky ones born to wealth and prominent social position. And the fortune he'd hoped to make with the oil boom of the early seventies died along with his investments and the family reputation, sinking into the mire of the Louisiana landscape. Oh, we never did without. We always had plenty to eat, even if it was pulled or netted from the freshwater Grand Lake Swamp or the river basin. And we always had enough to wear, even though it was only copied from a fashion magazine and sewed together on Mama's worn-out Singer.

We lived in a little town called Moisson, near Loreauville, Louisiana, inside the Atchafalaya River Basin. Baton Rouge was northeast, a good two-hour drive for those with the car, the gas, and the inklin' to travel. New Orleans was due east, with its multiple societies and closed social order. But no one I knew belonged to either the courtly, aristocratic society or the swarms of the debauched, roaming the streets of the French Quarter seeking thrills by night.

When I was twelve Mama came into her inheritance, and thereafter we spent each hot July in New Orleans, soaking up the culture Daddy had in mind for me to marry into. Mama was a Ferronaire, of the New Orleans Ferronaires, and had married beneath herself both financially and socially when a Dazincourt wooed and won her at one of the "white gown balls" for the socially prominent during Carnival the year she made her debut. Of course, the Ferronaires always married beneath themselves, everyone else being inferior.

Nonetheless, she and Daddy wanted something better for me than Moisson offered, so each July Mama, my best friend, Sonja, and I ate in fine restaurants, experienced opera in the Theatre for the Performing Arts, and plays in La Petit Theater du Vieux Carré and the Theater Marigny, heard the Louisiana Philharmonic Orchestra in the Saenger Theatre, and jazz in Tipitina's, the Maple Leaf, Muddy Waters, the Absinthe Bar, and Tyler's.

We toured horse-breeding farms for New Orleans's Thoroughbred racing, and the Fairground Race Track even though it was off season, trading on the Ferronaire name and Ferronaire connections. And we visited fashion houses, where Mama looked, studied, and mentally stored designs for the coming year. She was talented with cloth and needle like no one else. If she'd been a stronger woman, she'd have bucked Daddy and opened a shop. But maybe she liked the solitude of Moisson and her dependence on him.

Moisson had society of a sort. Local dances and church picnics and hay rides in the cooler weather of what passed for fall. But the concept of high society was beyond us all. Designer gowns and the private Carnival balls during Mardi Gras simply were not a part of our growing up. Without school, I would never have had the opportunity to meet the types of people who fit into polite society. And I certainly

4

would not have met the types of people who didn't fit into society at all.

I attended the Our Lady of Grace Catholic School in Plaisant Parish from the time I turned nine and Daddy decided I might someday become a beauty. It was his hope that I would attract the kind of man who could lift the family back up into its proper social and economic stratum. In other words, it was his intention to sell me on the marriage market to the highest bidder. Ferronaire connections would admit me to the debutante balls and the Carnival white gown balls of Mardi Gras. The rest would be up to me and the training I received at Our Lady.

It was because of Our Lady of Grace that I met both Montgomery and Sonja. It is ironic that the sisters gave me both my damnation and my savior. I was ten when Sonja LeBleu first came to Plaisant Parish. She was beautiful; a dark-eyed innocent with long, tapering fingers and beguiling eyelashes and a natural grace that put all the girls at Our Lady to shame when it came time to learn the dance steps popular in Creole ballrooms.

I was surprised that Daddy let me learn to dance. A stern-eyed closet Pentecostal in Catholic camouflage, he preached the danger of dancing, dating, sex, and sin most evenings at family Bible study. But that was before I understood about the marriage market and Daddy's designs on my future.

Sonja seemed born to dance. Her feet would learn the steps and her body would move into the proper forms as though she had already known what to do and had simply waited for permission to start. I wasn't half so lucky. Too tall for my years, and clumsy by nature, I had as much trouble learning to dance as I did learning to speak the Parisian French we studied three times a week. In both classes, Sonja outshone us all. And if she hadn't been a worse outcast than I, we probably would never have become friends.

Sonja was the lowest of the low in Louisiana society. One

step below mixed-blood Indians or white Cajuns, French persons with black blood in their lineage were considered outcasts. Practically untouchable. Called "high yellow" and "coon-ass," they had no chance to advance in proper society—unless they were beautiful and accomplished. Sonja was going to become both, move to New York, and pass for cultured but impoverished gentry. *Passé blanc.* Pass for white. Yankees, unfamiliar with the class strata so long established in the South, would not recognize nor care about Sonja's heritage, and she could make a good marriage into good green Yankee money. Or so the reasoning went.

Montgomery came to town the year I turned fourteen. I was too tall, too thin, and still suffering—as only the young can suffer—the continuing disgrace of the family name. My uncle John Dazincourt had been disbarred for graft (the monies involved being over and beyond the expected norm for a Louisiana politician) in a well-publicized courtroom scene only the year before. As he was the second Dazincourt uncle to be publicly discredited in recent years, the shame would have been unbearable but for Sonja. She just smiled her secretive smile, patted the back of my hand, and silently stood by me, waiting out the scandal. Even then, Sonja knew when to speak up and when to hold her peace.

Early that spring, as the scandal was at its peak, Sonja and I were eating lunch together on the school grounds of Our Lady, our plaid uniform skirts tucked beneath us, napkins spread across our knees, sitting apart from the other girls in their little knots all a-whisper. Closest to the pitted road, we had just finished our sandwiches and pears, and were wiping our fingers delicately on our napkins, when a motor sounded in the distance. A dirt-streaked antique Ford, its engine loud but smooth, pulled down the road and braked, showering Sonja and me with a fine powder.

A red-haired, blue-eyed man, his teeth strangely white in his dust-streaked face, braced an arm against the open window and leaned out of the car. His eyes fell on Sonja, and as always with the men of Moisson, they stayed there.

"Excuse me, miss. Could you direct me to Henri Thibodeaux's place? I seem to have made a wrong turn somewhere."

The engine roar covered all the sound from the garden, but I could well imagine the giggles and whispers. The sisters had often told us never to talk to strange men, certainly not strange, dusty, gorgeous men leaning out of expensive classic cars, looking at us like he was. Like a fox at bait. But they had also told us to use our manners. And ignoring the stranger's question and his obvious adversity was not the way to handle this situation.

I was tongue-tied as usual. But Sonja, her lashes downcast against the dust, smiled and directed the man to the front door and Sister Ruth, who stood there watching, her eyes like dark thunder clouds. The man tipped his hat—a curiously old-fashioned gesture—put the auto into reverse, and backed up the drive. Distinctly uncomfortable and red of face, Sonja and I retreated to the coolness of the classroom and the giggles of our classmates.

Later that afternoon, Sister Ruth came into the dancing classroom and interrupted. It seemed Sonja had responded in the correct manner when she sent the charming gentleman to the front door instead of answering his query herself. Sister Ruth, her black eyes sparkling, praised Sonja, and by proximity, me. It wasn't exactly the sort of tongue lashing Annabella Corbello had envisioned for us. It seemed the red-haired man had charmed even dour Sister Ruth—no small feat. But that was Montgomery. He could charm the bark off a live oak.

From the first moment I saw him, he enveloped my life, taking over the secret, intimate places where dreams nest in the heart of every young girl. Romance and passion bloom in these dark, moist havens, fantasies of rescue and stolen kisses, declarations of love and fidelity ever after, fantasies nourished by writers like Devereax and Lindsey and countless others who fuel the romantic expectations of this generation of women. These fancies would overtake me at the strangest times. I'd be working in the back of Daddy's veterinary clinic, washing out the pens of the few overnighters or postsurgical patients, and in would stride my imaginary Montgomery. Taking the hose pipe (that's southern for garden hose) out of my hand, he'd sweep me off my feet and carry me out of there, just like Richard Gere in *An Officer and a Gentleman.* Or so a typical daydream would go.

Of course, in real life the puppy poop and kitty vomit would have made walking precarious, breathing difficult, and romance impossible. But reality has little to do with the pirated dreams of a young girl. Montgomery became my life. I even took over the crabbing and catfishing from my brothers just so I could motor Daddy's flat-bottomed boat or the pirogue through the lakes and swamps and tributaries of the Atchafalaya River Basin towards Henri Thibodeaux's place in the faint hope that I'd get a glimpse of him working in the yard on the vintage autos the two men loved. I never got lucky.

Daddy, however, was pleased to see that I was making use of all his training, that I hadn't forgotten the swamp lore I learned at his knee. At least I made one man happy.

I had better luck in town, spotting Montgomery at local dances, escorting one of the parish's young beauties, dancing and sipping punch. I saw him at church for mass, and twice at confession. I went regularly on the same day at the same time thereafter, hoping to see him again. I saw him at the store buying bottles of liquor for one of the parties he and Henri Thibodeaux threw for the parish's young, wild, and rebellious set.

And I asked around. I learned all about this red-haired man with such uncommonly refined manners. He charmed everyone he met, from the parish priest, Father Joseph, to the man who swept out Therriot's grocery store. And I don't think he ever noticed me. Not once.

But when I turned sixteen, things changed. I changed.

One day I passed the tall gilt mirror in the entryway and stopped, frozen. Because the reflection wasn't me. It was Daddy's vision of me. And I was almost afraid of going back and getting a better look. But I did. And oh, God, I was fine.

Tall, yes, but in the way *Glamour* magazine called willowy, with long legs and a slim frame, and graceful as a ballerina. My face was delicately boned, with golden skin and gray eyes turned up at the corners—sloe eyes, they called them—and ash brown hair that was a riot of curls from the moist heat of August. I knew in that moment that my dreams could be reality. I could have Montgomery DeLande. I could. And I would.

Ten months later I graduated from Our Lady of Grace in a white-glove-and-lace-dress ceremony. Montgomery was in the audience. I knew, because Henri Thibodeaux's sister Anne was graduating, too, and it was common knowledge that she expected a proposal from Montgomery any day now.

But I knew different. The Montgomery of my dreams would never settle for some hoyden who would jump between the sheets with anyone who caught her fancy. Montgomery DeLande would only settle for the best. The finest. The most pure.

Thanks to my daydreams and the fact that no local boy had ever measured up to the perfection I ascribed to Montgomery, I was all those things. Pure and unsullied and ripe for the man with the patience and the skill to win me.

That night began our courtship. That night set me on the road to hell.

Montgomery and I were engaged on New Year's Day the year I turned eighteen. If a new cedar shake roof on the 150-year-old tidewater house I'd grown up in seemed a strange way to seal an engagement, no one mentioned it to me. And Daddy was ecstatic. His new son-in-law-to-be was all he'd ever envisioned. A man's man who could fish and hunt and restore a classic car as well as any man in the parish. And he had money. Lots of money. Money he was investing nearby in Iberia Parish in the new Grand Lake Resort. Money he wanted to invest in Moisson. Money he settled on Daddy and Mama in a financial arrangement that was never discussed with me.

I married Montgomery when I was twenty and had my first baby that same year, my second the next year, and my third before I was twenty-five. But long before my wedding day we were lovers.

Sex wasn't at all what I had thought it would be. Oh, at first it was a slow-building passion and the thrill of discovery. But later it became a frenzy and a fury, like a late summer storm from the gulf, drenching and violent. And after it was over, a desultory heat and a feeling of incompleteness.

Passion and desire were a part of my nature, built into my genetic code like the sultry heat of a moist night. There's something about southeast Louisiana and what it does to people. The awful wet heat and the rain and the smell of rich earth bring all the basic hidden needs out, close to the surface, so that passion and desire, obsession and rage, are intermingled and primed to a fever pitch. Always.

My honeymoon was a romantic week in the States and ten whirlwind days in Paris, France. We flew back to New Orleans on the Concorde—me drinking champagne till I was too tipsy to walk straight. As though he expected me to mutate into something strange and alien under the effects of the alcohol, Montgomery watched me with intense eyes. Eyes brooding and heavy with passion. Unaccustomed to the wine, I simply giggled, and Montgomery had to support me through the terminal to the waiting limo, where he poured me still more champagne.

It was a vintage limo, one that had been in the family since the sixties, and had been used in the funeral procession for President Kennedy. Silver-gray with rounded windows and leather interior, it lacked the modern conveniences of today's models, but it made up for the deficiencies in sheer luxury. As though he were starved, as though we hadn't made love in our Paris suite for most of the night, as though the driver didn't know what we were doing behind the closed privacy screen, Montgomery pulled away my clothes and made love to me on the drive out of the city. Over his shoulder, I watched New Orleans slide away.

The limo drove us through the sweltering city and into the countryside, through oak-lined streets heavy with moss and signs of marsh and age, for the final honeymoon weekend near Vacherie. Miles from that small town, we stopped in front of a two-hundred-year-old mansion with a two-story wraparound veranda and what looked like a family crest emblazoned on the front door—a bird of prey with bloodied talons.

A wisteria grew up beside the front door, a beautiful plant with fragrant blooms hanging down and buzzing with bees. The vine was the only foliage not pruned and clipped and shaped into balance with the other vegetation. Instead, it had been allowed to grow wild for years, wrapping its thin, wiry arms around the massive trunk and branches of its host tree. Almost lovingly it had encircled the tall timber, slowly strangling the massive trunk and branches with ever-tightening arms, till it choked the life out of the old oak. A slow graphic of life and death, both sensuous and cruel, the vine ran in long, spidery ropes across the ground, up the trellis, and over the circular porch at the corner of the house, as though if left to its own, it would eventually devour the house and grounds. As though some demented gardener had set it loose to consume the place. It was vicious and savage. I have always loved wisteria, especially this wild one.

Though Montgomery had not told me our destination, I knew where we were. I had been waiting for this part of our honeymoon, and I stared out through the darkened windows at the sculptured grounds. Shrunken from its once glorious past, the DeLande Estate was now five hundred acres of pecan groves, fallow fields, and horse-breeding barns for the DeLande racing stock. One of the few showplace homes spared from the burning ravages ending the Civil War, it was still kept entirely for the personal use of the founding family.

Unhurried, Montgomery helped me back into my clothes, smoothing the wrinkles with a practiced hand, his eyes once again sharp and scowling. "Come on, Montgomery. I'll be on my best behavior. I promise your family will like me."

He stared at me with an unreadable expression, his mouth tightening, and turned away, opening the door into the cooler air of the country. "That isn't my concern," he said. "My concern is that they'll like you too much."

Puzzling over that cryptic comment, I buckled my belt and slipped on my shoes, knowing I had angered him somehow, but determined not to show I cared. I wouldn't start out my marriage being intimidated. I would not become my mother. I wouldn't.

My father was a strong man in both personality and physique. Overbearing at times. Yet many women would have figured out how to live with the man and still conserve dreams and ambition of their own. They would have learned how to assert their own personalities into the home, while still keeping his love. I know. I had done it. The heroines in the books I read did it all the time. But my mother never had.

I smoothed the final wrinkles out of the dress we had picked up in Paris and smiled brightly at Montgomery. He glowered back.

While the driver unloaded the mountain of bags, Montgomery took my elbow and escorted me inside, introducing me to the house, a legendary place of long, cool hallways and twelve-foot ceilings, rich with family heirlooms, old rugs, and priceless art. It was a strange house, unbalanced and unnerving in the eccentric juxtaposition of furnishings.

Seeming to loosen up as we walked the cool, dark hallways, Montgomery pointed out the family treasures.

There were twenty-six tall-backed Frank Lloyd Wright chairs grouped around an ornate Louis XIV table in the dining room, and a collection of antique swords against the wall over the table. The steel had been sharpened and polished till it looked like it was used every day, yet was protected from the damage of pollution and damp by a locked glass door.

On the opposite wall was a glass-fronted, modern Scandinavian armoire twenty feet long and eleven feet high holding elegant Oriental vases and two-hundred-year-old china, still used by the family. The walls were painted matte black, textured with a sponge dipped in dark green enamel. A dark green coated the moldings, and matching green drapes fell twelve feet from the ceiling to puddle on the dark wood flooring. It should have been a dark room, but one whole wall had been knocked out for French doors which let in the afternoon light.

Worn Aubusson rugs covered the floors, and every room housed collections. On the parlor walls hung a collection of Picasso drawings, the modern shapes standing in sharp contrast to the antique furniture; in the music room were two Monets and a grouping of violins, an old Steinway—out of tune—and upholstered Art Deco chairs. Styles, periods, and colors were mixed and matched in odd combinations, with the cool dark green shade of the enamel flowing through the house like deep water, pulling the whole together.

We toured only the downstairs of the main wing, but already I understood that the DeLandes were a far richer family than even the Ferronaires. I wondered what Montgomery could possibly have wanted with me when he could have married into more wealth.

Nine of the DeLande children, several of their wives, and a round dozen grandchildren were waiting for us in the gathering room at the back of the main house. The walls of the room were mounted with deer heads and a Louisiana panther, endangered for decades. Snowy egrets with wings spread, or nesting with their young, and snakeskins moldered on the walls and shelves, ancient trophies of blood sport. And everywhere birds of prey. Horned owls and a half dozen eagles, some now endangered, barn owls and falcons and hawks, all high on a shelf that circled the room above the French windows. All were dusty and neglected. Some looked generations old, and I remembered the crestlike plaque on the front door—a bird of prey with bloodied talons.

Faded, deeply upholstered chairs and sofas sat side by side with austere hardwood benches, small tables—marked with numerous rings and small cigarette and cigar burns— at their arms. Even with the tall ceilings, this room was close and intimate, intense with DeLande personalities and DeLande judgment.

They sat on one end of the room as if our appearance in the doorway had interrupted an informal conference. Staring, they looked us over, evaluating, calculating, all gathered around the Grande Dame DeLande, the faded beauty whispered about over half a state for over half a century. I stared back unashamedly. She was still a striking woman, black-eyed and pale-skinned, with long silver hair entwined with a strand of pearls. Pearl enamel earrings, heavy with gold, pulled at her lobes, and on her left hand was a plain gold band and a monstrous emerald ring. She was dressed for dinner in emerald silk. All this I absorbed slowly, feeling the silence of the collected DeLandes as they studied me.

The rumors of this dark-eyed siren were numerous, most of them shadowy and twisted, with one similar, overriding component. That the last baby, Miles Justin, was not the direct offspring of Monsieur DeLande, but had instead been sired by one of his own sons in an incestuous relationship with the Grande Dame. That the Grande Dame, called that even then, had cuckolded the old man by sleeping with one of her own sons and conceived a child. And laughed about it to his face.

Enraged, Monsieur DeLande had tried to kill her and had instead been gunned down by one of his boys. The oldest at the time was seventeen. The Grande Dame had falsely confessed to killing her husband, but had never been charged, such was the power of the DeLande name. And no one knew which of her sons had fathered the baby or killed the old man. Or so one set of rumors went.

Another set painted her the heroine, saving one of her sons from death by shooting her husband when he went berserk and attacked the gathered family with a hunting knife. According to the proponents of this scenario, DeLande had been cuckolded, but by his own brother.

I was without opinion about the rumors and without the necessary daring to ask Montgomery for the truth. I was also young, foolhardy, and careless, confident in my own sagacity, unaware that I had little. I wrenched my eyes from hers, seeing in their depths that she read my thoughts and was amused, and perhaps a little angry.

Into the silence Montgomery spoke. "Nicolette Dazincourt DeLande. My wife." The accent on the last two words was challenging, defiant, and his jaw was out-thrust as he stared at the assembled grouping. I had accepted his reasons for the absence of his family at our wedding, but hearing his tone now, I wondered.

The room was silent for a long moment following Montgomery's announcement. Then one brother began clapping, slowly and distinctly, though whether it was for me or for Montgomery's statement, I never knew. Unwinding his long, lanky body from the seat of a straight-backed wooden chair, he stepped forward, his teenaged face intent and half-smiling, scuffed boots striking the wood flooring.

Taking my hand, he bent his lips to my fingertips in a gesture that would have been absurd in anyone else. Cocking his head, he smiled and said gently, "Miles Justin. The peacemaker." I had a feeling there was laughter in the depths of his black eyes, laughter that made the scene of greeting farcical. I smiled back at him, relieved.

A second brother, still seated, nodded, green eyes bright. "Andreu. The Eldest." It sounded like a statement of explanation or title, as though I should derive some special meaning from the words.

Another tilted his head. "Richard." Shorter and heavier than the rest of the men, he had nondescript eyes, neither blue nor green, but hard and unreadable.

A man with a rakish smile stepped up to me, pushing Miles out of the way with a rough movement, and pulled me into his arms, kissing me on the lips, hard. His eyes were on Montgomery over my head, and he laughed low, like a growl, as he released me. "Welcome home, little sister. I'm Marcus."

Montgomery stiffened beside me, and one of the sisters hissed. I thought it was Angelica, Montgomery's favorite sister, the only redheaded female in the bunch. Whoever it was, the sound released some hidden tension in the room and everyone laughed, approaching me en masse, for hugs and kisses and a closer look.

Cold and distant, or warm to the point of impropriety, Montgomery's strange family greeted me, while the Grande Dame merely watched, her eyes cool as her smile. My new husband finally led me forward and presented me to her. I could smell the scent of perfume as she lifted her right hand. But instead of shaking my hand as I thought she intended, she merely twirled her index finger slowly as a silent command for me to turn around so she might view me from every angle like a rare vase she might buy. Her dark eyes glittering, she smiled at Montgomery, and he nodded in return. But it was more than simple acceptance, and the hairs rose slowly on the backs of my arms.

I felt fortunate when the butler announced dinner before

16

the feeling could worsen, and we moved together toward the dining room, the Grande Dame on my left, Montgomery on my right. Miles Justin moved to pull out my chair, his smile wry and mellow, mature for his years. He couldn't have been more than fourteen.

The long stretch of table served us all comfortably, the youngest grandchildren having been carted off screaming to eat in the kitchen, as the sun set and cast shadows and prisms of light across the setting. Servants, quiet and elegant in dark jackets, moved discreetly in the dim corners of the room.

The conversation was purely southern, with a light smattering of horses, farming, the world economic picture, and a heavy dose of politics. Yet I seemed to fit in only when I was silent, though I knew a bit about horses and offered an optional course of treatment for a breeding mare with digestive problems. Only Miles Justin bothered to respond, asking for the recipe of the bran mash Daddy used to treat Mr. Guidry's delicate little Paso Fino.

After the "light dinner"—a sumptuous affair with six courses—the family retired back to the gathering room. Here I was silent, aware of Montgomery's increasing agitation. Members of the family came and went in singles and pairs, the Grande Dame the only one who was stable, never moving from her chair, her eyes following each movement, settling often on me and on Montgomery, who seemed to flinch each time he caught her watching him.

Twice when her eyes met mine I glared back, and this seemed to amuse her, but she acknowledged the expression each time with a slight nod. Late into the evening, long after the day's wine had faded, and long after the novelty of this complex and unpleasant family had worn off, the Grande Dame signaled to me. *Come here.* I don't know how she did it. She didn't speak; she didn't motion. But I knew I was being bid forward.

I came and sank onto a cushion at her feet. There were

dozens of these cushions strewn around the room, tassels loose and twisted or molting with age, all made from the same ancient and brown-stained Aubusson rug. I chose one with pale roses and gold tassels, fingering the fringe while this woman stared at me, and the remembered feeling of the afternoon returned. The hairs quivered along my arms and on my neck beneath my hair.

"You're breeding." It was the kind of thing a member of royalty might say to the lightskirt parlor maid just before she was dismissed. Scornful and contemptuous. I swallowed, because I had told no one except Sonja, and Montgomery had instructed me to remain silent about the fact to his family. Obviously he had decided to tell his mother, and she wasn't happy about it.

"No. He didn't tell me," she said, correctly divining my thoughts. "My family has a bit of the mystic about it. Sometimes we know things." She smiled at last, a real smile, the one that had ruled the Carnival balls in New Orleans for forty years, and I understood how she had won the power she now wielded in the lower part of the state. When she smiled this smile, she sparkled, like a black opal with fire at its heart. "When are you due?"

Feeling it was useless to contradict with a lie I knew somehow she would see right through, I said with all the dignity I could muster, "In seven months."

"Did my son marry you because you're carrying his brat?"

The insult was asked casually, as though it were not a foul slander; as though I should answer calmly. Instead, shaking with the temper I have fought all my life to control, I stood. Looking down on her, I said softly, "Your son and I have been engaged for two years. You were invited to the wedding. This baby was planned. I tell you this now because obviously you . . . he . . . told you nothing about me till the moment I walked in the door. I am not some floozy who trapped him into marriage."

18

Instead of responding to the tirade, she laughed at me, a tinkling sound. "Floozy. I like that word. Haven't heard anyone use it in years. No, you are not a floozy. Lineage?"

"Dazincourt and Ferronaire." I knew she could read the anger in my eyes, but she chose to ignore it.

"Oh yes. The Ferronaire scandal. I recall when your mother ran away and married so far beneath her. But your father was a handsome man, and many envied her. Myself included. You'll do. Tell my son he can relax. He's been as jumpy as a whore in a queen's bed all night."

I knew I was dismissed. Montgomery, who was standing right behind me and had heard every word, took my elbow and led me away. We went down two long hallways, one running the length of the main house, the other intersecting it near the kitchens, to our rooms. Montgomery's hand was so tight on my elbow that the feeling faded from my fingers and sharp runnels of pain traveled up my arm. I lost my way after the second turning, but Montgomery never faltered, his pace increasing as he strode, pulling me along an unlit stairway and left, down a final hallway to the lighted room at the end.

It was a sumptuous suite done in forest green and French country antiques, which under other circumstances I would have paused to admire. But I was angry. So angry I was shaking.

Our bags had been unpacked, our nightclothes laid out in some old-world kind of service, and Montgomery slammed the door behind us. Dropping my arm as though it burned him to touch my skin, he went straight to the bathroom. Seething, I followed.

"How could you? How could you not tell them? How could you not warn me?" He carefully squeezed out toothpaste, loading his brush, the water shooting so hard into the porcelain sink, it splattered onto the mirror above. "You never even invited them to the wedding, did you? Montgomery? Are you listening to me?" I jerked his wrist, knocking the brush from his hand, pulling him around to look at me.

His eyes were blazing with anger and with something else. Fear? I turned away quickly, shaking, turning off the jet of water and cleaning up the smear of toothpaste. He closed his arms around me from behind and laughed, a hysterical sound. His arms tightening cruelly around me, he pulled me back to the bedroom and onto the bed, taking me with a brutal ferocity. Frightened, I let him do as he wanted, not protesting even when he hurt me, plunging into me dry and unprepared.

In the books I read, those romance novels of undying love, sex always put a man into an expansive mood, made him smile and try to make up. But Montgomery lapsed into a depressed silence and uneasy sleep, and I feared to move, not closing my eyes till after midnight.

During the night I woke, perhaps hearing some sound, some echo, some ambient breath or rhythm alien to this place, to find two figures at the foot of the bed. I gasped, grabbing for the covers which had somehow reached my feet, pulling the sheets up over my breasts. Richard and Marcus stood there, watching me, and I flushed in the darkness, because I had fallen asleep naked, pinned under Montgomery's arm after the brutal intimacy of sex.

Marcus held out his hand to me and seemed surprised when I shrank back against the pillows. Some moments later, they turned and left, closing the door silently behind them. Beside me Montgomery's eyes glittered in the night, and I had the uncanny feeling he blamed me for the presence of his brothers in our room. Without a word, he rolled over and shut me out. I pulled on the nightgown I hadn't had time for earlier and fell back into troubled dreams.

Montgomery never answered my questions. When I brought up the subject of his family the next morning, he walked out the door, locking it behind him. I hadn't noticed the odd locking system on the door when we came up the night before, but it could be locked from the inside or from the outside, the choice of the one who held the key. Why hadn't he locked his brothers out last night?

Through the bedroom windows I watched the family gather on the back patio for breakfast, seeming like a solemn group, though I couldn't hear their voices. The Grande Dame was seated at the table nearest the French doors, which I realized were the same French doors of the dining room. Montgomery joined them, moving fluidly through the throng to the buffet and serving himself. He sat with a group of girls, and Miles Justin joined them, tossing a leg carelessly over the back of the chair as he sat, his denim-clad torso and boots standing out in the crowd of casually but elegantly dressed people.

I watched as my stomach growled and my breath fogged the window with anger. I watched as the crowd grew and as it thinned. I watched as the Grande Dame summoned Montgomery and Miles. I watched as Marcus approached and the men seemed to become angry, their body movements stiff and tight. I thought they might fight. I watched as the entire family moved away to the left and around a corner, leaving the cluttered tables for a small army of servants to clean. Then I found a chair and simmered, wondering if the entire episode had something to do with the visitation during the night.

Later that morning, Montgomery returned, carrying a tray in his right hand, and holding a bloodied piece of linen and lace against his neck with the other. He kicked the door closed, locked it with his left hand, leaving a smear of blood on the varnished wood. Grinning, he approached me with that panther's grace that all the DeLande men seemed to possess.

My eyes focused on the blood, which seeped past the frivolous piece of cloth and down his shirt. "Montgomery?" All the anger and seething of the solitary morning leached away at the sight of his blood pooling on his collar.

"Yes, my lady?" His voice sounded jaunty, full of life and eagerness, teasing me as he had when we were courting. His eyes were bright, animated. "Is my lady hungry?"

I took the tray, put it on the table by the windows, and stopped, uncertain.

"Well? Aren't you going to patch me up? Or did I wait through two years of nursing school to marry you for nothing?" His right arm clasped me around the waist and twirled me around the room as the blood flowed down into his shirt and stained my skin through our clothes. It was bright and sticky, and I couldn't take my eyes from it.

"Come on, beautiful wife. Do your duty and act as surgeon to your injured husband." He kissed me, his lips soft as they moved over my skin.

"What happened?" My voice was hoarse, and I cleared it.

"Cut myself shaving."

I almost laughed. It was the DeLande charm and I wanted to strangle him for it, fighting to keep all the anger I needed at hand. But he danced me toward the bathroom, mumbling something about Steri Strips and hydrogen peroxide against the skin of my throat.

He was almost giddy when he pressed me finally against the cool of the sink, and I steeled myself as I reached out and pulled the handkerchief away.

It was a knife wound about three inches long, and deep, stopping only because the blade had hit his collarbone. If it had gone higher an eighth of an inch, it would have slipped past the protection of bone and bitten deep into his neck, into his external jugular. The blood-smeared skin pulsed with the carotid, just beyond.

I swallowed and applied pressure with shaking fingers, searching the medicine chest for the supplies he had mentioned. They were there, along with clear, inch-wide tape like hospitals use to hold IVs and gauze in place on the human body. All the while his hands, now free from holding the cut, ran up and down my body, smearing the blood into my clothes and hair and skin, pulling at me and at my clothes, sticking as the blood became tacky. He mumbled as though drunk against my skin, making my job difficult, but I finally got the wound clean and dripped on the hydrogen peroxide. It bubbled deep and Montgomery gasped, biting into my neck and knocking loose the gauze I held.

"Stop it. I need to get this cleaned and bandaged and get the bleeding—"

"And I need you."

"Obviously." He laughed at the mockery in my voice. "When are we leaving?"

"Monday," he mumbled as he maneuvered me out of the bath toward the still unmade bed. "Take off your clothes."

"Tell me what happened." I was bargaining. Montgomery was having none of it. He pulled the damp, crimson gauze away and with bloodied hands pulled my clothes off, pushing me down on the mattress. His eyes met mine, and the light in them made me stop trying to stanch the bleeding. His breathing was harsh and he bit me again, this time on my breast, hard. I stopped struggling.

Montgomery sensed the change in me and became gentle, tender. He looked into my eyes as he made love to me, my body passive beneath his, his blood dripping onto my chest, my throat, into my hair, and puddling the sheets with his exertion.

My breath came fast and hard, not from passion, but from fear; my skin was cold and clammy, my hands and feet tingling. *Hyperventilation,* some remote and rational part of my mind whispered. Montgomery's eyes glittered with a strange, sparkling horror and laughter.

When he was done, Montgomery left me lying on the bed and showered. I could hear the water sluicing against the tile, thudding against Montgomery. Unmoving, I studied the molding around the ceiling, counting the swirls and rosettes as his blood dried on me and cracked. Carefully I kept my mind blank.

I had seen a rabid dog once, brought in to the clinic by a distraught boy who didn't understand what the insanity meant any more than he understood what the bites on his arms would mean later in terms of pain and shots and fear on the part of his family. The dog had writhed and fought and clawed once released, and I had ushered the boy out into the waiting room while Daddy got his gun and blew the dog's body apart. And that dog had Montgomery's eyes.

Dry and clean, his wound bandaged as well as I might have managed and a towel wrapped around his waist, he returned, bringing the tray to the bed. Plumping the pillows, he propped me against them, positioning me like a doll. And ignoring the blood and the stink of semen, he fed me.

I ate, afraid to refuse although I wanted nothing now. And then, still without explaining, Montgomery dressed and left, humming a little tune. The lock clicked.

I spent the entire weekend locked in my room. For my protection, Montgomery said later. Because I was too innocent, too lovely, and too much of a temptation for his brothers, and he would not share that which he chose as his own. Share with his own brothers? Share me?

I spent the weekend alternately furious and frightened, despondent and dejected. I was safe in the room as long as fire didn't break out or one of the brothers break in. But I was bored and lonely and God knows curious. Surely this family wasn't a danger to me. Surely I had misread both the situation and Montgomery's cryptic comments. And the rabid-dog look in his eyes . . . Surely. And yet . . .

When Monday came, we left without good-byes, driving down the curving drive in Miles Justin's antique classic car, the top down and a hot wind tangling my hair. I was so glad to be leaving that relief was a potent pulse beneath my skin. I looked back at the old house, its windows black holes like empty sockets in an old skull, the wisteria kinked and snarled like arthritic fingers reaching for the cavities.

Where just moments before, the front porch had been empty, Miles Justin now stood, his hip casually against the banister, watching. Even through the widening distance, his eyes met mine and he smiled. With all the grace of the

DeLandes he lifted his left hand and gripped the crown of his cowboy hat, one finger in the central dip. He raised the hat slightly. It was a kindness and a jest all at the same time, and I laughed as the drive turned and the wisteria hid my enigmatic brother-in-law from view, his hat still in the air.

I should have known. I should have understood.

CHAPTER

2

The wind was hot and arid, blistering as it whipped around the windshield, alternately sucking the moisture out of my skin, then forming a thick clabber on it, an oily, salty film. Even Miles Justin's fine-tuned, maroon red 1930 Cord L-29 Cabriolet was wearing after so many hours of unending travel. I had lathered sunscreen on the moment I saw the car, with its sleek antique lines, luggage rack on back, old-fashioned rumble seat, and convertible top down to the unmerciful sun. But the morning had already burned away by then, and the SPF 15 took its time about going to work. The overhead sun had pinkened my face and shoulders, my hair had been thrashed by the wind until it loosed from the braid I had started out with, and I was so miserable, I wanted to cry.

Montgomery, morose and controlling a barely concealed anger, and ignoring my tentative attempts at communication, hadn't spoken to me since rising from the French country bed. The one time I tried to touch him, he flinched away and moved his arm across his lap. Although I was no longer confined to our room, I was still a prisoner.

The anger I had initially felt at the incarceration had been snuffed out during the solitary hours of our stay, choked out by the erratic behavior of the man I had married. Romantic Paris was a tainted vision, a falsehood belied by this new Montgomery, this distant, volatile man. He even moved differently during our stay at the DeLande Estate, his fluid, effortless movements translating into the jerky motions of a caged, restless animal. The passion of the earlier part of our honeymoon was gone, replaced with a different emotion, a different passion, a cold, hurtful intensity I could not share.

As we drove away from the estate, I had hoped for a slow return to the lighthearted, loving relationship we had shared.

But as the miles and hours wore on, Montgomery seemed to sink deeper into the funk of his own making, and the weight of his silence settled on me like a somber shroud.

The landscape did nothing to lighten my mood. Although I usually loved the flat, watery landscape of the Atchafalaya River Basin, today the decay and rot that was always everywhere in the swampy wetlands seemed to expose a vista of Montgomery's soul, the hidden places within him I had just discovered, making me shiver in the broiling heat.

The Gulf of Mexico, with its salty tides, had been engaged in a life-and-death struggle with the Mississippi and Atchafalaya Rivers for some six thousand years, since the receding waters of the last ice age. A patient, endless war of brine versus fresh water, the flood tides of each squall, tropical storm, and hurricane brought in the sea to kill and maim the fragile life ashore. Fighting back, the Mississippi River Valley carried fresh water, topsoil, and nutrients south, reversing the salt content in the soil and wetlands and bringing back life to the damaged land.

So everywhere we looked, there were dead and dying trees, little more than moss-veiled sticks, pointing accusing, skeletal fingers at the cloudless sky. And then suddenly the road would turn in, toward the swamp marshes of a living section of wetland with its moss-draped green, dark with the feathery leaves of cypress and the darker foliage of black walnut, varieties of hickory, the old twisted oaks called cheniers, pecan, black gum, willow, wild vines and flowers, lotus and purple water hyacinth. At these powerful signs of life, my urge to cry would grow.

Twice, the twisting half-paved roads we traveled vanished under swamp, nature taking back what had been stolen from it, and man not deigning to respond. With the doubtful economy, the state would likely let the swamp keep its prize. Not even the latest maps showed some of these roads, remnants from the society that flourished in the Basin before the U.S. Corps of Engineers created the man-made levees that hold the river in its present course. On both occasions, Montgomery stopped, made a cautious three-point turn, and retraced our course.

The roads we traveled would someday be gone, sucked beneath the goo that pulled at the edges of the roadway, reclaimed by time and the watery Jell-O-like stuff that passed for land. We startled deer and slowed for lazy vultures picking at gray hunks of meat in the road. We passed choked waterways, ancient cemeteries—the above-ground sites encased in pristine white marble—abandoned houses, abandoned stores and railway depots. Alligators sunned themselves, an egret nesting ground was almost empty this time of day. There were few cars. Few people.

I stayed lost, but Montgomery never faltered at a turn or questioned a detour, moving across the land like a restive scavenger, looking for some elusive thing in the barren and fecund wilderness. His blue eyes, while never alighting on me, were never still, always roving over some parcel of land, some sugarcane field or abandoned industrial site, with mute concentration. At some point in the endless day, I realized Montgomery wasn't trying to get us lost or taking me on some cruel sight-seeing tour of the Basin's borders while my skin burned and peeled, but was on DeLande business.

Several times he slowed as we passed small open areas in

the foliage, marked with rusted and abandoned oil and natural gas pipes or wellheads. Once buried beneath water or sediment, the pipes had been discarded, left as scrap, by companies now out of business or deserting the swampland for more profitable oil sites. On several sites I saw signs, covered in vines or lying in weeds, painted with faded replicas of the DeLande crest, the predator bird with bloodied talons.

I almost asked Montgomery what species his family bird was, then shut my mouth. When I got back to my set of encyclopedias, I could look up the bird and identify it. I didn't have to ask him anything.

I pressed my lips together, feeling stubborn, and liking the sense of strength that came from defiance. Being stubborn was a Dazincourt trait. Half of what I had learned from my daddy was swamp lore and veterinary medicine. The other half was pure bullheadedness.

He had taught me to handle snakes and avoid the spines of freshly caught catfish. He had taught me to show strength of mind over useless compassion when it came to ending the life of an animal in pain. He had taught me to stand my ground when something was worth defending. He had taught me the value of principle and integrity and honesty. And when those values lost their meaning against the more important values of basic human rights and protecting the innocent. But he hadn't taught me how to handle my husband.

Another site, this one not marked with anything except the signs of past greed, was a vast tree cemetery, lying under a sheen of duckweed and still water, the slimy flowering plant parting to allow a nutria or muskrat to surface, its body sleek with water and muck. Tombstonelike tree stumps, useless as lumber, had been left behind by the loggers, testament to the rapacious avarice of the previous generations of the family I had married into.

For seven generations, the DeLandes had rebuilt a fortune lost after the Civil War, destroying the wetlands and reaping the profits with almost ruthless efficiency. Collectively the DeLande siblings and the Grande Dame owned more land in the southern half of the state than any other private family. More than most consortia. It had once been a rich heritage; nature and man had conspired to ruin it. Nature with salt tides and too heavy rains, flooding and hurricanes. Man with the blight of his selfishness and pollution. No one would drink the water that ran down the river basin. Bacteria and germs from human waste, and the hundreds of carcinogens and other pollutants, made it unpalatable and dangerous, as half a nation's waste ran out to the ocean through these channels.

It was called Cajun country, this southern portion of the state, and the wildlife and waterfowl, timber and other natural resources, had supported generations of trappers, hunters, moss pickers, lumbermen, fishermen, and in the last two generations, the growing oil and gas industry. Yet each man and each company who used the resources of this fragile area had raped the land in some way, leaving behind the evidence of his crime. And I was one of them now.

Still Montgomery didn't look at me or speak to me.

We had driven all day, stopping only when Montgomery needed gas, which was often. The Cord drank gas, and the old fuel gauge wasn't working properly. He never asked after my comfort or my needs, and the two times I ran to the unisex facilities in the little one-pump stations we found, I seriously thought he might drive on and leave me. But he waited, leaning against the roadster, watching the sky or a wandering family of raccoons. Once when I came out of the small bathroom, he was leaning over a fence studying a mare in foal, her tail swishing contentedly. Still he didn't speak.

As we drew closer to home, my thoughts turned more and more to the safety of my daddy's arms and the welcome I might expect if I left Montgomery and went home. I batted back my tears with swollen lids and bit my lips to keep from crying or begging Montgomery to talk to me. I wanted comfort, and I knew I could find it in my childhood home. And then I thought about the new roof, and Paris, and the Montgomery I had known before we went to the DeLande Estates. And again I fought back tears.

Near dusk, when the sun was dropping fast, a great orange-gold ball of fire hanging over the cypress groves and cane fields, tinting the world a delicate pink, I finally saw a familiar landmark. Bonnett's Meat Market and Grill. We were twenty miles or so outside of Moisson city proper, approaching on a road I had seldom been on, heading north. We had circled around the Basin, crisscrossing the back roads, and covered the distance home, taking more than twice as long as we should have. And Montgomery had not spoken to me once.

It had been three hours since our last stop. The gas gauge was on empty, I was hungry, thirsty, apprehensive, sun-burned, and miserable, hating this new Montgomery and damning my desire to ever marry him. More than a little bit of fear roiled at the edges of my mind as well. The vision of Montgomery's eyes, wild and rabid as he rocked on me and bled on me, still haunted me at strange moments, like a warning my mind couldn't let go.

Bonnett's was a local tradition in Moisson Parish, patron-ized by housewives and mothers in search of the best cuts of meat by day, and by local couples as an eatery and local men as a bar after dark. Bonnett's offered the best food for miles around, catering to both locals and the fishing tourists.

The odors that emanated from the smokehouse and grill were all the advertising Bonnett's needed. It was little more than a shack in front, added on to over and over, with dark little rooms opening off the original structure like ugly warts on an old man's hand. Unpainted and sere, with a sagging roof of rusted tin, it also offered a gas pump out front and a public toilet around back.

Montgomery pulled over in front of the pump and cut the engine. Without speaking, I pulled the chrome handle and stepped out, grabbed my bag, and headed for the back. The facilities, a unisex toilet and sink with no paper and no soap, were nonetheless cleaner than most. They were frequented by farmers, fishermen, passersby, and locals doing business at the few crossroads stores, who brought their own paper and were careful of the privilege of using Bonnett's facilities. Bonnett had once called the parents of a local boy caught urinating on the walls, and told them to clean it up. He had accosted more than one drunk who had misaimed, and tossed him out. The price of readmittance to the bar was to clean the john. No one had ever refused.

I had to wait, and spent the time trying to get the tangles out of my hair with my fingers and a travel brush I carried in my purse. Afterwards, I exited, water still damp on my freshly cleaned face, hair brushed and shining, a touch of lipstick in place to combat the sun damage on nose and cheeks, and another woman entered. I noticed she checked the place for cleanliness and seemed satisfied.

Instead of going out front and getting back in the sullen confines of the car as I had done all day, I went inside Bonnett's, clutching a five-dollar bill in one hand, my bag in the other. Montgomery could go all day without eating, but I was starving, and so was my baby. I intended to eat.

I stepped through the narrow door and down the hall, slipped past the stockroom on one side and the kitchen on the other, my mouth almost aching from hunger and salivating from the smells. Even though it was a Monday, the place was fairly busy, one of the warty little back rooms filled with a band of fishermen tourists celebrating a successful day on the Basin, and another filled with a group of local men from one of those stupid clubs. The Lions or the Tigers or Bears . . . Oh my . . . I smiled for the first time today.

Bonnett's was an old-time meat market, featuring the state's best boudin rouge, a blood sausage made with rice. They did their own slaughtering, cutting, smoking, and stuffing, serving up a variety of foodstuffs found nowhere else in Moisson.

Offering both hot meals and raw meat to take home and cook, the chef/butcher/owner, Billy Bonnett, dished out *tasso*—a highly spiced seasoning meat; *paunce*—stuffed calf stomach; three types of boudin—rouge, livery (heavy on the giblets), and lean chunk pork. He also offered *andouille*—another type of sausage, but made without the rice base of boudin—garlic sausage, hog's-head cheese, gumbo so rich it fed the soul as well as the body, boiled crawfish, cracklins, beef jerky, frog legs, fried vegetables from neighboring gardens, and three types of rice—dirty, brown, and the sticky white common to the area.

And cold beer. Lots of cold beer. Rumor had it Bonnett even kept some of the locally brewed beers in back in unmarked kegs, black beer so potent, it would curl a man's tongue, locust beer flavored with the long bean pod of the locust tree, and pale mockernut beer, said to be aged in mockernut hickory kegs. Of course, the local laws prohibited the sale of such beer. Yet rumor persisted.

Music came from the jukebox across the room, competing with the Cajun dance hall across the street. Levi's had the best live Cajun music in the area. Making it to the front room, the main room where the bar was and where all the food was served, I stopped, stung.

Montgomery, beer in hand, was leaning against the bar, a warped plank that served as meat counter by day and drink counter by night, bloodstained and aromatic but substantial enough to hold half a steer or several drunks. And he was talking, engaged in spirited conversation with a damp fisherman in coveralls, a young man in jeans and lace-up hunting boots, and Old Man Bascomb, a crawfish farmer. The conversation was in Cajun, a Houmas Indian dialect I could scarcely follow, but it was obviously a joke Montgomery told, because the men all roared with laughter just as I appeared.

Anger and hurt shimmered through me. That he would suddenly open up . . . with these men . . . Before I could react, Bascomb, a Cajun with seven sons and an accent so heavy, it bordered on the absurd, nudged Montgomery, and my husband turned.

The smile he flashed me was open and charming and almost indecently seductive after all the hours of his silence. *"Me sha,"* he shouted over the noise of the bar. Moving like a dancer, he crossed the room, took my hand, and pulling it to his lips, kissed the tips of my fingers. Not the top of my hand like an American aping French manners of the last century, but lifting my hand, he touched the underside, the soft fleshy pads, to his lips. Then he kissed me quickly on the mouth and stepped away, one arm around my waist, pulling me into a booth and calling to Bonnett to serve us.

Speaking Cajun like a native, he directed the placement of the dishes. There was a platter of boiled crawfish heavily seasoned with cayenne, a half dozen links of boudin made with lean pork chunks, dirty and sticky white rice in steaming bowls, fried squash, fried onion rings, and fried frog legs.

I couldn't accept his sudden reversal back into the man I had married, with the complacency he obviously expected. Tears puddled in my eyes before trailing down my face and dripping off my jaw.

The tears stopped him. He looked startled, horrified, guilty, and abashed in quick succession, and instantly he gathered me in his arms and pulled me onto his lap. Ignoring the amused stares and Cajun-laced catcalls, he rocked me in his arms, hiding my tears against his chest. Murmuring Cajun love words, he gentled me with his hands and voice as he might a young filly he was breaking. I couldn't follow half of his meanings and didn't try. I was just glad to have him back. And terrified of losing him again.

Finally he pulled away a bit, kissed the tip of my nose, and wiped my face with one of the harsh paper napkins Bonnett kept piled on the tables. With his arms around me, he reached for the tray of crawfish and pulled it closer. Choosing a large, red-shelled mudbug, he removed its head and peeled back the shell . . . and gently he placed the succulent meat in my mouth. It was a powerfully erotic sensation, the feel of his fingers on my mouth, the taste of the spicy meat, the lackluster lighting and mismatched furniture, the smattering of French conversation around the room, and the feel of his legs beneath mine.

His eyes met mine and he was no longer smiling, but intense. A feeling of almost electric heat passed between us as he slowly licked his fingers free of the juice from the steamed meat. Placing the head of the crawfish into his mouth, he sucked out the juice and tossed away the shell.

Montgomery fed me for an hour, refusing to allow me to return the favor, taking only a small bite now and then, but placing the bulk of the meal into my mouth with his fingers, letting me suck them clean. And his eyes never left mine. Burning eyes, brighter than a noon sky, radiating heat and hunger that the meal could not satisfy.

It was as if the weekend at the DeLande Estate had never been. It was Paris and New Orleans all over again, but now I sizzled beneath his hands with my own need, a need created by the days of want and fear and isolation.

Bonnett, who had the Frenchman's instinct for such things, stayed away while we ate, intruding only to plunk down two pitchers and mugs for us. A dark beer for Montgomery and tea for me. And the big, rawboned man intercepted the locals who would have interrupted the meal, calling them over to the bar with a Cajun phrase, leaving us in the half darkness and seclusion of the high-backed booth.

When the platters were mostly empty and the beer was gone, Montgomery picked me up and carried me out of Bonnett's, shouting to the patrons that he was still on his honeymoon and had better things to do than visit with the likes of them. Laughter and rough innuendo followed us out into the night, and Montgomery lifted me over the door of the Cord and settled me in the passenger seat, vaulting over the driver's door and revving the engine.

He took me home, saying nothing as the cool night breeze

billowed around me, tossing my loose hair and soothing away the day's heat. There was a different kind of heat now in the old Cord, feverish and steamy, leisurely and slow. We didn't speak on the drive, both of us perhaps content to let the heat build in the fiery silence, or perhaps afraid to short-circuit the gradually intensifying sensations with words that might accuse or condemn.

It was a magical night. Enchanted, as though a trance had been laid over us both and over the night air. The breeze, which had been hot and parched, yet thick with humidity so dense it curdled on our skin, was now gentle and mild, serene with the subtle scents of night-blooming flowers, and the sweet scent of the cologne Montgomery always wore. The moon was a silver sliver in a velvet sky. And the silence between us, which had been acrid and acerbic, was now redolent with a preoccupation of a different sort. Montgomery's fingers played over mine, smoothing the skin on the backs of my hands, tracing the tendons and bones in the darkness of the Cord.

The house Montgomery took me to was a renovated ranch-style, situated on a mound of earth in a protected and secluded cul-de-sac not far outside the city limits of Moisson. It was surrounded by live oaks covered with swaying moss, and old gardenias that filled the night air with their potent scent.

We parked in the covered carport to the right of the side entrance, and when Montgomery shut off the motor, an owl hooted into the sudden quiet. Crickets resumed their interrupted chirping, and the little breeze carried off the exhaust smells.

Montgomery looked at me and smiled a tentative smile. "I knew you would want to be close to your family, so I . . . This place was part of a small farm we bought last year. The DeLandes, I mean. And I took the house and the back five acres for us. There's a bayou out back a ways and a new dock. If you like it . . . Do . . . Would you like to see the house?"

A tentative Montgomery was a surprise. He was always the sure one, sanguine, almost arrogant. I knew immediately he was apologizing in the only way he knew. And then I heard the words. He had bought me a house.

I rose up and tried to see its outlines, but the darkness was complete, and Montgomery laughed. "Come on. If you like it, I'll install one of those security lights that comes on whenever anything near it moves, so we can see when we drive up late like this." He threw himself out of the car and came around to let me out, still talking about the house and the features he had added for me.

The power was on, and although I couldn't see the outside at all, the inside was stunning. About two thousand square feet of ranch-style house, it had been completely renovated inside, and I thought immediately of the cars Montgomery loved working on, restoring them to showroom perfection.

The side entrance was a mudroom with washer and dryer, pegs on the walls for raincoats or umbrellas, the shelves above already lined with the washing powder and cleaning supplies Mama used. I smiled, and he caught the direction of my gaze. "I hope you don't mind, but your mother said these were the best."

"They're fine," I said softly. "Perfect."

"Good." He pulled down an ironing board, hidden in the wall in its own little cabinet, the iron in a nook above. "You don't have to do your own ironing, and we can afford to send out the laundry if you want, but I know how you women will run and iron out a little wrinkle or something sometimes." He grinned, and I blushed suddenly, loving the man who had thought of that little detail. He led me on into the house proper.

The walls were white, stark in their brightness, but Montgomery assured me I could repaint or wallpaper if I wanted. "I put a decorator in Lafayette on retainer and set up credit in several furniture stores for you to furnish the house. I didn't know what you would like, so I left most of it empty."

The family room was big, with hardwood floors interrupted only by a single desk and chair styled for a man in one corner, a locked gun cabinet in the other corner, and a leather recliner before the windows. The kitchen was beyond, and I had never seen hardwood floors in a kitchen, but I liked it instantly. The cabinets went to the ceiling, white vinyl covering the doors, one section with glass doors that would show off special dishes. The appliances were white also, and I opened the refrigerator to see several bottles of the wine Montgomery had liked in Paris, cooling on a special rack. There were groceries as well, the kind of things my mama would have chosen.

Montgomery confirmed my diagnosis. "I got your mother to pick up a few things for us, but we have an account at Therriot's." Therriot's was the largest food store in Moisson.

I closed the door, the tears I had shed at Bonnett's threatening to return for a different reason. My hands were trembling. Montgomery seemed to sense my reaction and he hugged me, pulling me to the breakfast nook, his arm around my waist.

"I liked the breakfast room set, so I had it delivered, but if you don't like it, it can go back." There were white-painted chairs, four of them, and a round table, also white, beneath a simple light fixture. The furniture was situated in a nook with angled walls, reflected back from floor-length windows, no panes to interfere with the daytime view.

"It's perfect," I whispered, but before I was finished with the words, Montgomery had pulled me on, toward the front of the house, into the parlor. It wasn't a living room as such, too small for that designation. But it was elegant, with multipaned windows and deep-carved moldings at the ceiling and floor and on the windows. I could see it decorated already, with draperies that puddled on the floor like the tears that were puddling in my eyes again. I would do it up in gray and green and shrimp.

Or maybe we could put a piano in here instead. I put my

hand on my stomach, still flat but full of promise. It could be a music room for the children. The dining room was on the other side of the front entrance, an Oriental rug centered on the wood floor, a heavy glass table balanced on two wide concrete pedestals, centered on the rug. I remembered admiring the table in a storefront window in New Orleans some two weeks ago.

The tears rolled down my face and I hugged Montgomery. He had obviously purchased the table and somehow had it delivered here. Tall-backed chairs, styled after some Frank Lloyd Wright had designed, were situated around the table. It was beautiful. I watched our reflections in the multipaned front windows, turning slowly as if we were dancing.

The bedrooms were farther back, two bedrooms sharing a bath between, and a guest room with its own bath. I upped my estimate of the square footage to closer to three thousand.

The master suite was at the back of the house with two walk-in closets and a big bath with a whirlpool tub for two underneath a skylight. Even the shower had two heads, with enough room for two people to shower together. A bidet and a toilet sat side by side in the closed-off area for more personal and private activities.

Montgomery had bought a bed, a huge thing, its four posters carved with rice stalks like the plantation owners had made popular in days gone by. Two chairs faced each other across a small game table in front of the windows. These windows had blinds. I shook my head, the tears now gone.

"Like it?" It wasn't really a question. Montgomery could see that I loved the house. It was more of the final punctuation on the apology he was giving me.

"I love it," I said softly. "Thank you."

He flashed me that same smile that had stolen my breath away in Bonnett's and turned away. "You draw a bath or take a shower. I'll get in the luggage." And he was gone.

I walked slowly back into that magnificent bath, sat on the

edge of the tub, and turned on the brass spigot, listening to the water thud into the bottom of the tub. It was ceramic over steel, not some newer and cheaper material like fiberglass or plastic. And I watched my face in the mirror over the sinks, thinking about the man I had married.

He was much more complicated than I had known. Perhaps even a little . . . cruel. I was always honest with myself. Even when it would be safer to lie. But the cruelty had surfaced only when he had to confront his family, that bizarre, erratic, somehow unbalanced group of people. And vanished when enough time and space separated him from their influence.

I wondered at the rumors about the DeLandes and decided I should not ask, fearing again to see Montgomery's eyes glaze over like the rabid dog my daddy had killed. I feared that Montgomery. Shivering, I pulled off my sweat-streaked dress, noticing the splatters of crawfish juice and beer and catsup. I tossed the dress and the underclothes into a corner, sliding into the rapidly rising water. The tub bottom was dished out slightly, keeping my own bottom from sliding along the slick ceramic. I turned up the hot water, wanting to steam away the day, and tilted my head back against the padded pillow on the end of the tub.

I considered the man Montgomery had been for the past three days. And shivered again, little visions of the weekend piercing me like shattering glass. Montgomery, bleeding over me. Montgomery positioning me like a doll on the bed, moving my limbs until he liked the posture and location of each finger or toe. Montgomery feeding me like a child, holding the fork or spoon, refusing to allow me to touch the utensils. Montgomery locking me into the room and leaving me for hours. Montgomery refusing to talk to me, shutting me out from whatever misery and horror he reexperienced in that house, with those people.

I knew instinctively he had suffered for the three days we were there. Suffered and kept the pain all locked up inside. He was like a wounded child, abused by his family, yet still loving them all. The rumors beckoned. I refused the temptation. I wouldn't pry. If Montgomery wanted to block out the anguish, I would let him. If he ever wanted to talk about it, I would listen.

But right now I had my own memories, and they hurt. Like bleeding places on my soul, pricked by fragments of Montgomery's pain. I looked at each of them. Studied them as the water rose up to my waist, my rib cage, my breasts.

And I carefully gathered them all together, avoiding the sharp and hurtful edges, tucking them up like broken glass into a napkin. I held them in my mind, weighing them, uncertain what I would do with them.

I heard Montgomery enter the bathroom. Heard him remove his shoes and drop them near my discarded clothing.

Still I kept my eyes closed, focused on the bundle of hurt in my mind's hand, a hurt so real, I could see it, so fresh, it still bled. I knew I held something dangerous and frightening, something I would have to deal with over the years and couldn't just toss out like the broken crystal it seemed in my vision.

Heat steamed up around me. The water was cut off, leaving silence in its wake. Montgomery slipped into the tub across from me, and the water rose almost to my neck. I heard him sigh and felt him relax, his legs sliding around me, on either side of my body. He lifted my feet and placed them in his lap, his fingers massaging my arches.

And very carefully, very deliberately, I placed the broken things, the things that had hurt me, the things that were part of the new Montgomery I had met at the DeLande Estate, into a box in my mind and closed the lid. It seemed so real, I could feel the wood grain of The Box beneath my hands. I could hear the echo as The Box closed. And I walked away from the place where it was kept.

I wouldn't look at the things in that box until Montgomery wanted to. I wouldn't demand he explain. I would forget. I would close my eyes.

Some small part of my mind wondered if my mama had started out this way, hiding from something that hurt her, putting away the pain. Until it became a way of life to cater to Daddy, to deny herself a life that might have been different. But I turned away from that thought as well. And it was absurdly easy to do so, with the warm water lapping against me and Montgomery's hands rubbing slowly up my legs. I smiled, and without opening my eyes, knew he smiled with me.

We never visited the Grande Dame DeLande again, never heard from her except at Christmas and birthdays, though at one time or another one of the brothers would roar up the drive in some renovated old car and take over the guest bedroom for a few days or weeks till whatever business he was conducting was concluded.

In fact, except for the periodic changes in my bank account each time a child was born, I would never have thought about the Grande Dame at all. But each time I gave birth, a large sum of money was deposited into my personal account. And a second account opened in the name of my new child. "For their education," Montgomery insisted. And "Spend it," when asked about the money given me. Instead, with the help of a competent C.P.A. and my brother Logan, I invested it. By DeLande standards it wasn't much. But I liked my little nest egg and the security it gave me. The years rolled on, inevitable and inexorable, as though ordained.

Montgomery and I slipped into a regular and easy relationship like that of other married couples, I suppose. There were good times and not so good, but I didn't complain. Complaining didn't put potatoes in the pot, as my mama used to say.

She and I had never been close, in part because of the pithy little sayings she mouthed whenever I came to her with a problem. I decided early on in my own experience as a mother that I would never pass along the little sayings she had always preached to me. The snappy little lines that somehow made light of my worries and difficulties.

Montgomery and I chose a church and attended mass together. Montgomery joined several of those stupid clubs men join, became a Republican, and took up golf. I attended a local class and learned to make ceramics, discovering along the way that I had a talent for bringing out the intensity of color on porcelain. And I took up gardening. Montgomery built me a greenhouse out back, thinking that, like my mama, I wanted to get my hands in the dirt and watch things grow. I never told him different.

I had my first child, Desma Collette, seven months after my wedding. It was an easy birth, Montgomery coaching me and my doctor sitting back, letting me do the work. I'd never felt exhilaration like that before, the power, the pain, the indescribable joy when the doctor put the bloody, slippery little girl on my belly, all blending into one euphoric experience that could make me smile no matter what my current circumstances.

And when Dessie opened her eyes, her face all smeared with mucus and blood, and stared into my own . . . I don't care what the researchers say about the development of an infant's eyes, my little girl looked at me, focused on me, and knew me in that first moment. The bonding that is supposed to take weeks or months happened in seconds, and I had found my calling. From the first instant our eyes met, I knew I would never work as a nurse. I would never use the degree I had studied so hard for. At least not until all my children were in school and I could work part-time. I was a mother first, foremost, and always.

Ignoring the *tisk tisk* of my ob-gyn, I was pregnant again two months after Dessie's birth, still nursing my first child and walking swaybacked with my second. I read every book a mother could find on how to be a good parent, then discarded all the theories and felt my way through.

Dessie was baldheaded and fair-skinned with Montgomery's blue DeLande eyes. She laughed early, talked early, and walked early, all long before her first birthday. Precocious and gentle, she loved with abandon, preferring people to toys and my singing to TV or radio.

Dora Shalene was another kettle of fish entirely. She was dark like our mothers, the Creole heritage of the Ferronaires and the Sarvaunts confirmed in Shalene's black eyes and smooth black hair, her olive skin and high cheekbones. Demanding and self-absorbed, Shalene liked eating, holding her toys, and playing with her toes. In that order.

But I missed the first five months of Shalene's life, the bonding that took place between Dessie and me not duplicated at the difficult birth of my second child. Motherhood was stolen from me by a body that would not heal and emotions torn with hormonal swings. It seemed Shalene had already developed a complete personality by the time I was well enough to know her.

Establishing a relationship with the little dark-eyed child was difficult work, harder than reviving the tenuous bonds of my earlier intimacy with Dessie. But I worked at it, even resorting to the books full of theories I had so blithely discarded once before.

I invented games and put together puzzles, played house and dolls. Taught them to draw, the wild, colorful scribbles children put to paper. We constructed a life-style, we three girls, with special rituals and traditions, our own amusements and rewards. Perhaps every full-time mother could say the same, but I felt that the girls and I had developed something special, perfected a flawless model of family.

Montgomery intruded upon it only rarely. He preferred to watch with hooded eyes the lively tumult of our home. Even discipline he left to me, backing up my few threats with an unforgiving face and stern eyes, the twinkle that was usually present in the blue depths blanked out.

The only part of family life that Montgomery seemed to appreciate was the word games we played. Dessie, although especially articulate and with a vocabulary far beyond her years, had trouble saying "juice." Instead of asking for apple juice or grape juice, she asked for apple jewish or grape jewish. And Montgomery would laugh, encouraging her to continue the mispronunciation, sharing her difficulty with friends and family as if he was proud of it.

And both girls had trouble with "yeah." I wanted my children to say "yes" or "yes, ma'am." Not "yeah." Montgomery liked "yeah," I think to spite me. But I persevered, eradicating grape jewish from the vocabulary before Morgan was born. I wasn't so lucky with "yeah."

Morgan Justin was a peaceful child, sleeping through the night from the day we brought him home from the hospital. He liked to watch the world around him, being fascinated with his mobile, his stuffed bear, his food arranged in his colorful plastic bowl. He would study it carefully before shoving in his fingers and testing the tactile sensations just as earnestly. He particularly liked the grainy feel of pears, but he liked the color of strawberry ice cream. I often thought he would be content if he could ever find strawberry ice cream with the consistency of pureed pears.

My life seemed fixed and secure, Montgomery usually a giving, loving husband, if a distant and uncomfortable father. He bought me handguns, which he knew I loved to shoot, and set up a place away from the house for us to use as target practice. It was a dried-up gully, once a canal for oil rigs to travel on the way to the oil fields and back, but sealed off by the Corps of Engineers when they fortified the levee near Moisson back after the flood of '73. It had dried up in places over the years and left a rare dry channel about four or five feet deep at the back of the five acres we owned.

He bought me jewelry and clothes. We traveled extensively across the States, mostly on business for the DeLandes, but sometimes solely for pleasure. We toured the best vintners in the nation one spring and fall, dividing the country up into sections and driving it from one end to the next. I especially preferred the vineyards in northern California, but Montgomery fell in love with one in South Carolina, saying the soil was so like that in southern France that the wines could have been imported.

After the first few years, Montgomery began to travel more, leaving me with Rosalita and the girls, as he took on a greater share of DeLande business. He invested his own funds in land and new, speculative businesses across the state and up the Gulf and East Coast. I traveled a bit, too, to New Orleans to visit Sonja. But only once or twice a year. I didn't like to be separated from the girls for very long at a time.

Montgomery was seldom rough with me or cold, and then only when a DeLande male came to visit. When a brother pulled down the street in one of the DeLande trademark antique cars, wheeled into the drive, and appropriated a space in Montgomery's five-car garage out back, my palms would begin to sweat and a tightness would settle in my chest.

The strange irrational glint would appear in Montgomery's eyes, that radiant intensity, a cold brilliant sparkle, and he would withdraw from me. Watching me with empty eyes one moment, emitting a fierce repressed anger the next, he would change until there was only a thin patina of the Montgomery I had married. He became a brittle, quick-tempered man until the day his brother left.

And then he punished me. Sometimes even as the car that brought him was pulling out of the drive, as if Montgomery's reactions to his brothers was my fault. He punished me for a thousand infractions of rules. Rules I had never learned. Rules he had never shared.

Exotic or mundane, cruel or common, his punishments were varied and imaginative, from ignoring me, like the first time he punished me on our honeymoon, to more foreign, physical punishments. I lived through them, existing until he had worked out whatever demons blistered his soul. And afterwards he would love me again, the gentle man I had married reappearing suddenly, completely restored. As if he had been bewitched and the spell just broken.

Only Miles Justin never caused the conversion in Montgomery. He could show up a dozen times a year, and did, and Montgomery never changed. The title Miles had given himself the day we met seemed appropriate. Peacemaker. Even in my volatile husband. There were times I used to pray he would show up, during a visit by Richard or Andreu, when Montgomery would turn especially vile and hurtful. But he seldom did, preferring to come alone on weekends when school was out, more often in the summer, and always at Christmas.

He had a knack for picking out just the right gift for each of my children, either for birthdays or Christmas or just for no reason at all. One year he brought stuffed animals to Dessie, and a toy train to Shalene. Both girls were totally delighted, and he even managed to get them to play together with the toys, to share, when I had trouble just getting them to be civil to each other.

He was too young to drive the first few times he showed up on our doorstep, piloting the Cord we drove home on our honeymoon. Fifteen was the legally accepted age one could apply for a driver's license in Louisiana. But I never remonstrated with him. I learned quickly that the DeLandes were a law unto themselves in this state. Besides. I liked Miles Justin.

Over the years, the punishments began to appear at other moments, other times. When I displeased Montgomery in some way, or disagreed with him, or failed him. I learned never to say no. Not ever, over anything. But these moments were short-lived and fleeting, brief holes in the fabric of our marriage, and they fit into The Box, along with all the other pains.

It wasn't that I stopped being me. It wasn't that I stopped fighting to make life better, to make a safe haven for the girls and my son and myself. And it wasn't that it was all bad.

Most of the time, in fact, Montgomery was a wonderful husband. But there were times, dark moments, when Montgomery went away, and the stranger who inhabited his body and mind at such times was the enemy I feared and hated. These times I endured. Silent and pliant and uncomplaining. Patiently waiting for the Montgomery I loved to return and bring back the light.

He never explained the bizarre transformations. He never apologized. And I never understood. I simply tucked the memories into The Box. It became full over the years, full of remembered pain. But I seldom looked at it. I seldom thought about it. It was easier to stuff the latest indignity and hurt into The Box and slam down the lid, walking away as the echoes resounded on the walls of my mind.

CHAPTER

3

ॐ ॠ

I loved New Orleans this time of year. Once Mardi Gras
is over and the swarms of tourists go home, and before
the smothering heat of summer and the swarms of mosquitoes arrive—in that short space of time in March—is
the best time of year in the Crescent City. The time
when the residents themselves take to the streets and
meander down through the French Quarter, stopping at
the open cafés for beignets and chicory café au lait, or at
Johnny's for a po' boy made of fried oysters or soft-shell
crabs.

It was the time of year when daily rains washed out the
open drainage canals, taking away the stench of human and
chemical waste, when the bone-chilling cold of winter winds
blowing down from Canada along the Mississippi Valley
was only an unpleasant memory, when Lake Ponchartrain
sparkled like it was still viable instead of the dead sea it
really was. It was the time of year when the breezes blew the
soft scent of budding flowers, fresh coffee, hot beignets
frying in scorched grease, bubbling praline candy, the smell
of fried seafood, and the always rank smell of the harbor

together into the wonderful perfume that was New Orleans in spring.

Each year for several years I had spent most of March in New Orleans with Sonja shopping, eating, visiting friends, shopping, attending the numerous cultural and political events sponsored by the Rousseaus, and of course, shopping. I gave up a lot to placate the man I married, but I never gave up Sonja. I suffered for it, this friendship of my youth, but something wouldn't let me let her go. She was my guardian angel.

My visits to Sonja were oases of unrecognized and unadmitted freedom in the tight confines of my life. Bright moments of chatter and gossip and laughter when there were no kids hanging on to my fingers, no responsibilities demanding my attention . . . no husband demanding my compliance. Montgomery allowed my yearly pilgrimage because I came home refreshed and calmed and ready to assume my role as his wife. But he didn't like it.

We stood in the late morning sunshine outside of Petunias on St. Louis street, patting down the oversize brunch we had shared with two of Sonja's friends from NOW, the National Organization for Women. By combining our orders onto extra plates, we had feasted on two orders of *pain perdu,* also known as lost bread, which was French toast made with French bread and blanketed with powdered sugar and cane syrup. We had eggs Melanza and a Cajun sausage breakfast with both smoked *andouille* and boudin sausage, and eggs St. Louis. My cholesterol level would be sky high, and I didn't care. If there had been a piece of *pain perdu* left on anyone's plate, I would have claimed a mother's privilege and eaten the scraps. Petunias' *pain perdu* was one delicacy I could eat even when too full already.

I followed Sonja by instinct, my eyes half-closed, focused mostly on her lavender pumps in front of me, looking neither left nor right, to her car down the block, feeling the sun on my skin, oblivious to the world. I was relaxed and content, the pleasure of these last two days welling up in me like fresh water bubbling out of the ground in the swamp, clear and sparkling, as it smoothed the silt and bottom mold away from its entry to the world of light and air. I was pleased that I had not splattered any of the greasy food on my silk shell, pleased that I had two weeks of freedom to explore New Orleans, pleased that Montgomery had not tried to talk me out of this visit for once, pleased that I was full and lazy and possibly pregnant. I was only two days late, but already I was drowsy and peaceful and tender of breast, the way I get when I am "with child."

That was Sonja's term. But then she was so proper and demure these days. The public image Sonja maintained since marrying into the powerful Rousseau family, and the private wildcat I remembered from escapades in our youth, had blended into a sophisticated, politically minded young woman and mother. Still a wildcat who risked her neck and reputation, Sonja simply was more judicious in the causes she championed. Whereas in her youth she risked parental censure for joyriding with Montgomery and me in one of his antique cars, the top down, with a case of beer in the cooler in the backseat, these days she risked daily excommunication with her borderline liberal politics and her outspoken convictions.

Only because of Rousseau money and Rousseau clout did she avoid public reprimand from the more staid and conservative members of society. Meaning that she rubbed shoulders with such as the Ferronaires, and although she ruffled feathers, no one yet had the gall to put her in her place. Or try to. Her natural grace and delicacy of manner helped. Even in a protest march, Sonja would have been poised and self-assured and decked out in the latest spring Christian Dior or Yves St. Somebody, color-coordinated from the flower on her straw bonnet to the tips of her Gucci shoes.

So "with child" fit the image. My youngest daughter, Shalene, now five years old, would have said "preggers," proving to Montgomery once and for all that I am an unfit mother. I smiled faintly.

"Your watchdog is back."

"Hummm?" I mumbled, blinking my eyes against the reflected brilliance of the too white sidewalks, cracked shell tips peeking through the concrete. I managed to focus on Sonja unlocking the door of the white Volvo station wagon she drove.

"Your watchdog. Feel the leash?"

I sighed. "Poor analogy; I not on a leash. And you know it's for my protection. Montgomery hires them to keep . . . us safe on the streets. He doesn't like the crime and the car-jacking and—"

"Montgomery hires them to keep an eye on you, and you know it. But don't get your panties in a wad. I've gotten used to being tailed around the city by some two-bit detective in an old Falcon."

I moved around to the passenger side, feeling some of the day's intoxication slip away, but determined not to show it. "'Panties in a wad'? Old Sister Louey would have a hissy fit."

Sonja laughed. "Okay, avoid the issue. How is Sister Louey these days?"

Sister Louey was really Sister Mary Agnes, but she was the spitting image of Louis Armstrong and so the moniker stuck, handed down by five decades of students at Our Lady of Grace. "She's fine. A little frail, and gets lost in the rose garden, but doing well considering she's nearing eighty. And I'm not avoiding the issue."

We stood talking over the roof of the Volvo, traffic whizzing by and the occasional pigeon waddling over. Montgomery's hired watchdogs had been an issue for years with us, and although Sonja professed to hate them, it was a game to see who could spot them first.

"Then go introduce yourself to them and give them an itinerary. It'll make life easier on us all."

"Let them earn their money." I got into the car, slamming the door, and slowly Sonja followed. I knew it bothered her to have them always there, always just in sight, two cars back or parked down the street, but we had come to depend on them more than once over the years.

Like the time they stopped a purse snatcher from making off with our bags and a day's worth of shopping. The time they cleared the street after a drunk white man hit and killed a five-year-old black child and the crowd started to turn ugly. But it wasn't always a good feeling to have them there.

It was the odd sensation of being watched over and protected, guarded and photographed. The sign of movement from the corner of my eye. The presence of a certain car in several different locations during my day: at the curb out front in the morning, sighted two cars back on a drive, idling down the block after a late breakfast, and back at the curb out front in the evening. And once when I slipped on a slick slate walk and broke my wrist while trying to break my fall, Montgomery appeared at the hospital emergency room, alarmed and solicitous, though Sonja had yet to call him. And he was not supposed to be in New Orleans at the time.

On several occasions I spotted Montgomery in a crowd, or thought I did, turning away.

When I would return home from Sonja's, he would hold me close, too tight, cutting off my breath, reminding me I was his. Only his. And he would not share what was his. *God, I had learned to hate the sound of those words.* His loving at such times was harsh and punishing as he used my body to seal his ownership. To remind me of the vows I had spoken, vows he would not let me break. The delight I had in the day was gone.

"You should divorce the suspicious bastard and let me find you a good man."

I laughed, an almost normal sound. "And Montgomery and all his brothers could attend the wedding and fill my new husband with their forty-caliber good wishes. Right."

Sonja sighed and pulled out into traffic. "There are other men out there. Good men."

I smiled tightly. "One man in a lifetime is enough, thank you. Besides, I want nothing to do with some sex-starved male out to prove himself on the horizontal battleground."

Sonja darted me a look I pretended not to notice as I watched the mirror over the passenger seat for the car Sonja had spotted at least twice today. It was there, pulling into traffic and following us. A pea green, late model Buick Regal.

"Hummm. No Falcon. Montgomery hired me a better class of thugs this year. I'll have to be especially grateful when I get home." Even I heard the odd tone in my voice, and the slip angered me. A fast-blooming haze filled my mind, like a too large red rose opening on time-lapse photography. I didn't think; I just acted. "Pull over."

Without comment, Sonja pulled into a narrow one-way side street between two shops, the front end facing the wrong way. It was little more than an alley twelve feet wide, but open to the connecting street on the other side. Scribbling hurriedly, I folded a white piece of paper and reached for the door handle. There was just enough room for me to squeeze myself out without bruising the Volvo's paint job on the rough brick.

"Where are you going?" There was alarm in Sonja's voice, and I smiled. It must have been a nasty smile because she threw the car in park and struggled with the seat belt.

"I'm going to give them an itinerary, like you suggested."

Sonja stopped, her eyes wide, and I laughed, a strange ugly sound, full of anger, as I slipped down the alley to the street, the crumpled paper clenched in my fist.

"Don't piss off Montgomery!" The words bounced thinly off the brick walls enclosing the car.

"Sister Louey is probably having grand mal seizures right about now," I shouted back.

I looked for the Buick. It was idling in the middle of the street, blocking traffic. I smiled again, the muscles contorting my face, focusing on the man in the passenger seat as I threaded my way between two parked cars to reach him. His window was open.

I leaned over the window embrasure and propped an elbow on the window groove as horns began honking behind us. The man in the passenger seat, his face only inches from mine, was a green-eyed mulatto with an uneven goatee, his skin a rich brown shade, like wet pine needles. He drew back from me. The driver was white, black-eyed with full cheeks and a cigarette hanging down from his lips. Both were in jeans and T-shirts, and there were weapons on the seat between them. Brass knuckles, a blackjack, a short length of chain, a 35-mm camera with telephoto lens, and a silver semiautomatic handgun.

"How much do you earn?" I said, surprising myself.

The goateed one turned to the driver, his chin hairs quivering. The driver took his cigarette from his mouth. "Lady, you're holding up traffic."

I laughed, that strange hysterical sound that again shivered along my spine. "No, *you're* blocking traffic. And we can continue blocking traffic till New Orleans's finest arrive to clear the streets and find your toys—" I pointed to the collection on the seat "—or you can answer my question. How much?"

The honking behind us worsened as one driver leaned his palm on the horn, the two-tone note a strident sound, bouncing off the two-story buildings lining the street. At least two other drivers followed suit, and several cussed out the open windows. Yat and Cajun accents mangled the air.

"How much?"

Sirens sounded in the distance.

"Seventy-five a day plus expenses," muttered the goateed passenger.

I tossed the crumpled paper to his lap. "I just made your job easier." Turning, I ran back through the cars to the alley and the Volvo. A lone siren turned down the street. Still laughing, I crawled back into the Volvo, and Sonja gunned the motor, pulling us down the little one-way street the wrong way before I even got the door closed.

We pulled out into the brighter sunshine of the far street, just as a cloud covered the sun. A squall from the Gulf, perhaps, or just another of the city's slow rains. "What did you do?" It was an accusation.

My frenetic laughter slowed, growing shaky at her tone. Taking a deep breath, I said, "I gave them an itinerary. How fast can you drive?"

"Why?" She made a quick left and another right, pulling us out on a wide side street. I was lost. This was Sonja's town. I turned and watched for the pea green Buick, but it was nowhere to be seen.

"A fake itinerary."

"Shit." The unexpected profanity startled me, and I looked at Sonja. Her full lips were tight and her nostrils flared. I had a feeling she would have gone back for the goons if it weren't already too late.

"What . . ." Sonja ignored me, driving straight home, though we should have stayed in the Quarter shopping for an hour. Our next meeting was with the National Political Congress of Black Women, also gathering at Petunias, Sonja's favorite restaurant for small business parties and political get-togethers.

The euphoria drained out of me like rain gurgling down a rusted gutter. We didn't speak as she drove, and soberly I considered Sonja's opposing attitudes in the uneasy silence of the car. She had been goading me for years, trying to get me to stand up to Montgomery. Trying to get me to rebel against the restrictions and against the goons he hired to watch me. Then, when I finally did show a little spunk and fight back, she panicked. Sonja never panicked. Never.

And I never fought back. Not against Montgomery. That would have been dangerous, and I was too smart to risk that. Usually. Of course, there were things that I did and said that displeased Montgomery. Like the time I told him I didn't like his brothers—except Miles, the youngest and gentlest

DeLande—and didn't want them visiting. And the time, just a few weeks ago, when I asked him to hire a psychologist for Dessie because she had stopped eating and had withdrawn from the family.

There were times I displeased him in other ways. Like when my health was not quick to return after the birth of Shalene, or when he was feeling amorous and I was in a "womanly way," as Mama used to say, and not available. Then he was impossible to placate. Paranoid and accusatory.

He'd reach for me and I'd shake my head, because I knew how he felt about a woman during her time of the month. He'd draw back and growl, "Bleeding and not available?" And I'd smile a bit and nod.

In those few days he'd prowl around the house like a tiger in a cage or suddenly go out of town, using business as an excuse to get away from me. At least in the early years. These days he merely retired to the guest bedroom for the duration. And I had the master suite all to myself, luxuriating in the selfish pleasure of solitude.

I glanced at Sonja, her attention on the traffic and pedestrians. She looked cool, collected, so maybe she wasn't panicked. Just . . . worried. And angry. She kept glancing back down the road. No pea green Buick.

We pulled across St. Charles Avenue onto her street in the Garden District, one of those avenues of refurbished hundred-plus-year-old mansions with aged oaks and Spanish moss and a profusion of flowers blooming in the gardens.

New Orleans was an old city, with pockets of wealth and gentility nestled among acres of public housing, slums, and projects. Security agencies and private guards abounded in these wealthy enclaves. I wasn't sure the ambience of southern charm was worth the trouble or the property damage.

Instead of pulling down the drive to the three-car garage —once upon a time a stables and servants' quarters—Sonja parked the Volvo on the street in front of the Rousseau grounds, grinding the tire on the low curb. Cutting the engine, she sat, drumming her manicured nails on the leather wheel cover. The engine pinged into silence. A shaft of sunlight sparkled on the chrome of the windshield before vanishing behind cloud cover. The wind picked up, then died. And I was quiet. I waited. Seems like I was always waiting on someone or something these days.

"If you want to leave Montgomery, I'll help. But no stupid games like that again. Understood?"

I didn't respond to the command in her voice. I was used to masking my responses to commands. Mildly I said, "You've been pushing me to fight back for years now. I did. And now you say don't."

I stared out the window, not looking at Sonja, but aware of her regard. A bobwhite called in the distance. A second one answered close by. Sonja leaned back in her seat and exhaled.

"I've been trying to get you to see the cage you're locked into so you'd do something about it."

"So I'd leave Montgomery," I said flatly. I turned my head, her profile just visible in my peripheral vision. A flame of anger, quickly extinguished, scorched its way along my nerves.

Sonja nodded, scanning the street behind us for the sickly looking Buick. "But I didn't mean game playing. With Montgomery it's all or nothing. Either you give in completely and live under his thumb or you marshal all your defenses and fight. Divorce him. There isn't any middle ground."

I knew the truth of her words, but was surprised that she knew. "It sounds as though you've given this a lot of thought," I said slowly.

For a moment the car was silent. The bobwhite piped his plaintive message a second time, and the one nearby answered after a moment, as though he, too, had to think out his words. The air was getting close in the sealed car, but neither of us rolled down a window. We sat and breathed the stagnating air and didn't watch each other. Then.

"Four—five years ago. After Shalene was born and you were so sick."

I nodded. It took over a year for me to recover from Shalene's birth. The C-section had gone badly and I'd lost a lot of blood, none of which Montgomery would allow the doctor to replace with units stored in the hospital blood bank. Fear of AIDS and hepatitis was strong at the time in Moisson Parish as a kid injured in a freak accident had contracted AIDS from supposedly screened blood.

So Montgomery said no. No blood. I was too sick to care. After two weeks I left the hospital with a hemoglobin of 4.4—it was 12.6 when I was admitted. I was so weak, I couldn't care for my baby. I couldn't even make it to the bathroom without passing out on the floor.

Montgomery hired us Rosalita, a Hispanic maid with a heavy accent and no green card, and moved her into the spare bedroom to be housekeeper and nursemaid to the baby and to me. After two months I was still weak, and postnatal depression had set in. I spent most of every day in bed crying and feeling sorry for myself; I was out of control and spiraling down.

Montgomery was feeding me Valium and tranquilizers, and I could no longer sleep. Eating was a vague memory. I looked like death warmed over and I didn't care.

Out of desperation, Montgomery called Sonja. She drove down, packed me up, and drove me back to New Orleans for a two-month visit and recuperation. That was the beginning of my yearly jaunts to New Orleans.

"Montgomery never called me," Sonja said. I tensed, brought back from memories that were suddenly false, deceptive. "He showed up on my doorstep at six in the morning, half-drunk and looking like hell. He was desperate and offensive and, frankly, unbalanced." She paused, staring out the windshield with unfocused eyes. "He was there to beg, but he ended up threatening. You might say he laid down the law." She gave a brief smile, glanced at me and away.

"He told Philippe and me how sick you were and how much you needed help, so I told him I would drive down and get you and the children. He had other ideas. He told me I could take you, but the children had to stay with him. Insurance, I suppose, to make sure you would return. As it turned out, the children didn't need to go with you anyway. You needed rest." Sonja's fists clenched on the steering wheel. "But before he left, he told me what he would do to me if I ever let you leave him. He made his marriage to you my responsibility."

I looked quickly at Sonja. Her brows puckered, she pursed her lips, and I looked away, not really understanding where this all was going, but knowing Sonja never said anything without a reason. I wasn't too sure I wanted to know that reason.

"Before he left, he broke Philippe's fingers."

I flinched. I remembered the finger-splint Philippe wore and the pain he was in during the first weeks of my visit, so long ago. I closed my eyes.

She was silent. The bobwhite called again, and this time the one nearby didn't answer.

"He said if you ever left him, he would make sure Philippe would regret it. And that I would never look at a man the same way again."

I blinked and remembered to breathe. The smell of new leather and expensive perfume filled my nostrils when I inhaled the stuffy air. The bobwhite called again in desperation. A pigeon used the windshield for target practice; a purple and white smear ran slowly down.

Never look at a man the same way again.

I knew what those words meant. Sonja thought she did.

And the DeLandes could get away with it. They could send trouble to the Rousseaus, attack them financially and politically. Send hired thugs to harm instead of protect. Men who wouldn't think twice about taking a woman and using her till she hated the sight of herself and the touch of a man. All it would take was money and patience and the lack of conscience to see it through.

Sonja took a deep breath. "I'm willing to risk anything if it gets you away from that bastard. But no games. You have to mean it. You have to want it and no going back."

"Why didn't you tell me?"

Sonja looked at me and smiled. It was that girlhood smile, mischievous, seductive, and mysterious. "I just did."

She opened the door and got out, swinging her legs out of the car to the street. Standing, she bent over and looked back inside the car. "I'm leaving the car here so they can check the hood when they find it. It shouldn't take them long. They'll know we came straight home by how cool the engine is. And if they just park and take up a position to watch, we'll have a good idea that they haven't contacted Montgomery and aren't going to. Come on." She closed the door and started for the house.

After a long moment, I opened my door and yelled after her. "Why didn't Philippe press charges against Montgomery for the fingers?"

She turned as she inserted the key in the lock. "Because you're my friend," she yelled back. "And because we got the whole thing on tape with the security camera for you to use if it ever became necessary. I still have a copy in the safe-deposit box."

She vanished inside the dark entry. The clouds had thickened, bringing a false twilight. The bobwhite was silent. I knew Sonja had still not told it all. She always held back some little something for later. For impact. Though if pressed for more, she'd just smile and look innocent. Sonja was good at that. Looking innocent.

I realized what she had done for me all these years. The taunts were to make me see some new truth about Montgomery. The silence was to protect me from something I wasn't ready to accept yet. It meant I was another of Sonja's causes, one of those things she was willing to risk her neck over, like the nearly extinct Louisiana brown pelican and the nearly nonexistent black-woman-in-politics, and the women's shelter and the foster home program.

A spatter of rain marked the windshield, the wind once again picked up and scattered leaves across the lawn, tugging at my skirts as though to pull me out of the car before the storm hit. What would my little stunt tell Montgomery about me, about the state of my feelings—the ones I didn't look at too closely, the ones I ignored and pretended didn't exist? I shivered in the suddenly cold wind. And what would it tell him about Sonja? Would he take her away from me now?

I followed the tug of the wind to the front door and entered. The house was silent, Sonja at the window in the dark, watching the Volvo through the blinds. She didn't speak as I joined her there, and I didn't know what to say anyway.

Tires squealed down the street, an engine roared, and the pea green Buick, looking even more jaundiced than earlier, hauled up beside the Volvo like a car full of punks in a fifties drag race movie. In the sudden rain that blasted down through the trees, the goateed passenger leaned out and placed his hand on the Volvo's engine hood, then jerked his soaked arm back inside. Rubber squealing against the shell-based asphalt, they did a U-turn and blasted through the rain back down the street.

Sonja sighed, resting her head against the molding to the left side of the window. "Trouble. They've gone to Montgomery."

Leaving her there, I turned and padded slowly up the stairs to the guest room, my new pumps in my right hand, the wood banister smooth in my left.

Sonja was afraid. It was the first time I had ever seen her afraid. She was the only fearless person I knew. She could shout back into the mouth of a hurricane and bring it to a halt with the fire in her eyes. Of course, then she'd smile politely and say thank you. I smiled to myself and entered the room that was mine whenever I visited.

Sonja had never told me, but I knew she had decorated it with me in mind. It was covered with wisteria in washed watercolored silk. Wisteria twined on the comforter, on the settee by the window, wisteria-tinted stripes banded the drapes, bed skirt, and the accent pillows, with tassels of dark purple and white and green for the leaves.

Sonja was afraid. I thought no one but me was afraid of Montgomery. I stared at the phone, rubbing my upper arms as the air conditioning blew down from the ceiling vent. *Never look at a man the same way again.*

Two or so years ago, a woman had shot Marcus, Montgomery's brother, a half dozen times in a hotel room just off the Quarter. She was some little tramp he'd met on Bourbon Street and slept with a few times, off and on for several months. They had a fight, he hit her, and she shot him. The story was from Montgomery, whispered into the dark in our bed in Moisson. I had felt the lie even as he spoke the words, but I didn't know what parts were lie and what parts were truth. Still didn't, although I had done some digging on my own.

The girl's name was Eve Tramonte, and she had severed Marcus's spinal column with her first shot, and torn holes in his intestines with the rest. Paralyzed from the waist down with a colostomy bag attached to his side and no chance of ever walking or using the toilet again, Marcus was lucky to be alive.

The DeLande brothers had handled the situation, and although no charges had ever been filed, the girl had been *dealt with.* Montgomery's words. He had finished off that late night conversation by saying that Eve Tramonte would *never look at a man the same way again.*

He chuckled over the paper a few days later, the account of a crime involving three black youths from Chicago who had gang-raped a young woman in the Quarter and left her for dead. I had taken the folded paper from the ottoman after he left for work and found the write-up about the rape. I read the article.

I suppose I realized what it meant, the article about the rape. I stayed cold for days afterward, wrapping up in a blanket and sitting, holding my swollen belly and the child I was carrying within me. Morgan. My baby. I had understood. And done nothing.

Now, slowly, I reached for the phone and the slender address book beside it. The address book was covered in peach-colored silk, and had a slim gold pen attached to a gold and peach braided cord. A gift from Montgomery. Tears started at the corners of my eyes and threatened to fall, and all I wanted to do was cuddle up under the wisteria comforter and cry for a month. But although I turned blind eyes to things in my life, I had never run from anything or anyone. Not even Montgomery. And I wouldn't start now.

I had a friend from nursing school, Ruth Derouen, who now worked on the Rape Crisis Council. Quickly, before I could think it through and change my mind, I looked up her number and called her. Ruth worked second shift and was free to talk, as I had expected; she loved to talk, and had no ability whatever to keep a secret.

The phone call was a blur, with me sounding lighthearted and a bit silly, catching up on what had been happening to our classmates over the last few years, who had married whom, and had how many children, or moved away. At one point I brought up Eve Tramonte and asked after her now that she was recuperating. Ruth told me all about it, the ordeal the girl had faced and how she was fighting the disease, and on and on. Somehow I ended the conversation, or Ruth did, and I found myself holding the receiver, still standing in my stocking feet, staring at the phone. Carefully I placed the receiver in its cradle and sat slowly down on the floor in the dark room. Lightning flickered close by, and rain lashed the panes.

Eve Tramonte, a pretty half-Cajun, half-Indian girl of

twenty-two, had been attacked as she walked home from Jax Brewery, where she worked as a cocktail waitress. Three young black men had jumped her from the dark, abandoned entryway of an out-of-business restaurant, pulled her inside, and raped her repeatedly for two hours. Before they left, they had taken a six-inch, double-blade knife and raped her with that as well.

The whole time that she screamed and cried and pleaded, two white men, their faces hidden by bandanas like bandits in an old-time train robbery, had sat impassively and watched. One smoked through a slash in the bandana. The other drank. The drinker wore a cowboy hat and boots. And just before they vanished with the gang members, he tipped his hat like some well-mannered cattle baron passing Miss Kitty on the street.

The black teenagers had bragged about the exploit and the money the white men paid in order to watch the incident. They were now serving time. One had died in jail of AIDS. Eve Tramonte was dying of the same disease.

In the dark of the wisteria room, I reached again for the phone, dialing Montgomery's office number from memory. My hand shook slightly, the manicured nails colorless and shining in the lightning flashes. A tinny ring sounded, again.

I pulled the comforter off the bed, tucking the vine's arms around me, wrapping them as if they grew there, smothering me with their embrace. I was cold, so cold.

On the forth ring, LadyLia answered, her voice smooth and cultured. LadyLia, one word, two caps, was one-forth Italian, one-forth Irish, one-half black, with a Choctaw grandmother about four generations back, and Montgomery's right-hand man. She was fifty-four, accomplished, smooth, and capable, a paralegal with ten years specialized experience as a research clerk at Matthesion, Dumont, and Svoboda, New Orleans's leading investment brokers. In the five years she had been with Montgomery, she had made him a bundle with her suggestions on market investments. She put me on hold.

There were clicks, several of them, and I realized the call was being rerouted. Montgomery wasn't in the office. LadyLia wouldn't have told me either way. About ten minutes later Montgomery picked up. It was long enough for me to calm down and think, something I hadn't done a lot of today.

"Nicole."

"Oh, Montgomery. I'm so sorry. I've done the most stupid thing." The tears started falling, and I searched beneath the comforter for the pocket I carried tissues in, wiping my nose. "Sonja just finished fussin' at me and ... and ..." I sobbed, blowing my nose, the shakes back full force.

Never look at a man the same way again.

Montgomery was silent.

"I did a rotten thing, and I'm sure when you hear about it you'll worry somethin' awful." When I'm upset, the soft southern accent I always carry becomes heavy, and my words seem to drip with the rich drawl. I hated it. Montgomery loved it.

He was silent still, and I cried harder, shivering beneath the comforter with cold and dread, and some kind of respect for myself. I had never lied to Montgomery before, keeping silent not being the same thing as lying. And I was good at it.

"You know how you're always tellin' me I act before I think? Well, I did it again today. And Sonja just blessed me out about it, and I feel jus' terrible . . ." My breathing was the only sound on the line, so I blew my nose again just to hear some sound. "Montgomery?"

Finally he sighed through his nose, the breath sound caught and magnified by the transmitter. "What did you do this time?" It was a reprieve of sorts. I didn't delude myself that he didn't know all about it already, but if he was still talking . . .

I explained about the note and made it sound frivolous—which it was—and infantile—which it had been—and dangerous—which it could be. Dangerous to me. Dangerous to Sonja. "I know they are there to keep us safe, and Sonja thought I was jus' so unkind to tease them. I didn' mean to make them worry. Or you when they told you." I was babbling, and the accent was so strong, I could almost smell it.

Never look at a man the same way again.

At last I wound down. "Montgomery? Are you mad at me for being so silly? I know it was a schoolgirl prank."

"Nicole, you know I worry when you take off on these trips. You know that. But I'm glad Sonja at least had some sense. Did she tell you to call me?"

I sensed some kind of trap and hesitated. To cover the short silence I spoke in a small voice. "No. I jus' thought . . ."

"Well, you did right. You should have called me. And you should listen to Sonja and not go off half-cocked like that."

Relief shuddered through me. "I know, Montgomery. An' I'm jus' so, so sorry."

"I'd come get you now, but Richard is here"—he pronounced it in the Cajun manner, *Rushar'*—"and we're all tied up on the Fausse Pointe project. I can't get away."

I was glad. I hated Richard, and Montgomery knew it. Richard was a swaggering cold-eyed, bigoted man. When he looked at me I felt stripped and bare and dirty. But his presence gave me breathing room, and perhaps he'd be gone when I got back home.

"Will you be good from now on and listen to Sonja?"

"Oh yes, Montgomery, I promise. And when the—" I almost said *thugs* or *goons*, as I did to Sonja "—bodyguards check in, will you apologize for me? I didn't mean to make their job harder for them."

Montgomery laughed, sounding so much like the Montgomery who had courted me that something twisted deep inside me. I closed my eyes and sat up slowly, pushing the comforter away. "That's not what they said. They called you a few names I reckon you deserved." It was Montgomery now who slithered down into the southern-sounding vowels and chopped-off consonants. It meant he was no longer angry, and I sagged back to the floor and pulled the comforter over my head. "They got a ticket for holdin' up traffic. I told 'em I wouldn't pay it for their incompetence in losin' you. Don't worry, babe. They'll live. I gotta go. Love ya."

"I . . . love you, too, sweetheart."

He clicked off, and slowly I lowered the phone. I had skirted disaster by a narrow margin, I knew that. Of course, there would be a price to pay. There always was for a visit to Sonja's.

I shivered, thinking about that price. It would be a high one this time. Perhaps higher than I could pay. Not that Montgomery ever hit me. A DeLande would never be so crude. A DeLande was imaginative, and I had been on the receiving end of that imagination several times in the years since I married.

A soft knock woke me, gentle and persistent, but I snuggled down deeper in bed. Rosalita would go away if I stayed quiet long enough. She had her orders. But the knocking continued, and I turned my head to tell her to go away, burning my skin. Raising my head, I looked down. Carpet. I was on the floor.

It all came back then. The fake itinerary. Sonja's little revelation. Eve Tramonte. Montgomery. I had fallen asleep on the floor. The knock sounded again, and this time the door cracked open.

"Collie?"

I smiled, feeling the skin pull on my tear-dried face. When we'd been little, Sonja was Wolfie—short for Russian wolf-hound because of her Rusky-sounding name. I was Collie, short for Nicolette.

"Come in." My voice was rough with sleep. "I fell asleep on the floor." The crack opened wider, but it was dark in the hallway, even darker than in the wisteria room.

"The electricity's off. We've cooked out on the patio on

the gas grill, and if you can stand a meal of roast corn on the cob, roast onions and peppers, roast potatoes, grilled shrimp, and blackened trout, then supper's ready." Sonja's voice was hesitant as if she feared that Montgomery would appear and break more fingers. Maybe mine. Maybe hers.

I groaned as I pulled myself from the floor, stepping out of the tangled, twisted comforter just as I would have had the wisteria really grown up around me in the dark as I slept. "I called Montgomery. Everything's okay. Let me brush my teeth and I'll be right down."

Sonja moved into the room, glass tinkling on the bureau, and struck a match, lighting the hurricane lamp. I had never used it before, but there was one in every room. And extra oil and candles and batteries and a battery-powered radio. Standard hurricane supplies.

"You might want to change. Some of the Rousseaus are here. With the power out, everyone's brought something to add to the feast." She still sounded nervous, looking around at the flickering shadows that moved with the wick, as if she thought Montgomery might be hiding in the room to jump out and frighten her. "We'll eat by candlelight and lamp, off of paper plates. It's turned off cold, so you might want to dress warm."

I looked down while she was speaking. I might not have ruined my silk shell by splattering Petunias' good breakfast on it, but sleeping on the floor in it and dropping mascara tears down it had done the job just as well. The skirt was pretty well ruined too.

Sonja closed the door, watching as I stripped off the silk and pulled on a gray, cowl-neck cashmere sweater and gray slacks, washed my face in cool water to kill the redness left in my skin from the tears, and reapplied a touch of makeup. With my ash brown hair and gray eyes, the only spot of color on my person was the hot pink Isotoner slippers I stretched over my feet.

I talked while I dressed, and Sonja listened with her usual quiet intensity. She reacted only once, when I told her about

Eve Tramonte. She turned hollowed eyes to me and shook her head. Her face was flushed.

"You have a decision to make, you know," she said when I finished.

"No I don't." I shook my head, sliding a brush through my hair. "Montgomery was home that night. And I don't have any proof."

She looked at me strangely. "It sounded like Miles Justin and Richard. Richard's the only DeLande who smokes except Marcus." She was talking about the two white men who watched Eve Tramonte's rape.

"Proof." I watched her, setting the brush down on the counter by feel. "No proof. Just suspicions."

"You know who did it." Small pink spots appeared high on her cheeks. "You *know.*" Suddenly Sonja had on her crusade face—the one she wore to the Save Our Wetlands meetings; the one she wore when she went to a soup kitchen. Intransigent. Sonja was patience personified, but she would not compromise.

I nodded slowly. "Maybe."

"Maybe nothing. You can't just—"

"Never look at a man the same way again. Isn't that what Montgomery said to you? Well, what do you think he would say to me if I went to the police with what I guess—or what I *fear*, if we're being precise? What do you think some DeLande brother would do to me? If they are capable of watching Eve Tramonte be raped, then they are likely capable of anything." Sonja watched me with wide eyes like dark pits in the uncertain lamplight.

"And although Montgomery could protect me against anything, I don't know if he would." The words stuck in my throat. "I really don't know what Montgomery would do." Tears that I had thought all cried out surfaced again.

"Dinner's ready," she said, and turned briskly away, moving through the door and to the darkened stairs. A faint light flickered at the bottom of the staircase as I followed slowly.

The meal was tedious and uncomfortable, Sonja shooting me accusing looks and jumping at any odd little sound. I could sense the anger and fear that mingled in her mind. Anger that I wouldn't accuse the DeLande men of orchestrating and watching Eve Tramonte's rape. Fear of Montgomery.

And somehow I knew there was something else about Montgomery. Something she knew and wouldn't say, something she was hiding. Something Montgomery had done.

Later that night, when I confronted her about it, she told me to mind my own damn business. And she slammed a door in my face.

I had trouble sleeping that night, and it had little to do with the fact that I went to bed a little bit drunk, or that the lights flashed on at 3:50 A.M. and roused the household, or that I had slept for six hours on the floor. It had everything to do with Sonja's accusations against the DeLandes. And I hated Sonja for that.

Each time I closed my eyes I could see the scene. The tawdry little abandoned restaurant, the girl held down and forced. Over and over again.

The next morning I went home.

CHAPTER

4

Two weeks passed and I was able to put Sonja's fear and my own tears away in The Box in my mind where all my bad memories were stored along with the rebellion and the dangerous anger and the desire to say no. The Box was bigger now than when I first made it, and full. So full it creaked and strained under the pressure whenever I noticed it. Or whenever I needed to use it to hide away some bad thing I didn't want to look at just now. If ever.

I didn't have a need for The Box right then, however. Because I was pregnant—blissfully pregnant. And sure it would be a boy this time again. I had already called my family with the news, and spent some time on the line with Logan, my whiz of a brother, planning what I would do with the birthing money.

In the DeLande world, boys are valued higher than girls. Literally. Morgan had netted me one hundred thousand, and I was greedily contemplating the same largess for producing boy number two. My nest egg was a toy I never touched, but liked to play with just the same. It was like a game, with the same feeling of unreality as dealing poker with play money. I could get used to being rich, I decided, if my investments paid off as I hoped.

I was washing parsley and fresh lettuce greens and mint for the tea, standing at the sink with cold water running over my hands, the air conditioning humming full blast in the sudden hot spell, and the radio blaring a Garth Brooks retrospective hour, yodeling a melody into my sunny kitchen. I was listening to KCSO out of Morgan City, a station I only listened to when Montgomery was out of town on business.

Montgomery liked jazz and blues and considered country music a poor man's knockoff of the real thing. But country music was my secret vice, and I held it to me like a talisman, a reminder that I was still me. It was too soon, but I could have sworn the baby kicked in time to the music.

It was Friday, and Rosalita was gone for the day, and I felt free. She had moved out when she got her citizenship last year and married, but worked full-time for us to pay her way through college, even staying over whenever we needed extra help. So it was just me and my girls and Morgan and the baby-to-be for the whole weekend, and I could go where I wanted when I wanted. I could watch late night TV and talk on the phone to Mama and friends and eat in bed and listen to Garth Brooks if I damn well pleased. I turned up the volume, singing at the top of my lungs.

I had managed to forget the short stay at Sonja's. Forget the fight I had with her before leaving. Forget the door slamming in my face. Forget Eve Tramonte. Forget everything. At least while I was awake and the feeling of foreboding was shackled deep in my subconscious along with the strange dreams I was having.

And because I had come home early and pregnant, Montgomery had not exacted his usual revenge-price from me in the privacy of the bedroom. He had, in fact, been kind and gentle and wonderful. And I was able to ignore the faint tickling at the back of my brain that whispered everything was not all right.

I reached up and touched the one-carat diamond in my left ear. The right ear had a matching bauble. Together the pair had cost Montgomery twenty thousand dollars. He had a ring hidden in the study he didn't know I knew about. It was two and a half carats and probably cost more than the earrings did. I was turning into an avaricious little hussy.

Montgomery's generosity had extended to the girls as well. They had new clothes and new dolls from the shopping trip he took us all on when he picked me up in New Orleans.

He'd been euphoric, the letter confirming him as a deacon at Saint Gabriel's Church, the largest Catholic church in Moisson Parish, waving in his hand. The letter meant that Montgomery's long-held political ambitions were finally on track. If his agenda stayed on course, he would be a Louisiana senator in a few years, and we'd be living in Washington as one of the state's most powerful families. It had been more than two decades since a DeLande went to Congress, and Montgomery wanted to restore that part of the family's preeminence. I'd closed my mind to the memory of Eve Tramonte and let Montgomery's pride in his coming child and his image of the future wash away my fears.

I loved this Montgomery. If I could stay pregnant, life would be perfect.

A tug at my hem distracted me and I looked down into Dessie's and Shalene's eyes, big and solemn, one set blue and one set like milk chocolate. I caught my breath, turned away, and turned off the water, staring out the window at the sunny yard. It was nothing. *It was nothing.* Yet I felt cornered suddenly, as though a trap door closed over me and the sun went dim. Perhaps it only passed behind a cloud, or perhaps their eyes had in truth just sucked all the light out of my world.

A chill swept through me and slowly I leaned over, cutting Garth off in midnote. I dried my hands on a towel and squatted down, gathering my girls to me, each one in an arm, holding them close. But their bodies were rigid, and

Shalene pulled back. Dessie permitted the hug, stiff, but unresisting as usual.

That was another good thing Montgomery had done since I got home. He'd finally promised to look for a counselor for Dessie. She'd grown so thin, I thought she might starve. But the memory of Montgomery's acquiescence did nothing to ease the sudden dread I felt, and my breath was hard to catch.

"What is it?"

After a moment Shalene looked up, Hershey brown eyes determined. "We been talkin'."

I smiled, the stricture on my heart easing. She used the same words when she intended to talk me into some special treat. Ice cream? A trip into town for snow cones? "Yes?" I drew out the word knowingly.

The girls looked at each other, communicating as only children can, with eyes and body movements, content and intent written and read. "You bleedin', Mama?"

I pulled my hands to the front, turning them palm up and palm down. "No. I'm not bleeding. See?" I laughed, but the sound died as though torn from the air by the vacuum of their eyes.

"Las' year when you come back from A'nt Sonja's, Daddy said you was bleedin' and not lable."

Last year? Shalene had been only four . . .

"Available," Dessie whispered. "Bleeding and not available. And we had to play."

The trapdoor slammed down on me, icy iron teeth biting into bone and tissue and marrow.

Bleeding and not available. And we had to play.

I knew. In an instant, like sun-shattered crystal, I understood what they were saying.

Bleeding and not available. And we had to play.

Some part of my mind coldly and concisely began to put pieces together, weaving a whole tapestry from bits and shards of my life.

Bleeding and not available. And we had to play.

But . . . but. I shook my head and the tapestry unraveled.

"You have to play with Daddy?" I asked stupidly.

Both heads bobbed.

"And you don't like that? To play with Daddy?"

Two pairs of eyes watched mine: one set was steady and determined, the other steady and afraid. *Bleeding and unavailable* . . . Montgomery's words. Montgomery's phrase.

"What . . ." I swallowed past a suddenly dry throat. "What does Daddy do . . . when he . . . when he plays with you? Something you don't like?"

"He touches us. In our fannies. And he licks us there."

I sat down slowly on the floor as my knees gave out, my hands shaking like an old woman with palsy. The words whispered through my mind again, and the trap's iron teeth bit soul-deep. Shalene crawled up into my lap, her fingers picking at the buttons on my blouse. Dessie sat beside her on the floor and watched the fingers, her eyes never searching for mine.

Bleeding and not available. And we had to play.

"And he chokes Dessie with his thing."

My breath came short and fast. Bile rose, rancid and stifling with the remembered taste of semen.

I suppose some women don't understand the import of words spoken by children. And some have difficulty believing. Some simply never reconcile the two visions—the generous husband who gives diamonds and toys, and the beastly man who . . . who touches his children. But I did. I swallowed hard.

Into the silence of my once sunny kitchen I spoke. "How . . . What else does he do? Does he make you do?"

"He puts lipstick on us when you go to visit A'nt Sonja in New O'leans. And he makes us wear your nightgowns."

"The pretty ones," Dessie added in a whisper. Her head was down where she sat beside me, her blond-streaked hair hiding shamed eyes.

I stroked her hair, feeling beneath it the fragile bones of skull and brow, jaw and vertebrae. She was so thin.

I remembered coming home from Sonja's two weeks ago and going into a rage because my girls had been playing dress-up in my nightgowns. My beautiful silk lingerie. And I spanked both of them furiously, staying angry at them for days for such willful disobedience and disrespect.

Montgomery had unexpectedly—and uncharacteristically—intervened on their behalf, claiming they had asked to play dress-up and he had let them, not knowing that some things were off limits. He had apologized and soothed me, sending my chastised daughters away to play.

Shalene nodded officiously, reading my reaction. Then she looked at Dessie and back at me, took a deep breath. "This time when you was gone, Uncle Richard come to visit." She pronounced it *Rushar'*, as Montgomery did. As the Grande Dame did. "And Daddy gived Dessie to him to play with."

"Oh, Jesus," I whispered. The silence in the kitchen was charged, like the atmosphere before a lightning storm, rich in ozone and fear. And I could still taste the semen like a dull sour smear in the back of my throat.

"He hurt her real bad."

"Dessie? Is that true? Daddy . . . Daddy *gave* you to Uncle Richard?"

She traced the rough edge of the Mexican tile with her finger, following the grout. "I hate him," she said softly, not differentiating between her uncle and her daddy.

The silence built in the room, deep and rich like the silence of the swamp at midnight, heavy with waiting and the smell of rotted vegetation. Shalene looked up at me, her head bumping against the bottom of my chin.

"Daddy said you bleed. Are you gonna die, Mama?"

"No," I said, my voice a distant wind. "No. I'm not going to die." I looked down into their eyes, so trusting and afraid, limpid pools of fear and horror and pain. Taking a deep breath, I continued. "I want you girls to listen to me. You lis'nin'?"

Both sets of eyes fastened on mine, the vacuum I had detected in them sucking deep from some well of dependence on me. "Daddy's not ever going to hurt you again. You hear? Not ever." I remembered Sonja's words the night of the storm and the feast. *You have a decision to make.*

"See? I tol' you Mama'd take care of us," Shalene said, her tone superior.

"He said he'd kill her if we told," Dessie whispered, tears finally pooling in her blue eyes, like rain from a cloudless sky. "And then he'd give me back to Uncle Richard." The words were wrenched from her like the gasps of a woman birthing a child. She shivered in the heat, a tremor passing down her frail frame. "I don't want him to kill you, Mama. I'll go back to Uncle Richard, but I don't want him to kill you."

I grabbed my daughter, holding her close, and even now she stiffened against me in reaction. A reaction I at last understood. This time I didn't let her go at once, but continued to hold her, not moving, not stroking her. Doing nothing to remind her of a man who wanted to *play with her.* A long moment passed as her quivering worsened. And suddenly she sobbed in my arms, a violent anguished sound, slipping her own bony arms around my neck.

"You're not going back to Uncle Richard," I said, my voice a rasp in the back of my throat. "Not ever. Not even if I did die. But nobody's gonna kill me. Nobody." I rocked her slowly. "I'll take care of you. I promise. I promise. I promise." I rocked her back and forth, promising through a parched mouth, my voice hoarse and raspy, rough with unshed tears. My daughter cried and I held her, my own eyes dry and burning, as Shalene looked on satisfied and the sun passed behind the clouds and reappeared again and again.

Finally Dessie pulled away and stared into my eyes. Her face was red and swollen and . . . When had my child gotten so frail? So starved?

After a long moment she smiled. She had heard my promises and she believed. She believed in me. The tears I had held at bay pooled and threatened to fall. She reached forward and took my hand. Hers was cold, the bones as fragile as a bird's wing.

The girls stayed curled with me, there on the kitchen floor, my back against the oven. I could hear the clock ticking in the hallway; it chimed the quarter hour.

"I want you girls to promise me something, okay, *mes bébés?*" Dessie pulled away, fear in her eyes, and I recognized one of Montgomery's lines. *You have to promise me something.* "No. Not like that. Not bad. Not secrets," I said, understanding suddenly. "Something good."

Dessie waited, her breathing fast, her pulse a flutter in her throat.

"No more bad secrets. Okay? No secrets of any kind. You tell me everything. Even if you think it's bad. Even if you think I'll get mad," I added, thinking of my silk nightgowns. "Everything. Understand? And I'll listen. And no matter what, I'll never hurt you. Hear me? I'll never hurt you again."

The sun came back out a bit, the room mottled by sun and leaf shadow, moving in a breeze. Dessie nodded slowly. Shalene, too, though I could see the calculation in the eyes of my opportunistic second child.

"Me sha? Can you girls go—" the word caught in my throat "—play? Mama's got some thinking to do. Some planning. Can you do that? Go play in the yard? But stay close, 'cause we might be going away, to Nana's," I said, meaning my mama, "or out of town. Okay?"

"Forever?" Dessie asked, her face utterly changed, and I shook to my core at the desperate hope mirrored in her delicate features. My firstborn was lovely at that moment, showing a promise of beauty to come, an ethereal glow like a subject in a Rembrandt painting.

"I . . . I don't know. Yeah. I think so. I . . ." The memory of Montgomery laughing in delight over the news of our coming child, his face open and joyous, pierced me. "Maybe." The joy in Dessie's eyes faded, as though she had never really dared believe I would protect her, and I had lived up to her meager expectations.

"Don't say 'yeah,' Mama. Say 'yes, ma'am,'" Shalene said, catching me at the grammar game we played.

I managed a smile. "Yes, ma'am. I think we're going away. Maybe forever."

Dessie looked again deep in my eyes and slowly nodded, hearing the prevarication, but trusting the promises. Needing the promises. Pulling Shalene up, she turned away, and they headed to the back door. It opened with a creak of paint-coated weather stripping Montgomery had promised to replace. Hand in hand they stood framed in the blaring sunlight of the backyard, heat pouring in like a hot *roux,* sticky and clinging, stinging the skin with sweat.

"Dessie?" They stopped and turned back, faces obscured in silhouette against the vicious sun. "How long? How long has Daddy made you . . . do those things with him? How long has he . . ." The words faded away.

She shrugged, her too bony shoulders rising against her T-shirt. "Forever."

I shuddered as the door closed behind them. Curled into a fetal ball and wrapped my arms around my shins, holding myself tight against the memory of the last quarter hour, the word tolling in my mind like a funeral bell. *Forever.*

I don't know how much time passed before I got my breathing under control, but I could hear the girls playing, Shalene's screams loud and laughing, Dessie's much softer and tentative, the giggles a curious counterpoint to my gasping sobs. The sun continued to dapple the kitchen floor, the clock continued to chime the quarter hours, the girls' voices continued to echo the awful words in my mind.

How could I not have known? How could I be so blind? I searched for clues in my memory, my mind skittering around like a blind rat in a box.

The girls had often begged me not to go to Sonja's. Cried when I left and clung to me when I returned home. But didn't all children? I had occasionally left the bedroom to check on the baby during the times when I was bleeding and not available to Montgomery, the master suite door squeaking on its tight hinges. *Hinges Montgomery never oiled,* my mind whispered. Once or twice I had found Montgomery in the girls' room, curled up on the big bed they shared, telling them a story. But so what? Fathers tell their children stories when they can't sleep or have bad dreams.

But Dessie—my precious Desma Collette—had stopped eating. Was starving herself to get away from the agony of her life. Had withdrawn into herself and held the world at bay. How had I not known? Where were all the clues? The little things the child psychologists tell a mother to be on the lookout for?

Finally I pulled myself from the floor and washed my hands under hot water to warm them. I fixed a pot of strong coffee and watched it perk, although my ob-gyn had forbidden me caffeine for the duration of my pregnancy. I needed the stimulant. So I could think. So I could plan. So I could absorb the dreadful truths my girls had spoken. My fingers shook as I held my cup, sitting at the breakfast table, looking blindly into the backyard.

The wisteria Montgomery had given me as a wedding present and planted beside a cypress sapling was in bloom. Already its wiry arms had encircled the young tree, climbing to its height and reaching for the sun, fighting for light and water and root space in the sandy soil. Idly I wondered how long before my beauty strangled its host tree to death. That thought still sharp in my mind, a frozen image, I reached for the phone and dialed a number at random.

"Hello?"

Like a child myself, I had called my mama. Tears started again at the sound of her voice, and I could scarcely speak. I had been crying a lot lately, but then I was always emotional when pregnant. "I have a problem, Mama. Can we talk?"

I stood and walked to the sink, dumped out the cold cup of coffee, the dark fluid a brown stain spiraling down the white porcelain. Pouring a fresh cup of coffee, I added a large dollop of cream and sugar, moving mechanically as I told her what the girls had said.

It was disjointed and uncertain and I burned my mouth on the too hot liquid as I spoke, watching my wisteria through the glass. I shared my hurt, my fears, my pain, my uncertainty, and through the whole sordid story she was silent, asking only clarifying questions now and again when I stumbled over words or wasn't clear on a point. Finally I trailed off into embarrassed silence, tears dry on my face, sipping the now cold coffee over my burned tongue, ignoring the discomfort.

"What do I do, Mama? What do I do? I need . . . Can I come home for a while, Mama? Can the girls and Morgan and I come home? I need some time to decide what to do. And some breathing space."

Tisk, tisk, tisk. Her tongue made that admonishing sound she'd used to keep me in line when I was a child. It could shame or cheer me, depending on the circumstances in which I found myself. This time I smiled. "I think you're making a big deal out of nothing."

My smile faded. Her voice was soothing, slow and drawling with the vowel sounds drawn out, and I could hear the dishes clinking in the sink, the TV on in the background.

Laughing shakily, I wiped my eyes. Mama could understate an earthquake. To her there was no such thing as a problem, just inconveniences.

"Montgomery is a good husband, isn't he?"

I stilled, not certain where she was going with this line of thought.

"Now, you just calm down, and think this through. You don't want to anger your husband. And you should be ashamed to doubt Montgomery. Why, he's the finest man to all of us. Did you know he gave your daddy a new bass boat last month?"

My coffee had cooled, and a film of oil and cream sheened the top. It, too, needed to be thrown out, but I just held it. The girls ran across my line of vision and climbed the tiered monkey bars, swinging bare legs off the ground. "Mama. My girls said—"

"Well, they're just children, and you know the kind of tales they make up. I used to tan your backside when you'd come home with some wild story. They'll forget all about this silliness in no time and be on to some other little game. You shouldn't be concerned over something like this. I'm sure it's just the pregnancy making you so upset."

I sat my cup down on the table, missing the saucer and sending it clattering and sloshing across the painted wood top. "My girls—"

"Marriage isn't always easy, sweetheart. You should try harder to please Montgomery. You know he's going to be a senator someday and you'll be living in Washington, attending parties with ambassadors and the president, although I hope we have a good Republican in office when you go. It would be such a shame to have a Democrat in the White House." She sighed.

While she spoke, I watched the puddle of coffee and cream crawl slowly to the edge of the table, widening and spreading as it moved. "My girls—"

"I just envy you all that excitement. And I'd never endanger your marriage by allowing you to run away and come back home. Why, Montgomery would be furious with us. Now, you just put all this behind you and make up your mind to trust the man you married and everything will work out fine."

My eyes were dry and wide, the coffee spilling over like tears and splattering on the floor. "Mama, did you hear anything I said?" My voice came out breathy and incredulous, with half-hysterical laughter propelling the words. I stood slowly, pushing myself away from the table. "I said Montgomery has been *touching my babies!*" I screamed the last words.

"Don't you raise your voice to me, young lady. You're not too old to show some respect. Of course I heard what you said. But so what? It happens all the time. That's no reason to go running away. Men do these things sometimes. It's in their nature." Her voice rose, shaking. "We women have to be the strong ones. We have to bear these things."

With numb legs I found the chair and sat back down. "Did you have to bear these things?" I whispered.

The silence was sharp with shock. I could hear her take a breath as though to speak, and then release it. "Of course not." She sounded insulted. "But it'll all work out. You'll see. They'll forget. You just be patient. I have to run now." Her voice brightened. "Your daddy is pulling up in the drive, and we're going to do some catfishing in his new boat. Doesn't that sound like fun? You thank Montgomery for us again. It's a beauty, and your daddy is so proud, he could pop. 'Bye now." And she hung up the phone, satisfied she had solved my little inconvenience.

I sat for a long moment, then stood again and found a rag, ran some water on it, and wiped the coffee from the tabletop and the floor. Mechanically I rinsed it again and folded it carefully across the divider between the twin sinks. *Men do these things sometimes. It's in their nature.* "Not to my babies, they don't." I poured a last cup of coffee and sipped it black, although I prefer double creams and sugars.

Then I called Sonja.

I worked the half-rotten vegetables and oatmeal, vermiculite and eggshells, into the compost, breaking the black clay and mixing in sand, the decaying vegetable matter a slick film on my goatskin gardening gloves. I had two compost bins. One was two years old, the contents of which I packed around new azaleas when they went into the ground. The other was fresh, full of last night's leftovers, and last week's, and last year's. It stank of methane whenever I lifted the thick black plastic that secured it from scavengers.

The girls were subdued, playing with toy trucks at my feet in the dirt, making roads and castles and tunnels for the vehicles to pass under. Dessie made the best tunnels, packing the soil firmly over the arch of her foot, using a stick to scrape away the loose edges and easing her toes back out. Shalene wasn't patient enough for the delicate task, and her tunnels usually fell; her specialty was roads decorated with twigs for trees along the sides and rock gardens and stick bridges.

I rose up, feeling the pregnancy in my lower back early this time. Or maybe it was just age. "It's dead. It can't get you now. You can go back and play in the yard."

Both girls eyed the dead rattler on the garbage can lid. It was in two pieces, the head and about three inches of neck in one spot, the rest of its fifteen inches writhing on sun-heated metal, where red ants hitched a ride.

Twin screams had alerted me to a problem, and grabbing the hoe at the back door, I had run on my bare feet to kill the snake. It wasn't very big, sunning itself on a bald patch of ground, but the smaller the snake, the more potent the venom, or so I'd heard.

I encourage black snakes and garters, green snakes and king, but rattlers, moccasins, and coral snakes, I killed no matter the size, no matter the environmentalists' prattle. A poisonous snake could be deadly to a child. I averaged two kills a year. The biggest was during the year I was pregnant with Morgan and a six-foot rattler crawled up into the yard to catch and digest a bullfrog. I wasn't afraid of snakes, although rats and spiders were another story—the girls were terrified.

"It's still squigglin'," Shalene said.

"It'll squiggle for hours," I said, immediately adopting Shalene's word. "If you two are going to shadow me, I'll be in the greenhouse next. Want some iced tea?"

They chorused agreement and I stepped into the house, checked on Morgan sleeping in his playpen in the family room, and poured three plastic tumblers full of my mint brew. The girls' tea was sweet and dark; mine came from a separate pitcher, decaffeinated and no sugar. I was back to following doctor's orders, the morning's rebellion over. The morning's revelations, however, hung across my shoulders like a lead-weighted shawl. *Montgomery* . . .

I closed the door, taking the tray of tea and gingersnaps across the patio and yard to the greenhouse that Montgomery had put together the year we were married. In it were the herbs Rosalita and I cooked with, the spring lettuce and tomatoes, year-old azaleas I had rooted from last spring's clippings, and bulbs ready to go into the ground.

I loved bulbs, daffodils and irises, tiger lilies, gladioli, and day lilies, even bluebells for the color and heavy blooms and the fact that they were low-maintenance. Contrary to Montgomery's belief, I didn't love gardening, but working in the yard did leave me refreshed and satisfied at the end of the day.

After an hour of fertilizing, weeding, watering, and thinning out the plants that would go into the yard and summer garden, the girls and I returned to the yard and the swing set. We were still there, tired, giggling, dirty, sweaty, and Morgan's cloth diaper a muddy disaster, when Sonja pulled up in the yard and cut her motor. The girls squealed and ran, hugging their aunt Sonja, who stooped and hugged back, disregarding the dirt that stained the white of her crisp linen blouse. I followed more slowly, carrying Morgan. When I reached her, she looked slowly up, as though she had to brace herself to meet my eyes over the heads of the girls; her own were wounded.

I had left New Orleans angry. But although our last words had been acrimonious, I had known she wouldn't turn me away when I needed her. Sonja never held a grudge, and she had the coolest, clearest head of anyone I had ever known. She should have been a lawyer instead of just marrying one. She could follow any argument to its logical conclusion. Yet she could see both sides of that same argument. I needed that ability right now, as my own clear head had grown dull and blurred.

"Thanks for coming."

She nodded, stood, and reached into the backseat for a suitcase. "I had to stop in town for a toothbrush and . . ." Her voice trailed off. She tried for a smile and failed, took a deep breath. "I see I should have picked up some detergent and bleach too. How in the world did you all get so dirty?"

"Mama killed a rattler, A'nt Sonja."

"A diamondback," Dessie added. "Come see. It was still squiggling." She took Sonja's hand, and Shalene tapped the suitcase. Sonja set it down and took her hand as well. Both girls pulled her back to the garbage cans in the section of yard I used to recycle and work the compost. The snake, hours dead, lay still, covered with red ants. Sonja shuddered delicately.

"Your mama used to kill snakes for me, too, back a long time ago when we played together." She sounded proud and I smiled. "She's not scared of anything. Not even dirt," she added as she looked us over.

"Bath time, girls," I said softly.

"Can we get in your tub," Shalene asked, "and turn on the bubbles?"

It was a treat for them. When Montgomery went out of town on one of his trips, I let the girls bathe in the master bath, the Mr. Bubble rising three feet above the water level when the whirlpool jets agitated it. It was a pain to clean up, but they loved it.

"Yeah, okay, if you promise to go right to bed afterward, no whining, no complaining."

"Yes, ma'am, Mama," Shalene said, catching me using the word I was trying to break them of. "Not yeah."

"Yes, ma'am, then. Do we have a bargain?"

The girls each shook my hand solemnly and took off for the house, squealing and jumping and shouting about bubble mountains. In the ensuing silence, Sonja regarded me over Morgan's head, her feelings masked.

"You okay?"

"I am now." Swallowing back the relieved tears, I managed a smile.

Sonja took Morgan. "I'll bathe the little one and you shower. We can talk tonight."

Sonja was used to boys, having been raised with brothers and with twin four-year-olds and a two-year-old at home on the Rousseau grounds. When she could, she adopted my girls to fill the void at not having a daughter at home as well. Sonja held Morgan up, inspecting the diaper as we walked to the house.

I sniffed. "He needs changing."

"No kidding." She grimaced. "God, what did you all do? Take the hose and make a mud bog, then roll around in it?" Without waiting for an answer, she went on, "Bath first, young man, then bed. He been fed?"

I nodded. "Picnic in the backyard. That's plum and bananas on his hands and chin, and I think there's some more in his ears."

Sonja glared. "Maybe you better give me a pickax to chisel it all off."

We parted ways in the hall. I carried her suitcase to the guest room, heaved it onto the bed, and opened it. Sonja could never pack for short time periods, and this trip was no exception. Before I went in search of the girls, I hung up her folded blouses and dresses so the wrinkles would fall out. It was a kindness; she performed the same service for me when I visited. But I never carried a gun in my suitcase. Wrapped in a pair of jeans was a snub-nosed .38 and a box of ammunition. Sonja hated guns. But she brought one to my house. . . . What was she afraid of? Montgomery? Quietly I rewrapped the .38 and went to my shower.

We talked till after midnight about Montgomery and the girls and my mother's bizarre response and my options. It all boiled down to options . . . and the decision I had to make to leave. The decision I had already recognized, and half promised to the girls as they sat curled on my lap on the kitchen floor. Sonja kindly did not mention Eve Tramonte and the decision I had refused to make implicating the DeLandes, but it hung on the air between us, unspoken and powerful.

"Wouldn't counseling work? I mean isn't there someplace Montgomery could go and get counseling and we could stay together? All of us."

Sonja nodded, a strange tension in her eyes. "Counseling would help. Maybe. But he'd have to want it. He'd have to want to change. Child molesting isn't a choice a man makes each time he reaches for a child. It's an addiction, an obsession that lasts his whole life. From the very first time he succumbs to that need, he's hooked. Like an alcoholic with a genetic predisposition. And there is no AA for child molesters, Collie. No detox. Montgomery would have to want to change more than anything else in the world. You have to decide if he loves you enough to make the changes. To admit that he has a problem. And in the meantime you have to decide how to live."

"Montgomery would never move out."

"Change the locks. Get a legal separation."

I shuddered to think of Montgomery's reaction to such a move on my part. I remembered his reaction the first time I said no to lovemaking. I never said no again.

"Look. You have choices." She ticked them off on her fingers once again. "Separation and counseling; either he moves out or you do and take the children. Divorce. Or you could go through the court system and let the state deal with Montgomery. Put his ass in prison. Let the other inmates show him what it feels like to be abused."

"He'd never go to jail. The DeLandes have too much power and too much money. They'd find a way to implicate me in some crime and take my children away from me. You know that."

"And he won't move out?"

I shook my head, my eyes on the wineglass turning slowly in my fingers. I had opened a hearty merlot bottled in the south of France, about thirty miles from Spain. It was so earthy and rich, you could taste the very soil of the region in each sip.

I shouldn't have opened the wine. It wasn't good for the baby, all that caffeine and alcohol I had ingested that day. I held the glass up to the light and tilted it, watching the way the world changed color when viewed through a thin film of wine.

"Move onto the Rousseau grounds, then." I looked at her quickly. "You and the kids. We've got that guesthouse. It's small, just two bedrooms, but the connecting den could be a nursery for Morgan. You could stay as long as you want. Till you decided what you want to do. It's empty. You'd have to bring furniture, but it's yours if you want it."

Sonja had spoken the last words slowly, as if she thought I might stop her at some point and refuse, accuse her of trying to break up my home and my marriage as I had the day I left New Orleans. That awful fight. I knew she hated Montgomery, although I had never learned why. Not even then, in the heat of anger. But even with all the attempts to get me to leave him, she had never pushed. Never made trouble. At least not until that last night. I smiled wryly.

"I had Lois Jean bring her sister to work this afternoon before I left. They started on the guesthouse. It'll be clean and livable in a couple of days."

"I thought Montgomery put you in charge of his marriage. I thought he threatened you."

"And I thought I told you I'd help any way I could as long as you didn't play games. I'll get you an injunction to keep him away from the property, and Philippe will hire a guard to make sure we're safe. And Adrian Paul, my brother-in-law, can handle the separation and divorce. . . . And then I'll find you a new husband."

I laughed. "You had to go on and add that, didn't you?"

Sonja grinned unrepentantly, lifted her glass in a salute,

and swallowed the last mouthful. "No matchmaking. I promise." She was serious. She wouldn't interfere.

"I have enough problems in my life right now without another man." The clock chimed the half hour. Twelve-thirty A.M. "Can we decide later? I'm tired." I set the wineglass down beside the nearly empty bottle, the crystal sounding a dull chink in the silent house. "I'm so tired, I could just curl up and die." Tears pooled in my eyes, as they had in Dessie's eyes earlier today, and I wished for my own mother so I could cry it all out as she had.

"You remember the time we were playing in the woods and I stepped in the nest of snakes?"

I nodded. We had been twelve or thirteen, wild and daring with the reckless courage of youth, always running the three miles or so through the woods to visit, or taking the flat-bottomed johnboat the shorter distance across water. On land, Sonja always went first, carrying a stick to take down spiderwebs. I followed with a dull, short-bladed machete Daddy gave me to kill snakes. The day Sonja stepped into the nest of snakes, we had been exploring a new path along an old bayou, many miles from home and in unfamiliar territory.

Sonja had stepped off the path, gone down in a hole covered with leaves, and come up screaming. Her foot had swelled up almost instantly, and seconds later, as I half carried her back along the path, her breathing became difficult. She started having chills, and I had known she was about to die.

"You were scared to death of Old Man Frieu. He couldn't half speak English and he fired that old shotgun off in the air whenever he saw us on his property. And he killed all those dogs."

There had been a rash of dog poisonings in the area, and everyone blamed Old Man Frieu. He hated any dog on his property and kept pails of antifreeze in his yard. Dogs loved it, the sweet taste of the pink liquid. And after they drank it, they died a horrible death. But no one could prove the dogs had drunk antifreeze from Old Man Frieu's place. And besides, there was no law against leaving the stuff out in pails.

"But you ran right up to him, even after he fired that shotgun, and knocked the gun out of his hands. And you made him come help me. You saved my life."

"Old Man Frieu saved your life when he took us straight to Daddy in his boat. Not me." I could still see Sonja cradled in Old Man Frieu's arms as the flat-bottomed boat scudded through the marsh. Wrapped in a filthy blanket and struggling for breath, Sonja had turned blue, her eyes glazed and her leg swollen and running red. Old Man Frieu had shouted for her to "breathe, damn yo', breathe," in both Cajun French and broken English, stroking her forehead as I piloted the boat, watching from the tiller.

Daddy had taken one look at her and gone to work. The veterinary versions of snakebite antivenin and epinephrine and oxygen had kept her alive until the ambulance arrived.

I shrugged. "I got mad." I remembered Old Man Frieu's face when I knocked the shotgun away, picked it up, and turned it on him. I had never told anyone that part, scared of the law and the fact that I threatened to shoot him. He was a wee little man, all whiskers and smelling of onions and whiskey, brandishing his shotgun and cussing me in Cajun. I was a good head taller than him even then, and I might have hurt him. I half grinned at the memory of him standing there mad and admiring and agreeing to help.

"You were even smart enough to kill one of those rattlers and toss it into the boat so the doctors would know what kind of antivenin to use. Well." She stretched and rolled her shoulders to relieve the strain of sitting for so long. "It's my turn to return the favor. I'm scared to death of Montgomery. Of all the DeLandes. But I won't let you face this alone." She stood and placed her hands into the small of her back, arching back and groaning. "See you in the morning."

She padded back toward the hall, her loose socks puddled around her ankles. I stared out the windows, my reflection looking back at me through the darkness, pale and weak and not the least bit heroic. "Sonja," I called.

She stuck her head back in from the dark hallway. "I'm pregnant."

I thought she might swear. Instead, after a long pause, she said, "Aunt Sonja to four of your brats and five Rousseaus. Huh. Congrats." And then she disappeared.

There really was little choice. By the end of the week everything was packed, the moving van was backed up into the yard. The girls and Morgan and I were heading to New Orleans. They were excited; even Morgan picked up on the scent of adventure. I was terrified.

I left the house nearly empty. Took most all the furniture, all the financial records, all the clothes except what belonged to Montgomery. I did leave him the couch and television, his recliner, his VCR and gun cabinet, the dresser, and a bed. Our bed. I couldn't stand the thought of sleeping on it again. I also left the girls' bed. After what they told me during the days we packed, I knew they needed a fresh start, and I intended to take them shopping so they could pick out what they wanted.

Sonja moved us all, my girls, Morgan—the baby-to-be—and me into the guesthouse on the Rousseau grounds, a six-room cottage we shared with Sonja's gray, long-haired Persian cat, Snaps. I didn't take to cats as a rule, but this one claimed us, and the girls loved her.

The cottage was a gingerbread-style clapboard with multipaned windows and heart of pine flooring and tall ceilings and fans that turned slowly to dissipate the spring heat instead of central air. It was overgrown with English ivy and honeysuckle and climbing rose, and it needed a coat of paint beneath the clinging vines. But it was secluded and private and not visible from the road, with its own carport and a rope swing hanging out front, tied high in the boughs of a massive sycamore. The back porch had a washer and dryer hookup and an ancient chest-style freezer. It was shady and cool and open to the breezes, and the scent of gardenia and wisteria blew in through the open windows. I never saw the wisteria. But I smelled it that first day, rich and sensual, innocent and intimate, like a young girl's dream of romance, like making love with a stranger who never closed his eyes.

CHAPTER

5

Bleeding and not available. And we had to play.

The words were a litany thrumming through the edges of my mind, the rhythm and texture of the syllables an enervating incantation sucking the light and the life out of me. I couldn't eat, thinking of Montgomery and the girls. I couldn't sleep. And when exhaustion did finally claim me in the early hours of each day, The Dream would claim me as well. I had The Dream every night until we moved, and often thereafter, and it was so real, my skin burned upon waking. In it, I was the rattler I had killed, twisting and blistered on the hot metal of the garbage can lid, writhing and exposed and feeble as fire ants tortured me. I would wake up gasping, clawing at my skin, still hearing the words.

Bleeding and not available. And we had to play.

I was paralyzed and useless, and tears came too easily. I found myself slipping back and forth between crippling numbness to an intense awareness, where my attention would be caught by some small thing like a frosted glass pitcher or a toothbrush or a mint leaf in the greenhouse. I would stand there, staring at it, my mind blank. It was a form of mourning, I think. And it was Sonja who saved me.

I felt like a puppet, one of the wooden kind with painted faces and jointed arms and legs, dancing a numb ballet as Sonja pulled the strings. I was wrong when I said she would make a good lawyer. She would, however, have made a fine general.

On day one, the day we moved to New Orleans, she moved us into the cottage and stored the excess furniture in one of those concrete block storage facilities, dumped off the financial records with a C.P.A., hired a security guard through the security company that protected the Rousseau grounds via electronic surveillance and various monitors, got a quote on wiring the small cottage, and talked to two lawyers.

Sonja was deliberately making my decisions for me, pushing me around, rushing me from subject to subject, from one logical thought process to the next, trying to jar me back to her reality and the decisions I had to make. It worked. On the day we moved I began to listen, to disagree, to think and feel again.

She even made an appointment for the girls and me with a counselor who specialized in sexually abused children within the family. I still couldn't call it what it was. Incest happened to other people. Low-class, white-trash, drug-addicted, alcoholic unwed mothers with scuzzy live-in boyfriends with torn, dirty jeans and greasy hair and . . . Oh, God. Not me. Not Montgomery. But . . .

Bleeding and not available. And we had to play.

I couldn't escape the words awake or asleep, and suddenly I didn't want to. I wanted to look at the words, see them, fondle them in my mind until they no longer had power over me. Over my girls. And I finally thought I might succeed, on that first night in the Rousseau cottage, my back against the unfamiliar mattress, a fan turning lazily in the ceiling of shadows above me. That night I slept. Long and hard and dreamlessly, and I woke up knowing where I was and what I had done and smiling in the half-light of the early day. I took a deep breath, the first in days. I was free.

The hurt and the shock were still there, powerful and binding, like the heavy links of a ponderous, rusted chain, but I was no longer shackled by them. I thought I might even manage to crawl out of them.

I still followed Sonja's directions on day two of the move to New Orleans, but now I followed clear-eyed and determined, under my own power, lucid and rational. I even disagreed with Sonja about the girls' schooling and saw the slow smile that curved her lips when I took that decision away from her and chose the school myself. That smile said, *It's about time.*

I decided to send the girls to a Catholic school, enrolling them in Saint Ann's Catholic School for Girls. It was located well outside the city on ten acres of sculptured grounds surrounded by old magnolias, oaks, and a high brick fence. It looked safe, and although it would mean a far drive each morning and evening through New Orleans's notorious traffic, I enrolled them on Friday, the morning of my second day. Then I went to see my lawyer.

I dressed with special care that Friday morning of the interview with the nuns and my new attorney. In a silk peach two-piece outfit of vest and baggy pants, with a contrasting aqua jacket and taupe shoes, I looked my best. Or at least as well as one can look after a week of no sleep and too many nightmares, a surreptitious move across state, and a slight case of morning sickness.

I left the girls with Lois Jean, Sonja's housekeeper, and a young girl from down the street who often looked after Sonja's boys to earn extra money. Cheri was a night student at the University of New Orleans. I hated to leave the girls and Morgan so soon, but I was satisfied Lois Jean and Cheri were acceptable short-term guardians.

Montgomery had never let me drive myself to New Orleans for one of my visits, claiming I didn't maneuver well enough in dense traffic. But I had no trouble negotiating my way in the late-model Toyota Camry I used in Moisson whenever he left me the keys. It was listed in my name. It was paid for. It was mine.

I was delighted with the sisters of Saint Ann's. They offered a curriculum rich in the arts with a strong emphasis on languages and literature. They turned out young women who knew how to interact with other peoples and cultures. They were a fine learning institution, but frankly, I best liked them for the fence and the grounds of the enclave. I knew the girls would be safe at Saint Ann's for the last few weeks of the school year. Yes, I was pleased with the sisters.

Less so with the choice of Adrian Paul Rousseau for attorney. I would have preferred to choose a lawyer for myself, but Sonja insisted he was the best, and I suppose that quality can't be judged by running one's finger along the yellow pages' list of practicing attorneys in the greater New Orleans area.

The Rousseau Firm was housed in an old building a few miles from Tulane University, a former warehouse or mill of some sort. The Rousseaus had renovated the old-brick exterior with French windows and doors covered in black wrought iron, and hundreds of small evergreen plantings at strategic spots on the grounds.

I parked close by the front entrance, checked my makeup, and locked the doors. Only as I reached for the brass door pull did the enormity of what I was doing hit me. I was seeing a lawyer about Montgomery. I stopped in the shadows. *I was seeing a lawyer about Montgomery.* My breathing came shallow and quick, and I struggled to control my reaction as a tingling started in my fingertips. Slowly I opened the door and passed from the damp warmth to air-conditioned comfort.

The interior of the once cavernous building had been partitioned into offices, and I followed the directions on a brass plaque to the part of the building that housed the Rousseau Firm. It was on the first floor, hidden behind a set of carved doors that formerly protected a monks' retreat.

Immense roughhewn things, counterbalanced on brass hinges, they probably weighed a ton, but opened to the pressure of my hand.

I paused, the ease of opening the huge doors triggering a memory. There was something, somewhere in the back of my mind, clamoring for attention. It had been signaling me for days, trying to rise to the surface. Something about doors. And then I remembered The Box. The Box I had fashioned on my honeymoon and stored in the recesses of my memory. The Box where I stored all the things I didn't want to look at. All the things I didn't want to remember. I didn't want to think about The Box just now. Maybe later. Much later.

My palms were moist. The monks' doors swished shut behind me, cutting off the rest of the world.

Within was a small waiting room, tastefully decorated in shades of shrimp, charcoal, and white, with a receptionist's desk at the far end. I took a slow, steadying breath. Adrian Paul met me in the center of the room, as though he had been watching for me to arrive.

I took him in with a single glance and was mildly surprised. He was attractive in the dark, Creole way of the Rousseau men, his eyes direct and penetrating, his manner competent. I wondered if they taught that look in law school. The Lawyer Look 101, followed by The Judge Look 202.

Yet his hair was too long for the typical lawyer, and he wore no suit coat, just a white shirt open at the collar, his tie loose, and dark slacks. And he wore dark, soft-soled shoes like a runner might wear on his daily miles around the track.

Taking my hand, he greeted me and led me over to the receptionist's desk. "Nicole DeLande, this is our office chief of staff, Bonnie Lamansky. She runs things around here."

"Bonnie." My voice sounded almost normal, not breathy or weak, and I took comfort from that, though my breathing was still too fast and my mind was suddenly on overdrive. It was as if my body thought I was facing disaster and danger.

"Mrs. DeLande. It's nice to meet you." It was a perfectly inane greeting on both our parts, but Bonnie's seemed sincere. I, on the other hand, wanted to be anywhere but here. She was a short, stout woman, about fifty, with silver-gray hair and sparkling blue eyes, dressed tastefully in charcoal as if the decorator had left strict instructions that she not violate the decor.

She was the kind of woman who had never met a stranger. I admired the trait, not possessing it myself. While Bonnie would be able to settle into instant conversation with anyone she met, I would stumble through the pleasantries of a stranger's discourse, hiding behind convention.

"Bonnie, if Mrs. DeLande calls with a problem or a concern, she's to be put through immediately. This is one call you don't hold for me at any time if she says it's urgent."

I almost smiled, relaxing a bit. "Sonja got to you already, I see."

He shook his head and led me down a hallway to his office, carpet muffling the sound of our footsteps as well as the voices from the two offices we passed. Besides the conference rooms and the law library, there were four offices. It was a family business; the patriarch of the Rousseau Firm was Rupert Rousseau, the father of a family of lawyers and the fourth generation of Rousseaus to practice in the New Orleans area. Gabriel Alain was the firm's criminal law expert, Sonja's husband, Philippe, was the civil law expert, and Adrian Paul took care of people like me. "My sister-in-law is a . . . formidable woman."

It took me a moment, then I realized he was still speaking about Sonja. "You are kind," I murmured, to his back.

He shot a look at me as he pushed open the door to his office and stepped aside. It was a conspiratorial look, amused and light, as though we shared visions of Sonja only we two could see.

"Diplomatic. Not kind."

"Ah." I smiled back, relaxing even more. "Let me guess.

She told you to be waiting for me when I arrived. Personally. Did she tell you what to say and what to wear too?"

Adrian Paul laughed, a rich sound like hot fudge melting down the sides of vanilla ice cream. I had a feeling he didn't laugh often. But it was that laugh that decided me; I would accept him for my lawyer. Maybe it wasn't much better than running my fingers down the yellow pages, but I somehow trusted the man who laughed that laugh.

I passed him entering the office, and the scent of the man struck me. It was strong and rich and authoritative. Dependable. It wasn't sweet. Not a cologne. Not Montgomery.

The sensation of moving the monks' immense doors with the palms of my hands returned, however, as I stepped inside the office. I could almost feel the wood grain against my skin. My hands seemed to tremble. Looking down, I saw that my hands were calm and stable-looking. Steady.

His office was not what I had expected. There wasn't a power desk with a manager's leather office chair behind it, facing two smaller, vulnerable-looking chairs for the client/supplicant to use, all backed up with bookshelves full of law books and framed sheepskin diplomas on the walls. There was nothing typical about Adrian Paul's office.

There was an old, Spanish table, massive blackened wood inlaid with mother-of-pearl, and carved with spirals and leaves in the heavy stumps of legs. It sat at an angle to the door, situated so it faced the tall windows and a small private courtyard beyond. The chairs were all alike, comfortable-looking, low-backed, upholstered in a charcoal flame stitch. Three of them were grouped in front of the table-desk with a small tea table holding coasters and a box of tissues for the thirsty and the emotional.

No bookcases. No diplomas. No awards. Just a well-used leather sofa, a TV, and a sound system. And on that beautiful table-desk, a bonsai tree beside the brass-framed picture of a beautiful woman. I supposed she was the wife he had lost last year to leukemia. Camilla. And they had a son,

JonPaul. Sonja had filled me in on the particulars of his life in an attempt to convince me that Adrian Paul was the lawyer for me.

He waited while I looked around, as though aware I would judge him by this space, and he was willing to give me the time to reach a conclusion. Instead, I used the moment to calm myself. *I was seeing a lawyer about Montgomery.* I focused on the tree.

"How long have you had it?" I asked, my gaze on the tree. It wasn't an old one, all twisted and gnarled and ancient, but it was beautifully made, God and the hand of man creating something glorious. In the wild, only the fiercest elements of nature and the valiant heart of a tree could create a bonsai so windswept and pliant.

Adrian Paul walked into the room behind me, his head cocked and a brow lifted. "You know something about bonsai." It wasn't a question.

In bonsai etiquette, one never asked, *Did you start it?* One never implied or questioned that the current owner might not have done so. Nor did one ask, *How old is it?* possibly forcing the current owner to admit that he did not control the growth of the tree from the beginning. One asked, *How long have you had it?* allowing the owner to tell as much as he chose about the history of his tree. My question indicated an awareness of that proper protocol.

"A little. My mother took a course once and we had dozens. Or rather they had us. She sold them to an Oriental landscaping company in Mobile twice a year." I remembered the care she lavished on the trees, staying for hours in the greenhouse, often until after dark. But I didn't want to think about Mama just yet. Perhaps not for a long time. There was too much pain involved in her recent rejection of me and my children.

I realized suddenly how little I knew about my mother. We had never talked or shared our feelings. I had always been a Daddy's girl, hanging around the veterinary clinic, tagging along whenever Daddy would let me go on a call to an outlying farm, or taking care of the clinic when he was out. I had avoided my mother and her aphorisms as much as possible.

Had Mama told Daddy about Montgomery? I could have called him at the clinic and cried on his shoulder, circumventing Mama altogether. But I hadn't. I hadn't called Daddy even once. Perhaps it had something to do with the new roof Montgomery had put on the house when we became engaged, and the financial agreement the two men had worked out. A bit archaic, that financial agreement over the marriage of a daughter. And a bit sinister. Did it mean that I could never go home?

The monks' door began to open deep in my mind, my hand guiding its passage. My breath quickened again, and the tingling was back. I wanted to wipe my palms down my jacket. Adrian Paul was speaking.

"I've had this one for ten years. My wife bought it just after we met, from Irv Eisenberg in the Quarter. But the one in the courtyard"—he gestured to the windows, which I realized were really French doors covered in black scroll ironwork—"is over seventy-five years old."

I walked to the doors and spotted the small tree, off center in an exquisite ornamental garden. The brick walls around the small space were six feet high, with no outer entrance. They were covered with vines and English ivy up to within two inches of the top of the brick, where the greenery stopped abruptly. Something of the garden reminded me of my life, close and claustrophobic.

The tree was placed so that the direct afternoon sun would not hit it, shaded by the brick and the foliage of a young redbud tree. It was standing in its elegant pottery dish, gnarled roots twisting up through a bed of moss and bare earth that was rich in peat moss and compost. A traditional bonsai, stunted and twisted with age and the hands of its creator and subsequent caretakers. Its leaves were dark green, miniature, each placed so it contributed to the strength of the whole.

"A Japanese black pine," I said, not wanting yet to release the subject and turn to the reason I was here. *I was seeing a lawyer about Montgomery.*

Adrian Paul was standing behind me, so close I could smell the musky scent of his skin, serene and earthy. "It was started by Kensei Yamata, a house servant brought back from California after the gold rush days by one of the St. Diziers. This was his last, started only a few years before he died.

"Would you like something to drink? Coffee? Tea?"

A jolt passed through me, identical to the one that almost stopped me as I entered the building. My hands were wet, and the room seemed to darken. The tingling in my palms spread. "No. Thank you." I spoke without thinking. "I managed to get myself pregnant just in time to find out my husband was molesting his children." The words were harsh, quick, caustic with anger that strangled me. I swallowed it back down and took a deep breath, determined to control my reactions, to think logically and to reason my way through all this.

I was seeing a lawyer about Montgomery. Hysterical laughter bubbled up my throat, and I forced myself to breathe slowly, counting off the inhalations. Time was moving in slow motion around me, and I thought for a moment I might faint.

Adrian Paul moved quickly and indicated a chair, his face concerned. "You need to sit down then." I almost laughed that hysterical laugh, his response was so typically male. Yet his concern was a balm to my fractured emotions. He could see I was frazzled and frightened, and he was trying to make it all easier on me. He was trying to make it all seem effortless and light. I managed a grin, the hysteria I had held in check dissipating a fraction.

"I'm not that pregnant," I said, sounding droll. "Actually, a decaf would be nice if you have it." He nodded and reached to a small intercom and phone on the Spanish table-desk. "Two creams, two sugars."

He raised an eyebrow at my extravagance, but placed the order with Bonnie, and we sat, both of us in the grouping of chairs in front of the exotic table-desk. "Sonja told me a little about your situation," he said as I settled myself, "but why don't you tell me everything again."

Fear washed over me as a wave on the Atlantic would wash over a small girl, knocking her down, tumbling her against the ocean bottom, sucking the air out of her lungs. As sand abrades flesh and leaves it stinging from the salt water, I felt abraded by the sudden terror, and I remembered the dream of the snake.

"If I know Sonja, she told you more than a little bit. She gave you every detail and then told you how to advise me," I said softly, fighting to breathe. I could feel the monks' door firm against the palm of my hand, and I struggled to remember what my mind was trying to tell me. But I must have looked almost perfectly fine, composed and calm, because Adrian Paul laughed again, pausing as Bonnie brought us each a cup and saucer with a tray of real cream and sugar. I fought for control. And after she left, he sipped and waited for me to talk.

Somewhere, somehow, I found the words. I opened my mouth and phrases and sentences limped out, disjointed and disordered. The words came out stunted, like the tree I watched as I talked. It was painful, overwhelming, to talk about the last week. To say out loud what I had learned about the man I had married and thought I knew, and the lie we had lived together. *I was seeing a lawyer about Montgomery.* My breath was too fast, tight in my throat, and the tingling in my hands spread up my arms.

Somehow I managed the narrative without resorting to the box of tissues on the table, pausing only when he asked a question, or I couldn't find the breath to continue. I had heard of panic attacks and consoled myself with the diagnosis. But it didn't help me regain control.

I drew strength from the young bonsai on the table as I talked and sipped, my eyes seldom leaving it. The tree had been tortured to create something beautiful. I thought of my girls and the torture they had been through, and I ached for them. *For the girls.* The thought came unbidden. For the girls I could do this. *I was seeing a lawyer about Montgomery.*

When I ran out of words and the ugly narrative stammered to a halt, there was silence in the spartan office except for the scratch of pen on paper. My breathing was easier now. The tingling, stimulated by hyperventilation and panic, eased. I placed the empty cup and saucer on the little table, and I felt a comradeship with the china cup. I was just as barren. Exhausted. I glanced at my watch, the ruby and diamond one Montgomery had given me when I became pregnant with Morgan. The stones reminded me of blood in the artificial light of the office.

We had talked for over half an hour, or I had. Adrian Paul had taken notes on a yellow legal pad, the script an illegible scrawl outlined with irregular margins and with smaller groups of words in the upper and left margins with arrows pointing here and there. My voice was worn and parched, and I felt as though I had been drained through a sieve. All the emotion washed away like a wound flushed free of filth and detritus.

Finally the pen stilled and Adrian Paul looked up. "You had no idea that Montgomery had been abusing the children?"

I flushed and looked quickly back at the bonsai, my breath again too short and the tears I had thought conquered threatening to spill over. A mother's guilt, unlike other emotions, can't be so easily expunged. I blinked to clear my vision, and Adrian Paul placed a tissue in my fist. I caught a single tear on the tissue and damned myself for my weakness.

"I keep asking myself . . . how I could have missed it. I keep looking back over . . . everything . . . and trying to see the clues a mother is supposed to be able to spot. . . . The sex play with dolls . . . or with each other. The mood swings ... the fear ..." My breath gave out and the bonsai wavered, its arms seeming to dance in the current of my unshed tears. "There was nothing," I finished in a whisper.

I could feel the monks' doors again beneath my hands, and they were opening. It was a waking dream, a strange feeling of my mind operating on two separate levels, one in the office with Adrian Paul, the other in some forgotten dreamscape that my subconscious thought wildly important. A light was burning beyond the doors, a red haze filling the air. It was surreal and illusory and I dragged my mind back to the office, not wanting to see beyond.

"Nothing except Dessie's not eating. And Montgomery ... promised ..." The word hung in my throat, trapped for the lie it must have been. Understanding sprouted at the base of the lie and spread. "Promised to get her a counselor," I whispered. The tears stopped pooling, and my vision slowly cleared. The air conditioning came on, blowing from a ceiling vent down across my shoulders. "He promised to get her a counselor." I could hear the mockery in my voice.

"Would he?"

I shook my head, loosing a strand from the careful chignon I had twisted up that morning. "I suppose not." My fists seemed to clench and unclench of their own volition.

"I don't think so either. He would have been exposed too easily." Adrian Paul met my gaze and smiled a half smile, as angry and sad and worn as I felt inside. "If it makes you feel any better, the girls were party to the secrecy, however innocently. They hid the abuse from you too."

That was a new thought. A new pain. It lanced into me and I gasped, "Why?"

I stared into his eyes, black on black like a still pool of water deep in the bayou. "I don't understand why." My voice broke again, and the darkness of his eyes wavered like rippling water through my tears. Tears that still hadn't fallen, perhaps because they were falling inside, filling up the hollow void in my soul.

"Because they were forced to be bad little girls. Because Daddy said to keep a secret. Because he likely threatened them or promised them good things like toys to keep them silent. Because they loved him and feared him. Because they knew it would hurt you somehow, and they didn't want to do that." Adrian Paul watched me as he spoke, his eyes calm and composed.

"Shame and fear mostly. Child molestation isn't about sex any more than rape is about sex. Both are about power and fear and violent control. Both are mental and emotional assaults as well as physical."

"Will they . . . get over it? Ever?" The tears finally fell, half a dozen of them, caught in the tissue I had mangled with my twisting hands.

Adrian Paul smiled as I sniffed. "You believed them. You got them away. That's a first step."

We both knew he hadn't answered the question. That no one could.

"What do I do now?"

"What do you want to do now?"

"I don't know. Sonja doesn't think that counseling will help him."

"I doubt it. Unless he sought it himself."

" 'He has to want it,' " I said, quoting Sonja, " 'more than anything else in the world.' "

"Did Montgomery ever hurt you? Ever beat you?"

The laugh that escaped my mouth was raspy, a shocked coarse sound, the hysterical laughter I had been prone to lately, but shut off abruptly in midpeal. "The DeLande men have never beaten a woman. They don't need such *superficial, primitive* measures," I said. "They have other ways of getting the point across."

"Such as . . . ?" His voice was low and even, almost uninterested in its imperturbable serenity.

I focused on the bonsai. It was a Tropical Mimosa, a delicate tree with feathery leaves that closed up tight at dusk and opened again at dawn. I was surprised how readily the species' common name came to my mind. Its flowers would open early this summer, and tiny hard buds were already visible on the branches.

I stood suddenly, my knee bumping the small table, rattling the china cups in the saucers. The French door opened beneath my fingers, and the scent of New Orleans in the morning hit me, fishy and polluted, and yet somehow reassuring. Adrian Paul didn't comment on my presumption, perhaps accustomed to audacious women after his years of dealing with Sonja.

I stood just outside the office, the sun full on my face, my hands on the wood molding to the left, and the unopened door to the right. "A DeLande uses his *imagination* to . . . curb a wayward woman." A bird chirped, hopping across the brick wall top, surveying its domain. "Once he took all of my clothes away because I disagreed with him in church, in front of the priest. I had a pair of shorts, a T-shirt, and no clean underclothes for a week." My voice was emotionless and hoarse, as dead as though I were reading from a stodgy nursing journal, some stuffy article on the proper way to treat postsurgical cholecystectomy in the morbidly obese patient.

"I learned to live without a car because he took away the keys so many times. Half the time groceries are ordered over the phone and delivered, or Rosalita picks them up. I shop for clothes through catalogs and have them shipped to the door." I paused, the breeze puffing against my face and stirring the leaves of the redbud tree. I wondered how the air found its way past all the brick and vines.

"Once he took away my children." I stopped, shaking, my breath coarse, my voice suddenly guttural and bitter. The bird flew away. "He'd sent the girls to stay with Rosalita for a few days. I had no idea what he'd done with them. I actually thought . . . he might have . . . hurt them. And Montgomery let me think it . . . terrifying me, I suppose, into submission and silence." I took a deep breath.

The monks' doors were suddenly so real, I could feel

splinters in my flesh, rough and tightly grained wood on my hands. I pushed open those doors, flooding my mind with the red light. Inside was The Box. Montgomery's Box. The Box I made on my honeymoon to contain the Montgomery I didn't like. The Montgomery I didn't want to see. Inside were all the bad things in my life, all the secrets of my marriage.

I was surprised at its size. When I made The Box, it had been smaller, neater, like a lady's hatbox. Now it was larger, rough, broken in spots . . . as if something inside had kicked out like an angry horse in a too small stall.

I suddenly realized that Montgomery had done to me the same thing he had done to the girls. They had kept his secrets, kept silent about his abuse, hidden it for years out of fear and terror. And so had I.

"Oh . . ." I took a deep, steadying breath. "And God forbid I should say no to sex or displease him in bed." I gripped the French door and framework in Adrian Paul's office so hard, my nails pierced the layers of paint and pressed into bare wood. I looked up at the sun and blinked, blinded. Adrian Paul was behind me, so close I could feel his body heat on my back, but he didn't touch me.

"You have no idea how painful sex can be if someone wants you to hurt. Pinching and biting, twisting skin and flesh." I laughed again, the sound this time hard and strident, no longer hysterical. No longer weak. I opened The Box.

"I've been made love to . . . No. Not made love to." I breathed deeply. *"Fucked."* I paused at the obscenity, tasting the unfamiliar word on my tongue, sharp and coarse and stinging.

"I've been fucked against door molding until the bruises were black and my back was so sore, I stayed in bed *sick* for three days." I closed my eyes against the too bright sun, focusing on the replica it created on my eyelids, orange and red, its outlines faltering and waffling. "I've been fucked on the kitchen cabinet top, the flame going on the stove so close, it blistered the skin on my hip. And I've got the scars to prove it."

I laughed again, liking the sound, grating and husky and brutal. "I've been fucked in the whirlpool tub, my head held underwater till he was done . . . and I almost drowned."

My breathing was hard, like a bellows in a blacksmith's forge. But I felt better, I felt . . . free finally. A wild splendid freedom. And I could think. I could decide. It was my life. *Mine.*

"Why did you stay with him?" There was still no emotion in Adrian Paul's voice. I smiled and knew it was an ugly smile. All teeth. Savage.

"Most of the time he was so *good* to me. He *pampered* me like a woman desires to be pampered. As though I was of great value and fragile as the finest spun crystal," I said slowly, the mockery thick on the words like sap running down bark. "He was generous and giving and a *good man in the community.* And he only went bad on me when one of his brothers had been to visit. He started drinking when they were around . . . and he changed into one of them. It took days for him to get over the effect they had on him. And he was a *good father, too,* or so I thought. He tended to ignore the girls in the *affection* department, but he provided for them well. Far better than I could have alone.

"No. Montgomery never beat me with a closed fist. He never had to."

I wasn't crying. I was dry-eyed and hollow. And so cold I shivered when Adrian Paul took me by the shoulder and led me back inside, the door clicking shut behind me. I couldn't look at him. I didn't want to see his face.

He ordered more decaf, extra cream and sugar, and wrapped my frigid fingers around the warm cup when it arrived. From somewhere he pulled an afghan and placed it around my shoulders. He was silent and attentive until the shock wore off. I had never told anyone about the dark side of my life with Montgomery, the things I secreted in The Box. I seldom even looked at them myself. Yet now I had not only looked at them, but hung all my dirty linen out for the neighbors to gawk over, as Mama used to say.

How *could* I have stayed with him? My mind came back to the question, fingering it as a blind woman might finger a shawl to detect the weave of crochet.

"Let's talk about your options." Coolly professional, his voice was detached and calm as he outlined those options, how Montgomery could counter each, and his own personal recommendation. The one time I glanced at him, his eyes were devoid of warmth or emotion of any kind, but the tightness along his left cheek and the way the corners of his mouth pulled down as he spoke belied the composure in his voice.

Adrian Paul was angry. Furious. He was angry for me and for my girls. Angry over the abuse. It felt good to have someone angry *for* me.

He encouraged me to start proceedings today, certain he could get the paperwork to a judge and signed by Monday morning. It was for my protection, he said. But I was simply too empty and exhausted to say the words he wanted to hear. I had a decision to make. And I wanted to be clearheaded and sane when I made it. "I'll call you tonight," I said softly as I stood and walked to the door. "Thank you for your time. . . ." My voice trailed off.

"Nicole. Don't let him defeat you. Don't let him—"

"Thank you. And my name is Collie. Only Montgomery and my mother call me Nicole." I walked out of his office and closed the door.

There was a sound behind me in Adrian Paul's office. The kind of sound an angry cat might make, low and growling. Followed almost instantly by another, sharp and cracking, like something breaking, glass or the cups we had used for coffee.

I walked down the hallway, past Bonnie, who was talking

on the phone, and out the heavy monks' retreat doors on their magical hinges. I found my car by instinct and sat inside in the pressurized heat from the solar buildup trying to get warm. Trying to feel again. I wasn't successful.

Sometime later, I inserted the key and drove off, amazed that my hands were steady enough to control the Camry. I was no longer shaking, having left the tingling and sweaty palms on the other side of the monks' doors along with the false dreams and false visions of the marriage I thought I had. Now I was simply numb.

The last hour had stolen my energy, leaving me limp and weary. Pulling the rearview toward me at the first traffic light, I looked at my face and reached for the makeup bag in my pocketbook. I needed a complete makeover. I felt like the "before" shot in a fashion magazine advertisement. I added a bit of lipstick and powder, blotted my lips to lessen the color, and then gave up.

I should have gone back to the Rousseau grounds and the sanctuary of the little cottage, but I was determined to make my other stops. I had promised myself before I left the cottage that morning that I would complete the itinerary I had scheduled for the day. In my own way, I intended to make sure Montgomery didn't defeat me. Finding the energy from somewhere, I ran my other errands before I drove back to the cottage and collapsed.

I slept the rest of the day, the girls playing wildly in the yard with the Rousseau twins, Mallory and Marshall trampling the flowers and the undergrowth in the backyard, their screams loud and innocent through the open windows. Lying stretched out on the sofa, a pillow under my head, I dreamed of the snake again, and I woke screaming silently, my breath strangled and crying, my fingernails having torn rows of weals down my arms.

Later that evening I remembered the last part of my conversation with Adrian Paul. My options.

I was sitting on the front porch of the cottage, in the

wooden swing that the gardener had hung earlier that day, the supporting chains croaking softly against the screws in the roof beam overhead and on the arms of the swing. One leg was stretched along the cushion seat, the other down, my bare toes pushing against the wood flooring. A grand daddy longlegs picked his way across the floor to investigate my toes, and I wiggled them a bit to scare him off. I don't like spiders, and I don't care how Funk & Wagnalls encyclopedia might classify them, a grand daddy longlegs is still a spider to me.

The scent of the citronella candles I had placed on the porch railing kept away the worst of the mosquitoes, and a mocking bird made his raucous calls, the repetitive sequence somehow soothing. It was dusk and the girls were bathing in the claw-footed tub, having climbed up a stepstool to get in. I could hear their giggles and whispers and shouts as they pushed tugboats and sailing vessels through the water.

Morgan played on a pallet at my feet. He was a peaceful child, slow to walk and bored with crawling. He preferred to lie sucking his thumb, watching the roof beams so far over his head. He wasn't developmentally slow, he merely lived at his own pace, observant and quiet. I thought he might grow up wise and thoughtful and kind. Odd for a DeLande man. I could see him a priest. Or a lawyer . . .

You have a decision to make, you know.

Sonja's words, echoed by Adrian Paul at the end of his list of options. He was right. I couldn't close my eyes to what Montgomery had done. To what Montgomery was. I had to respond to the damage he had visited on the girls. And on me.

I could handle the situation any number of ways, but Adrian Paul had recommended one course of action above the others. He had suggested that I file for separation and divorce based on Montgomery's abuse of me and the girls. In the same document, I would state the number of children from the marriage and ask for custody based on child abuse. That would provide me with an immediate temporary restraining order to keep Montgomery away from the children, and grant me temporary custody. A temporary restraining order was good for ten days and could be renewed each time it ran out, without a new hearing.

I wondered if a judge's decree would be binding against a DeLande. It didn't seem likely.

Of course, then I would have to prove Montgomery was an unfit father. Prove it in court. And obtain a permanent injunction keeping him away from the children and away from me forever. Finally, if necessary or if I wanted to, I could file charges with the district attorney's office, charging Montgomery with carnal knowledge of a juvenile . . . and rape if it proved to be true.

All this I would have to do to protect the girls. But I knew good and well that no woman ever left a DeLande. Not in one piece. And certainly not with the children. There was precedent. Others had tried and failed. Running away had never worked, not for the wife of a DeLande. The law was my only hope, paltry as it was.

We could have started the procedure before I left the office earlier in the day, but I couldn't think clearly. I couldn't decide if Adrian Paul's way was the best. I knew the resources available to the DeLandes. I knew the power they wielded in the state, the financial resources they could bring to bear against me and any charges I might file against Montgomery.

Also there was the fact that I had never told anyone about my marriage. About Montgomery's punishments and Montgomery's subtle violence. I had learned to live with it for the children's sake. For the life-style he could give them which I could not duplicate. Not on a nurse's salary.

But I suppose my dreams and my needs were the final culprit. I had wanted Montgomery to love me. Like all fool women, I had thought my love would eventually change him from the man formed in his mother's house to the man who had courted me.

I had time to decide. Five days before Montgomery would be back in town. Five days to put a new life together for me and my children. Montgomery was in France. He never called from overseas. He would have no way to know I had left unless someone was watching the house for him—a possibility but not a very strong one. I think Montgomery trusted me at home.

I laid my head back against the swing and watched the ceiling with Morgan, wondering what he saw there in the beams and slats of the porch roof, letting the soothing motion of the swing tranquilize and comfort me. It was solace at the end of this dreadful day. My emotions were still raw and scored from the interview with Adrian Paul. I was left with a tendency to laugh when it wasn't appropriate, or to tear up when I should have been laughing. But I was better. Calmer. And I had survived this awful day.

Tomorrow would be hard too. I didn't want to face it. I didn't want to look too closely at the vile things I was learning, or endure the changes in my life. But then, I didn't want my peace of mind back at the cost of the girls' suffering. I knew I would follow Adrian Paul's advice and sue for separation and divorce. I should call him, tell him to start proceedings. But I wouldn't. Not just yet.

I closed my eyes and allowed the swing to slow and stop. I heard Morgan yawn and sigh. Heard the girls climb out and dry off, their footsteps loud and hollow on the wood floors as they ran to find nightgowns.

They knew they were going to the doctor tomorrow. An appointment arranged by Sonja and Adrian Paul to check them for venereal disease and physical signs of sexual abuse. Not that there would be any. Unless one of them had been penetrated . . .

They liked their doctor in Moisson. Dr. Ben. He was a

late-middle-aged pediatrician in semiretirement who had moved to Moisson Parish for the hunting and fishing he loved more than practicing medicine. He kept an office three days a week for the income to practice his hobby. But for this examination I had insisted on a female doctor, and Sonja had agreed. The doctor would examine the girls while under videotape and write a report on her findings. She had already agreed to appear in court to testify if the need arose.

Afterward, for a treat, we were meeting Sonja and the twins for lunch at Van's on St. Peter's Street. Van's was a great, old-fashioned, neighborhood-type restaurant tucked away in the Vieux Carré, which served some of the best po' boys in the city, sloppy and heavy eating, rich with gravy or cheeses or fried seafood, and my mouth watered at the thought.

We would need the fortification. Because the counselor was the next stop. The counselor who would try to help the girls deal with what Montgomery had done to them, help them to face it and accept it and fight back. Help them to live with the pain and find victory over it, instead of letting them sweep the abuse into the back corners of their minds. That kind of forgetfulness was dangerous. I had heard the horrors of women who later remembered the abuse, the memories surfacing in self-destructive behavior, damaged emotional relationships, sexual dysfunction, and lost lives.

But this counselor was more than just a healer. She was also an instrument of the case against Montgomery. She would videotape the sessions with us all, both those with the girls together and alone, and those with me included, the family counseling sessions. And behind a one-way mirror, an assistant would take dictation. The notes and the tapes together would comprise the bulk of the evidence for court.

Both the doctor and the counselor were expert witnesses

who had been approved by the Louisiana court system in the past. If it came to a trial, they would testify against Montgomery for us, and face the battery of attorneys Montgomery would undoubtedly hire for his side. I would have felt sorry for them if they weren't charging an arm and a leg to be so supportive.

The girls ran through the screen door screaming and fell against Morgan's pallet, one on either side of him, tickling him and making baby talk. My little man giggled at the tickling, and then watched them sleepily. He looked at me and smiled his old-man smile, as though amused at the chatter and spirit of children.

"Story time, Mama, before Morgan falls asleep," Dessie said. She looked up at me from the pallet, a grin stretched across her face, a different child from the little girl of last week. We were just a bit over twenty-four hours away from Moisson, and already she was coming alive. She had even eaten supper, part of a muffelletta I had picked up at Norby's on the way home from the Rousseau Firm. A seafood muffelletta, almost twenty-seven inches around, the bun stuffed with steamed shrimp and crab and fried oysters and lettuce and tomatoes and some kind of gooey soft cheese melted all through it. Dessie had eaten an entire portion, sliced like a pie, and two glasses of juice. Her little belly was rounded and firm at the unaccustomed quantity of food.

I smiled down at her in the dusky light. "I'll need a flashlight. You know where it is, *me sha?*"

"I'll get the f'ashlight. You get the book," Shalene said, and both girls left Morgan at a run. He met my eyes again and smiled his secret smile. I leaned forward and hoisted him to my knee, settling him just as Shalene returned and sat to my left on the swing, flicking on the flashlight. Dessie took the right, handed me the book, and began to play with Morgan's toes.

The sunlight was mostly gone, but we read for an hour in

the unsteady light of the flash in Shalene's hands, the story of David and Goliath. It was Dessie's favorite, next to Robin Hood and Sleeping Beauty, and I wanted to remind both girls that the little guy could win.

It was after nine when they went to bed, curled up together on the old guest bed from our house in Moisson saying their prayers. That was another thing I should do this weekend. Tomorrow. Take them shopping for new furniture. I could afford it. I had the money. Nearly forty thousand dollars in cash, deposited in the First National Bank of Commerce after the sale of the diamond earrings Montgomery had given me, and the ring he had hidden.

It was one of the things I had accomplished on the way home from the Rousseau Firm. I had hocked some jewelry. Of course, when referring to forty thousand dollars worth of diamonds, one would never be so gauche as to say *hock.* Except me.

The girls finished, crossed themselves, and pulled the covers up to their necks. Morgan snored softly from the next room, the little den that just barely held all the paraphernalia a baby needed.

"Night, Mama," Shalene said. I smiled at them in the darkness, the duck-shaped nightlight the only illumination. "What you gonna sing us tonight?"

I cocked my head, considering, one finger tapping my cheek. "Ah. How about this one? Jesus loves the little children," I sang. "All the children of the world . . ."

They closed their eyes—part of our long-standing bargain —and my voice filled the small room, escaping out the opened windows. I could hear feminine voices in the distance, which neared and then quieted as I reached the end of my song. Likely neighborhood women out for their evening constitutional. My voice dropped and I slipped from the room.

Wandering back to the small sitting room, I was reaching for a lamp when a soft tap sounded at the front door.

Montgomery. The wooden door was open to the night breeze, the screen door offering pitiful protection.

I remembered what Adrian Paul said about Montgomery and custody. It didn't matter what my husband had done to us; if he hadn't been served with papers, officially he could take us back. Or take *them* back. Silently I moved for the bedroom and the gun I had brought.

CHAPTER

6

~~~

"Collie?"

I could have wept with relief. Or killed Sonja for frightening me. "Next time use the phone," I hissed. "I almost shot you."

She laughed that rich contralto I remembered from our girlhood, so mischievous and sensual. "You don't have a phone, remember? Open up. I have someone you should meet."

I went to the door, lifted the useless metal latch, and let them in, Sonja and her guest. Flipping on the two lamps that had lit my family room in Moisson, I also pulled up a kitchen chair before I turned to greet them.

"Collie?" Sonja sounded nervous, and my hackles instantly went up. "This is Ann Nezio-Angerstein, formerly of the New Orleans Police Department." I lifted my brows. I had a bad feeling what was coming next, and I was getting a bit tired of Sonja running my life. No matter that I had screwed up while running it on my own. I glanced at Ann, waiting for the other shoe to drop.

The former cop was of average height with auburn hair

and a smattering of reddish freckles across her pale-skinned nose. She was dressed in a slim-fitting business suit, pants and vest with low-heeled shoes. I put her at about her late thirties. "She's a detective."

Even though I half expected it, a shock went through me and I quickly looked Ann Nezio-Whatever over again from the perspective of her profession. I dubbed her Ann Hyphen, because I knew I'd never get that mouthful out in one piece. This time I did a more thorough inspection. She was wearing little makeup, was fit and toned, and wore her hair short, cut in a bob like Princess Di had worn before she married the guy with the ears. She was older than I had first thought; I placed her in her early forties. She needed new shoes; the heels were worn on the pair she was wearing. The ex-cop had an air of quiet confidence, the kind of confidence that wouldn't waver even if she were alone on a dark street corner in the middle of a riot.

She grinned at me. "I pass inspection?"

I could feel a flush start at my toes and heat its way north. "Oh God, I'm sorry. Please come in, sit down; I didn't mean to stare." I had actually walked around her checking her out. My mama would have been mortified, swearing that she had taught me better. "Would you like a col' drink, 'r some tea?" My southern drawl slithered through the words, strong with my embarrassment.

She sat, moving smoothly onto the straight-backed kitchen chair. "No, thanks. You know, that was one thing I had to learn about you people when I came here. A cold drink always means a soda, a pop means a Popsicle. You don't say 'I'm buying groceries,' you say 'I'm makin' groceries.' And you don't chuck out the baby with the bathwater, you chunk it out. You guys have a completely different language down here." She smiled pleasantly at me, set her briefcase at her feet, and folded her hands in her lap. She looked composed and expectant and utterly at her ease. Personally, I had never "made groceries" in my life, but I chose not to contradict her. After all, she was a guest in my house.

I looked at Sonja, my brows halfway to my hairline as I took the overstuffed armchair. That left Sonja the sofa beside the floor lamp, and she sat down gingerly. She was pulling against her long false fingernails, a sure sign of nervousness, and suddenly I understood.

"You hired her, didn't you." I sounded flat, hard, and rude, and I should have been ashamed. But I had no control over any part of my life anymore anyway, so why not just . . . chunk . . . Miss Manners and say it like it was. "Didn't you." Sonja flinched at the tone and broke off one of those expensive fake fingernails. She stared at the ragged nail, her chin quivering. She looked like she was going to cry.

"You didn't know?" Ann Hyphen's face went through a strange sequence of emotions before she scowled at Sonja. She had one of those "you have been wasting my time, lady" looks on her face.

"No. Of course I didn't know. Sonja the lawyer, general, and generic busybody has taken over my life and runs it as she darn well pleases."

I closed my eyes so I wouldn't see Sonja's face. She looked so woebegone as she picked at the ruined nail. And she looked a bit afraid, too, as if this time she knew she had gone too far tampering in my life. "Oh God," I sighed to the ceiling. "I wish I wasn't pregnant. I need a glass of wine. A bottle. After today, it might take a whole case. Tell me, Sonja. What else have you done that I don't know about?"

"You drank wine last week," Sonja accused, tearing off the ragged nail and ignoring the question.

"Last week I was being rebellious. Now I'm being good. Speaking of good, are you?" I asked Ann Hyphen, which was rude, but so what.

"I do have excellent references, which I would have brought had I known this was an interview. I'm really very sorry," she said. "If you are interested in continuing my services for the purposes of following and investigating your husband, I'll be happy to bring them."

I didn't respond. Instead I glared at Sonja. "Continue

your services? *Continue?"* Sonja glared back. "Just how long ago did you hire this woman?" Sonja looked back at her nails, smoothing the nine remaining perfect edges against her slacks. A tense silence built.

Some moments later, Ann Hyphen stood. "I can send a bill to Mrs. Rousseau for my services to date." Still Sonja looked at her nails, her mouth clamped in a defiant line. "And if I can be of any—"

"Oh, sit down," I sighed, losing the battle to my childhood friend. "And don't mind me. I'm punishing my favorite dictator for meddling, not you. It's your job to meddle. Are you reasonable?"

"Two fifty a day plus expenses," Ann said promptly, sitting back down.

"How much do I owe you to date?"

"I fully intended to pay Ms. Nezio-Angerstein's bill if you weren't satisfied with—"

"Put a sock in it, Wolfie. How much do I owe? And how long have you been on my payroll?"

"I have an itemized bill—"

"Good. Let's see it." I seemed to be doing pretty well without Miss Manners and her onerous list of dos and don'ts and proper etiquette. Interrupting people was a heady experience, powerful, a vastly underrated achievement; it cut wasted inanities out of the conversation exceptionally well. It was an art form for Yankees, I'd heard, but I figured I could hold my own.

Ann Hyphen passed me a typed statement. I barely glanced at it except for the bottom line. Twenty-nine hundred dollars plus or minus a bit of change. "You've been on the job awhile. You take counter checks? I just opened my account today." I got up and went to find my new checkbook, passing behind the sofa where Sonja sat. She had conjured a nail file from somewhere and was smoothing the rough nail, her face intent, still ignoring me.

I felt intoxicated suddenly, even without the bottle I was denying myself and the baby. Intoxicated, sloshed, wasted, stoned, looped, plastered, and intensely free. The feeling of freedom had been growing all day and was blooming now, rich and lush, like a hothouse orchid. I took a deep breath and laughed. It was reckless laughter. An angry tone. I was going to divorce Montgomery.

I found my pocketbook, took it back to the sitting room, and pulled out my new checkbook. "So—"

"Mrs. DeLande." Ann Hyphen was pretty good at interrupting too. But then she was a transplanted Yankee, so she should have an edge.

"Yes?"

"Mrs. Rousseau paid me a two-thousand-dollar deposit."

"Well, isn't my busybody friend just oh so generous. You'll have to refund her money, honey, because I'll pay my own way, thank you very much."

Suddenly Sonja relaxed back against the sofa and laughed softly. "You aren't even a little bit mad, are you?"

I considered for a split second. I should be. I wanted to be. Anyone else would be. But . . . "Nope." I handed Ann Hyphen the counter check, her name left carefully blank so I wouldn't insult her with my opinion of women who hyphenated their last names. "Don't cash it till after two P.M. I want to make sure it clears. So. Wha'd you find?"

Ann Hyphen looked from me to Sonja and back again, the counter check held firmly in her left hand, a bemused expression on her face. She shook her head and folded the check. Lifting the briefcase from the floor to the coffee table, she clicked the locks.

"Mrs. Rousseau hired me to follow your husband—he was your husband, wasn't he?" Ann sounded dubious, but at my nod, she went on. "One Montgomery B. DeLande?" I nodded again. "She hired me to find out where he went, what he did, who he saw, et cetera. Do you wish to continue the same services?"

"Sure. Why not? But not indefinitely. I expect regular reports and accounting—"

Sonja stood in the middle of my sentence, stretched to her

full five foot two inches, and headed to the kitchen. "God, you people disgust me. Where's that wine you can't drink, Collie?"

"Bottom cabinet, left of the sink. Most of Montgomery's South Carolina stash, although I left him a couple bottles." I looked back at the detective. "Let's see what you got."

I don't think the Second Coming would upset Ann Hyphen too much. She calmly put the folded check in the top pocket of the briefcase and handed me a manila folder marked DELANDE, M.B. at the top along with the date she was hired. Still feeling wired, I opened the folder and stared.

Slowly the sensation of champagne bubbling in my bloodstream leached out of me. The anger, the laughter, the feeling of freedom, all drained away, leaving me empty again. I was staring at five-by-seven photographs of two people. One was Montgomery.

I moved methodically through the stack of photos, studying each meticulously before moving on to the next. I didn't really need the time to look closely at each picture. I seemed to absorb the details of each one instantly. But my hands were slack and clumsy, and I used the time spent staring, finding the muscle control to move on to the next.

Sonja moved into the kitchen doorway, bracing her right hand up high on the framework to listen and strain for a glimpse of the photos.

I made it to the end of the stack, not quite sure what I was feeling. With some clinical part of my mind, I analyzed my reactions as I evened the edges of the stack of photos as one might even up a stack of playing cards. My whole world should have been tumbling down around my feet like a line of upright dominoes falling in every direction because one of them had been tipped over. Instead I felt . . . detached.

Montgomery was having an affair. And this stranger knew it before I did. It was a silly reaction, to care that a private investigator had uncovered Montgomery's perfidy and that Sonja had made it happen. But I did care. Carefully I went through the stack of photographs again, isolating two that showed the woman's face most clearly. Zoom-lens shots, with the light glowing from her face. She was utterly beautiful.

Sonja moved up behind me and stared at the shots. I ignored her. She shouldn't have done this, hired an investigator to invade my life. Montgomery shouldn't have done it. He shouldn't have deceived me. I closed my eyes.

Abruptly I was back at the monks' doors, my hands on the rough wood, dull red light flowing through the crack from the room within like a red fog. It was easier this time, to shove aside the doors and enter the forbidden room, to cross the floor and approach The Box. Touch the lid.

The lid hung open, the wood splintered and brittle, dried up like kindling wood. Things had been slithering out of it all day, from the moment I first opened it in Adrian Paul's office. Ugly things. I had been watching them, almost dispassionately, as they paraded grimly past me all day, losing their power as they moved in front of my memory. The Box was almost empty now. But it was still The Box, a hiding place, a secret vault.

Carefully I took all the feelings I had for Montgomery, all the anger, all the hate, all the guilt and shame, all the passion and love and need that had kept me with him all these years, and I put them in The Box. And closed the lid.

The Box looked better now, the wood newer, refreshed, the splintered holes healed over. It looked secure. A new lock, shiny brass, gleamed on the front, with a key sticking out. As I twisted the key, the lock clicked.

I turned and walked away. Eventually I'd have to deal with The Box. And with Montgomery. But not now. Silently I walked across the room and out into the cool places beyond. And I closed the monks' doors, sealing away The Box.

"Who is she?" It was my voice breaking the silence. Calm, emotionless. Glacial and almost indifferent.

"Glorianna DesOrmeaux. A half-Cajun, half-black female, nineteen years of age, who earned her GED at adult day school last year." Ann passed me a typed sheet filled with the particulars. "She lives at the address you see on the second line. It's a duplex in New Orleans proper, a residence purchased by your husband for her four years ago when he bought her from her mother."

There was a silence following Ann Hyphen's last words. The kind of silence that fills the air after a thunderclap on a cloudless day. The PI seemed to realize she was dropping bombshells with amazing accuracy, and she waited for me to digest the fallout.

Cats have an unerring instinct for grand entrances, and Sonja's gray-haired Persian was a master. Into the silence of the small sitting room she padded at a graceful trot, using the cat flap in the bottom of the screen door, leaving it swishing behind her. With a single flex of muscle she jumped onto the coffee table, walked sedately over to me, and deposited a dead mouse on the tabletop beside my knee.

I took a deep breath, the first one in several minutes. Under other circumstances I'd have run screaming, but my legs, numb and deprived of oxygen, wouldn't let me. Instead, I simply looked at Sonja and whispered, "I don't do rats."

Sonja nodded, her face pale and her dark eyes huge. I knew then that she had not heard Ann Hyphen's report until now; she had not seen the pictures; her reaction was as stunned as my own . . . and perhaps a little guilty. She walked from behind me, a bottle of Montgomery's favorite white wine, Cruse Vineyards 1989 Vidal Blanc, in her left hand, and picked up the mouse by the tail.

I closed my eyes against the sight of the dead rodent. Instead I saw Montgomery kissing Glorianna on the walk in front of her house. Strange. I didn't seem to react to the vision. All my feelings were in The Box. My emotions had been on a roller coaster all day. This absence of feeling was a blessing, I suppose.

Water ran in the kitchen, shut off with a rattle of pipes. A slow squeak followed and a soft pop as the cork eased from the bottle top. Then a gulp. I could have sworn Sonja was drinking out of the bottle, but moments later she entered the room carrying a tray with the bottle, three glasses, and my pitcher of decaf iced tea.

Elbowing a prowling Snaps out of the way, she set the tray down, passed out the glasses, and sat back down on the sofa.

"What do you mean, 'when he bought her from her mother'?" I asked. I was amazed at my own sense of calm, and wondered if it was real or if it was going to shatter suddenly like a mirror, giving me seven years of bad luck and cutting me in the process.

"Have you ever heard of the practice of *plaçage?*"

It seemed familiar to me and I cocked my head, trying to place the term. It was loosely translated "placement" in French, but the classroom I was seeing in my memory wasn't Sister Mary's French class at Our Lady of Grace, it was the stark history room occupied by Sister Ruth. "I can't place it." I shook my head and glanced at Sonja.

She was staring at Ann Hyphen, her full lips closed, her eyes wide, as the color slowly drained from her face. She started to tremble, and her rayon blouse was in danger of being stained by the wine. If not her blouse, then my upholstery. She brought the glass to her lips and drained it in one convulsive gulp, then set it on the table in a single snapping motion that should have broken the stem.

In a flash of collaborating intuition and memories, I understood. All the feelings I should have felt over Montgomery and his mistress washed over me, distress, shock, bleak melancholy. But they were not for Montgomery. They were for Sonja. A sense of loss for the hurt little girl who was sneered at and insulted by the lily white cliques at Our Lady of Grace.

"*Plaçage,*" Sonja said, as though reciting, her voice soft and almost bewildered. "The pre–Civil War practice of Creole and Anglo slave owners. They would take a beautiful black or mulatto slave as mistress, and then to save the . . . outraged sensibilities . . . of the white woman to whom they were married, they would free this slave, buy her a house, educate her and her children, pay her bills . . . provide for her future and her children's future. . . ." Sonja licked her lips. I remembered then the first time Sonja told me the story of her heritage.

It had been the year we turned eighteen, the last July that she, my Mama, and I spent in New Orleans together, soaking up good food and culture and, for the first time, good liquor. Sonja had not driven up with us, but had come later on a Greyhound bus, her luggage stored away in its cavities like nuts in a chipmunk's jowls.

On our second night we'd all gotten drunk at a new restaurant and bar near Tulane U., as a tropical storm blew out its weakened fury in rain and small hailstones that rattled against the brick and windows. The staccato sound competed with the jazz band playing on the stage. And I recalled the shock I'd felt when she first said the words.

"My great-great . . . great grandmother was a black slave. Brought over from Africa when she was twelve or so."

I remembered the rumors and the hissing from the girls in class as they tried to warn me against the pretty, dusky-skinned woman/child who came to school one year. "High yellow," they had whispered, and "Coon-ass." "So what?" I had whispered back. Sonja had pretended not to notice or hear the exchange, but she must have. She became my friend.

I had watched Sonja that night in the bar, her mouth moving as if someone else were forming the words for her, hesitant yet studied, long pauses where she took a breath. Her chest, always fuller than mine, even at eighteen, rose and fell beneath her shirt.

"She was . . . purchased by a planter named St. Croix and freed four years later under the concept of . . . the practice of *plaçage*."

Sonja stared out over the crowd, a jet-eyed beauty, casting an unconscious spell over every man in the place. Even with Mama there—a stern-eyed chaperone no matter that she also was two sheets to the wind—several men had sent over drinks, hoping for an introduction. Sonja accepted the drinks, but not the offer of company.

"Her half-white daughter was presented at the quadroon balls fourteen years later and made quite a . . . stir." Sonja smiled softly. "She was called Antoinette.

"I have a picture of her in my things somewhere. A daguerreotype made late in her life. Antoinette was beautiful even then. Proud. White features in the blackest of faces." Sonja's voice was melodious, her words slightly slurred, as if the liquor had worked its magic and made her mellow. "She had long curly, curly hair worn up in ringlets."

Sonja's fingers demonstrated an upswept hairstyle, carelessly loose with hundreds of tiny tight ringlets on her face and neck. And she was smiling as if she could feel the stiff curls beneath her palms. Mama and I watched, fascinated.

"Antoinette's quadroon daughter was presented at the balls not long before the start of the Civil War, in 1857, I think. Her second . . ." Sonja's brows creased in thought, and I wondered why she was telling all this, in front of Mama, when she had never mentioned it before. And then I realized she told it only because Mama was in the room. Mama was a barrier between us, a protection should I react badly. "No, I think it was her third cousin was the highest bidder. Her name was Amorette. Amorette LeBleu, because she had such dark skin and blue eyes."

"I thought you said she was free." I could have kicked Mama for disturbing the narrative.

Sonja looked at her in mild surprise, as if she had forgotten we were there. A little like a child awakened from a daydream filled with imaginary characters who were real a moment ago, and then vanished.

Mama realized her mistake. "I . . . I thought you said that Antoinette's mother was free, so . . ."

The waiter walked up just then. Sonja smiled and accepted another admirer's gift, a pretty yellow confection with a pink umbrella tilted to the side and a red plastic sword piercing a shish-kebob of citrus fruit. Sipping it, she watched the play of light and smoke and heat against the cheap crystal. And she was silent.

"She was free," I said, recalling the short history lesson given by Sister Ruth just the year before. "They all were. Called the *gens de couleur libre,* the free men of color. There were some eighteen thousand of them living in New Orleans at the start of the war. 'They had a culture like no other on earth before and no other since,'" I quoted Sister Ruth, willing Sonja to continue. And I almost said, "Don't chicken out on me now, Wolfie." But I didn't.

Sonja smiled as if she'd heard me anyway, and after a moment took up her story. "The sons of 'colored' women with white protectors were educated in Paris and went on the grand tour. Some . . . many," she amended, sounding a bit like a teacher herself, "stayed on in France, where skin color had less significance, marrying white women and becoming doctors and poets, writers and lawyers, artists . . . The daughters, if they were educated at all, were educated by the nuns, like us." She smiled quickly at the glass and took several sips.

"But they received their real education at their mother's knee, taught to run a small household. Taught to please a man in and out of bed. *Plaçage* didn't return a woman to slavery. She kept her free papers. But her . . . *services* were purchased in a financial agreement pounded out by her mother and other female relatives, and by the white boy's father and his lawyer. Much like a marriage agreement in those days, and it was almost as binding."

I had realized Sonja was talking for Mama's benefit, not mine, explaining the history of the "colored" society in New Orleans prior to the Civil War. And perhaps she was also finding a means to avoid talking to me. I remembered the taunts Sonja had endured on the playground at Our Lady. And I remembered the way I took up for her back when we were children. Did Sonja think I would regret our friendship because of her revelations? Sonja could have been pure black or a purple Martian with pink polka dots and I would still have loved her.

"If the white protector wanted to end the relationship, he had to provide a sum of funds to support her until she could find another protector. He was also legally constrained to provide financially for any children by him, which were conceived under the original agreement."

Sonja shrugged. "At any rate. . . ." She drank the last two sips, reached for another glass, and sat back with it. This one was a blue ice medley, half-melted and dripping with condensation. "At any rate, Amorette was pregnant when the war broke out, and St. Croix sent her and her two-year-old son to Paris to wait out the conflict. The war lasted far longer than the zealous secessionists expected, and Amorette was forced to go into business for herself. She opened a dress shop and did rather well for herself, but that's another story."

Sonja finished off the drink. I had seldom seen Sonja drunk. She was a weepy drunk, one of those maudlin beings who cried and moaned and got sick all over the bar floor, spending an evening with her head in a toilet, instead of partying with her friends. And she was well on her way there now.

"Anyway . . . anyway. She came back to New Orleans in 1867. A wealthy woman. With two . . . exquisite . . . octoroon children. St. Croix was dead. So was his white family. So was *plaçage.*" Sonja's lips twisted. "The girl, Ava Juliet, married a white Yankee colonel and moved back north. *Passé blanc.* The boy was Armand LeBleu. My grandfather."

Sonja had looked up at me, her eyes wary and apprehensive, unfocused from the alcohol. "The rumors were all true, when we were in school. My grandfather was one-eighth black."

I shrugged. "So?"

There was silence in the bar suddenly as the band came to a halt, put down their instruments, and took a break. And

Sonja laughed. That rich contralto, seductive and alluring, inherited from generations of women taught to please men; women who turned out best at pleasing themselves. She reached for a fourth drink, but Mama took it away from her. It was one of those smooth motions a mother learns when she has toddlers who constantly reach for the fragile or the dangerous or the forbidden. Sonja didn't seem to notice, her hand falling back limply to her lap.

Sonja had looked at me from across the table, smoke drifting between us, her eyes shadowed and intense and very drunk. "So. I'm eighteen. Ripe for *plaçage*. A hundred years ago, it would have been the only way I could have made my way in the world. The only way open to me with my *tainted* blood . . ." Sonja seemed to be holding her breath, waiting for me to say something, and that confused me.

"I've always been proud of you, Wolfie." Sonja seemed disappointed, and I felt I'd failed her somehow. The narrative had been for my benefit, and I'd missed Sonja's point. And she'd never enlightened me. I had never been able to pry out of her the purpose of her revelations that night. She'd not spoken of it since, refused to even acknowledge it had taken place.

I looked at Sonja, her face nearly as drunk now as it had been that night all those years ago. Her eyes still avoided mine. Moving uneasily on the sofa, Sonja pulled her knees up, tucking her feet beneath her. She drank deeply of Montgomery's wine, poured herself another, and drank it down as well. I knew she was remembering that night in the chrome and mirrored yuppie bar when she'd bared her soul and I'd failed her.

Sonja didn't look at me, her eyes unfocused and her lips trembling slightly, just as they had that night so long ago. I wasn't sure why she was so upset then, or why she seemed so upset now. But I didn't think it had to do with Montgomery's mistress or the practice of *plaçage* or even her family history. Instead, I knew it had something to do with me.

Snaps, perhaps feeling slighted by the inattention, jumped from the edge of the coffee table where she had been observing the three humans with haughty disdain. Settling on my lap, she rolled once, rather like a dog exposing her belly, but gracefully, and emitted a noisy rumble of a purr.

Satisfied with her perch and pillow, the cat flexed her claws into my leg through the jeans I was wearing. Flex out, pierce the fabric, tighten, and relax back into the sheath. Flex out, pierce the fabric, tighten, and relax back into the sheath. Again and again. Sonja seemed fascinated with the process and with the three small stains of rust-colored blood Snaps drew on the first try.

Thunder sounded in the distance. Snaps paused, tilted an elegant ear, and flexed again.

A moment later Ann Hyphen cleared her throat. Sonja and I both jerked and looked at the PI. Her face was amused. She had been talking, apparently, and only just realized that neither of her audience was listening. "So. You want to hear the rest of this or what. It's your money."

I almost grinned, glad to have the distraction. "Shoot. And take the bottle away from Sonja. She's . . ." I almost said "not a pretty drunk," but replaced it with "had enough."

Ann lifted the bottle away from Sonja, setting it close to my knee. "Well, after the history lesson, let's just say the DeLandes revived a form of *plaçage* two generations back. If they ever discarded it. Royal DeLande had a mixed-race mistress and four children by her. Two of his sons, including Montgomery's father, Nevin, had mixed-race mistresses and children. And so far as I can tell, Montgomery and at least one brother have continued the tradition. Andreu's . . . ah, ladyfriend lives next door to Glorianna, in the other half of the duplex.

Ann looked at me, waiting perhaps for some reaction, the wife scorned or hurt or bitter. But I'd done all the reacting I could today, in front of strangers. And somehow this new lie, this new atrocity, didn't sting, not when placed beside the knowledge that Montgomery had abused my girls.

For an instant, almost in a flash like a vision, I saw Dessie's eyes the day she was born and the doctor laid her across my stomach all bloody and slick. She was still as helpless as at that moment. Helpless before Montgomery.

Sonja's attention was on the empty glass in her hand, and her lips were moving as if in rehearsal for some speech.

"Can you prove it?" I asked, my voice carefully emotionless. "Can you prove she's his mistress? Prove it sufficiently to satisfy a judge?"

Ann nodded. I could see the motion from the corner of my eye. "And I'm available for court time at reduced rates. Most divorces don't take long once a judge sees the kind of evidence you're mangling right now."

It took a moment for her meaning to sink in and I glanced down. Almost as bad as Snaps, who had drawn droplets of blood through my jeans, I had twisted the folder with the five-by-sevens into funnels and cylinders so many times that the manila was permanently bent.

"Sorry," I said absently. "Would our personal financial records help?"

Ann's head came up fast. "You have financial records?"

"No." I shook my head. "The C.P.A. Sonja hired has them. As well as photocopies of the books from his office. We made them the night before we left Moisson." Watching Sonja, I leaned forward, squashing Snaps, confiscated a scrap of paper and a pencil from Ann's briefcase, and scribbled the C.P.A.'s phone number and name. After a moment I passed the curving folder back to her as well.

"Would you be so kind as to take these for me now? I don't want the girls to see them."

"I could turn them over to your lawyer if you like."

I nodded, my eyes still on Sonja. Sensing she had been dismissed, Ann Hyphen stood. Snapping the locks on her briefcase with one hand, she smoothed the wrinkles out of her slacks. Her untouched glass of wine on the coffee table sloshed, sending yellowed circles of reflected liquid light quivering across the table.

I wondered briefly where Sonja had thrown the dead mouse. The back door had been shut, and I hoped fervently Sonja hadn't simply tossed the thing into the trash.

"I'll need a signature on a new contract, one with you as my client instead of Mrs. Rousseau." I nodded slowly. "Since you don't have a phone yet, shall I contact Mrs. Rousseau periodically? My usual practice is every third day unless something interesting comes up."

Something as interesting as Montgomery messin' with his babies? Something as interesting as Montgomery buying and keeping a beautiful young woman as his mistress? I nodded again, my eyes still on Sonja.

"When did you get the pictures? Montgomery was supposed to be in Paris on business."

"That may be the case. I haven't seen either of them for the last seventy-two hours, and the duplex looks empty, like houses do when people are on vacation. Lights coming on at prearranged times, that sort of thing. I thought I might . . . ah . . . visit the premises, but Miss DesOrmeaux has a fairly sophisticated security system. The best I could do was look in the windows when her neighbor wasn't home.

"The photos were shot the day they left. They loaded up quite a bit of luggage and sped off. Traffic was light, so I wasn't able to follow them far. I'm trying to find out now if they have used their passports, and what flight they were on." Ann Hyphen pointed to the folder. "It's all in here."

I nodded again.

"Well." Ann Hyphen looked back and forth between Sonja and me. "I'll be in touch. And Mrs. Rousseau has my answering machine number should you need to contact me. I'll let myself out."

The screen door shut behind her. She called out to the security guard whom Philippe had hired to watch the grounds. I had seen the man a couple times, backlighted as he made his rounds in the dark. Mostly belly with bandy legs throwing bent and crooked shadows across the ground, he could have made a good dwarf character in the Dungeons and Dragons games university students play.

Sonja was no longer talking to herself, but was twisting the empty glass around and around. "You want to tell me the rest of it?" I asked.

"No."

So. There was more. "When you talked about *plaçage* that night in the bar . . . when we were eighteen. About your family history . . ." I chose my words carefully. "You sounded rehearsed. Like you were reading a script."

Sonja didn't look up, but turned the glass upside down, watching the last drop of wine descend and collect at the inverted lip. It didn't fall.

"I reckon I had said all that to you so many times in my mind, I damn near had it memorized."

"When are you going to trust me with the rest?" I murmured.

Sonja stood. "See you in the mornin', Collie." And she walked off without responding, although I knew she had heard me.

Snaps and I sat in the overstuffed chair listening to her footsteps as she made her unsteady way across the twenty or so feet of bare earth between the cottage and the main house. Afterwards we listened to the silence.

Except for country, I was never one for music, preferring the quiet to the raucous and demanding beat of someone else's rhythm. Snaps had her own rhythm, purring steadily as I stroked her, my mind mostly blank. Perhaps I should have been shocked at what Ann Hyphen told me. And in a way I was. But it was the shocked reaction one might feel when one heard something awful confirmed. Something one had known all along, intuitively. Something one had expected, but hoped wasn't true.

Sometime after midnight I lifted Snaps and placed her on the floor where she shifted from sleep in a sensuously long stretch, again flexing her claws, this time into the thick Chinese rug beneath the coffee table. I was stiff, too, and after a moment, I followed the cat's lead and stretched myself. Up to the ceiling fan turning lazily above, out and down, my hands sliding along the rug until I was prone. Relaxing slowly, I looked at Snaps. Her expression said I needed work to do it right, but it felt wonderful to me.

Before I went to bed, I checked the screen door. In the morning I would have the screen reinforced with wrought-iron grillwork and have a good lock put on it so I could leave the front door open at night. And I'd reverse the screen door on its hinges so they were inside and couldn't be removed quietly for easy access. I closed the door and snapped the meager locks. Maybe I was being paranoid. But it might help. It might keep the girls safe until . . . until what? I had no answer, and no answer came to me in my sleep.

Tacoma Talley, M.D., was in her fifties, short, slender, and brusque as a drill sergeant with me. Gentle and tender with the girls. She had us escorted to the back, bypassing the noisy waiting room full of hacking, coughing, squalling children and their irate mothers, to wait in the relative quiet of a playroom. The big room was filled with bright-colored plastic toys, the kind that could easily be washed between infectious children. A cardboard kitchen set with plastic dishes, puzzles, and a medium-sized ball. It was the clear plastic kind that made a hollow echo when it was bounced against the floor, a sound like the photon torpedoes on "Star Trek." The playroom was a perfect place for us to wait. The girls could amuse themselves, and I could watch, without my own trepidation showing and rubbing off onto them.

Dr. Talley had put aside an entire hour for us, but an outbreak of flu had changed her Saturday schedule. We had to wait. Shalene played hard on the wooden rowboat, rocking the heavy contraption back and forth with determination. Dessie grew more distressed by the minute, her hands shaking and cold, her feet dragging as she walked slowly around and around the room. Finally she curled up on my lap and buried her head in my shoulder. I stroked her gently, trying to control the tears in my eyes. It wouldn't do for my babies to know just how horrible I thought this exam would be.

Adrian Paul had talked to Dr. Talley when he and Sonja set up the appointment, preparing the way for the girls and for me, explaining what sort of abuse the girls might have suffered and when. And at whose hands. I don't think I could have said the words out loud to anyone. Not again.

When Dr. Tally finally arrived, she paused at the door and studied us individually, seeming to sense the distinct and diverse wounds we each possessed. Sticking her head back into the hall, she said something to a nurse before coming fully into the room. Shalene's loud rocking stilled. Dessie stiffened in my lap.

Dr. Talley pulled up one of the child-sized chairs and sat waiting while Shalene circled widely around her, found my knee, and curled my free arm around herself. It was like watching her wrap up in a cloak, the way she took my hand and swirled up against me.

Despite her slender build, I had the feeling that Dr. Talley was in poor shape physically, not from abusing her body deliberately, but from simply ignoring its need for exercise and nutritious food. And perhaps from long hours without proper rest. She obviously loved her patients.

"Hi, girls. My name is Tacoma Talley, but most of my friends call me TT." Shalene giggled against my neck and risked a look at the woman whose name reminded her of a toilet. I smiled. "I'm just a doctor, but a lady doctor. And I need to check you both over, listen to your hearts and take some pictures and maybe a little blood from your arms later. Did your mother explain what I would be doing?"

Dessie nodded her head and buried her face deeper in my neck. "I don't want you to touch me down there." Her words were muffled. Desperate.

The tears I had been controlling fell onto her head, and I hugged her body close to me, my eyes staring into TT's.

"I don't blame you," the doctor said softly. "I don't like to be touched down there either. It's . . . embarrassing. But I won't hurt you. Ask your mother. It doesn't hurt when a doctor looks. She has it done at least once a year."

Dessie stiffened, pulling back a bit. I quickly wiped away my tears and sniffed. "It's true, *ma belle*. I have a doctor look at me down there at least once a year. And it doesn't hurt when they touch me." I smiled, although I knew my lips were shaking. "When I was pregnant with you girls, I got looked at real often, exactly the same way as Dr. TT's goin' to look at you."

Shalene listened intently, her concentration absolute as she studied TT's words, her body language, and their significance with a thoroughly avaricious eye. "Do we get candy after? Dr. Ben gives us candy after we go see him."

TT smiled. "I don't keep candy, but I do give away frozen yogurt coupons from the little store next door. They have waffle cones." TT had pegged Shalene for the covetous little wench she was. I smiled at her over Dessie's head, tears still shimmering in my eyes.

"Two," Shalene bargained.

TT nodded her head. "Okay. If you go first."

Shalene stuck out her hand, her left, but who cared, and they shook on it. The nurse opened the door and put her head inside, following it with a tray.

"You girls like juice? I like grape best," TT said, as if she were a child herself. She passed around the paper cups, saving the one on the corner of the tray for Dessie. Her eyes met mine, and I read her expression; she had put something in the cup to settle Dessie. A powerful *thank you* must have shown in my own eyes, because TT gave me her one and only smile of the day. All the other smiles were for the girls, and she gave them unstintingly.

Shifting Dessie, I sipped my juice, giving her the one on the corner of the tray. Grape was the best juice TT could have chosen. Dessie's favorite. I remembered the grape "jewish" she had asked for as a little girl, and I hugged her once, just for me.

Shalene passed her cup back and extended her hand imperiously. "I'm ready. Come on."

TT grinned. "You must be ready for that yogurt."

"Two," Shalene reminded her.

"Two. Come on, yourself. Through this door is my doctor table." I followed, carrying Dessie, who still sipped her juice. She had eaten little breakfast, and I hoped the drug would work on her quickly.

The exam room wasn't what I had expected. Painted in bright, primary colors with cartoon-style alligators and raccoons and skunks and birds, it was a jungle swamp scene. Even Dessie was impressed, her head swiveling on her neck as she took in the room. TT lifted Shalene up on the table and told her to pull off her shirt.

My youngest daughter handed me her money belt to hold during the exam. It was one of those special gifts picked out by Miles Justin one Christmas. He had brought a soft doll for Dessie, and a money belt for Shalene. It felt fat and full. I wondered if she stuffed it with tissues like a teenager stuffed her training bra.

I sat on the only chair, Dessie's too long, too bony legs dangling around me.

The first part of the exam was simple, the ordinary part of any childhood exam, with heart and blood pressure and reflexes, bright lights in eyes and ears and belly pokings. And then TT explained about the stirrups. Designed just like stirrups on a pony saddle, there were two sets, small and smaller, on chrome swivels at the foot of the table. And a video camera, its red light on, positioned between them, beside a goosenecked lamp. There was a Dictaphone as well, with a headpiece like operators wore hanging loosely around the doctor's neck. TT taped the entire exam.

She explained the stirrups to Shalene and instructed Shalene to take off her shorts and panties and stick her feet into the stirrups. Shalene looked at me as if for permission, and I managed a grin. A grin that faded and died as I watched my baby girl receive her first gynecological examination. The speculum was tiny and the doctor's gloved hands compassionate.

TT described, analyzed, and clarified each part of the exam in a no-nonsense voice as she took culture swabs and put them into bottles of media. She looked up at one point and met my eyes.

"Hymen is intact. No evidence of infection or previous lacerations." I closed my eyes and remembered to pray a thank you to the God who heard my prayers.

Dessie was watching intently, but her body was settling easily into mine as the drug took effect. She seemed fascinated by TT's every move, and even as her eyelids tried to close, she struggled against the drug.

"Can ladies really be doctors, Mama?" she asked finally.

I was startled. "Of course ladies can be doctors. They can be doctors or nurses or lawyers or carpenters or bricklayers or anything else they want to be. The only thing they can't be is daddies," I added before I realized the slip of my tongue. I nearly froze, and TT met my eyes over my daughter's head again, then focused on Dessie.

Dessie looked up at me and smiled as if I had said something wonderful, not something stupid. It was the same smile she had showered on me the day the girls told me about the abuse. The day all the sunlight seemed to vanish from my world. "Good. I don't ever want to be a daddy. But I could be a doctor like TT."

I smiled back at her. "I think that would be wonderful, if that's what you decide you want to do. You can think about it for a few years, though, and make sure about all that. Okay?"

Shalene was sitting up, reaching for her panties. "TT didn't hurt," she said, her voice almost contemptuous. "I don't think it was worth two yogurt cones, Mama," she added in a whisper as if TT couldn't hear. The doctor's lips twitched. Shalene eased off the table and walked to me, stepping into her shorts with each step, and taking back her money belt. She strapped the taupe wallet around her waist before she pulled on her shirt.

Dessie slipped from my lap and walked slowly to TT, their eyes meeting. She pulled her hair back from her neck and let it fall.

"It's okay, Dess. She didn't hurt. Not like Daddy when he—" Shalene stopped and looked up at me, then back to the doctor, her eyes wide, her face horrified at her slip. She had told her daddy's secret.

"It's okay. TT knows," I said.

Shalene looked at me, back at the doctor, and back to me. Then she looked at the table with its pony stirrups, her young mind drawing conclusions. Silently she finished dressing and took Dessie's place on my lap.

Dessie looked steadily at the doctor. "My daddy hurt me. But Uncle Richard hurt me more."

Dr. Talley stiffened almost imperceptibly. Her lips were tight, her face pained. Even though she had heard the story from Adrian Paul before she ever agreed to see us, she still reacted. As quickly as it appeared, the pained expression vanished. She nodded and smiled at Dessie. "Well, I won't hurt you."

Dessie nodded and climbed up on the high table, TT letting her as if she knew Dessie needed to do it herself. "Did your daddy ever hurt you?" my daughter asked.

TT tensed, looking deeply into Dessie's eyes. After a moment she said, "Yes. He did." The camera was still rolling, but TT didn't care. My little girl needed to hear the truth. And TT gave it to her. Tears filled my eyes again.

Satisfied, Dessie slipped off her shirt and allowed the doctor's probing instruments and lights. TT finished the exam with only doctor talk, long words separating her from the little drama being played out in the room. But there was a change in her tone when she slipped a small, clean speculum into Dessie and focused the light inside.

She silently took cultures. Then, "Vaginal exam reveals hymen to be disrupted. There is evidence this disruption occurred two to three weeks previously, with a small vaginal laceration remaining, approximately two centimeters long and two millimeters deep on the posterior wall. Infection is present, cultures and gram stain to follow.

"Dessie," she said. "Do you itch down here some? Have to go to the bathroom a lot? Yeah? Well, I'm going to give you some medicine for that, okay, sweetheart? I'm done. You can get up now."

My world slowly spun to a stop as Dr. Talley's words settled into the visceral depths of my mind. *Vaginal exam reveals hymen to be disrupted.* My daughter had been raped.

"Not raped," TT said, her eyes on my girls through the open door of her office. Shalene played on the wooden rocking boat, and Dessie dozed on a vinyl exercise mat in the corner as we talked. Relief washed over me, bringing tears back to my eyes with her words. "I would imagine it was done by a finger or a foreign object of some kind. If there hadn't been infection, the laceration would have healed over by now."

"What was it caused by? The infection." When she looked at me strangely, I asked, "Neisseria?" referring to Neisseria gonorrheae. "I was a nurse. Was it—"

"It wasn't gonorrheae. According to the gramstain, it was a staph infection, so the cream I gave you will be sufficient to clear it up. But I have a question. It's none of my business, but how in hell did you not know what was going on? I know what your lawyer said, but usually a mother has some indication that abuse is taking place."

I realized that was a question I would have to answer often in the coming months, and with the thought, a pain started in the pit of my stomach between my ribs. A dull ache that burned. I couldn't catch my voice. Putting my hand against my stomach, thinking of the baby, I wondered just how all the pressure would shape my unborn child.

"My . . . husband. Only mol . . . molested . . . my babies when I was having my p . . . in a womanly way. He had taken to sleeping in the guest bedroom. . . . The girls never told me. I never guessed." I stood and walked over to the doorway, watching Shalene's frenzied rocking.

A fierce anger surged up from the burning in my gut. "I would have killed him. . . . I would have killed anyone I found hurting my babies." I turned around, facing the doctor, whose face was clinically interested, but whose eyes were bruised. *"Anyone."*

TT nodded. "Good." She stood and walked to the doorway. I moved back as she approached, into the playroom. "I'll send a final report to your lawyer. Do you intend to press charges?"

"My lawyer will have to decide." It was an evasion, but I didn't care. The anger still burned in my throat. "Shalene, *ma souk,* come on," I said, using the harsh Cajun version of "my sweet" or *ma sucre.* "We can have that yogurt now." I stooped over Dessie, trying to wake her, and she looked up at me groggily, rubbing her eyes with the back of her hand.

"Yogurt?" she repeated hopefully.

I smiled. My baby wanted to eat.

CHAPTER
7

The girls were not interested in Van's so soon after yogurt, so we stopped at a furniture store for them to pick out beds. They settled on twin four-posters with canopies. Beds that could be bolted together while they still wanted the security of sleeping together. Later, when privacy became a necessity, the beds could be separated and the large single mattress replaced with twins.

I think the reason they wanted the canopies was the window display at the second store—a large four-poster with a frame above, mosquito netting draped artistically over it. They both insisted that they be given some of the "fuzzy stuff" to go on their new bed as well. I shuddered to think how crowded the small bedroom in the Rousseau cottage would be with the towering posters. But if the girls wanted it . . . I even paid a premium to have the bed delivered before the close of the business day, and because the store wouldn't take one of my counter checks, I had to pay cash, seriously depleting my small store of emergency funds.

We arrived at Van's fashionably late. The French Quarter

bar and restaurant was situated on a corner, with multiple entryways of tall French window-doors. Van's was a perennial favorite with the locals and the tourists, a big family-style dining room with a floor of broken marble in shades of pink and gray with dark grout, plain wooden tables, armless captain's chairs, and a padded bench that ran the length of the back wall. The ambience was casual and relaxed, always busy. Even though it was located in the biggest tourist trap in New Orleans, Van's served some of the best food in the city.

In the back, on the wall bench, where two wooden tables were pulled together, sat Sonja, looking cool and collected and chic enough for the Commander's Palace Restaurant. The twins were with her, Mallory and Marshall restive and wiggling in their booster seats. Down from her, at the other end of the long table, sat Adrian Paul and a beautiful child who looked as if he had been cloned out of Adrian Paul's genes, like a miniature mirror image of my soon-to-be lawyer.

Lunch at Van's should have been an anticlimax after the visit to Tacoma Talley and the furniture store. A restful anticlimax. But I forgot to factor in Sonja's penchant for rummaging around in my life, taking my decisions away from me. I might make Philippe a widower yet. She had invited Adrian Paul to lunch. Sticking her nose in my business again. I wondered if she had signed a contract with him in my name, the way she had with Ann Nezio Hyphen Angerstein.

I started a slow boil, my eyes on Sonja, willing her to glance up so I could scorch her with my look. She didn't comply, although she knew I was staring at her. A slow blush started beneath her collar and rose.

The girls ran ahead, pulling out chairs and chattering away. I stopped, looking at the tableau, watching the girls fight over Van's last booster seat. Not who could have it, but who had to sit in it. Adrian Paul introduced himself to the girls and mediated the dispute before he looked up at me.

And his face fell. He closed his eyes and sat back on the bench, groaning.

"Machinations again, Sister-in-law?" His voice was weary with accusation, and I felt better knowing that someone besides me suffered with Sonja's interference. "I thought you said she asked me to be here."

"She would have. I just missed mentioning it to her before she left this morning." Sonja was unrepentant, a mischievous grin in place as she watched our faces. "You forgot to call him last night."

Adrian Paul sighed and massaged his forehead. It sounded like he mumbled, "My brother is a brave man."

Pulling up a chair, I sat and rested my arms on the table. "I was rather busy last night. Remember?"

"You could have called this morning."

"Sonja. Butt out."

Her grin got wider. We both knew I was licked, but I wasn't quite ready to concede the battle.

Even though I had already appropriated a place at the table, I turned to Adrian Paul and asked, formally, as the sisters at Our Lady had taught us, "Adrian Paul, may we join you and your son—JonPaul?" I queried midsentence, and at his nod I continued, "—for lunch? We're starvin'," I said, drawing out the words in Hollywood mockery of a southern accent. "Or at least I am. Oh," I added casually, "and would you do me the honor of representin' me—" I stopped, looked at the girls, and quickly revised my wording. Shalene was entirely too interested in this adult conversation. "—in the state of Louisiana?"

Adrian Paul looked from me to Sonja, who lifted her brows innocently. I ignored her totally, and Adrian Paul smiled at my performance.

"Of course, we'd be delighted to have you join us," he said, falling into the small game. "My son and I always prefer congenial company to dining alone." He nodded his head as if thinking. "And I'd be honored to represent you, Mrs. DeLande." He glanced down the table at Sonja and said pointedly, "Would you like to retain the appointment Sonja made for you on Monday morning at ten, or would another time be preferable?"

As the corners of his lips turned up, I glared at Sonja and wondered how much life insurance Philippe carried on her. And if he'd miss her when she was gone. But this was a game, Adrian Paul and me against Sonja. . . . We didn't stand a chance.

I smiled sweetly and said, "Monday morning at ten would be quite convenient, Mr. Rousseau, but any future appointments scheduled by my *overbearing dictator* are to be made *null and void.* I will handle all my own business from now on, thank you very much." This last I stated to Sonja, who smiled a cat's satisfied smile. I went back to ignoring her, nodded to my lawyer, and looked after my girls.

Leaning over to my left and then to my right, I pulled their chairs closer to the table, hopefully avoiding future spills. I hoped the waiter had a mop handy. With all these kids, it was axiomatic that we'd have at least three spills. I had once conducted an informal study to determine how many spills per meal per child took place in any public setting. My study concluded that over the course of one meal, there was a minimum of one spill per every two children, with the averages going up as the prices on the menu rose. I placed the girls' napkins in their laps and pulled their ice water within reach before I settled myself.

The girls were watching Adrian Paul's son with unabashed curiosity. JonPaul—I decided to call him JP, as Sonja did, as there were entirely too many Pauls in the Rousseau clan—was dark-eyed and olive-skinned, with a very French nose and thick brows. Father and son were even dressed alike in khaki shorts, oversize T-shirts, and Docksides with no socks. He was a very pretty child. All JP needed to become a flawless miniature of Adrian Paul was a brush-cut beard. His father had not shaved this morning.

Shalene laid her head against my arm, and I slipped it around her shoulders. It was a simple movement, a mother's touch, instinctive and casual and innocuous. A shy Shalene was a rarity.

JP watched the move with the kind of profound ferocity usually reserved for a hungry animal studying bleeding prey. It was disconcerting. As was the unconcealed anguish in Adrian Paul's face as he in turn watched his son. Our waiter interrupted before I could grow embarrassed enough to remove my arm from Shalene's shoulders.

He moved between the tables like a downhill skier dodging slalom poles, calling out to Sonja. "You ready to order now, Miz Rousseau? This all the people you expect?"

I wasn't a regular, like Sonja, but I'd eaten Van's home-made fried onion rings till I was ready to bust on more than one occasion, washing them down with a Dixie Blackened Voodoo Lager beer, a New Orleans claim to fame.

Sonja ordered for us, taking over as usual, but as usual she managed to remember what everyone's favorites were. She was all southern woman at that moment, putting her well-groomed fingers on the waiter's arm, smiling up into his eyes. Adrian Paul watched the demonstration, his face strangely bleak and empty. It was obvious he was remembering his wife, and his pain was so fresh, I looked down, purposely rearranging paper napkins and tableware.

A street musician, standing on St. Peter's, warmed up his fingers on an old, tarnished sax. Strangely enough, he slipped into a bluesy rendition of "Love Me Tender." Dessie sleepily mouthed the words as our waiter wandered back to the kitchen, writing on the small order pad.

"My mama died."

The girls turned to JP, his eyes large and solemn as our table fell silent, and then the table behind us. "She had leukemia and she died jus' before Cris'mas." His voice carried, and a table farther down caught the silence, the hush spreading like a contagious disease through the room. His face was intent, his eyes huge and serious, as he waited for our response.

The overhead fans created an artificial breeze. The sax player on the sidewalk drew a small crowd.

Adrian Paul's jaw tightened, and I had the impression he had stopped breathing. JP's eyes were on me and the arm I still had around Shalene. Suddenly I felt guilty . . . ashamed. My dark-eyed daughter turned and looked up at me a moment as if asking permission, then slipped from the booster seat Adrian Paul had forced her to take. Squatting down beneath the table, she duck-walked, maneuvering diagonally between human and inanimate legs to the far end of the upholstered bench, where she surfaced, her curly head silhouetted against the lacy curtains and bright noonday light.

Every eye was on my daughter as she pushed against Adrian Paul with both hands. She moved him one space down the empty bench and claimed the place he vacated, wiggling until her back was firmly positioned against the dark green upholstery. She was fully aware of the silence of the restaurant, playing it for all it was worth . . . and I was terrified at what Shalene might blurt out. Impetuous at the best of times, she could be downright dangerous when she was the center of attention.

In the sharp silence, Shalene leaned over and took JP's hand, dark eyes meeting dark. Shoving her head a bit forward on her neck, indicating the importance of her words, she asked, "Does your daddy hurt you?"

"No." JP looked surprised.

"It's okay then. Our daddy hurt us, but we got our mama. Long as you got *one,* it's okay. 'Sides—" she paused, her head cocked to one side, "—we can be your mama. Dessie?" she asked, seeking confirmation.

After a moment, Dessie nodded. "Okay. We can be his mama. But *we don't* need a new daddy," she said pointedly, looking up at Adrian Paul.

"His su'si'tute mama. Till his daddy marries him another mama," Shalene clarified. The people at the next table laughed softly and went back to their meal. The normal social sounds of diners resumed, glass clinking, murmured conversation; a child to the front spilled a glass of something. Adrian Paul and I both began to breathe again.

JP looked at me and smiled slowly. My lawyer blinked quickly several times, swallowed, and nodded to himself, his eyes on the children's clasped hands. I glanced quickly at Sonja, proud of Shalene and relieved she hadn't done something really bizarre. On the other hand, I felt sorry for the little boy. Shalene as a substitute mother was enough to raise the hairs on the back of my neck. She was almost as bossy as Sonja, and she was only five.

Adrian Paul looked up at me, that quirky half smile in place. "I guess this makes us family. I imagine Sonja will insist I give you a family discount."

"Pro bono," Sonja amended. For free.

"Sonja. No." I said, feeling a flush start. "Adrian Paul, please. I fully intend to pay all my bills. I don't want special favors just because we're both scared of Sonja." Sonja laughed, and only when I heard the sound did I realize what I had said. But I didn't take it back.

Adrian Paul laughed with her, that deep, rich sound I had heard in his office, his eyes still on his son, firmly under the power of Shalene. "In the remote eventuality that . . . the ex . . . doesn't pay all expenses, *pro bono.* I think it'll be worth it."

Thinking of my forty-thousand-dollar checking account, I smiled wanly. Sonja had outmaneuvered me. Again.

"Can he spend the night, Mama? 'Cause we got our new bed comin'." Shalene put her arm around JP's slender shoulders, much as I had done to her earlier. The look she gave him, however, was more the look that a child gave a stray dog she wanted to take home.

"If his daddy says yes," I answered absently. "He can go to Mass with us in the morning."

Shalene was a born manipulator, shameless and brazen, wielding words to maneuver people's emotions. Seeing Shalene in action was a little like seeing a five-year-old

Sonja. I contemplated my future with dismay; I'd have two of them rearranging my life.

I looked down at Dessie, now mouthing the words of a Mills Brothers tune, her eyes half-closed. The medication given to her by TT was still strong in her system, and she looked sleepy. Tantalizing traces of the tempting beauty she would one day become were apparent on her face.

Would my girls start looking at men differently, feeling the loss of a father who taught them all the wrong things about love? Would they adopt the first man they saw and reach out to him in the only way they knew or understood? Physically? Or would they perhaps avoid men and the physical factors of a normal male-female relationship? Or would they carry around an unreasoning anger against men all their lives? . . .

I shuddered and looked down at the plate of onion rings the waiter plunked down in front of me. And barely made it to the ladies' room. My meager breakfast came back up fast. But even after my stomach emptied, my body continued to discharge its contents, dry heaves lasting a good five minutes while Sonja held my head and placed cool, damp paper towels on my face and neck. It was a time-honored tradition in the South, the wet towels. A mother's remedy that really did work to kill nausea.

Pregnancy's phase two for me. I spent the first month or two of each pregnancy blissfully happy and content, rubbing my tummy and humming little songs. Then came the nausea. For several months I'd see food or smell it and lose whatever was in my stomach. Following the attack, I'd have a craving for whatever it was that had set off the spell, and I'd eat ravenously.

Some women would have retired to bed for the rest of the day, sipping tea and eating crusts of toast after losing a meal. Not me. I wanted the onion rings that had sent me running. I ended up eating a double order of Van's homemade rings all by myself, and a whole po' boy. One of Van's specialities, fried oyster, dripping with catsup and hot sauce.

Sonja had never handled other people's nausea well. Still green, she sipped coffee and shot me murderous glances for spoiling her meal. She couldn't even stand to watch us eat. Of course, I hadn't asked her to hold my head over the toilet, in the unair-conditioned ladies' room, playing nurse and ending up ill herself. But I figured she deserved it. And I thoroughly enjoyed my meal.

The visit to the counselor was the easiest and best part of our day. Dr. Hebert, pronounced "A-bear," in the Cajun manner, was a jolly older woman with a big smile and round cheeks, dressed in a T-shirt, a red split skirt, and tennis shoes, her legs unshaven between. Her long gray hair was pulled back into a ponytail secured with a blue rubber band. She looked like the quintessential grandmother, and with her singsong Cajun accent, she captivated us all. The girls christened her Abear, and the sobriquet stuck.

There were Winnie the Pooh prints on the walls, and pillows and stuffed animals scattered all over the office/playroom, including two monstrous stuffed giraffes, eight feet tall, whose heads touched the ceiling. They were made from a skeleton of steel rods concealed by foam rubber and bright plaid fabric. Hand and footholds climbed up the front legs, fluff tails in the rear, buck teeth and pink tongues over our heads. A scarlet tuft of hair nested between the upstanding ears. A bit of literary license on the part of the maker. Very effective. The girls climbed up and talked to doctor Abear from the safety of the high perches, immediately establishing a rapport with the grandmotherly counselor. There was no trauma in talking to Dr. Abear.

During the session, I kept looking back over my shoulder at the one-way mirror hiding the video camera and the assistant taking dictation. Yet my uneasiness faded as I realized that the doctor would be able to help my girls. They answered her questions freely and talked about their father. Only the good stuff this time. Dr. Abear wanted them to remember that there was good stuff intermixed with the bad.

I wanted to remember that too. Montgomery had been good to me so often. Flowers. Jewelry. Perfume. Trips to France, and once to Spain, to try the vineyards on the border. And he knew just how to touch me . . . *and how to hurt my babies.*

My eyes fell on the sets of dolls in the glass-fronted cabinet across the room. Anatomically correct dolls in various shades of plastic skin tones. I shuddered. I knew that the following interviews and counseling sessions would become harder to deal with as my girls and I became more comfortable with Abear. She would progress from capturing the simple things on video camera to capturing the more difficult things. She would progress from discussing the differences between the truth and a lie—as she was doing now—to asking the girls to show her—using the anatomically correct dolls—what their daddy and uncle had done to them.

It was obscene, what my girls would have to relive in this room. And yet these tapes might prevent forcing my daughters to testify in court about the abuse.

My lips tightened. I spent the rest of the session watching my fingers twist in my lap.

JP went home from the restaurant with Sonja and spent the first two hours of his visit playing with Mallory and Marshall. By the time we pulled up in the yard, the boys were dirty, sweaty, scraped, and unmanageable, just the way kids are supposed to be. They greeted us from the top of Sonja's magnolia tree, the thin, supple branches bent with the boys' weight.

Most magnolia trees grow up thick and heavy with big, waxy leaves. But those trees that manage to survive in the shadow of older, taller trees grow up slim, the foliage sparse, the branches exposed in a marvelous jungle gym of ladderlike climbing apparatus.

The girls burst out of the car and, climbing like chimps, followed the boys up the tree, giggling and screaming. "Stay close to the trunk," I shouted. "The limbs can't hold your weight out on the end." The boys laughed and shook the branches in answer.

Snaps leapt to the hood of the Camry and watched the children's antics, tail tip swishing. She looked amused at the clumsy humans in a cat's domain.

Sonja and Cheri were just getting Morgan and Louis up from their naps, Louis fussy, Morgan placid and lazy-eyed. His temperament was simply too even for him to be a real baby. I knew the next one would be a holy terror to make up for it.

Thumb in mouth, Morgan grunted as we walked back to the cottage, his head bobbing over my shoulder, eyes on the magnolia blossoming with noisy children. Pointing with four stubby fingers, he grunted again.

"What do you want, *mon bébé?*" I murmured, pausing on the bare ground, my eyes on his face. "Hum? You want something?" He grunted again, still pointing. "Well," I sighed. "Maybe someday you'll learn to talk and ask for things. It's too bad you don't talk yet, isn't it? Then I could understand, and you could have whatever you want."

My tone was innocent and musing, and the look he threw me was murderous. I knew my baby could talk if he wanted to, and I'd stopped "understanding" his baby talk weeks ago.

Entering the cottage, I noticed the new bed, already delivered by the furniture store. Someone had made up the bed with sheets and comforter, mosquito netting across the canopy, and two pretty little throw pillows. Sonja. No delivery boy would have done so nice a job. She had even tucked my luggage back beneath the bed.

I smiled as I unfolded the playpen onto the front porch and jailed Morgan in its center where he could watch the older children playing Tarzan in the trees. Now he could see the object of his desire and think about the importance of language and walking versus being a baby forever. I could tell he didn't like the way things were going.

I changed clothes, found the mosquito repellent, and joined Morgan on the front porch. Sitting in the swing, using my toes to gain a faint motion, I watched the children and tried to relax. Sipping iced mint tea, I contemplated my money situation, my thoughts a sharp contrast to the abandoned gaiety of the children. I had close to three hundred thousand dollars invested in stocks, bonds, and certificates. It sounded like a lot of money, but I knew it wouldn't go far in the raising and education of four children.

Part of Adrian Paul's list of options and advice had been Montgomery's legal responsibility to provide child support, even if the law never let him see his children again. The cost of the doctor, the counselor, and the children's education would be—should be—his responsibility as well. But I knew the DeLandes. I had listened in during dinner conversations for years as Montgomery and one brother or another worked out ways to avoid paying what they owed.

Two years ago they cheated the state of Louisiana out of hundreds of thousands of dollars in penalties and fees for the cleanup of DeLande chemical spills over the last seventy years. If they could defraud the state through legal chicanery, they could surely do worse to me.

Suddenly I felt chilled. Montgomery knew where my money was invested. Could he get to those funds? Take them? The swing came slowly to a stop. Monday, before I saw Adrian Paul, I'd change brokers and transfer all my investments to new vehicles. Longer-term investments would make it harder for Montgomery to touch the money, even if he hired a hacker to steal it all by computer.

The children's education had been provided for in the birth gifts. The DeLande tradition. I was executrix of those trusts. Control would revert to Montgomery, however, should I die. And to Andreu, the Eldest, should he die. I needed to change that, making my mother— No. Not my mother. Sonja. She was a meddlesome, nosy, officious snoop, but I knew that Sonja could provide for my children and educate them if I was not available.

That meant I would need a new will too. And I would have to establish permanent custody to protect the children. To keep them from falling back into Montgomery's hands. Sonja again.

I rubbed my head with both hands, sliding my fingers through my hair, massaging my scalp. So much to do. At least I had Sonja to take some of the burden. My meddlesome friend would be kept busy the rest of the summer, probably in hog heaven because she would have the opportunity to poke around in my life, rearranging things to suit her. Much in the same way she would rearrange her furniture. I kicked the porch boards with my toe, sending the swing into motion again.

At least I wouldn't have to go to work any time soon. Alimony wasn't something I would accept from Montgomery, but even without alimony, I would not be penniless. If I changed my portfolio from growth funds to income funds, and lived off my investments, I could gross as much as thirty thousand a year. When I added in child support payments based on Montgomery's income and net worth, we five should be fine.

I dropped my hands, putting them on my stomach, and opened my eyes. And almost laughed out loud. JP was standing on the ground beside the porch, his eyes boring into Morgan's, his hand outstretched. Whispering, crooning to my son just as he would to an apprehensive puppy, he encouraged Morgan to walk.

Morgan stood, pulling himself up on the mesh playpen wall, fingers gripping the padded bar at the top. Little "he he hu he mmmmm" sounds grunted from his throat. He laughed.

Picking up his left foot, he pivoted, let go of the padded bar, and walked the eleven little baby steps to the far side of the pen, squealing with delight.

When my mouth finally closed, I was grinning. It was obvious the little dickens had walked before; that was no toddling first attempt. I walked over, lifted him up by the armpits, and sat him diaper-first into the dirt beside JP. "If he walks, he can play. If not, he sits. Understand?"

JP grinned his dirt-smeared consent, held out a hand to Morgan, and helped him rise. "He's a big boy. He can walk. My mama was going to give me a baby brother, but she died first." He looked up at me, smiling. "I'll take good care of him." Together they crossed the yard to the other kids, who were now playing Hula Hoop and hopscotch in the dirt.

The girls were already as dirty as the boys. It was a matter of honor. They shrieked when they saw Morgan walking, and the baby was passed from finger to grimy finger as each of the older children took a turn walking Morgan around the yard.

I sat on the swing and watched. Montgomery would have been proud.

Carefully I put that thought away. It was one of the good things Dr. Abear wanted me to remember about my husband, that he was always proud of his children. But his betrayal was too fresh, too painful, to savor the good things yet. Especially since Montgomery would never see his children again. Not if I could help it.

Grass didn't grow in this much shade. Mosquitoes, however, flourished, along with filthy children for them to bite. I called them back and uncapped the mosquito repellent I had brought out earlier, smearing the white goo into the dirt that coated them. They looked like Stone Age children by the time I had finished smudging them.

Sonja stepped out her back door while I worked, watching the scene with amused eyes as she walked over. "I ought to make you bathe them all. God. How could two kids get so dirty?" Instead of the white T-shirts above red and white striped shorts they had worn to Van's, Mallory and Marshall were now wearing uniformly brown clothes, the original colors buried beneath the filth of a day's play. Five pairs of shoes and socks, long discarded, were beneath the magnolia tree. The children all had grubby little black toes and fingers, faces so smeared with sweat and soil that gender could not have been determined by anyone but a mother. Multiple black rings adorned their necks; even their ears were filthy.

Sonja sat beside me on the swing, helping me propel it with her toes. She was barefoot, and even her toenails were perfect, rounded and smooth, painted an opaque fleshy tint. She was the kind of woman who never had a hair out of place, was always correctly dressed for whatever was happening around her, and whose mascara probably didn't even run when she was caught in the rain. Other women hated that quality of perfection. I admired it.

"Hungry for onion rings," I murmured, taunting. Okay. So maybe I hated perfection a little.

She hurled one of those ladylike "go to hell" looks my way, all slanted eyes and downcast lashes. One of those "if looks could kill" expressions. I just grinned.

We watched our six charges chase frogs and lightning bugs around the yard as the sun set through the tops of the trees, turning the world all glowing and rosy for a while. The swing creaked softly, and mosquitoes buzzed around our heads as the light died.

Sunday came and went in a slow blur of rain and lashing winds as a sudden cold spell destroyed the myth of an early spring. Cartoons followed early Mass, stories followed cartoons. It was a first and final restful day before the week that Montgomery was scheduled to return. My three children and I curled up in the cottage, huddling beneath the comforter we had bought for the new bed, pulling the mosquito netting closed for the false sense of security it gave us.

Monday and Tuesday passed quickly as the girls dressed in plaid uniforms and red sweaters, joining a long line of Kewpie dolls for their first day of school. It was all strange to them, and I wondered how they would handle the atmosphere of Catholic school after the loose ambience of public school. Predictably, Dessie loved it and Shalene hated it. But she'd adjust. Eventually.

I found a new broker in the Rousseau building. He was congenial, did not claim to know any of the DeLandes, and was positively ecstatic at the prospect of a new client. One with almost three hundred thousand dollars in liquid assets. He started salivating when I walked into the office, rushing to take my jacket, offering me tea or a col' drink or coffee. I think he would have offered to slash his wrists had I wanted a drink of blood. It was pathetic really. And I enjoyed every minute.

My appointment with Adrian Paul went smoothly, as well. Ann Hyphen had been in touch with him and with the C.P.A. who leased offices in the Rousseau building. They had uncovered proof of Montgomery's deception and his financial support of Glorianna. And their child. My children had a half sister. There was no doubt that the courts would allow a divorce on the grounds of adultery with all the evidence Ann Hyphen had uncovered. I supposed that meant I would eventually have to use my PI's real name.

Taking Adrian Paul's advice, I sued for divorce on the grounds of adultery and sued for custody on the grounds of child abuse. That was a claim I would have to prove in court, but for the preliminary papers, my accusation was sufficient to issue a restraining order against Montgomery, without having to mention the sexual aspect of the children's abuse.

There was a separate paper prohibiting Montgomery from disposing of any assets. "So you can get what you deserve," was the phrase that Adrian Paul used in explaining the injunction. The words had an ominous sound. The DeLandes always made sure that others got what was coming to them. One way or another.

The papers were signed by a judge late Tuesday.

As Wednesday approached, my palms began to itch and

sweat. The morning sickness I was plagued with so seldom worsened to the point where I couldn't eat. I couldn't even smell food without running to the toilet. Tea and crusts of toast became my main diet, like ordinary mortal women. And I had to listen to Sonja gloat.

On Wednesday Montgomery's plane landed and Ann Hyphen watched as Montgomery and Glorianna walked into the air-conditioned coolness of the terminal, arm in arm, laughing and giggling and joking. A PI accomplice got a dozen clear shots of the happy couple, two of them kissing, before a strange man in a business suit appeared. After that everything went to hell in a hand basket.

Montgomery went one way, the man and Glorianna went another, kissing and cooing as if they had arrived together. Ann, using a miniature video camera, got the entire exchange on film, while the hired investigator who was working with her got still shots as he followed Montgomery.

Ann's assistant lost Montgomery in a crowd of English tourists. When he and Ann rendezvoused later in the terminal, he informed her that my husband had also managed to avoid the uniformed sheriff's deputy who was waiting at Montgomery's car to serve him with the separation and custody papers. The car was still there. Montgomery wasn't.

As I studied the shots taken by the two PIs, I began to shake. I knew that man. And I recognized the look on Montgomery's face.

Richard DeLande had met the plane. And told Montgomery about me. I knew it. Somehow the DeLandes had found out about the papers. Montgomery knew I was going to divorce him and try to take away his children. And he intended to punish me. I knew that look. God. *He was going to kill me.* Or worse. I remembered Eve Tramonte and the lesson she was taught. . . . And I remembered Ammie DeLande.

The day Ammie left Marcus for another man was too

bright, too cold, for southeast Louisiana. Usually winter was damp with lowering clouds, sparse stinging rain, and cold dismal winds. But Ammie took off in the sunshine.

Within hours the five DeLande brothers had gathered, and because word had come that she was heading west, they assembled in Moisson. They had weapons and maps and too much liquor, and I kept to the back of the house with the girls, playing quiet games until the men left.

Three days later, the brothers returned, arriving in two groups, bearded and rank with swamp smell, gamy from filthy clothes and unwashed bodies. They raided my kitchen, took over the bathrooms and three bedrooms, showering and eating and falling asleep in a matter of an hour.

My house was a wreck, but the odor of old whiskey and the violence that sparked in their eyes warned me to stay silent. I did. Even when they dropped bloodstained clothes in piles on the bathroom floors.

The girls and I stole the Camry keys from Montgomery and slipped from the house while the men slept, staying at Mama's overnight. Montgomery punished me for leaving, but the safety of my girls was paramount.

I wondered about Ammie for years. Wondered if she survived her punishment.

"No woman ever leaves a DeLande." Richard's words, overheard as a threat before they left to follow Ammie. Overheard again on their return, before the brothers fell asleep . . . with satisfaction grating in Richard's voice.

A mother always sleeps lightly, aware of the slightest sound, a change of breath patterns, a cough, the almost silent sound of a child sitting up in bed. Even in Moisson I slept lightly, except for the nights when Montgomery used the guest room. Being closer to the girls' room, he always cared for them then . . . on those nights when I was *bleeding and not available.* But once Montgomery vanished from the airport, I found that I slept even lighter than usual, rising often in the night to check on the children, the doors, the windows, waiting for the watchman on his rounds.

When the day of Montgomery's return passed with no word from him, my ability to sleep diminished until I slept no more than half an hour at a stretch, catnaps broken incessantly by the noise of nonexistent intruders. I was waiting for Montgomery to appear in a rage because he had been served with papers . . . or heard about the papers and their contents through DeLande contacts in the court system.

The day of Montgomery's return came and went. And the day after that. And still Montgomery had not surfaced. Deputies had gone to our home and to the office with the papers. They had even gone to Glorianna's empty apartment twice. No Montgomery.

In almost a frenzy of anticipation and nervous energy I pulled my Singer out of storage and stitched together new curtains for the cottage, made two new jumpers apiece for the girls, and little T-shirts for Morgan out of the remnants.

He glared at me as if he knew that floral cotton prints were not manly, but I figured that I'd dress him as I pleased until he decided he could talk. He had forgotten how to move around on two feet again anyway, holding up his chubby little arms when he wanted to go somewhere. He did a lot of sitting now that I had wised up to his stunt. But the appearance of JP on Friday stimulated his memory and he was toddling around all over the yard within minutes. Morgan was crazy about that boy. So were the girls.

I also slipcovered the kitchen cushions and made big fluffy pillows for the girls to lounge around on in the sitting room. My nervous industry went further, to cleaning the cottage, rearranging Philippe's tools in the garage, and washing all the cars. Philippe bore it all with his characteristic patience, quietly replacing all the tools in their proper place as soon as I left.

Making out a new will took up two hours, and starting the

paperwork establishing Sonja and Adrian Paul as permanent guardians of all my children in the event of my death took up four more. The latter required that I make legal depositions. But at least my children would be safe . . . *if* Adrian Paul and the Rousseau legal firm could dodge the DeLande legal maneuvers. An iffy proposition at best.

Wednesday and Thursday I was busy each waking moment. Sleep took up another three hours each night. For forty-eight hours I heard nothing. On Friday the trouble started.

It was all benign at first. Two phone calls to the Rousseaus after two A.M., with no one speaking. Just hoarse breathing. Then two more during breakfast. Prank stuff. Silly. But we all knew that Montgomery was behind the calls.

By ten A.M., Sonja had accepted a bid from the security company to have the cottage wired into the security system of the main house. A rush job, but with a full crew, possible. Ann Hyphen checked out the system and pronounced it basic, but acceptable. Her grading embarrassed the young salesman who had claimed it to be "top of the line," "state of the art," "the best." He instantly found important business elsewhere.

Just having the security system gave me a semblance of safety. The cottage was wired so the windows could be left partially open, the sensors five inches above the sill. The reinforced screen door was secured into the system instead of the wooden door behind it, so I could have air flow in the unair-conditioned cottage.

On Friday the damp, rainy weather we had suffered through all week cleared by midafternoon, leaving cloudless skies and brisk winds, carelessly tossing the azaleas and stripping off the few remaining dogwood tree blossoms. White petals swirled across the streets, and we shivered still in sweaters by day and flannel pajamas by night.

I picked up the girls at the end of the school day, changed their clothes in the car, and drove them to the videotape store for a copy of *Honey, I Shrunk the Kids* and Walt

Disney's animated version of Robin Hood, the one where the hero in tights is really a squirrel or a fox or something. Then we went to the grocery for frozen pizza and popcorn, planning a highly nutritious meal to be eaten in front of the TV in true American tradition. We got back into the car after loading up three plastic bags of high-fat necessities.

My two satisfied little girls—pleased that they had out-witted their old mom when they also talked me into some Fiddle Faddle—climbed into the backseat and strapped in as I went around the front of the car, glancing in as I did. Slowly I came to a halt.

On the front passenger seat there was a bouquet of tiger lilies. Tiger lilies like I had planted in my backyard in Moisson. Double-petaled and of rich red hue. Out of season. Mine hadn't bloomed yet.

I had locked the car. I was sure of that. And Montgomery didn't have a key. I had taken his when I left Moisson.

So, I reasoned as I stood in the too cool wind, my hair whipping in time with the white-petaled breeze, Montgomery had followed me from Sonja's to the girls' school, to the video store, to the grocery, broken into the car and deposited the flowers, relocking the doors. Flowers that bloomed and died all in one day. There was something ominous and threatening in the choice of flower.

I went on around the car, opened my door, and tossed the flowers onto the pavement. I was shaking, a bone-deep vibration that quivered in my fingers and pulsed up into my body. Terror so strong, I could hardly start the car. Terror for my girls. Montgomery now knew where they went to school. He could take them anytime. And because he had not been served with papers, there was nothing illegal in his taking them. I couldn't stop him.

As I drove away, I deliberately steered the wheels over the tiger lilies. I could leave messages too.

I watched the rearview on the way home, looking for repeat appearances that might mark some of Montgomery's thugs in a chase car. I even took back roads where scarce traffic would expose a tail. But there was nothing. No tail car. No thugs. Maybe Montgomery figured he'd made his point. He had.

That night late, he made his second move. A DeLande never struck on only one front. Two- or three-pronged attacks were their forte.

I was hyperalert, half-awake, half-asleep, when I heard the crunch of sand and gravel beneath someone's feet. I reached in the darkness for the 9mm handgun on the bedside table. I kept it locked up while the children were awake, but on the day Montgomery disappeared at the airport, I began sleeping with the gun near me, like a night-light or a teddy bear. Once the sun set, it was never more than fourteen inches away from my hand.

My late night visitor wasn't stealthy, but was picking his way carefully in the darkness. Even with the cold spell, I was sleeping with the door open, bundling the children up under blankets, putting them in thick socks. All this so that I could hear what went on outside. My visitor's footsteps were almost loud in the darkness.

I eased the safety off and threw the covers to the foot of the bed. It wasn't the guard. His tread was heavier, a bit uneven. It wasn't Sonja out at this ungodly hour. These steps were sliding, making little *shuss* sounds over the dirt with each step. A hot sweat started beneath my armpits.

Curling my knees to my chest, I rolled off the mattress and padded quickly to the front room. The footsteps stopped, just beyond the porch. I stood behind the doorframe, like cops do on television. The knock was so loud, I jumped.

"Collie?"

Shaking, I thumbed the safety back on before I answered, walking to the front door. Sonja was standing on the ground, off the porch, out of the way of the crisscrossing security beams, her robe held tight to her chest, big bootee-style slippers on her feet. The kind that never fit right and seem to drag with each step.

I took a deep breath and exhaled slowly, realizing only then just how frightened I really was. "It's two in the morning. Next time start talking on your way over here." My heart was beating an erratic tattoo against my rib cage. I bent over to ease the pain in my lungs. God. I was going to kill her yet, whether I intended to or not. This was the second time in days I could have accidently shot her.

"Why? You sleeping with that damn gun now?"

"Matter of fact, I am. Wouldn't you?"

Sonja didn't answer that one. We both knew she hated guns. "Phone's for you. Cut the system and let me in. I'll sit with the kids. JP in bed with the girls?"

I almost told her I wasn't taking calls, just to be difficult. But she beat me to the punch. "It's your mother," she said softly.

Stabbing the deactivation code into the security panel beside the door, I turned the two locks just as Sonja stepped onto the porch.

"She sounds upset."

My heart was back beating funny, and a burning started between my ribs, an ache that was becoming almost familiar. Pushing open the screen, I stepped onto the porch, moving aside as Sonja entered the house. "Somebody hurt? Daddy? Montgomery didn't—"

"Jeez, girl, it's cold in here. I don't know. I didn't ask."

"Reactivate the system," I said, dropping the handgun onto the table. Flying off the porch, I sprinted to the main house, my bare feet icy and bruised with the first step.

"Phone's off the hook in the kitchen," she stage-whispered after me. I heard the door close and the locks click into place.

Slamming the back door against the wall, I entered Sonja's house. Using the doorframe as a pivot point, I did a one-eighty and picked up the phone from the countertop. "Mama what—"

"You . . . You . . . How could you do this to us?" She was

crying. And the bottom seemed to fall out of my world. Sonja's too bright, yellow kitchen darkened and I slipped to the floor, pulling the spiraling cord after me.

"Montgomery didn't . . . He didn't hurt you—" Cold air blew through the open door, cooling my sweat-wet body.

"You ungrateful little bitch," she hissed through her tears. "Montgomery wouldn't hurt a fly buzzin' round his head. But he's mighty upset with you. How could you do this to him, Nicole? How could you do this to *us?* How could you leave him?"

"Mama. Wait a minute. I don't understand. Montgomery didn't hurt you?"

"Of course not. Don't be silly, girl." Her tears were turning to anger, and I was bewildered.

"But he called you." I struggled to understand.

"He was here. He said you cleaned out the house while he was gone away on business and moved in with that high yellow coon-ass you were always bringing around."

"Mama—"

"He's just *devastated.* He looks *awful.* Why have you done this to the poor man? To *us."*

"Mama," I said again, louder.

"He's always been so *good* to you and the children. He's always been so good to *us.* We had an agreement and you *ruined* it, damn you."

"Mama, will you listen to me! Mama! Put Daddy on the phone."

"Don't you bellow at me, young lady! You ought to be ashamed of yourself. I'm still your mother, and you're not too old to show some respect. And your daddy has nothing to say to you. Nothing at all."

She sounded furious suddenly, but not half as angry as I. Red-hot rage burned in my mind like a wave of glowing lava, melting everything in its path. "Mama. Did you forget that little conversation we had a couple weeks ago? The one where I told you Montgomery was . . ." The breath expanded in my chest. My hand fisted. *"Montgomery was messin' with my babies."*

There was silence on the other end.

"Did you tell him why I left him? That the good, kind Christian man I married turned out to be a *child molester?"* I grated out the last two words, pounding against the wall with my fist. "Did you tell him that? Or did you forget all about my *little problem?"*

"Of course I didn't tell him that. I wouldn't sully his ears with such nonsense. And that's no reason to leave a man anyway. I told you. Sometimes a woman has to be strong."

I'd heard that one before, and it was even uglier the second time around. Because she believed it. "Mama. If Daddy had crawled into bed with me at night and put his hands all . . ." I swallowed, fighting anger and revulsion ". . . all over me . . ." tears started to fall ". . . and forced me to perform oral sex on him . . . would you have stayed with him? Would you have let him . . . hurt me that way?"

She was silent again, the sound of her breath ragged and hoarse.

"Is that what happened to you, Mama?" I whispered. "Is that why you married the first man who looked at you twice and moved you away from all you had in New Orleans and all you were as a Ferronaire? Is that why you dropped out of school and moved to a little tiny Cajun town in the middle of godforsaken nowhere? Were you runnin' away? Were you runnin' away 'cause your daddy *touched* you?" My voice had dropped to a whisper. "And because your mama *let* him? . . ."

"I don't have to listen to this trash," she said. Her voice was low, like the growl of a vicious dog. "I don't have to. I don't know who you're sleeping with, girl. Montgomery says it's a *black* man." Her voice dropped lower, the words savage and primitive. "One of the LeBleu girl's high yellow friends. Well, anyone who sleeps with a *nigger* is no daughter of mine."

I was stunned. The word sounded foreign in my memory, the coarse syllables of it. *Nigger*. A word she had never allowed in our home. A word she had beaten Logan over once upon a time. A word exposing a part of my mama that I had never seen before. An ugly side. A side she had covered up all these years with a facade of honeyed sweetness and with proper protocol, all the right phrases and all the right moves. That too thin veneer of Ferronaire gloss.

Softly I said, "I'm not sleeping with anybody, Mama. But you should know. Your grandchildren have a two-year-old quadroon sister. Montgomery has a . . . lady friend."

She sucked in her breath.

"She's a pretty little thing, Mama. I've seen pictures."

Mama said nothing. Only the panting of her breath crossed the miles to me.

"Don't call here again, Mama. Not late at night. If you want to talk to me or to my babies, you can keep civilized hours and phone at a decent time."

I could almost see the angry tears glittering in her eyes, her chin uplifted and aristocratic, her manner regal and stately as she accepted the insult of being told she had called unpardonably late. Slowly I stood, the room swimming in my tears. "Night, Mama."

Replacing the receiver, I laid my head against the wall. Tears icy cold on my face. Tears falling and splattering on Sonja's too clean, too cheerful, too yellow flooring. I sobbed.

"Collie?"

Quickly I wiped my face with the back of my hand and turned, blinking.

"Come here." It was Philippe. Dour, dependable, unflappable Philippe. Standing in the kitchen doorway in his robe, hairy calves exposed beneath—worse than Dr. Abear's hairy legs, I noticed needlessly. His arms were open. I fell into him, boneless and wounded, bleeding inside as if my mother had stabbed me over and over again. And I sobbed against his chest, damning my pregnancy, which made me so weepy. And damning Montgomery. And damning my daddy for not taking the phone away from Mama. And trying to damn my mama, who seemed to have wounds of her own.

I cried until Philippe's robe was saturated and mucus ran mixed with my tears. I sobbed until my voice broke with the strain. I sobbed until my breath groaned in my throat, and each time I inhaled, my esophagus shuddered with pain.

I cried until I had no more tears left. I cried until the sound of a voice penetrated and I realized we were sitting on the floor, Philippe's back against a kitchen cabinet, me in his lap. And shame flooded through me.

"Cesté bon, ma sha ti fum. Cesté beiun, ma petite chou, ma sha ti fe."

I hiccuped and laughed shakily, pulling away. I blew my nose on the Bounty towel he passed me, and when I spoke, my voice was rough and clogged with tears. "Cajun? What happened to that terribly proper French you Rousseaus usually use?"

Philippe shrugged, a very Gallic gesture, the very proper Frenchman, even sitting on the floor at two in the morning holding a crying, disheveled woman. "Go back to the cottage, *me sha*. And don't tell my wife we have been sitting on the floor in each other's arms all this time. She is a very . . . emotional woman."

I laughed at his flagrant understatement.

CHAPTER

8

"Why?"

When I didn't answer, Adrian Paul placed his cup on the little table between us and leaned forward, resting his elbows on his knees, his interlaced fingers hanging down between them. "Why do you think your husband would physically harm you?"

I watched the bonsai on the table-desk, its leaves a delicate green, the hard little buds I had noticed on my first visit here softer and larger now. A paler green tint of flower petals showed through the pale green of the bud casing.

I sipped my coffee. Decaf. Bitter and acrid-tasting. I'd give a whole lot for the right to drink a good strong cup of Community Coffee, dark roast with real cream and—

"Nicole."

I jerked, met Adrian Paul's eyes, and slowly set the cup and saucer down on the table beside his. "I'm sorry. I was daydreaming. About coffee. Real coffee," I sighed.

His lips twitched, but he didn't respond to my plaint. "Why do you think your husband would hurt you?"

"Because I've left him," I said finally, putting into words

174

my fear and the sense of futility that had gripped me in the early hours of the morning. "'No woman ever leaves a DeLande.'" I looked at him quickly, and then back at the tree. It needed a leaf pinched off, a small one that was hanging loose at an odd angle. "'No woman ever leaves a DeLande,'" I repeated. "It's a saying . . . a homily they use."

Adrian Paul waited, his pen and yellow legal pad on the table beside his cup. He wasn't taking notes. He was just listening.

"I guess I should tell you about Ammie. She was Marcus's girlfriend. Or wife. I never got it straight even though I met her twice—the first time when he brought her to visit. I was between babies—" I smiled "—and she was pregnant with her second. Big pregnant." I made a circle with my hands to demonstrate how rounded she had been.

"She was the single most beautiful girl I'd ever seen. Redheaded. Scarlet really, with big lavender eyes and golden skin. I don't know where he found her. She had a southern accent, but not a regional one. Not Texas or south Louisiana. I suppose she could have been from east Alabama. Or—" I stopped. "I'm babbling."

Adrian Paul hadn't moved.

I really wanted to pinch off the offending leaf. Sonja would have. Instead I folded my hands in my lap. Very proper. The sisters would have been pleased. I took a deep breath.

"I never told anyone. But Ammie left Marcus. Came through Moisson on her way to Texas. She was with a man, but I didn't see him; he stayed in the car." I stopped and looked at Adrian Paul. How could I expect him to understand when I never had? "She told me she was leaving Marcus, that she was tired of sharing—whatever that meant. She gave me her destination—Daingerfield, Texas—and I don't know why she did that. We weren't friends. Not at all." I paused, remembering again the still, cold day, too bright with winter sun. "It was January second, two years ago this past winter. She said she was fulfillin' a New Year's resolution and that she wouldn't be back. And then she left.

"The next day, four of the DeLande brothers landed on the airstrip outside of town and came to the house. The DeLandes have a family helicopter," I added needlessly. "Someone had told them where she was goin'. She told two other DeLande wives that I know of. And the men all went after her." I paused, watching the little leaf, so lost at the bottom of the branch. "Montgomery too.

"Three days later they came back. The men, I mean. They had blood all over their clothes . . . and Ammie wasn't with them." I looked at Adrian Paul. He was very still, his eyes showing no emotion.

"I started to go to the sheriff, but DeLande money elected Terry Bertrand to office. Montgomery and he were always goin' off huntin' and fishin' four, three, two times a year. They even went to Montana once for . . ." I stopped and stared into Adrian Paul's dark, empty eyes.

"I didn't even know her real name," I said, my voice low, my hands twisting in my lap. "I think she was Marcus's common-law wife. I watched the papers for mention of somethin' . . . anything. I even asked Richard's wife later if she knew about Ammie. I didn't know how to find out what happened to her. But I learned this. 'No woman ever leaves a DeLande.' Not by running away."

Adrian Paul's eyes were shuttered. I focused back on the bonsai, suddenly irritated with the out-of-place leaf.

"I can make some inquiries for you. If you let me. Discreetly, of course. But it might mean you would someday have to testify about what you saw."

I nodded, giving him permission. I had thought a lot about Ammie lately, wondering if I'd disappear someday.

"Why didn't *you* run away from Montgomery instead of coming to Sonja? You didn't have to repeat Ammie's mistakes and inform the entire family of your travel plans. You're bright. You could have flown to Reno, gotten a quickie divorce, left the country, and disappeared. You have money, and there are plenty of places you could go where no one would find you."

I shook my head, surprised he hadn't thought it through. "No. Only people who live out of cardboard boxes can disappear. The rest of us have Social Security numbers, passports, and money that can be traced. And any computer processor in any government office anywhere in the world can trace you if the price is right. The DeLandes do business all over the world. They could find me. They *would* find me.

"I did think about cashing in all my investments and living off the funds, paying cash for everything. No paper trails to follow," I explained. "But the government keeps eyes out for people who live on cash. Drug dealers, you know. And I won't deprive my children of a decent life-style if I don't have to.

"The DeLandes can find anyone anywhere," I repeated, "so running wouldn't help. Out there—" I indicated the rest of the world with my hand "—I don't know anyone. Here I have family." I smiled. "Well, I have Sonja. I have a life. And by staying public, I might have a chance to be safe. That is, as long as I don't remarry.

"Andreu's first wife, Priscilla, actually divorced him, but she never remarried. She lives outside of Des Allemands in a conservatory, as a lay sister, I think. He watches her, but he leaves her alone. Of course, she had to give up her children." I looked at Adrian Paul again and leaned forward slightly. *"I won't give up my babies. And I'm not interested in a life of religious seclusion."*

"You're going to twist that finger off if you're not careful."

I looked down. I had pulled so hard on my wedding ring that the finger beyond it was grayish from lack of blood. I eased the ring off the bruised finger and looked at the flawless gold. Held it up to the light so I could see all the leaves and flowers and vines carved into its broad surface. I hadn't looked at the ring lately. It was a fine piece of artwork, sculpted in Paris according to Montgomery's specifications. Wisteria that was cunningly shaped to follow a seamless band. Without comment, I pushed the band back on.

"So. You think Montgomery would let you go if you left him the children. But you're not willing to do that. Therefore you think he will come after you," Adrian Paul summarized.

It sounded so simplistic put that way, and I knew it would never be simple. Not with Montgomery. "Eventually he'll come after me," I agreed. "But I want to see if he'll let me go. I want to try it before I run. Because once I disappear, it will mean a life on the run for as long as I live. For as long as my children live." I had tried to visualize such a life. But I couldn't envision how people live when they had no home, no people they could call their own. And I think I was more afraid of being alone than of facing Montgomery. The feeling of futility that had shrouded me all day returned, sharp and crisp.

"Priscilla had to convince Andreu that she wanted a divorce. I'll have to convince Montgomery."

Adrian Paul shook his head, no more convinced than I was. "We can get you more protection. More security."

I shrugged, watching again the little leaf that wanted to go its own way, instead of being a polished part of the homogeneous whole. And I liked the little rebel leaf suddenly. It was as if it had grown there, out of place, just for me.

"Are the children in any danger?"

I actually smiled. "Only if Montgomery gets them back."

"Let me talk to Philippe. If more security guards would help, then we'll get you more. Do you have a gun?"

"Several," I said wryly.

"Do you know how to use them?"

I bristled at the arrogance in his tone. The big strong man talking to the helpless little lady. "Yes. I do know how to use them. All of them. Extremely well."

Adrian Paul grinned. "Forgive me. I didn't mean to insult you."

"Yes you did. But it's okay. After all, you can't help it. You're only a man."

"Touché." He laughed and I smiled again, pushing away the feelings of helplessness that seemed to clog my mind like a low-lying fog. He stood and I followed suit, picking up my bag.

"By the way. Is there some quick and easy way to open a locked car door without a key?"

"Yes." Adrian Paul's eyes grew very still and intense. "Why?"

It seemed terse questions were the trademark of Rousseau men. I told him about the tiger lilies on the passenger seat of my car, and he sighed. "Yes. There's a tool called a shim. A flat, thin piece of metal, roughly eighteen inches long, shaped like a ruler but with a notch in it. It takes an experienced user all of five seconds to open a car door. But there are ways to protect yourself from all that. Security systems and such. I think you should consider getting one."

"And I think it would be a waste of time and money. Montgomery would find a way to get in if he wanted to, security system or no." I thought about the cottage and the security system there. It was good for advance warning. But it wouldn't ultimately protect us. Not against a DeLande. "I will, however, consider it. At least I won't be surprised when someone's put something in the car. I'll have a siren to inform me of the fact."

I looked back at the little leaf and hoped Adrian Paul would let it continue to grow. Going its own way in the world, rebellious, independent. And alive.

We said our good-byes, all the little polite, inane things people say when it's no longer just business, but the relationship isn't personal either. And I walked out.

I spoke to Bonnie as I left. Today she was dressed in a shrimp silk suit, still color-coded to the office decor. I would love to see her in purple or crimson or some clashing color, maybe with a big sunflower tucked behind her ear. I wondered if she dressed the same way at home, a big beige bathrobe to fit the beige tile in the bathroom. A blue dress to match the wallpaper in the dining room.

I smiled at my whimsy as I pushed the outer doors of the Rousseau Firm and checked the parking lot for idling cars or strange men just standing or sitting around. The lot was empty. My car was parked up close, and I unlocked the door hurriedly before slipping inside.

On the passenger seat was a book.

Not that it would do any good, but I locked the doors before picking up the book. It was a frayed, ancient edition, so old that the title was obscured on the worn leather cover.

It was a book of love poems, passionate and romantic verse and sonnets by John Donne. I flipped to the page marked by a small, tarnished brass bookmark. It was old, too, in the shape of a broken heart, mended. Tears filled my eyes as I read the poem Montgomery had whispered to me once at night, long ago, when our loving had been fierce and wonderful and sweet. I could hear his voice as he murmured the words, soft as a summer's breeze against my skin in the late evening darkness, a full moon overhead.

> Come and live with me, and be my love,
> And we will some new pleasures prove
> Of golden sands and crystal brooks
> With silken lines and silver hooks.
>
> There will the river whispering run
> Warmed by thine eyes more than the sun.
> And there the enamored fish will stay,
> Begging themselves they may betray.
>
> When thou wilt swim in that live bath,
> Each fish, which every channel hath,

> Will amorously to thee swim,
> Gladder to catch thee, than thou him. . . .

Tears filled my eyes as I read the poem Montgomery had quoted to me. There were silk ribbons marking other pages throughout the book. I flipped through, reading snatches of love poems, familiar and exquisite.

Closing the book of poetry, I replaced it on the passenger seat. And I drove away. I couldn't force myself to leave a message of my own this time. Perhaps this could be the first of the "good stuff" that Dr. Abear wanted me to remember.

The next morning, when I took the girls to school, there was a rose on the hood of the car. At lunch, a small book of love poems again. This time sonnets by William Shakespeare. And a small bouquet of gardenias tied with a silk ribbon and a gold chain. It fit perfectly around my neck.

Montgomery was courting me. The fact made me shiver.

That day, late in the evening, a sheriff's deputy told his story to Adrian Paul and me while lying flat on his back in the emergency room of Charity Hospital. I don't care what a good decorator might do to cheer up an emergency room, they still all looked drab and wan to me, colorless and medicinal and frightening. Even when I was studying to be a nurse I had hated emergency rooms, the bustle and turmoil, the fear on family members' faces as they waited to hear the worst about someone they loved.

Adrian Paul and I stood at the side of a stretcher, its back angled up to form a chaise lounge three feet off the floor. Police, all grim-faced and hostile, worked around us, taking reports, patting the deputy's arm, talking into radios that crackled and spat like angry cats.

Montgomery had been on his way out of the New Orleans office of DeLande Enterprises, LadyLia by his side, when the deputy, recognizing Montgomery by the photo attached to the papers, approached. He stopped, slapped Montgomery with the papers, said his little piece, and stepped back, his job completed.

"His face never changed," the deputy said. "He didn't blink. He didn't stop smiling. But the nex' thing I knowed I woke up in the gutter underneath all these papers I'd just served him with." He handed over the legal papers signed with the judge's signature to Adrian Paul. They were torn into four neat pieces.

"The sonabitch—'scuse me, ma'am—beat hell outta me." He held up his left hand and displayed four fingers, temporarily splinted together until a good "hand man"—an orthopedic surgeon who specialized in hand repair—could take a look at the X rays.

The deputy's face was unmarked except for the bruised lump on the side of his head. But he had four broken ribs and he moved his legs gingerly as if Montgomery had kicked his genitals.

"His face never changed. He never blinked," the deputy repeated. "But Mother Mary Fuck a—ah, excuse me, ma'am. But shit. I ain't never seen no eyes like to his in my life. Like lookin' at the devil hisself."

The deputy moved his torso on the angled stretcher and grunted as a spasm of pain crossed his face. After a moment he found his voice. "Ma'am, that's one mean sonabitch you married. I wouldn't want him coming after me. No way in hell."

I shivered all the way home afterward, fighting a burning pressure in the pit of my stomach, a pain that threatened to overwhelm me. If Adrian Paul talked to me, I didn't hear. If the sunset was beautiful, I didn't notice. I just kept seeing Montgomery's face, the way it always looked as he punished me, blue eyes burning with a cold flame.

My husband had been served with Service of Process, summoned to appear at a court proceeding fifteen days from now. And he had attacked an officer of the law in the performance of his duties. There was a warrant out for his arrest.

When Adrian Paul helped me out of the car in front of the cottage, he passed me a card. It was to James McDougal's Auto Alarm Systems, out in Metairie. I took the card in nerveless fingers and followed him to Sonja's back door.

She fed me hot brandy in milk while the Rousseau brothers talked security. I watched them move as if we were all underwater, every movement exaggerated, sluggish, every sound muffled. Shock could have this effect. But knowing a medical explanation didn't explain the sensation away, didn't return me to the regular world.

I rubbed my baby through the abdominal wall and fought down nausea that the brandy simply wasn't strong enough to battle alone. *I had a decision to make. I had to decide to leave.* To run as Adrian Paul suggested. But where the hell could I go that Montgomery with all his connections couldn't find me?

Yet if I stayed here, the Rousseaus were at risk as well. Would Montgomery attack them too?

I clenched my fists and pulled on the wedding ring I still wore. Sipped brandy in milk, the crystal snifter coated with caramel-colored liquid. The feeling of futility I had endured all day closed around me like a noose, strangling the strength out of me. Choking to death the essence of who I was. Who I became the day Dessie was born, and she looked up at me with big blue eyes, and I swear to God, smiled. I was a mother. And I couldn't protect my children.

Slightly drunk, mouthing prayers to a God who seemed to be very far away at the moment, and crying silent tears, I let Sonja put me to bed in the wisteria room upstairs in the main house. The girls bunked in with the twins in the cavernous room they shared with their hundreds of toys. Morgan slept with Louis. And for the first time in weeks, I slept soundly.

The next morning I got my last gift from Montgomery. An old copy of the *Book of the Dead*.

It was sitting on the hood of the car, little cat paw prints circling around it, clearly marked in the dew that had fallen overnight. Montgomery or one of his hired minions was getting past the security guard at will. Philippe doubled security, hiring a second night guard to patrol the space between the two houses, the garage, the cottage entrances, and the drive.

And for a week we heard nothing from my husband. I read the copy of John Donne poems, all the pages Montgomery had marked with silk ribbon strips. I knew my husband loved me. I accepted that he didn't want to let me leave. And when I read all the poems he had marked, I understood that there would be no convincing him to let me go. No quiet divorce. No amicable separation. Not from Montgomery.

Only the law could protect me now.

Yet the feelings of helplessness that had plagued me seemed to dissipate with this knowledge, this acceptance. A germ of new feeling began to bud inside me, just a tiny hope, a tiny belief. That perhaps I could protect my children alone. That perhaps the God who had left me here with three children to protect had given me the way, the power, the strength to accomplish the goal. If I could only find it.

One week later, almost to the hour from the moment that Montgomery had been served with papers and had attacked an officer of the court in retaliation, my husband began his assault. A strange man, dark-haired and dressed—despite the heat—in a three-piece business suit, showed up at Saint Ann's. He was urbane and relaxed and carried a note from me to release the girls into his custody.

The note was handwritten in a style so close to my own extravagant scrawl that my own mother would have accepted it as genuine. But the mother superior at Saint Ann's was no pushover where the safety of her girls was concerned. Not even when faced with all the charm and authority a DeLande male could bring to bear. She refused to release the girls to him until she could confirm the authenticity of the note. And when Saint Ann's phone lines were mysteriously out of service at that particular moment, her protective instincts were aroused.

She sent her assistant—a postulant in gray wool—running through the heat with three errands: to remove my girls from class and take them to Sister Martha in the dispensary for safekeeping; to find a pay phone and call Sonja's house, the number on the "in case of emergency" card in her file; to copy down the license number on the dark gray rental car outside.

The man, left kicking his heels in the entry hallway while the mother superior supposedly summoned the girls, must have realized that he would not get his way. He took off, tires grinding into the shell-based concrete used to pave the drive.

Sonja and I rushed to the school while the mother superior called the police, Sonja driving the Volvo through traffic like a maniac, me holding on to the dash with one hand and the door with the other. I never once condemned the risks she took.

We couldn't prove it, of course, but the man the sisters described sounded like Richard. The cops could do little, even with the license tags, because the rental car was listed in the name of a woman. Eloise McGarity. Whoever that was.

I just held my girls while the cops talked and the mother superior stalked around in a fury. Her stiff calf-length habit made outraged sounds as layers of starched black cloth rasped against starched black cloth. Her eyes were spitting sparks.

I was forced to tell her about the sexual abuse suffered by my girls at the hands of their father and their uncle. Perhaps the very same man who tried to take them from the school.

I had the rare opportunity of actually seeing a nun steam. I think that had she been alone, the mother superior would have indulged in some old-fashioned cuss words before she settled down to pray for Montgomery's soul.

I took the girls home for the day. The school year was

almost over, only a few days left, and I suppose I could have removed them from school altogether. But I rediscovered the Dazincourt stubborn streak inside myself. It had lain dormant all these years, quiet and tranquil, but it had been roused the night the deputy was attacked.

I wouldn't let Montgomery destroy my girls' lives. I would protect them.

I took to carrying the Glock 9mm handgun with me wherever I went, concealed beneath my clothes. I didn't discuss this with my lawyer, who might have tried to dissuade me. I didn't even know if Louisiana had a law against carrying concealed weapons. And I didn't care. I wore a lot of jackets in the hot, steamy weather.

And I stopped praying. I'm not sure exactly when I stopped expecting God to protect my girls. My prayers had changed on the day we moved from Moisson. They had changed from "God, please protect my babies," to "God, please help me protect my babies," to silence. But I think God was with me. Waiting in the stillness.

The girls and I continued our twice-weekly counseling sessions with Dr. Abear, sometimes together, sometimes separately. The cost was amazing, and I watched my forty thousand dollars dwindle for weeks until Adrian Paul found a sympathetic judge and attained a court order forcing Montgomery to reimburse me for all pertinent expenses or risk seizure of his property. Dr. Tally, Dr. Abear, and the girls' schooling fell under the heading of "pertinent." DeLande Enterprises paid up without a demur, in a check signed by the Grande Dame DeLande herself.

Ann Hyphen, however, wasn't considered pertinent. I still signed out checks once a week to her and the C.P.A. as they tried to find more proof of Montgomery's liaison with Glorianna DesOrmeaux and her little daughter. Ann had captured a single photograph of the mother and daughter the day Montgomery returned from Paris. Montgomery's child was breathtakingly beautiful. Neither had been seen since that day.

I passed through phase two of pregnancy more quickly than usual, and although I was only three months along, I no longer suffered with nausea and dry heaves at the sight and smell of food. I was instead weary, lethargic, and enervated, taking longer naps and sleeping hard at night. I was drowsy during the day, and could nap anywhere. On the sofa, at the kitchen table, on the porch swing.

The need for sleep forced me to depend on the security system and the hired guards for early warning. The new guard was named Max, and he stopped in every evening when he came on duty to speak with me, the .38 policeman's special hanging on his hips. But even with his presence, I kept the 9mm close by, strapped to my ever-enlarging waistline.

At the end of the second week following Montgomery's disastrous encounter with the sheriff's deputy, Snaps disappeared. The girls missed her first, complaining that she didn't come to bed with them one night. But since JP was once again snuggled down between them, and since that meant greater roughhousing in the canopied bed, I assumed the cat simply got smart and slept beneath the front porch. In the morning, however, her food was untouched. And I knew that Montgomery had taken her.

On Sunday morning we went to early Mass, waving good-bye to Max, who had wandered the grounds all night, chain-smoking unfiltered Camels in an attempt to appear older than his twenty-one years. He was a good kid, bespectacled with short-cropped hair and a too thin mustache, but very gung ho.

We hadn't chosen a church to call home yet, but attended Mass at the Saint Louis Cathedral. It was a tourist trap, and we passed several other churches on the drive, but the history and beauty of the old church kept bringing me back. The streets were almost empty in the half-light of dawn, and the church was nearly empty as well. A few well-dressed, bleary-eyed retirees, stopping off for a dose of religion following a night of partying, a few families with sleepy-eyed children, and a few dozen adults, alone, were scattered throughout the darkened sanctuary.

Besides Mass, the cleric taught a short lesson on the beatitudes, the part in the Scriptures about the meek inheriting the earth. No one had been more meek than my girls, and I thought it grand to consider them as heirs. I'd give them the Atchafalaya River Basin as a home base, and maybe the Grand Canyon for a vacation change of pace. My fantasies brought a smile to my lips midway through the sermon. The priest smiled back.

The music was good, the rich strains of childhood's memory. There was none of this new stuff, with difficult lyrics and impossible melodies. I felt reborn, standing in the half-dark church, singing as the rising sun streamed in through the stained-glass windows, organ notes bouncing off the old taupe and cream plastered walls, candles twinkling off gilt and brass, and off-key voices raised in praise.

After the service, I picked up Morgan, propped him on my left hip, and took Shalene by the hand, Dessie trailing behind us as we walked down the aisle to the outer doors. The girls were prattling on about ways to get JP a new mother. A permanent one. I laughed when Shalene suggested that Adrian Paul buy him one.

And was still chuckling when we passed Richard on the way out. He smiled at me. An amused smile, as if I were a precocious child caught in a prank. He nodded his head at me as I swept past, then focused on Dessie, his eyes hungry. Possessive. I almost pulled my gun and shot him, standing there in the cathedral in front of God and all the saints. Instead, I did the only thing I could. I took the priest's arm in front of the church and dragged him along after me.

He was young and obviously thought he was being attacked by a woman with an obsession fixated on priests. He spluttered and pulled away till I leaned close and told him I was being stalked by an ex-con, a rapist, and that I just saw him loitering in the church. He believed me and took up

Shalene and Dessie in his arms, speeding our progress to my car.

I wondered if lying to a priest was worse than lying to someone else, and determined that the next time I went to confession, it would be at another church. I was willing to perform whatever penance was necessary for the deception, but not willing to risk facing the same man under the seal of confession.

We made it to the car and pulled out onto the street, passing Richard's 1955 blue-on-blue two-door Chevy. It was two cars down, its custom paint job sparkling in the sunlight. He probably had planned to leave me a little gift, and desisted when he saw the new security company sticker on the Camry's window.

I could scarcely breathe, my heart beating so fast, it seemed to thunder. Not in fear. But in recognition of the violence inside me. I could have killed Richard standing in the cathedral. I *wanted* to kill him.

When we reached home—by a series of back roads to make sure we weren't followed—we found Snaps. She was lying on the cottage's front porch, hogtied with blue fluorescent fishing line, her four feet and tail knotted together. Her fur was matted with blood at both front feet where she had struggled, biting herself to win free of the cording. Her eyes were listless, her breathing short and fast, and she looked terribly dehydrated.

The girls followed silently as I sat Morgan inside the cottage and carried Snaps to the kitchen. I deactivated the security system with one hand and reactivated it as I moved through the house, making sure no one had been there. I set Snaps down on the kitchen table and started rummaging in the cottage for supplies. In the bathroom I found two pair of scissors, clear tape, a razor to shave off the fur, a claw clipper so she couldn't scratch me, hydrogen peroxide for cleaning, and finally the antibiotic cream. Returning to the kitchen, I dropped the stuff with a clatter and tied on an apron.

"Go change into shorts, girls," I said without taking my eyes from the Persian. I lifted the matted fur to check her wounds, and the girls didn't move. "I need you girls to help me help Snaps. Dessie, would you please open out Morgan's playpen and stick him into it? I don't want him running all over the place. Shalene, bring in some towels from the bathroom, the white ones. Clean ones," I added. "Oh. And, Dess, after you put Morgan up, bring me some of the leftover linen. That's the wide-weave cloth, the tan stuff that you think wrinkles too easily. Then you two change clothes and come help me. Hurry."

Both girls moved this time to obey. I don't think they would have followed orders had I not given them commands that were calculated to help the cat.

I wished I had some morphine to dose Snaps; it was going to hurt like hell when I clipped the fishin' line and pulled it free. The skin had swelled and closed over the fluorescent blue line in several places. Besides morphine, I needed an IV with D5W, saline, maybe some silk for stitching. . . . *Damn.* I needed Daddy. Or at least his well-stocked surgery.

I found the sterile bandages in the back of a kitchen drawer with the needle-nosed pliers, instead of with the other medical supplies. Moving will do that to you, I suppose.

Shalene brought the towels, Dessie the linen. "Go change. Hurry," I said without looking up from the cat. "I may need you." I hadn't meant to sound terse, but at least both girls moved like greased lightning, as Mama would have said.

I placed Snaps on clean white towels, doubled over beside the sink, and clipped and shaved the matted hair off the swollen ankles and tail. Snaps lay unmoving. An unnatural state for any cat.

Both girls were back at my side so fast that I didn't have to ask if they had folded and hung up their Sunday clothes. They were half-naked, dressing as they watched, and I remembered how I had stood watching Daddy in the surgery when I was their age.

Snaps's paws were slightly gray beneath the fur, showing a decrease in blood flow. I could only hope that removing the blue line would restore the circulation. If not, then Snaps might lose all four feet. "Damn," I whispered. Neither girl fussed at me for cussin'. I paused. I could pile all of us back into the Camry and go hunting for a twenty-four-hour emergency veterinary clinic. But I didn't. Instead I put water in the kettle on the gas range to heat.

And that was perhaps significant in retrospect. It marked some tenacious, defiant part of me rising to the surface. Some aggressive, assertive component of my soul that resolved to protect whatever was mine. No matter what.

It was vaguely familiar, this new/old part of me. It was the same part that had carried me through the time that Sonja was snakebit in the swamp. It was the part of me that faced down Old Man Frieu and took away his shotgun. A little rusty, but still tough for all the years unused.

Carefully I clipped Snaps's claws. The slight jerk should have caused her enough pain to bring her around, or at least make her flinch. When it didn't, I knew that Snaps might not make it. Before I clipped the fishing line—it looked like ten- or fifteen-pound test line, the kind that fishermen use when they are going after big-mouth bass—I poured diluted hydrogen peroxide over Snaps's feet.

A dilution of one to four first. Then a dilution of one to two, the bubbles only slight. Then the pure stuff. And a thick white froth bubbled over the shaved and swollen flesh. Snaps finally jumped, her body jerking roughly as she reacted to the cleansing pain. A faint "meew" escaped her mouth.

"Dessie, you dressed?"

"Yes'm."

"Go to the bathroom. Find the little plastic pipet I used to clean the tile in Moisson. You know, the one I dripped bleach with."

"Yes'm."

"You know where it is?"

191

"Yes'm." She started to run.

"Dess?" She stopped and looked back over her shoulder. "Bring the bleach too." Her bare feet pounded around the corner. "Shal?"

"Yes'm?" Her voice sounded hollow, a small, forlorn sound.

I looked away from Snaps, down into her face. "You gonna be okay?"

"Is Snaps?" she fired back, her voice stronger.

"Maybe. If we're real good. You wanna help?"

She nodded.

"Good. Get me a glass mixin' bowl out from under the sink." The kettle began to sing. "And turn off the kettle, will you, honey?" The shrill note slowed and stopped.

She clattered around beneath the cabinets as I found the salt and the sugar, and added a few pinches of each to a wide-mouth crystal juice glass. I added cool water from the bottled spring water in the refrigerator, swirled and tasted the salty/sweet mixture, then added a bit more sugar. The layman's version of D5W and saline. Distilled water with five percent dextrose and 0.9 percent salt.

Dessie ran back into the room, the small disposable pipet in one hand, the bleach weighting down the other. I picked her up and sat her on the cabinet beside Snaps's head, poured out a dollop of bleach into the mixing bowl Shalene handed me. She was rubbing her head, having bumped it under the cabinet, but she didn't complain.

I added water from the kettle on the stove, swirled the bleach mixture, and depressed the bulb on the pipet, aspirating a large amount of bleach through the tip, then dispelling it, cleaning the pipet. Finally I rinsed the pipet with my homemade D5W and handed the almost sterile pipet to Dessie.

"I want you to dribble a little of this clear stuff into Snaps's mouth. Okay? Like this." I filled the pipet and delicately expelled its contents over the cat's dried-out tongue, between her slack jaws, moistening her mouth and lips and encouraging her to swallow. I counted to ten out loud slowly as I did, and then repeated the procedure. Snaps didn't respond. "I want you to try it."

Dessie took the pipet. "Do doctors do stuff like this?"

"Yeah, but to people."

"Yes, ma'am, Mama," Shalene corrected almost absently.

"Yes, ma'am, then. Shalene, I need you to cut this linen." I cut a long strip, showing her how it was done. A two-inch-wide, two-foot-long strip from the pieces left over from when I had made a new maternity tunic for church last week. "I need ten of them. Can you do that?"

She took the scissors and demonstrated, her little fingers working on the fabric. It would be ragged, but serviceable. I dropped the first linen strip into the bowl of bleach. "Drop each of the strips you cut into this bowl and swirl it around so it gets wet. Okay?"

Shalene nodded, her tongue held firmly between her teeth as she worked. Bleach fumes filled the kitchen. I turned on the overhead fan to dispel them.

"Don't get any of this bleach into your eyes." I turned on the spigot and splashed water into a cereal bowl, placing it beside her as well. If you get any on your hands, rinse your fingers in here. Okay? It's water."

Shalene looked up, saw the water, and nodded briefly before she returned to work.

"Dess, you okay?"

"Yes, ma'am. But Snaps won't swallow. It's goin' all over the towels."

"Don't worry. Snaps will swallow. I promise." Instantly I felt like a fool. Daddy had known never to promise me an animal's life. Never. *Dumb. Very dumb.* But I didn't retract the words.

Instead, I took the small pair of fingernail scissors I had gathered earlier and dropped them into the bleach mixture, swishing them around to sterilize them too. Rinsing them and my fingers beneath the bottled water, I realized what faith I was putting in the company that provided our drinking water.

Carefully I snipped a strand of fluorescent blue fishing line. With the first snip of the scissors, the line *sizzz*ed through the cat's flesh, loosening several revolutions.

"She swallowed, Mama. Snaps swallowed."

That could be a good sign. Or not.

"Dess, can you stop a minute? I need your help for something else."

"But, Mama. She swallowed."

"I know, *me sha,* but I need you to hold her head. She could bite and—"

"Snaps never bites," Shalene stated firmly, looking up from her scissors. "Never."

"Okay. Maybe not, but I want Dessie to go find my gardening gloves. They're by the washing machine on the back porch."

Dessie jumped to the floor, deactivated the security system, and ran, coming back with my old goatskin gloves, stained and wrinkled with age and soil, curved into dried claws like mummified hands. "Put them on, sweetheart," I said as I lifted her back onto the cabinet. "And hold Snaps's head so she doesn't . . . ah . . . jerk and hurt herself," I finished, shooting a look at Shalene. I closed the back door, reactivating the system.

Dessie stuffed her small hands into the gloves and grabbed Snaps's head, choking the poor cat. "Like this?"

I repositioned her hands so that Snaps could breathe. "Like this."

Dessie grinned a gamin smile. Lovely. My heart turned over at the sight. She had smiled so seldom in the past year. I swallowed and went back to work. "Dess, I'm goin' to pull this fishin' line off of Snaps's feet. You hold her, ya hear?"

"Yes, ma'am." She sounded definite. Quite determined. "Then I go back to wettin' her tongue, right?"

"Right," I murmured as I took the blunt end of the ten- to fifteen-pound test line in the pointy end of the needle-nosed pliers and unwrapped one loop of line. Snaps didn't flinch.

Slowly, using my fingers to push back the swollen flesh, I removed the line from Snaps's feet and tail, snipping loose the knots that held it all in place. The thick tail popped loose midway through, lying limp and seeping blood on the doubled-over towels. It took me five minutes to remove the line, and there was over two feet of the bloody stuff when I finished and dropped it into the sink.

The line hadn't been so tight when first applied that it cut off the cat's circulation to her feet. In fact, had Snaps not fought her restraints, her flesh would not have even been abraded.

Snaps finally began to fight about halfway through the procedure as pain brought her around. But Dessie held her well, and neither one of us was bitten. I cleaned the wounds with more hydrogen peroxide as Dessie steadied the weakened cat's head. I pulled on the desiccated flesh, even snipping a bit of blackened skin away with the fingernail scissors to get into the deeper wounds.

"Okay, Dessie. I'm done," I said as I rose up and stretched, pulling at back muscles held too long in one place, with a baby displacing the load. "Ohhhhh . . ."

"The baby?" Dessie asked sympathetically as she pulled off the stiff gloves.

"Yeah—Yes, ma'am," I corrected before Shalene could. "The baby."

My blue-eyed daughter smiled and picked up the pipet, slowly squirting my saline-and-sugar solution into Snaps's mouth. On the third try, the cat swallowed. Dessie's eyes met mine, hers glistening with . . . what? Delight? Bliss? A little bit of heaven? I smiled back at her.

"You can do anything, Mama," she said softly. "Anything."

I laughed shakily, realizing that the handgun had bruised

my ribs beneath my jacket and apron. "Keep it up, *me sha*. I have to change right quick. Shalene, you okay?"

"I got six cut so far, Mama," she said, pride in every syllable.

"Good. I'll be right back." I stripped off the apron and jacket as I walked through the house, automatically checking the windows, the security panel, and Morgan in his playpen out front, as well as the driveway. Everything and everyone was in its proper place.

Locking the Glock 9mm in the bedside drawer, I stripped off the long linen tunic I was wearing and tucked the key to the bedside table into my bra. I pulled on a loose cotton dress and padded back into the kitchen barefoot.

"Snaps is drinkin', Mama. Watch," Dessie commanded. She was right, which meant my time was limited. I rinsed all ten of Shalene's linen strips beneath water from the kettle and dropped the bloody scissors and pliers into the bleach for cleaning. Once I smeared antibiotic cream into the gouges on Snaps's ankles and tail, I was finished with the most painful part of the procedure.

Finally I placed sterile bandages on the cat's wounds and bound them with damp linen strips. By the time I was done, Snaps was stirring, trying for more sugar water with a tongue that moved thirstily. I held her and let her drink, supporting her body so her feet took no weight. I don't think she noticed.

It took two days for Snaps to recover enough to try to walk on her own, and when she was ready, I taught the girls how to use a towel to support her body when she moved, so her feet never got too much of her own weight. We bought enough cat food and treats to spoil her rotten, and several weeks worth of cat litter.

The girls also picked out new, bright blue bowls for litter, water, and food. And a new collar and leash. I didn't have the heart to tell the girls that Snaps would probably refuse to be walked on the leash.

BETRAYAL

On Monday after we found Snaps, Montgomery didn't show up for the court proceedings scheduled to establish a legal separation. A second bench warrant was issued for his arrest.

Four days after we found Snaps tied on the front porch, Max was killed.

CHAPTER

9

He was on the back porch, sunlight striping his face as it filtered through the vines. There was a sticky, dark pool of blood beneath him. His feet, propped against the washing machine, were shoeless, one sock half-off. He had been dead awhile. Hours. The stench of old urine and feces, which stained his navy slacks, was strong in the early morning heat.

The girls, dressed for the last day of school, were behind me, eating Cherrios at the kitchen table, stroking Snaps, who was stretched out on the table between them, waiting for her portion—the sugared milk in the bottoms of the bowls. Carefully I pulled the back door closed, reactivated the security panel protecting this entrance, and leaned my face against the molding, panting softly.

My bedroom shared a short wall with the back porch, and I had slept through whatever had happened here. I had gone from sleeping scarcely at all to sleeping too hard, too deeply. Taking a deep breath, I moved past the kitchen table to the security panel at the front door. It was activated, the green light steady.

Morgan was standing up in his playpen in front of the door, a stuffed bear in his left hand, a chicken-shaped rattle in his right. With those strange old-man eyes, he watched me as I circled the house, checking the windows, stripping off the oversize T-shirt I slept in and strapping on the 9mm.

The leather hip holster was heavy and rough against my bare skin, but I put it on first, my hands shaking with tremors as I remembered Eve Tramonte. I knew better than to think that a DeLande had dirtied his hands with the tedious murder of an unexceptional security guard. They picked their personal victims with great care. Like Ammie. Max meant nothing to them; he was merely a message to me, most likely delivered by hired hoodlums from out of state.

I stepped into lightweight navy cotton knit slacks and resettled the holster, pulled on a long, sleeveless tunic to match, and slipped my feet into canvas slides. Lipstick and a comb through my hair helped the last of the tremors diminish. I was appropriately dressed for the police. Foolish perhaps, but Mama's training died hard. "A lady is always appropriately dressed for callers," she used to say.

"Girls. Come brush your teeth. And change back out of your school clothes, into play clothes. You're not going to Saint Ann's today." My voice was shaking, but I managed a smile as they ran into the bedroom.

"Why not, Mama?"

"Shhh. She might change her mind," Shalene whispered.

"You're going to play at A'nt Sonja's today. With Cheri if I can find her on such short notice. But no TV. Understand?"

"Can we go to the park?" Shalene asked.

"No." Fear blossomed through me, entangled with the vision of Max on the back porch, his chest drenched with blood. "No. You stay indoors today. Come on. Quick. Off with the uniforms." I hung the freshly cleaned school plaids back on hangers in the closet we all shared, tossed T-shirts, shorts, and little red Keds to the unmade bed as the girls brushed their teeth. Shalene's Keds slipped off and snarled in the mosquito netting. While they were still half-dressed, we all trooped over to Sonja's, Morgan squirming beneath my arm.

We passed a shoe, a scuffed black oxford. A patch of dark soil, splattered all around, was just beyond. And twin furrows where heels had been dragged over the ground. Neither girl noticed.

I didn't knock at Sonja's. I just used my key and let us all in. I shoved the girls inside, slammed the door, and turned off the alarm system, reactivating it immediately before I even turned around.

Sonja and Philippe stopped, cups halfway up or down, and stared. "Are the twins up yet?"

Sonja nodded and put her cup back into its saucer. Philippe's clinked down a half second later.

"Go upstairs and play, girls. Go on." They tore through the kitchen and up the back stairs, screaming for Mallory and Marshall.

"What." It was more of a command than a question from Philippe.

"Philly, she's going to faint."

I smiled just before the room blacked out completely. Philly. What a perfectly unsuitable name for the serious Philippe Rousseau.

Philippe caught Morgan. Sonja caught me. It seemed she was always catching me as I fell these days. Literally or figuratively.

"Collie?" I could hear her calling me as I came to. I couldn't have been out but a moment. "Jeez. You've never passed out before."

"Shall I call an ambulance?"

"No," I whispered, my mouth cottony-dry. "The police."

"Why?" Trust Philly to never waste a word.

"Max. He's dead."

Philippe swore and moved away, his slippered feet sliding on the floor. Sonja sank down beside me where I lay with my eyes closed, and held my hand. It seemed only moments later that a siren sounded in the distance.

I moved my dry tongue over my lips and said with a half smile, "You better take the holster off me, Sonja. In case they decide to search me." Sonja snorted and pulled up my tunic, yanking on the holster buckle. "And can I have a glass of water, please. And a good strong cup of coffee. To heck with doctor's orders."

The day passed in a flurry of useless questions, repetitive questions and innuendo by the officers on the scene, their superiors, the homicide investigators, and the head of the security company. They never searched me, but they all seemed to find it difficult to believe that Max had been killed in the yard and dragged to the porch. They seemed to want to believe that I killed him in my bed and dumped him out the back door. I was very handy as a suspect, I suppose.

The twin furrows in the yard and the dirt-filled oxfords finally convinced them that I might be innocent. It would take a stronger woman than I to garrote Max and drag him to the back. Max hadn't even had time to pull his .38 before he died. They found two sets of strange footprints in the yard and dozens of Max's unfiltered stubs.

One killer was heavy and wore a size-ten Reebok. The other was smaller and lighter and wore very old Air Jordans. There were no other clues.

The security company immediately assigned us a new security guard. This one carried a .357 and walked like a linebacker. Big, solid, and experienced. He cost an arm and a leg, but I didn't demur at the expense. No more freshman guards. I even demanded that the company replace Max's partner, the bandy-legged guard who limped around the grounds. He was too old to fight the kind of men that DeLande money could buy.

Adrian Paul, summoned by Philippe, stayed for several hours, talking to the police and watching the crime scene techs work. He said he would find a way to force Montgomery to cover the cost of the security protection. If not right away, then in the divorce settlement. I didn't bother to grace that comment with a reply.

Ann Hyphen stopped by, dropping off some papers she said I needed to see. She hung around, too, watching the excitement. I hoped the loitering was on her own time.

I stayed propped up on Sonja's sofa, alternately napping off the horror of Max's death, and repeating answers to the police. At the end of the afternoon, the cops wanted me to come downtown and answer some more questions. Adrian Paul told them to charge me with something or get out. It was obvious to everyone that I had endured all I could handle. The possibility of bad press resulting from forcing a pregnant woman to come in for questioning when she was conspicuously innocent made them change their minds. They finally left me to sleep the heat of the afternoon away in Sonja's den, the TV flickering with colored images, half-seen each time I rolled over.

A storm off the coast in the Atlantic, just south of Cuba, swirled into the familiar comma shape of the summer's first, early, tropical storm. According to the TV news meteorologists, Ada was heading north and west at a leisurely pace, an afternoon stroll. In reality, she sheared off the tip of southern Florida and moved into the Gulf, howling with chaos and outrage.

From my berth on the couch, I watched as the police finally left, hauling Max's body off for a postmortem. The press, which had grouped around the entrance of the Rousseau property, soon decamped as well, dispersed by the head of the security company himself with a half-true story told on live television.

The evening news told the tale of the brave twenty-one-year-old security guard who gave his life protecting a family from thieves. Probably desperate lowlifes in need of drug money, if not New Orleans's version of the Manson clan out to kill and maim just for the hell of it. I'm sure the security company's profits skyrocketed as frightened residents signed up for such selfless and necessary protection.

I turned off the TV and didn't watch the reports. I wasn't ignoring the fact of Max's death. I was simply numb. Numb and cold and empty inside. I wasn't afraid anymore. Just bare and lifeless, like the long stretches of swamp where loggers had stripped the life out of her.

Somehow I kept the news of Max's death from the girls, telling them only that he had been reassigned and replaced. They accepted the tale with little response, too busy with the twins to care much.

Once I finally dragged myself awake, Adrian Paul, JP, and we four DeLandes ate supper with the Rousseaus. Philippe grilled chicken breasts, salmon, and shrimp kebobs on the gas grill, over mesquite coals. The girls and I contributed boiled corn on the cob, dirty rice from Mama's old family recipe, and homemade pecan ice cream, which churned under electric power.

Dessie, Shalene, and Adrian Paul added ice and rock salt to the churn as needed, chatting noisily on the back deck. The twins and JP made mud pies under the watchful eyes of my youngest daughter, still taking her self-assigned duties as substitute mother very seriously.

The boys decorated their mud pies with rocks in the shape of smiley faces, offering to trade anyone a bowl of ice cream for their brownies. Only JP didn't seem surprised when no one fell for the ruse.

Slowly, under the influence of the massed Rousseaus and surrounded by happy and contented children, I began to come alive again. After supper, the men told "old Frenchman" jokes. In another part of the country these would have been old Polish jokes, or old Jewish jokes, or old Indian jokes. And I laughed at the unsubtle humor until my sides ached and the misery inside eased.

Although Sonja insisted that we stay the night in the safety of the main house, as soon as the new security guards arrived at ten P.M., Adrian Paul and I carried my bunch back to the cottage and bed. They were as dirty as little field hands, but what the heck. I could wash the sheets.

I was saying good night to Adrian Paul at the front door when he stopped, one hand on the door, one hand on the frame. His dark eyes were solemn and intense, his face grave, and my stomach did a flip-flop. I didn't need the complication of romance in my life.

"I owe you an apology."

"Oh?"

"Yes," he said slowly. "I didn't believe you when you said you were afraid of your husband. Because he had never beaten you. I thought you were . . . ah . . ."

"Crazy?" I supplied helpfully, relaxing slightly. This didn't sound like a come-on. This sounded like lawyer talk, not romance.

"Exaggerating."

"Um." I grinned. He smiled back, a half smile.

"I'm sorry. Grievously sorry. But I do think your troubles are over. These guys look like they know what they're doing." He glanced back, and I watched over his shoulder as the two new guards covered the grounds with paramilitary precision, marking off routes and checkpoints, verifying radio signals, and conversing in low voices. They did look capable. And the weapons they carried looked deadly. We should be safe.

We should.

But I didn't share Adrian Paul's confidence. Not anymore.

"I'll pick you up at ten in the morning. Wear shorts. It's supposed to be in the upper nineties."

"Ten."

Adrian Paul squinted at me in the dull porch light. "The girls didn't tell you?"

"No, the girls didn't tell me. Tell me what?"

"We're all going to Betty Louise's tomorrow and then to lunch at Van's again."

"Oh, we are, are we? Whose big idea was this?" I glared at him. "Sonja's?"

Adrian Paul grinned at me. "No. Not Sonja. Sonja Junior. You do know that Shalene is going to grow up just like her, don't you? She can already twist me around her little finger. It's scary actually." He shrugged, a bit embarrassed.

"Ten, huh?" I yawned hugely. "I suppose I can drag myself out of bed and be ready by then."

He nodded and turned away, paused, and turned back all in the same motion, laughter lurking in his dark eyes. "I think you'll make a great mother-in-law."

"I beg your pardon?"

"Shalene has decided she likes being JonPaul's adopted mother and ordered me to propose to her."

I groaned.

"We're engaged."

"Good. How soon can she move out?"

"Not soon, thank God. Louisiana state law says I have to wait on her to grow up first."

"I'd rather you took her home tonight."

He smiled back at me in the darkness, backing away, shaking his head. "Not on your life." Raising his brows as if he just had a thought, he stopped. "And that makes you a ready-made grandma."

I closed the door on his laughter, and after checking the cottage once more for safety, I looked out on the back porch. Someone had cleaned off the blood. There was only a dark stain where Max had lain. I clicked off the back porch light, pulled off my clothes, including the 9mm I had strapped back on before dinner, and drew myself a bath.

A bubble bath with scented bubbles and candlelight, soft country music on the radio, and the gun on the toilet top. My hair pinned to the top of my head, I relaxed in the huge claw-footed tub, pushing the stress of the day away. All this tension wasn't good for the baby. Seems I was saying that a lot lately.

There were charges issued against Montgomery for assault on the sheriff's deputy, for missing our court date, and now he was wanted for questioning regarding Max's death. There was a good chance that the DeLandes would all lie low for a while. Maybe Adrian Paul was right. Maybe I would be safe here for a time.

I wanted to believe that. I tried to believe that, as the warm water soothed away my tension and eased the muscles in my lower back. I smiled slightly as the candle flames moved and scented bubbles popped slowly around me. Maybe. Maybe I was safe.

That night I slept hard and long, waking up bleary-eyed and groggy only when the girls and Snaps climbed into bed with me. Snaps was walking almost normally, the bandages like little warm-up leggings on each ankle. Her tail, however, had a kink in the tip that might not ever straighten out. The cat walked up my body and stuck her nose into my face, her whiskers tickling and her purr a deep rumble as I tried to ignore them all.

Shalene pulled the covers off, dislodging the cat and removing any pretense that I might still be asleep. "I'm gettin' married, Mama. So I can be JP's mama."

"So I hear." My mouth felt like someone had dusted it with moldy talcum powder during the night. I rose up, hunting for the clock. "What time is it? Oh, God." I fell back into the pillows, groaning, the clock still in my hand. "Nine o'clock. Have you girls eaten breakfast?"

"Yes'm. Pop-Tarts. Dessie had b'ueberry, and I had strawberry. Morgan wanted one, too, so we put him in his playpen and gave him one. Dessie changed his diapers first," she added. "He did a big stinky. You gettin' up today, Mama? My fancy's comin' to take us to the k'doon doll lady."

From that monologue I understood that Morgan had scattered Pop-Tart crumbs across the playpen, and probably had filling smeared across his face and hands. Sonja Junior was giving orders again. She was taking this substitute mother role very seriously. I hoped it would blow over soon.

"Go brush your teeth and draw a bath. You both went to bed dirty last night." I rolled gracelessly out of bed to the floor, still groaning. "I'll strip your sheets. They can wash while we're gone." The girls took off.

"Mama, there's a gun in here," Dessie yelled from the bathroom.

The bedside table was empty; I ran my palm over the smooth tabletop. No steel gray 9mm. And then I remembered the bath the night before, candles, country music, and a gun on the toilet top. I had forgotten to bring it to bed with me. I had left a loaded gun out in plain sight where any of the children could have picked it up and blown somebody's head off.

The girls knew about guns, and they knew better than to touch one. They had even been taken out to the dry gully behind the house when Montgomery and I went to target-practice. But still . . . A loaded gun left lying around. Dumb. Very dumb. Sonja would have used some very choice words to tell me just *how dumb*.

I walked quickly to the bathroom, the night's false feeling of safety shattering around me as I moved. *I was being hunted.* The thought rocked me. The flowers, the poetry, the *Book of the Dead,* Snaps . . . Max. I was being hunted.

I took the gun from the toilet top and turned on the bathwater, ignoring the curious eyes and the questions the girls were asking. "Get in the tub." For once, Shalene didn't argue.

I left them climbing up the short stepladder into the tall tub, and went to change. And to lock up the 9mm.

I was being hunted. How long would I be safe?

The day was overcast and sweltering, with tropical storm Ada wrecking havoc in the Gulf of Mexico. She was sitting in place off the coast, disrupting shipping, slapping offshore oil rigs around with rough blows, and being a major problem to the coast guard and the meteorologists.

We were all dressed in shorts, T-shirts, sneakers, and sunscreen, with rain slickers piled on the porch swing just in case, when Adrian Paul pulled up in the drive and circled around to the cottage. I had never noticed this car. Only the BMW he drove the evening he took me to the hospital to talk to the deputy Montgomery attacked.

Now he was driving a classic. A fairly rare 1974 carmine red Triumph Stag. The hard top was off for the day, the roll bar exposed, the rag top available should Ada suddenly veer inland. I had always liked Stags. They were built as luxury touring cars, equipped with air conditioning, leather upholstery, and all the bells and whistles and conveniences of the seventies.

No DeLande would have owned one, of course, except perhaps Miles Justin. The cars weren't rare enough, for one thing, and they weren't American-made. Most of the DeLandes preferred classic American cars. Only Miles Justin broke the unspoken policy, owning two Jaguars and at least one Lotus Elan.

I dropped Morgan off at Sonja's while Dessie, Shalene, and JP were strapped down in the backseat. Shalene shared a seat belt with her adopted son. Her second choice. She first insisted that she be allowed to sit with her "fancy." However, Adrian Paul prevailed, and I got to ride up front with Shalene's fancy man.

The weather was bearable only because the sun was hidden. But even with the sun obscured behind a cloud bank, the day was muggy and damp, the breeze generated by the Stag's progress marvelously welcome.

A visit to see Betty Louise was a treat. She made one-of-a-kind porcelain dolls and sold them in the French Quarter four times a year. Although her studio was based in the western part of the state in the little town of Westlake, she spent time in New Orleans catering to wealthy and elite doll collectors. Her creations were numbered and stamped editions that cost up to three thousand dollars. And every single one was a quadroon beauty.

Betty Louise could have been one of her own dolls, full-lipped with upswept silver hair trailing down in tiny ringlets. She was black-eyed and olive-skinned, and spoke with a heavy southern accent, so rich and fluid that it flowed like nectar. Or melted butter. Or rich cream.

But when one of her more audacious customers would broach the subject of racial history, the doll maker merely shrugged her shoulders, rolled her eyes, those huge expressive eyes, and said, "Ah. We never know what we are, do we? You can't tell by skin color, you know."

A few years back, when Sonja was pregnant with Louis but still hoping for a girl, we went to see Betty Louise on one of her infrequent trips to the Crescent City. Alone in her shop, Sonja had told the artist her own racial history, while I looked at the ten dolls she had brought to sell. Betty Louise had listened to Sonja's story of *plaçage,* and interracial relationships, and the end of the Civil War. Then she laughed one of those deep alto laughs that endeared her so to her customers.

"Little girl," she said, her voice slow and languid, "when that war for southern independence expired its last wheezing, miserable breath, eighteen thousand free men and women—and who knows how many children?—left New Orleans and scattered on the far winds. 'Colored' people who looked white. Most headed north to Yankee country where they could *passé blanc* and marry into the established white community.

"And that didn't count the thousands of free *gens du couleur* who were living in small towns and plantations scattered across the lower part of the state. And that also didn't count Charleston, South Carolina. There were thousands more 'colored' folk there too." She had nodded her head, her hands busy stitching a blue velvet jacket to fit a twenty-four-inch tall, half-dressed quadroon doll on a stand beside her. The doll's head and breasts were all one solid piece, cleavage and naked bosom a rich mahogany brown.

And with the history lesson, she had sidestepped the

entire question of her own racial history. And left the racial composition of the rest of the country in limbo. So much for the KKK's and Skinheads' claims of racial purity. According to Betty Louise, we were all mixed race. And might as well enjoy it.

I smiled at the memory as we glided through the city on the smooth suspension of the Stag. Was it independent rear-wheel suspension? I couldn't remember. And didn't really care. My days of having to listen to car lovers discuss the merits and value of individual automobiles was over.

The wind of our passage snarled the girls' hair, and I spent five minutes bent over the seat trying to get the tangles out while Adrian Paul hunted for a parking spot. He found one four blocks away and pulled into it. We'd have to walk, but one never parked illegally in New Orleans unless one wanted to have the car towed immediately.

We followed two women to the back of the bookstore, where Betty Louise had set up shop. Both women carried dolls, one with a broken arm, who cornered the doll maker instantly. In a loud yat accent, she complained about the awful accident that damaged her doll. "Could it be fixed. Could the arm be replaced. Her cat had knocked the doll off the shelf, you see."

I walked away from the conversation and watched my girls. Both walked slowly along the wall of dolls, twelve this time, dressed in the velvets and lace and pearls and sparkles of a bygone era.

Dessie's eyes filled with tears, and Shalene was at a loss for words, her mouth open. For minutes they moved slowly up the aisles of dolls, and back down, studying each specimen intimately. They each finally stopped in front of a particular doll. Thank God it wasn't the same doll.

"How much does she cost?" Dessie whispered, blinking back her tears.

The doll was slightly over eighteen inches tall, dressed in blue velvet with lacy, ruffled petticoats exposed up the open front of the wide skirts. The dress left the doll's shoulders bare and showed a hint of décolletage beneath lace. She was wearing a matching jacket trimmed with fur and carried a wide-brimmed hat with no crown. She had dark hair piled high on her head in finger curls, with thousands of tiny tendrils framing her face. And she had dark chocolate skin and big blue eyes, just the color of the velvet.

I lifted the small booklet attached to the doll's wrist and read, "Maya Louise. Twenty-eight hundred dollars."

The doll Shalene coveted was dressed in green silk, her slips a contrasting old lace. The hat on her head was tilted to display light brown eyes in a light brown face. Her hair was lighter brown as well, kinky wavy, exposed through the open brim of the hat. She looked saucy and flirtatious, the old-world coquette.

I checked the tag and read, "Charlsee Louise. Two thousand, five hundred, seventy-five dollars."

"That's more than Daddy makes in a whole year," Shalene said, finally closing her mouth.

Betty Louise laughed, coming up behind us. "You want to hold her?"

"Could I?" Shalene turned, looked into the black eyes of the doll maker, and fell silent. I had a feeling something passed between the two dark-eyed females. Something on a level I couldn't follow. Something old and rich and primeval. Something that excluded me. An elusive hint of déjà vu, like something out of ancient times. Goose bumps rose up on my arms, lifting the small hairs like fur on a cat's back.

Shalene turned and went to the sofa that sat against the wall of the tiny shop and wriggled her way to the back, her legs outstretched before her. She did it without being told. Betty Louise turned her gaze to Dessie, and after a moment, my eldest child followed and sat beside her sister. It was uncanny. I wish I had that kind of control over them.

The exotic doll maker lifted the doll in green silk that had so entranced Shalene and carried her over to the sofa. "Are your fingers clean?"

The girls presented spotless hands, and the artist sat

Charlsee Louise in Shalene's lap, arranging the thick skirts and raising the movable arms. Then she returned for the doll in blue and sat Maya Louise on Dessie's lap, repeating the procedure with the blue velvet skirts.

JP stood beside the arm of the sofa, as spellbound by the dolls as the girls were. If it hadn't been sissy stuff, I think he would have asked to hold a doll too.

"You should feel very special, girls. Madame Betty Louise doesn't let just anyone touch her dolls," Adrian Paul said. I doubt the girls even heard him, they were so entranced with the creations on their laps.

Betty Louise looked up at him and smiled that slow, sensuous smile that some southern women cultivate. A warm smile that seems to simmer just below the surface like mulled red wine in a kettle. "I missed you and your lovely wife on my last visit, but I haven't sold the dolls she ordered. I brought them this time as well. And I do hope Camilla is well."

I turned and walked away before Adrian Paul could respond to the veiled question. It was obvious that Betty Louise had known Camilla Rousseau, and did not know that she had died.

I checked the price tag on two other dolls. One sold for almost two thousand, the other for almost three. Trust my girls to go high-end on any purchase. It was clear to me that they had each picked out a doll to take home. I had never cared much for dolls, but even I recognized the "look" in the eyes of a doll lover. More than five thousand dollars for dolls they couldn't play with, but could only look at. I could almost hear my checking account groan under the strain.

Oh well. At least I had Morgan. Him, I could teach to fish, and shrimp, and shoot. And maybe the girls would outgrow the doll stage . . . I could hope.

Adrian Paul paid for both dolls over my protests and ushered us all out to the Stag. Ignoring my objections as if they were nothing more than pesky mosquitoes buzzing around his head, he settled the kids into the backseat and put the dolls in their wooden carrying cases into the trunk.

"Listen," he said, his face drawn and tight. "My wife ordered and paid for two dolls when she went into remission last summer. Betty Louise doesn't grant refunds, only exchanges. So I exchanged the dolls Camilla ordered for the ones the girls liked. It didn't cost much." A corner of his mouth turned up. A bitter smile. "Surely you can't deny me the pleasure of treating my fiancée to a small token of my affection."

When I didn't respond, he left the passenger door open so I could get in if I wanted, climbed into the driver's seat, and started the car. My last words were drowned by a deep engine note, the *thrummm* of a well-tuned V8.

Defeated by the noise of the dual mufflers, I crawled into the auto, pulled the door shut, and sulked. As we drove back past the bookstore where Betty Louise had set up shop, a movement caught my eye.

Miles Justin. His long, lean legs were encased as usual in skintight denim, his ankles, booted in snakeskin, casually crossed. A charcoal gray cowboy hat was pulled low over his eyes, shadowing his face and the collar of his western shirt. Leaning a shoulder against the recessed doorway of the bookstore entrance, his arms were crossed in an attitude of ease. Just a man waiting for someone. And he was smiling. A knowing smile. A smile just for me. As we drove past, he raised his left arm, grasped the crown of the hat, and lifted it. We turned a corner and swept out of sight.

Miles Justin had been my friend. Not Montgomery's friend, but my friend. And the girls' as well.

In the early years of my marriage, when Montgomery traveled so extensively on DeLande business and I was left at home alone and pregnant, or with a small baby and pregnant, Miles would motor into town in his favorite classic car, the 1930 Cord Montgomery had borrowed on our honeymoon.

For weeks he would stay with me, especially that first summer of my marriage. We spent almost every day on the bayou behind the house, fishing or crabbing off the dock or simply lying in the sun and watching my belly grow. In the mornings we would walk to the dry gulch out back and target-practice with an array of guns filched from Montgomery's gun cabinet. In the evenings we would clean and carefully replace the weapons we had used.

On cloudy days we visited my friends and family and even helped out at the veterinary clinic. We watched movies on the VCR when it stormed. When our boredom grew so great we couldn't stand it anymore, Miles drove me down to Chaisson and Castalano's and bought a fourteen-foot aluminum johnboat and a thirty-horsepower Mercury motor. I thought it was an extravagant purchase for a fourteen-year-old boy, but when I said so, Miles lifted a dark brow and said, "Who do you think paid for the Cord? I do have an allowance, you know. And I don't think a small purchase like a johnboat is going to strain it appreciably." After that, I kept my mouth shut.

We set out in the "small purchase" to explore the bayou country. It was all old territory for me, waterways and pathways I had explored as a child. But the bayou never stays the same for long, changing constantly as storm and wind and heavy rains sculpt new shapes in the land. Together we motored and poled all over the easily accessible parts of the Basin, talked with French trappers and out-of-state sport fishermen, and once, even an alligator poacher who expounded on the fine points of trapping or shooting the biggest gators.

We survived a few scrapes and unexpected storms together that first year. We even survived a run-in with Old Man Frieu and the business end of his shotgun. That was the day I realized that the DeLande charm was a genetic trait, not something Montgomery had developed on his own.

I watched as my fourteen-year-old brother-in-law smiled lazily up at the squint-eyed old Cajun, doffed his hat respectfully, propped his booted foot on the dock we were trying to tie up at, and convinced him we were both harmless and the best company he'd had in months. The old man fell for it.

I smiled at that memory, the wind created by the passage of the Stag across the city pulling at my braid and tossing loose strands of hair about. Adrian Paul smiled back. The girls and JP were shouting happily in the backseat.

Miles and the old man became such good friends that we went back several times, visiting the dock at the minuscule shack where Old Man Frieu made his summer home. It was an incongruous matchup, the short, filthy river-rat Cajun and the polished DeLande stretched out on the dock at sunset, fishing, drinking the old man's homemade beer, and playing cards.

The old man had a knack for poker, and Miles once ended up owing Frieu nearly a thousand dollars. The old man hadn't been happy to learn that Miles had gambled with money not in his pockets, but on the far side of the levee. And when Miles disclosed that he was a DeLande and therefore good for the amount, we had to contend with the old man's shotgun again. It seemed that Frieu didn't care for the illustrious DeLande name. Would, in fact, rather shoot a DeLande than take his money.

We got back home in one piece, however, and Miles made the trip back again with the cash he owed. Alone this time. He made the trip in record time, knowing I was worried, wringing my hands at home, envisioning a hundred ways the old man could do away with a DeLande of such tender years. I kept picturing Montgomery's face when I told him I had led his baby brother into danger.

Miles left the money on the old man's kitchen table, a stack of hundreds with a brand-new skinning knife stabbed through them into the wood beneath. On top he left a note, although neither of us thought the old man could read. It said, "The word of *this* DeLande can be trusted."

Miles didn't think the old man needed money. He had

wallpapered the wood slat walls of his shanty with money. Hundreds of ones, fives, and tens, and even a few twenties scattered around for decorative effect. And he had at least four shotguns and several hunting rifles hanging on the walls as well.

A week later, Old Man Frieu pulled up at the dock behind the house, tying off a brand-new ten-foot johnboat with a twenty-horsepower motor. His grizzled face was wreathed in a toothless smile, and he gestured for us to come with him, using both hands in the French fashion, palms close together, facing his chest.

"Com', you. Ah sho' you a one t'ing you neve' see b'fo'. Com'. Ge' sleep'bag. Ge' supplie'. Com'. Com'."

With a modicum of supplies, we boarded his small, flat-bottomed boat and allowed him to take us off into the swamp. We spent three days living off the land and watching the alligators mate from the safety of a hidden campsite known only to the old man, and two trustworthy DeLandes. The huge reptiles were most dangerous in mating season, males occasionally charging a boat that entered the sacred water.

Alligators mate underwater, only their heads in the air, and it's an energetic white-water experience for both parties. We had shoreside seats in the shallow-water mating site.

The old man never mentioned the money delivered by Miles. Neither did we. But Miles and I often spoke of the old man and his swamp lore and his summer shack papered with money.

My smile faded. Miles had been my friend. So why had he followed me into the Vieux Carré. Was he simply taking orders from the Eldest, as I knew all the brothers did? Or was he tailing me as the hired thugs once had? Or was he going to be a part of another punishment . . . like the one delivered by the DeLandes to Eve Tramonte and Ammie?

I was shaking. Shaking so hard that Adrian Paul noticed,

even with his attention on the road and traffic. "What?" He sounded like his brother Philly.

So I told him, talking softly, keeping my voice inside the front seat, not letting the words drift with the breeze to the children in the back. To my surprise, Adrian Paul was not upset.

"Good."

"Good? *Good?*"

"Good," he repeated. "It means that they intend to keep it in the family now. My guess is that Max's de . . . ah, accident was a mistake. Hired men going too far. And anything that brings in the press is going too far. They'll lie low awhile. Let you see them, let you know that they're around. Then, when they realize that you aren't going to run and aren't going to come back, they'll change tactics again. Probably financial or legal maneuvers." He smiled at me, his teeth flashing in his lightly tanned face.

I hadn't yet told him about Eve Tramonte. And I figured I better tell him. Soon. So he would get rid of thoughts like that.

We never made it to Van's, stopping instead at a little luncheon spot in the Quarter for a quick, early, and inexpensive lunch. It wasn't much, but I insisted I be allowed to pay for the meal. A twenty covered the entire bill, so I still felt guilty at the thought of the price of the dolls. Only later in the day did I realize that, being a lawyer, Adrian Paul would probably find a way to tack the cost of the dolls onto his bill for legal services. The bill he intended to force Montgomery to pay. That brought a smile to my lips and lessened the guilt I felt at the price of the dolls. Montgomery could afford to pay for Betty Louise's entire collection with his pocket change.

After lunch, we went to the Barataria Unit of the Jean Lafitte National Historical Park to learn about the history of the dolls the girls had picked out. They were not much interested, but I loved it. I even managed to forget Miles Justin and his polite salute for a while.

Adrian Paul took us to the library and the park, and Shalene insisted that her fancy should buy JP—and her, of course—a swing set for the cottage yard. "Children need lots of essersise, you know," she said. Adrian Paul gravely agreed that was so, and promised to consider the matter carefully. I rolled my eyes.

It was late afternoon when we stopped for the day, and I had missed my nap. Exhausted, I left the kids—including JonPaul—with Sonja and fell into a weary sleep.

Three hours later, Ada, fickle and flighty as all tropical storms, swerved inland and smacked into the coast. There was little warning. Less time to prepare. Thank God the cottage had old-fashioned storm shutters. Philippe helped me get them closed only minutes before the storm hit.

Adrian Paul, traveling upstate to visit friends for the rest of the weekend, had left JP with the girls. Secure in his personal belief that the DeLandes would lie low for a while, and trusting the weather predictions that Ada would most likely stay put in the Gulf, then dissipate, he motored north. He was able to get one phone call through to us before the storm struck and all the phone lines went down.

The electricity followed soon after, and an early night fell on the cottage. A night punctuated by hail the size of marbles, lightning flashing across the turbulent sky, and a storm surge of twelve feet that smashed against the levees.

The Crescent City is slowly sinking beneath the Gulf of Mexico. Already a foot below sea level, she depends upon levees and meteorologists' early warning to protect her land and people. As the night progressed, I hoped the levees worked better than the early-warning system. Ada stalled over the coastline, gathering strength at the very moment she should have been dissipating and dissolving under the weight of her own fury.

As true night descended, Ada's winds rose in pitch, a howling, violent sound. I pulled the mattress off of my bed, wedging it over the bathtub, stocking the steel basin with an extra flashlight, my smallest battery-powered radio, extra batteries, two candles, waterproof matches, tea, bottled water, snacks and cookies, fruit, two pillows, and a blanket. I wondered if there would be room for the kids should they need the protection. On the floor beside the tub, I put extra blankets and pillows for me. Finally I tossed in a change of clothes for each of us.

The tub was heavy iron beneath the white porcelain, sturdy and substantial enough to survive even if the cottage didn't. It wasn't unheard of for an entire family to wait out a hurricane in the family tub. It was the safest place for people and the basic survival supplies they would need after a major storm.

In the front room the girls held their dolls in the light of a flickering hurricane lamp, it's globe so old that the light from the wick bent around hand-blown imperfections and bounced off bubbles in the glass. The heavy red base was cut crystal, filled with scented red oil, and when the light touched it, it cast a blood glow. Snaps prowled nervously in the pool of light, weaving her way across the table, the back of the sofa, and my lap, until she finally settled in JP's lap, purring urgently, her bent-tip tail swishing. The girls' radio, a bright pink contraption with dual speakers and a carrying handle, ran on four D-size batteries. Propped on the table beside the sofa, it crackled softly in the background with weather updates, news reports, damage estimates, Coast Guard reports, and the rare Cajun melody.

Tornadoes, with the sound of far-off freight trains running out of control, roared and shrieked. Lightning struck again and again, thunder shaking the house. As wind shook the little cottage, I read *The Wizard of Oz,* my voice fighting to stay above the piercing rush of the gale. At seven o'clock the radio station went silent, its tower smashed by the angry wind. I changed books, setting down *The Wizard of Oz* and picking up the *Illustrated Children's Bible.*

Just before eight o'clock, a tree in the front yard surrendered to the storm and fell on the house, rolling across the porch with an almost human scream of wood splitting and rending. The whole house shook. We all ducked, the children screaming. Snaps sprinted under the table and then under the sofa. And I waited for the basso thump that let me know the tree was at rest. After long minutes the wood screamed again and the tree hit the earth.

I almost decided to take the children to the main house, but with the tornadoes, the two-story house was in even more danger of wind damage than the cottage. I tried not to think about my own fear, concentrating on easing the terror in the children's eyes. I even tried to tell jokes, but I had never been very good at that, and the attempt at humor fell on unappreciative ears.

A leak started in the roof when a branch pierced through. I found a bucket by the back door to put beneath the trail of water. As I set it down, I noticed a rusty red stain in the bottom where Max had bled into it. The water plinked down, a hollow metronome, as rain mixed with old blood and turned the water rosy.

We huddled around the lamplit sofa table, Morgan sleeping peacefully on my lap, the older children all wedged into a corner of the sofa, still holding on to the dolls. I don't think Betty Louise intended her creations to be so ill used, but then, if she was still in the city during this storm, perhaps she, too, was snuggled up with one of her dolls.

I tried to distract the children with songs and word games, but it was difficult to talk over the roar of the storm. We were all too jumpy anyway. We would start one game, play it a few seconds, and fall silent at the sound of something crashing outside. I began to worry about the danger of fire in the cottage should a tree fall and knock over the hurricane lamp. Fire and rain. Wasn't there an old James Taylor song about that?

One time, it sounded like a tree fell on the carport and

crushed my car. The shrill sound of tearing metal was bright and sharp against the deeper sound of wind lashing against the shutters. Water trailed down through the front windows, and I piled towels on the floor to catch the moisture.

As the wind increased in pitch I sat on the sofa with the children, and Snaps piled on top of me. Snaps having decided she didn't like being alone beneath the sofa in the dark. We sang "Jesus Loves Me" and "Michael Row Your Boat Ashore" and "A Hundred Bottles of Beer on the Wall," and waited for the indistinct eye of the storm to settle over the cottage and give us some respite from the constant noise. I found a new station on the radio, which claimed that the eye was hovering over the center of the city, only miles away.

At the height of the storm, the cottage gave and shifted, as if it might break loose from its moorings and whirl away, taking us with it, just like Dorothy and Toto. Another tree cracked and split, smashing into the side of the house, hanging on the remnants of the ruined porch.

The cottage gave again. Creaked mightily. A sudden draft blew through the room.

I grabbed the children in my arms and rushed to the bathroom, shoving JP to the back of the tub under the mattress and dumping Morgan into his arms with the cat. I was reaching for Shalene when the tree broke loose and landed in the yard. A powerful crash knocked me off my feet.

The shutters smashed loose from the front window, breaking glass and admitting the fury of the storm. I shoved the children behind me. Rushed forward. And stopped.

A long leg followed the wind inside. Raging, as frenzied and brutal as the storm he seemed to have brought inside with him, Montgomery forced his way into the house.

Crawling through the shattered window casement, he whipped shards of glass throughout the room. Wild-eyed and streaming wet, he knocked the remains of the window and shutters away with a splintering roar.

Cursing and reeking of whiskey, he waved a dripping handgun. Blood streamed down his face, too red, too bright, diluted by the rain. Almost absently, he reached up and pulled a sliver of glass from a wound in his forehead, tossing it aside. He smiled at me, his face a rictus, twisted with victory.

I wasn't wearing my gun.

I stood in the doorway—the girls behind me, partially protected from the wind by my body—and met Montgomery's eyes across the expanse of wind-sprayed room. He laughed, a savage sound, as vicious and violent as the storm at his back. His eyes on me. His teeth bared. Blood running down his face. Into his clothes.

I took a step toward the gun I had left locked in the bedside table.

Through the window behind him crawled Terry Bertrand, the sheriff of Moisson Parish. Grim-faced and hard-eyed, he was out of uniform, dripping on my Chinese rug. Off duty, he answered to Montgomery's bidding, waiting, his eyes cold and hard.

And then I realized the desperation of our situation. The storm was nothing. Here stood the real threat. Montgomery.

Montgomery had become a powerful man in Moisson Parish what with graft as common as crawfish and his passing out lavish campaign contributions. The law would protect him. No matter what he did.

Montgomery's eyes were bloodshot, savage, spitting blue flames as he moved toward me. He stopped in front of the table where the children's books were piled, and the lamp. The light was fitful in the wet wind, casting living shadows across his face.

He raised his arms. Brought his fisted hands thundering down on the tabletop. The .38 forgotten in the grip of his right hand. Splitting the old wood. Sending the hurricane lamp rattling across the table, plunging us into darkness.

Lightning flickered through the night, sharp and ragged. Rain blew past the window, splattering inside, the drops hard and brisk hitting the wood floor.

"In south Louisiana, a woman don't leave her husband easy," Montgomery whispered into the blackness, his raspy voice seeming louder than the wind. "Except in a coffin."

CHAPTER

10

Terry Bertrand ignored Montgomery and took charge, with a flick of his flashlight, returning light and sanity to a world gone black. The sheriff's face was skeletal in the reflection of the beam, all planes and angles and wet shiny skin.

"You'll need to come with us, ma'am."

"Montgomery was served with papers. There're warrants out for his arrest. He attacked a deputy," I said, my words coming through clenched teeth, pleading with the cop to do his job.

"You'll need to come with us, ma'am," he repeated. His voice was cold. Implacable. The sound of a man who will not listen to explanations or reasonings. The sound of a man set upon a course of action, who looks neither to the left nor to the right. Who believes he is always right, always justified, always correct in his own beliefs.

The beam of the flashlight caught Montgomery as he swayed and sat, landing hard on the sofa, his eyes suddenly confused and lost and empty. Terry's mouth tightened. "You'll come with us, like a wife should, back to her home and husband, or we'll just take the children and leave, ma'am. Your choice."

Fear slithered through me. "I'll come."

"Wise decision. I'll help you pack, ma'am."

The sheriff followed me into the bathroom, where the children waited in the beam of their own flashlight. Morgan was crying, more in anger and abandonment than fear, from his dark bed in the tub. The girls were terrified.

Lifting the edge of the mattress, I took Morgan from JP's arms and carried him to Terry. "If you'll pack for the baby, I'll take care of the girls."

After a moment, Terry nodded, but not before I saw the options flit across his eyes, one of which was that I might take the girls and run out the back door. Holding Morgan, Terry directed the beam of his light into the rest of the cottage. Satisfied that I couldn't get away without passing either him or Montgomery on my way out, he went to the little den that had become Morgan's room. He seemed to know his way around. He hadn't seen JP.

I leaned into the tub. "JP?" The little boy stuck his head out from beneath the mattress. "We need help. Could you be brave and strong and help us?" His dark eyes waited, dull and frightened as he peered past me to Shalene. The shadows in the dark house were alive, shifting and mesmerizing, promising terrors and apparitions to come. "JP?"

Slowly he nodded.

"I want you to stay here, in the tub where it's safe, with Snaps. We have to leave with Dessie's and Shalene's daddy. And the sheriff. Can you remember that? Their daddy and the sheriff?"

"I don't want to stay here alone," he sniffed. "I'm scared."

"I know, *me sha*. But we need you. Shalene and Dessie need you to stay here and tell somebody where we are. Please. Stay here. Okay?"

Slowly he nodded, his face crumpling in tears. He pulled Snaps to him, the patient cat unprotesting.

"You can keep the flashlight and the radio. When you hear

the front door slam, you can turn them on. Okay? Thank you, *me sha.*" I pulled the mattress back over his head and pulled the girls to their room. Fumbling in the bedside drawer, I found a second flashlight and flicked it on.

"Pack some panties, your nightgowns, and some toys. Quick." I pulled a suitcase from beneath the girls' bed, opened it, and spread it out on the mattress.

"Do we have to go?" Dessie was crying, her face as frightened as JP's. Shalene looked angry; that stubborn look I hated to see was settling into her features.

Kneeling, I took both girls, pulled them to me. "It's all right. I'll get us away again. I promise. But don't tell Daddy that I know about what he did to you. Okay?" Neither one responded. I shook them gently, forcing them to meet my eyes, a hand under each chin, the flashlight cradled in my thighs. "Okay? Trust me."

They finally nodded, and Dessie wiped her face. I handed her the flashlight. "Hurry. Pack. Like you were going to spend the weekend at Nana's," I said, referring to my mother, who had kept the children from time to time in Moisson.

While they pulled out a few games and coloring books and concentrated on underclothes and nightclothes, I ransacked the bureau for play clothes.

I could hear voices in the front room. And the sound of furniture breaking. Montgomery in a rage and out of control. I shivered. I had never seen him like this. The pain-pressure that I had been fighting for weeks was back, heavy and burning between my ribs. Heartache. And fear.

On top of the toys and books and the untidy pile of play clothes, I tossed clothes for me, grabbing things in the darkness that felt right. T-shirts and maternity skirts and wide-leg shorts. In the back of the closet, my hand found something rich and sleek. Luxurious. Silk. My nightclothes. The elegant ones Montgomery had loved me in. The ones from Paris. The ones he had forced the girls to wear . . . I tossed several onto the growing pile. Toiletries from the bath for the girls and for me, toothbrushes and paste, shampoo, soap.

Running into the bedroom, I wrapped the 9mm in a nightgown, found extra shoes, then ran back into the light before I could be missed. I shoved the gun in its silk wrapping into a corner of the suitcase. The weapon held fourteen rounds. No time to find the extra clip.

Could I use it if I had to? It was a question I had never allowed myself to ask. And I realized that I had no answer. *Where the hell was he taking us?* I pushed the thought away.

I found rain slickers and rain hats and extra shoes. Terry reappeared in the doorway with a diaper bag and Morgan in one arm. Morgan was screaming in fury now.

"We have to leave now, ma'am."

I wrapped the girls into slickers and shoved their hair into the hats.

"My doll," Shalene screamed, and they both jerked free of my arms to find the quadroon dolls. I could hear them rustling in the darkness. Lightning struck in the yard outside, so close I could feel the shiver of electricity even inside the house. As the sound of thunder faded, there were thumps and chatter from the bathroom, heard above the wind.

I closed the overstuffed suitcase, sitting on the top to force it down. The girls ran back in, carrying the expensive dolls. I knelt beside the girls again and pulled them to me. "You can't take them with you, *mes bébés*. They'll get wet and ruin. I'm sorry."

Shalene, still stubborn, pulled away, lifted the hem of her slicker, and secured the doll beneath its protective folds, ruining the curls of the lavish coiffure. She dropped the hem. Her face dared me to object, and instead, I laughed. It was shaky, but it was laughter. Dessie treated her blue-costumed doll the same way and smiled at me, delighted. I hugged them both. "Okay. Remember. Trust me." I could feel their nods beneath my chin.

The rain was hard and driving, pelting us like sharp

stones. I realized then that there was hail, small and irregular-shaped, like thimbles, mixed in with the rain. I was almost lifted from my feet by the wind, and my slicker, a utilitarian version of a lady's raincoat made from heavy yellow plastic like the girls', flapped hard at my calves.

Ada beat us as we walked through the front yard, the footing precarious, the water standing several inches in some places. I saw the bodies of the two security guards in a puddle beneath a battered tree, bloody and tied together, but moving weakly. I had not thought that the men would show up in weather like this. They must have thought that Montgomery would not show up in the storm either.

And only then did I remember the security system and the twelve-volt battery, the backup power source I had payed extra for. The final defense against intruders who might snip the electrical supply to the cottage. The alarm should have gone off when the window was shattered and again when the front door opened for us to leave. I wondered how much Montgomery had paid the security company flunky who had left him a way in. My car, its own alarm silent as well, was crushed beneath a tree under the metal carport.

Once we were out from beneath the trees, the fury of the storm hit us full strength, knocking Shalene off her feet. Montgomery grabbed an arm on each girl and jerked them roughly along after him. The .38 was nowhere to be seen.

Dessie looked back, to make sure I was still with them. Lightning ripped the sky. Thunder crashed and rumbled.

Terry carried Morgan and the diaper bag beneath his slicker with his left arm, and my too heavy suitcase with his right. Neither man watched me as we fought our way through the storm. They knew I would never leave my babies.

I slipped and fell once, catching myself on a fence and a fallen, ruptured tree. Splinters tore into my palm. My clothes, exposed to the storm for a moment, were soaked.

Finally, after what seemed like miles, the men stopped at a Land-Rover, and Montgomery pushed the girls into the backseat. Terry set the suitcase in the back luggage area and then handed me solicitously into the front passenger seat. He lifted his slicker and placed Morgan in my arms. There was no sign of a baby seat.

For a moment, his eyes met mine, cold and hard. He closed the door, shutting out the wind and driving rain, and disappeared into the storm. Montgomery climbed into the Land-Rover, revving the sturdy V8, and drove us into hell.

Tree branches swayed their arms in a primeval dance, lashing against the purple sky, shifting weirdly. Constant lightning flashes were a strobe against the plum-colored clouds.

Shielded behind the protective shutters, I hadn't seen the storm and the strangely painted clouds. Violet and amethyst, lilac and orchid, like a Van Gogh painting of nature gone berserk. It was barbaric, this hurricane, this netherworld Montgomery forced us into, with wind rocking the Land-Rover on its heavy suspension and the fierce storm shrieking and roaring its howling voice, drowning out any attempts at speech.

Around us trolley car lines thrashed madly, like neon snakes writhing on the air. Flogging the wind with sparks, they spit fire like gyrating, demented flagellates.

New Orleans is perpetually prepared for storm, with all electrical and phone lines underground, the traffic lights on cast-iron poles at every corner. But in places, the wind had pulled the electrical service boxes loose from the sides of houses, such as the old mansions that had been wired years after construction. Loose wires hung in trees, twisted with moss and leaves. Small fires burned. The clash of the elements, air and fire and rain.

Everywhere trees were down across the road, old cheniers and sycamore, black walnut and ornamentals. The smaller trees, Montgomery simply drove over, the tires of the Rover digging into the wet bark, the cab tilting at crazy angles, like a carnival ride. Branches snapped and broke, dragging at the undercarriage. The larger trees caused setbacks, up one-way streets, across trolley car tracks, as Montgomery fought to get us out of the Garden District and out of the city. Wipers slashed at the sheets of rain, offering rare moments of clarity in a watery prison. The whole world was wet and weeping.

The streets were littered with broken glass, trash, and papers. Traffic lights had been pushed over by fallen trees. Some few were still working, blinking their commands from the roadway or from the concealing foliage, others were smashed on the asphalt.

Emergency vehicles flashed red, blue, yellow, their sirens competing with the wind. We passed a police cruiser, its black body a shadow in the night, and the thought flashed in my mind. *Take the wheel, shove it hard left. Hit the cruiser. Beg for help.* And then on its heels, other thoughts. Montgomery with a gun, attacking the police. Montgomery with my babies as hostage. Morgan bludgeoned against the dash, torn from my arms by a collision made unpredictable by the slick road surface and blasting winds. The lack of a child seat left my youngest at the mercy of my arms and luck. The cruiser raced on by. My girls slept on and off, heads and bodies and legs entangled, dolls still grasped in limp arms.

And all the while Montgomery muttered and whispered and drank straight from a bottle of Jack Daniel's he held in one hand as he drove. He never once looked at me. But his words enveloped me, a constant low undertone.

"She was right . . . damn her . . . give her the girls . . . should have . . . do it right this . . . love her . . . can't kill . . . nothing . . . damn her . . . kill . . . bitch . . . do it right this time . . . love her . . . big house . . . she was right."

After we passed the city limits, the eye of the storm hit us. An oasis of silence in the world. A silence so strong and deep that my battered ears strained again for the sound of the wind, missing the roar and the scream of the storm which had become our reality.

The girls whimpered and shivered in the steamy dampness of the Rover. Even Montgomery quieted, his knuckles white on the steering wheel. Everywhere, the branches became still, shop signs, tilted by the wind, swung back to the vertical and stopped. Trees were canted and bent, arched and split, dropped like a can of pickup sticks upended by a child. A few of the foolish came outside, staring at the wreckage and the starry sky, shouting and squealing. The wise waited out the eerie silence, knowing that when the eye passed, the storm would resume, stronger and more angry than before.

Perhaps ten minutes passed before the wind hit again. And in that awful silence I prayed that the eye of the storm had passed over the cottage. For at least a few moments. Knowing that if the storm died even for a few seconds, Philippe would have come, would have found the broken shutter, the shattered window. Would have found JP huddled in the tub and taken him back to the main house.

I wasn't foolish enough to think that Philippe would get word out to the authorities about the girls and Morgan and me. And Montgomery. Not during the eye. Even after the storm, the police would have too much to do to look for us.

Too much damage. Too many homebound and elderly people without water and power and medical supplies. Too many injured. Too many dead. They'd have looters and violence. Human violence spawned by the violence of the storm. There would be no time, no men, no desire to comb the city for us.

We were on our own.

The storm hit again with the force of an angry god striking the earth. A pulsing, throbbing wind, alive, furious, buffeting the Land-Rover, sending it rocking on its suspension. Trees that had been balanced precariously on roofs and cars and buildings were hammered in the opposite direction by corkscrew winds. They crashed to the ground, to the road in front of us, behind us.

A tornado sat down right in front of the Rover, the whirling maelstrom ripping into a van, whipping it around and around, flipping it over and tearing it apart, slamming pieces of it against a storefront. Shattering the building's windows out. And then it was gone. Montgomery steered the Land-Rover past the spot where the van had whirled in the wind. He never even slowed down.

He drank steadily as we passed through a small town on the outskirts of New Orleans, hit I 10 and moved west, then turned off the interstate. Once again he muttered and cursed. He wasn't taking us home. He was taking us north. Following the storm.

For hours we traveled, into territory I didn't recognize, wouldn't have recognized even had it been light. Some of these towns were less prepared for major storms. Above-ground electric wires burned in the trees or lashed the air or snapped and popped on the road, steamed in the puddles. Traffic lights were strung on cable—some few still working. They were swirling and spinning on their connectors, flashing a mad and clumsy jitterbug. Others were snarled in the electric and phone lines, twisted around trees, or smashed to the street. One was sitting in the front seat of a parked car, still carefully changing from green to yellow to red.

I watched Montgomery as he drove, his eyes narrow, never still, his fingers gripping and loosening on the wheel, his breath coming fast and harsh in his throat.

He was drunk. Drunker than I'd ever seen him. The kind of drunk it takes days to achieve. Or weeks. But he was in control. He was still able to maneuver the Rover. Still able to negotiate the narrow roads and downed trees.

Slowly, as the hours passed, the storm outpaced us, howling up the Mississippi River Valley until it finally turned east and rushed toward the Atlantic on trade winds. The awful roar that had hounded us softened and eased. Montgomery turned on the radio as the winds began to die, and we listened to the report of damage and death and mayhem.

There was massive flooding in the coastal areas not protected by levees, some towns under four feet of water with uncounted missing and dead. The scant warning hadn't allowed the residents time to prepare or to get out. Damage estimates were sky-high and still climbing. New Orleans had six known dead, and the hospitals were swarming with the injured and the wounded. The National Guard had been called out to protect against looters; already the arrests had begun.

Using my teeth, I pulled splinters from the pad of my hand. And licked away the thin, watery blood that ran from the deepest holes. My entire palm was bruised.

A strong wind whipped the clouds from the sky, revealing a brilliance of stars seldom seen in the state, the haze of obscuring smog blown away, competing city lights doused. And still we moved north, up curving two-rut roads. Leaving the destruction behind, we came into areas untouched by strong wind and heavy rain, the streets damp but clear of broken limbs and debris.

Near dawn, we passed a crossroads and turned west. *Dear God . . . where was he taking us?*

Half an hour later, with a gray light brightening the sky behind us, we turned in to a side street, then another. And another. The asphalt was cracked and pitted, potholed. And then there was no blacktopping at all. Only a two-rut track between trees, muddy, rough, overhung with low, dripping branches and moss, the sound of morning birds and tree frogs sharp and piercing on the clear air.

A house appeared, at first no more than a dark stain lit by headlights. Old asbestos siding, gray or pale green. A crumbling porch. A well house. Weed-choked yard. Wisteria and honeysuckle smothered a tree. The place looked abandoned, deserted. As if it had stood empty for some time.

Montgomery pulled to a stop and extinguished the headlights. But not before I saw the plaque. The DeLande bird of prey. Wings spread, talons bloodied. Montgomery cut the motor and got out.

I carried Morgan through a light rain, across the cracked and broken concrete stepping stones, each in the shape of a four-leaf clover. Each with at least one cracked-off leaf. Luck run out? Or deliberate vandalism? Some of the cracks looked fresh, the concrete edge bright and sharp against the slick mold coating the rest of the space.

It was fresh damage, these breaks in the stepping stones. Someone had been here recently. In the surface mold of one stone were tread marks. Someone had driven up to the front door. Montgomery preparing a prison for us? Or a DeLande doing it for him.

Montgomery held the neck of the Jack Daniel's bottle and the key in one hand. With the other, he steadied Dessie, who was tossed over his shoulder, pretending to be asleep. He opened the door and stepped back, allowing me to enter. Unconscious gentility. Even drunk. Even not quite himself . . . he was polite. The fact was somehow more threatening than the hours of whispered threats. I stepped inside.

The place was stuffy and dank, the walls molded and damp, wallpaper peeling in the corners. The furniture was mismatched and threadbare. A rustling in the kitchen. Rats? There was one main room, a combination living room, dining room, kitchen, with two bedrooms and a bath opening off the side. Montgomery flicked a switch, the click of the old plastic precise in the undisturbed air.

There was power here, in this renovated shanty, dim lights, a 1940s stove and refrigerator. A single window-unit air conditioner. Electric fans were scattered around the front room, the kind that swivel, placed so they would direct cooled air to the bedrooms and the bath. Neither the air conditioner nor the fans were running, contributing to the dank, stale feeling of the small house.

Montgomery dumped Dessie on the moldering sofa, pocketed the keys, and drank again from the bottle, the dark liquid sloshing in the bottom. His eyes were blue suns blazing, the veins like bloody lightning, jagged, stabbing through the yellowed orbs.

He had not shaved. A day's growth of beard, always a shade lighter than the red of his hair, caught the glint of the single bulb overhead. Gold, mixed with the red, threw sparkles of light from his chin and jaw. His hair was too long, unkempt. Dark from the rain. Without a word, he turned away and went back outside.

Quickly I sat Morgan on the sofa beside Dessie, returning her worried look with a smile I didn't really feel. I walked through the house. No phones. No phone jacks that I could see. If they were there, they were under the furniture.

Montgomery sat Shalene on the sofa beside his other children, dropped the suitcase I had packed, and shut the door. There was a finality to the sound, definite and irrevocable. Punctuated by the sound of a lock clicking into place. We were locked in.

Before Montgomery could turn around, I picked up Morgan, checking his diapers and rummaging through the bag Terry had packed for him. A dozen cloth diapers, premoistened towelettes, baby powder, a pacifier, which Morgan never used. No baby food. Morgan was wet. I took a diaper and the towelettes to the coffee table.

The girls were awake now, and silent, eyes wide with fear as they looked from Montgomery to me. Back and forth. And Montgomery stood over me, watching and waiting. I reached for Morgan.

"Who is he?" Montgomery's voice was low, a slurred undertone.

I was silent, thumbing loose the safety pins, rolling up the diaper, wiping Morgan's bottom.

"Who's the sonabitch you're sleeping with?"

I opened out a fresh diaper, folded it, and lifted Morgan's feet, sliding the clean cloth under his body. A bit of powder.

"The one Miles saw you with? That him?"

My hands were shaking as I slid the pins into the cloth and secured the diaper around Morgan's body. Clear plastic pants over the diaper.

Montgomery took a long swig from the bottle, his throat moving with each swallow. I glanced quickly away. "Answer me, Nicole." The bottle was almost empty.

I sat Morgan in Dessie's lap, putting her arm around the baby's fat tummy, and walked to the window unit. The air was stagnant and moist, and I stabbed at the buttons, grateful when the old air conditioner hummed and sent out a current of cold. This air smelled as stale and wet as the rest of the house, but after a moment, it freshened a bit.

I could feel Montgomery's eyes on me, hot and possessive. I left the cold and moved through the small house, turning on fans. The place was clean, almost scrupulously so, except for the pervasive mildew and mold. The bathroom was a 1950s housewife's dream, with ceramic fixtures, a pedestal sink, and six-foot-long tub, all smelling faintly of pine oil. The floor was red and gray tile, cracked and worn.

"Girls, the bathroom's clean. You need to go?" I was pleased that my voice was steady. I was utterly terrified, but the girls would never know.

Moving slowly, they crossed the room, keeping a wide berth from Montgomery, as they always did when the smell of whiskey was potent and Montgomery was angry. *They were afraid of their father.* Not the normal respect-fear of a child for an authority figure. But real fear. The terrifying paralysis of the habitual victim. The thought was new and disturbing. The signs subtle, almost imperceptible. But I could see it now, see the fear. The dread. The wary distrust. How long had my girls been afraid? Had I not noticed, or just ignored the signals?

Dessie carried Morgan, her brother a wriggling shield between her and her father; she passed him to me. I stood in the doorway as they used the old toilet, a barrier between them and Montgomery.

"Wash your hands. You hungry?"

Both girls nodded. Shalene flushed the toilet, the old chain innards clanking as too much water purged the bowl. I slipped past Montgomery and rummaged through the kitchen. The little fluorescent bulb overhead did little to brighten the dark-paneled cabinets.

The room had been cleaned thoroughly, but little mouse pellets ran along the edge of the countertops at the backsplash, and a bag of chips—one corner chewed open—held even more. I found two family-sized cans of ravioli, and although it wasn't much of a breakfast, I heated the contents and served up five plates—which I washed first—and five Tupperware glasses of presweetened Kool-Aid.

We all ate, even Montgomery, the girls and I saying grace over the meal before digging in. It was messy eating for Morgan, who discarded his spoon and picked up the slippery pasta with his fingers. The sight of my son, blithely smearing tomato sauce all over himself, made me smile. I never once looked at Montgomery; he didn't take his eyes off me.

After the meal, I washed all the dishes again, swept up the mouse pellets, and finally tucked my exhausted daughters into bed. Morgan and the damp, bedraggled dolls snuggled down between them. It was dawn, but none of them had rested well in the Land-Rover. I knew they would all sleep.

At last, I turned to Montgomery.

"I asked you a question, Nicole." His voice was a rasp, coarse and hollow.

I moved past him, careful not to touch him, and went to the bathroom, desperate to relieve myself. I pushed the door closed and turned to the toilet. The door crashed open behind me. The knob breaking through the wallpaper and wallboard.

I stopped. Didn't turn around. This was a new version of an old game. Tame Nicole. Carefully I opened my clothes, relieved myself. The sound was clear and distinct in the little room before I flushed and the torrent of water drowned out the last little sound.

Refastening my clothes, I walked past Montgomery, still not meeting his eyes, and opened out the suitcase. The 9mm was still wrapped in the corner of the case, camouflaged in the delicate, watered silk. The plum and lavender and orchid shades of the nightgown were remarkably similar to the color of the hurricane-torn sky only hours earlier. I had to find a place to hide the weapon.

I stacked games and coloring books on the coffee table, separated the girls' clothing, making stacks of underpants, shorts, T-shirts, shoes. I carried their toothbrushes and the other toiletries to the minuscule bathroom, arranging everything on the shelf above the toilet. With each trip, I passed Montgomery, silent, my eyes averted.

Then I turned on the bath. There was no shower, but plenty of hot water. I added a teaspoon full of bath crystals, scented like black raspberry.

The soft water caught the crystals and instantly melted them, bubbles rising, glinting in the harsh light. While the water rose, I went back to the suitcase and closed it, dragging it to the second bedroom.

I had put the children in the smaller room, and was pleased that it had a TV, the old-fashioned kind, a black-and-white with aluminum foil wings attached to the ears of the antennae. Neither girl had ever seen such an old model, but I had no doubt that they would figure out how to work it.

In what might laughingly be called the master suite, I unpacked my things beneath Montgomery's constant glare. The only sound in the little house was the sound of whiskey sloshing, bathwater falling, and my small movements. The faint rattle and clank of the air conditioner could scarcely be heard from the front room.

I put my outer clothes into the second drawer of a bureau; it was a meager wardrobe. No style at all. Sonja wouldn't have survived with the scant items. I almost smiled at the thought.

I opened the top drawer and reached for the plum nightgown. Montgomery laughed.

"Were you going to shoot me, Nicole?" His voice growled, whiskey-rough.

I stopped, my fingers inches from the silk.

"Were you going to aim your little toy at me and pull the trigger?"

I took the silk in my hand. It was empty. The 9mm was gone. I said nothing, simply shook out the crumpled silk nightgown and carried it with me to the bathroom.

Montgomery must have searched the suitcase while I ran the bath. It was the only time he could have disappeared for a moment and I wouldn't have noticed.

With Montgomery standing in the door to the bathroom, drinking and watching, I stripped off the damp clothes I had put on the day before and dropped them in the sink. And then I bathed.

My husband stood and drank from the limitless bottle, his eyes like twin blue coals on my skin. I was far enough along in my pregnancy that my breasts were full and rounded, my nipples darker and heavy-ringed, my belly just a bit full.

His breathing changed as I bathed. Deepened. Became rough and harsh, as if he sucked in air between clenched teeth.

I submerged in the extralong tub, washing my hair. Letting him look. And rinsed myself afterward by cupping my hands beneath the stream of water and dousing clean water over me. Slick and refreshed, I stepped from the tub, wrapped a towel around me, and rinsed the tub free of scum before pulling on the plum nightgown.

I was combing out my wet hair, standing in front of the pedestal sink at the small mirror, when Montgomery attacked.

He grabbed my wet hair. Twisted it around his fist and bent back my head. I could see the long length of pale throat exposed in the mirror. My eyes appeared deformed, the skin was pulled so taut.

Montgomery smiled at our reflections. Tightened his hold on my hair. Put down the bottle.

He ran his thumb up and down the sweep of my throat. Slowly. Gently.

Encircled my throat with his long, slim fingers. Slowly. Gently.

"Don't make me damage you," he whispered, pleading, his voice whiskey-scented, soft against my skin. "Just tell me his name." His words came slow, unhurried, patient. "Or is it Sonja? You two always were so very close. Is it more than that now? You finding what you need between that high yellow, coon-ass's pretty thighs?"

His voice deepened. And his fingers tightened on my throat. There was no air. I knew better than to struggle.

"She tell you about me while she was bringing you pleasure? Or was it that lawyer brother-in-law after all? The one Miles Justin likes so much. The one that gave my girls those dolls."

He pulled me to the bedroom, stumbling, my head held back in his grip, my scalp tingling with the pain. All I could see was the dirty gray stippled ceiling. Someone had once tried to brighten it with sparkles. The crystals still glinted in the dim light.

He pushed me to the bed. Handcuffed my hands to the bed frame.

I had told Adrian Paul that a DeLande never used his fists on a woman. I was wrong.

Teeth, fists, the flat of his hand. He beat me. Concentrating on my face, my ribs, my breasts, my back. I never knew you could hear a bone as it broke. But you can. Each of three ribs. A single crack, separate from the sound of fist on human flesh. More personal, more private. An intimate sound. An intimate pain. And through it all, the words like a litany, "Tell me, Nicole. Tell me the truth."

Montgomery bent back my fingers, my elbows, my shoulders, unlocking and rearranging the handcuffs each time he moved me. He pulled my arms from the shoulder sockets, dislocating my left arm. I had never felt pain like that before. Didn't know that numbness and agony could exist in the same tortured flesh.

That was the only time I cried out. Uncontrolled. Unable

to hush my cries. Not even when Shalene burst into the room and beat on Montgomery, her fists a tiny tattoo on his thigh. Not even when Montgomery backhanded her across the room, threw her into the front room, and slammed the door. Not until he unlocked the cuffs and pulled on my arm, forcing the joint to slide back into place, could I stifle my moaning.

And then the other part of the punishment began. The personal part. The part to make me remember who I was. What I was. And what I was good for.

I held the injured arm across my chest as he used me. Trying to keep it immobile and still as he rocked on the bed, heaving over me, his blue eyes never leaving my bruised face. Tears I could no longer command spilled down my jaw, pooled in my ears, slid across split flesh, the small amount of salt in the tears bringing a tiny flare of pain, sharp and stinging.

He muttered again, as he had in the Rover. ". . . kill her . . . can't . . . love . . . give them . . . house . . ."

He had lost all semblance of reason, yet he held his insanity with a tight rein, constraining and controlling it, like a rabid dog barely restrained by a leash. His eyes blazed like hot flames, blue-hot torches, deranged. "Tell me, Nicole. Tell me the truth."

After what seemed like hours, he grunted and rolled off me. I pulled up my knees and curled to my side, cried silently into the sheets. The room, with the door closed to the cool air, was sticky hot. A glaze of sweat, left from his body and my pain, was slick and oily across my skin. "Tell me. Tell me who he is. Tell me the truth."

I couldn't tell him. I couldn't tell him that I knew he had molested his children. I knew if I did . . . I knew my punishment would be worse. Much much worse than this.

So I just cried, silently curled into the striped sheets, thin and worn and limp. My bruised face, broken ribs, and aching shoulder held still against the movement of the sobs.

I heard him, felt him, move away. He rolled from my

body. The DeLande grace. Even drunk he moved like a dancer. A predator. A cat, still hungry, even after feeding.

I heard him suck on his knuckles, the skin broken where he had bruised them on my body. Heard him slip on his pants, the zipper sharp and crackling in the room. He slid a cuff around my uninjured wrist and pulled me up on the mattress until he could clip the other cuff to the bed frame. Before leaving the room, he threw the sheet up over me. I could feel the heat of his eyes.

"Just tell me the truth." Whispered.

It went on all day, the slow punishment. But he didn't hit me again, either with his open hand or with his fist. It was the old punishment, the pain coming from the ribs that ground beneath his weight and in the strength of his embrace. Lips that couldn't take his kiss. And every so often, he'd whisper, "Tell me. Tell me who it is. Tell me the truth, Nicole." Or he'd mutter again, the crazed refrain from the hours of the storm. I don't think he knew he said the strange phrases, or made the bizarre threats.

But he never once, in all his rough handling, injured the baby I carried. His baby. Somehow he didn't doubt its paternity.

Toward evening, the end of the long, sweltering day, I looked him in the face for the first time, meeting his eyes, my own eyes passive. He was less drunk now. And he seemed calmer. Almost uncertain. Puzzled. As if he was waiting for something or faced some dilemma, riddle, or secret. His eyes probed my face, questioning. But this time he didn't ask. He was silent.

"I need to go to the bathroom," I said, my voice low and even.

Slowly he rose up from the bed, removed the cuffs, and tossed them to the floor. He pulled the snarled sheet up from its place on the floor, shook it out, and wrapped it around me, the plum gown long ago ruined in his rough hands.

He followed me into the bathroom and shut the door, watching me with unwavering eyes. Without asking his permission, I turned on the tub water when I finished with the toilet, cold water this time, to fight the heat and slow the bruising. When the tub was full, I flushed the toilet, watching the torrent of wasted water.

Then I dropped the sheet and stepped into the cold tub. I rested back, neck-deep, wishing for the whirlpool I'd left behind in Moisson, and for the Epsom salts I'd left behind in New Orleans. Yet the cold water alone eased the worst of the aches. Twenty minutes later I pulled the rubber stopper loose with my toes and crawled from the tub, stiff and nearly shivering.

For the girls' sake, I applied a bit of makeup and combed out my tangled hair, inspecting the visible damage in the small mirror above the sink. Both my eyes were black, the bruising only half-hidden by the concealer. The lipstick too bright, too pink, against my pale skin. My hair had dried in the bed, its luster dulled and the part on the wrong side. Uneven.

Working out the tangles with only one hand jarred the broken ribs, brought silent tears to my eyes. Midway through, Montgomery took the comb. Gently he pried apart the rat's nest of tangles and snarls. Patiently. Just as patiently as he had beaten me earlier.

Finally my hair was smooth and he picked up my brush, pulling it through my hair again and again, the rhythm almost the same as when he slapped my face with his open hand. Stroke. Stroke. Stroke.

"The girls must be hungry," I said to stop the awful cadence.

"The freezer is stocked."

I nodded and stepped away, leaving the sheet, the towel my only concession to modesty. I noticed my dirty clothes, the ones I had left in the sink that morning, were piled in the corner. I kicked the sheet into the small pile.

Back in the bedroom, I pulled on shorts and a T-shirt, letting Montgomery help me when I couldn't get the shirt on over my head alone. He even used the remnants of the plum gown to fashion a makeshift sling for my arm, securing it to my side. Before I left the room, I picked up the handcuffs from the corner and handed them to him, again meeting his eyes. He seemed bewildered for a moment, and then heat darkened his face and he walked away.

In the main room, I hugged both girls, praised them softly for being brave, warned Shalene against trying to help me, and changed Morgan. Dessie had cared for him all day, feeding him Kool-Aid in his plastic cup, peeling bananas, giving him Pop-Tarts and milk. He was contented where he sat on the sofa, pulling at the curly hair of Shalene's doll, watching us all with his wise, steady eyes.

I found shrimp in the freezer, at least twenty pounds, and broke off a huge chunk to boil. There were salad greens in the refrigerator, tomatoes, fresh parsley, carrots, cucumbers, yellow squash, potatoes, eggplant, and three kinds of peppers. The kind Miles Justin always brought when he came to visit. I stared for a long moment at the multicolored mild peppers. *Had Miles prepared this prison for me?* I closed the refrigerator door. Ranch dressing, unopened on a shelf, decided my menu.

With Dessie's help, I made a salad while the shrimp boiled. It was then I realized that there were no knives in the kitchen. No heavy dishes, no glass dishes. Everything was plastic and Tupperware. *No weapons at all in the little house.* Dessie figured out how to use a Salad Shooter so we could cut the salad vegetables.

I found mousetraps and silently handed them to Montgomery. Just as if we were home in Moisson, he located peanut butter for bait, armed the traps, and stuck them in corners and behind the refrigerator.

We ate in silence. Montgomery watched me as we ate, his eyes sharp, hawklike, in the house's poor lights. *There were no lamps to throw. Nothing heavy to batter a man.* He watched me all evening, sitting at the table, his hands slowly turning the empty Jack Daniel's bottle around and around on the tabletop. The sound was grating, loud in the silent kitchen, steady and rhythmic.

One-handed, I washed the dishes, then washed out Morgan's diapers and hung them to dry over the backs of the kitchen chairs. I noticed a door in the corner by the refrigerator, probably a back door leading from the kitchen. It had appeared as only an empty space before I noticed the small latch. Not even a knob, just a latch. No lock.

I bathed all three children, dressed them for bed, read them two stories, and sang them a lullaby. My breath was short from the broken ribs, but they didn't seem to notice. It was just like being back home in Moisson, except for the tension that crackled in the air and the constant pressure of Montgomery's eyes on my back.

Late, I went to bed. It took all the courage I had to force myself back to the mattress where my punishment had taken place.

Even though I was exhausted, sleep didn't come. My ribs ached with every breath, I couldn't find a comfortable position on the thin, lumpy mattress, and each time I woke with the pain, I found Montgomery's eyes on me in the darkness. Glittering. More clear crystal than human blue.

The next morning, my pain was worse, the stiffness so severe that I couldn't roll out of bed without Montgomery's help. He half carried me to a hot bath and left me to soak for an hour while he fixed breakfast for the children—pancakes and syrup, applesauce, and scrambled eggs.

He fed me where I sat in the tub, carrying each bite to my mouth, holding the juice cup to my lips. Wiping my mouth gently when the juice burned or the syrup dripped. He smiled at me lovingly. Each movement was deliberate, smooth, paced. And silent.

There was something ominous in his solicitous attention, his careful consideration. As though Montgomery liked me helpless with pain and totally dependent on him. The fear, which I had held at bay throughout the beating and punishment of the day before, blossomed, flourishing under his disquieting kindness, nurtured by his tender notice.

After the meal, he reheated my bathwater and stripped off his shirt. Reaching beneath the hot water, he massaged my feet, my calves, my back. Perhaps it was only my fear that made it seem as if his fingers lingered on the fragile, delicate bones of my neck. As if measuring each vertebra for its tensile strength.

I knew then that my punishment wasn't over yet. It had scarcely begun.

CHAPTER
11

All morning Montgomery left me alone, not touching me once, except with his eyes. Eyes that never left me. With my good arm, I folded diapers, made baby food by pureeing cooked vegetables in a heavy glass blender, washed out the girls' dirty clothes, played games with the children. Montgomery carried out two dead mice, caught during the night with his baited traps; reset the traps.

Once, late in the morning, Shalene came running into the kitchen, her cotton panties and shorts rolled in a tight wad where she had tried to pull them back on after using the toilet. "Mama. I'm stuck," she said, demanding help and pointing to her exposed backside.

I dropped to one knee and pulled loose the wad of twisted cloth, patted down her smoothed-out shorts, and glanced up at Montgomery. His eyes were on my fingers, where they rested on Shalene's bottom. Odd eyes. Hungry.

I looked away, patted Shalene's head. "Go play, *me sha.*" A mousetrap snapped closed from behind the refrigerator. A mouse squealed, flopping horribly in its death trap. Finally it quieted and died. I rose from my knees and went back to the sink.

My punishment resumed that afternoon.

It was sexual. All of it. Exotic and inventive and painful. Intimately painful. "Tell me, Nicole. Tell me who it was. . . . Tell me the truth."

I was silent throughout the ordeal, grunting only when the pain was sharpest. I kept my mind blank, my face impassive, my eyes unfocused. But every once in a while, I'd see that look in my mind. Montgomery's eyes on my hand where I touched my little girl. The hunger there. The need. And I knew that I had to get away.

The whiskey remaining in Montgomery's system slowly burned away during that long day, taking his remaining anger with it. His punishments grew less inventive, less painful, his eyes grew more confused. Silence always seemed to confuse my husband. Or defuse him maybe.

But still he kept muttering, "Tell me. Tell me his name." A litany so urgent, it was like a prayer for salvation. He had stopped the muttering, the diatribe of half-spoken, half-heard threats.

That night he fixed supper for the girls and me, letting me rest on the sofa with Morgan. He thawed some chicken breasts, baking the meat with new potatoes, served up a salad and homemade cornbread. He even cleaned up the kitchen afterward, and carried out the dead mouse. I didn't know he knew how. Either to cook or to clean up.

He helped me bathe the girls, his face free of the expression I had witnessed earlier. Except once. It flickered across his eyes and vanished, so fast I nearly missed it. Desire. For his babies.

I had seen the same expression flit across his face for years, gone so fast, I could never identify it. But I recognized it now. And I hated him for it.

I had to get away. There had to be a way to get the girls to safety. But there were no weapons. No car keys. No phone.

Once the girls were safely in bed, Montgomery drew me

another bath. Hot. Scented with my bath crystals. He watched me disrobe, climb in the tub, sink down, and sigh. And he left me alone.

For an entire hour he left me, taking the Land-Rover for supplies. Groceries. Washing powder for Morgan's dirty diapers. He didn't leave me a towel, and he locked me in the bathroom. But that hour alone was pure heaven. And the means to our escape.

When Montgomery came back in, I was sitting in the reheated water, carefully massaging my bruised left shoulder. The tendons were aching and sore, and I could follow the swollen ligaments from clavicle and shoulder blade down my upper arm, the strained tissue hot and tight with pain.

He unlocked the door, checked the floor for signs of water. Seeing the puddles, he looked at me, his face set. I shrugged, splashing the hot water. "I had to use the toilet. You forgot to leave me a towel."

Montgomery walked into the tiny room, seeming to squeeze out what air there was in the steamy hot space. Water still beaded on the toilet seat. He shook his head and went for a towel, but the set look was gone from his face.

He cleaned up the mess, passed me a fresh towel, and watched me dry off, stepping from the tub to the damp towel he had left on the floor. His eyes were calm and amazingly sad.

He made love to me that night. No punishments. No pain. And he kissed me as he had so long ago. Tenderly. With passion. As he had when he was courting me, teaching me. Before sex became a sport and a sometime punishment.

After loving me, he stroked my back and my hair till I was calm. He produced a drugstore bag and wrapped my ribs with a tough fabric binding he had picked up for me, something specifically designed to stabilize broken ribs.

I didn't tell him that no one used them nowadays. And the pressure did feel good. A little stifling perhaps. And perhaps that's what he intended. He fed me aspirin and Tylenol, two tablets each, and put a plastic glass of ice water beside the bed in case I got thirsty in the night.

Water condensed on the plastic and ran down the sides, puddling on the bare wood of the abused bedside table. It wasn't my table, and the wood top was scored with other rings and cigarette burns. But it bothered me to see more damage to the old surface. I went to sleep. So did Montgomery.

In the morning, I put my plan into motion.

I fed the girls and Morgan, smiling and joking with them. Touched them often. The tension that had been in their faces for two days melted away. I packed the children a lunch. Sandwiches for the girls, a divided Tupperware for Morgan filled with pureed squash, pureed bananas, pureed chicken, pureed potatoes. The same food we had been eating, but creamed in the blender. I packed a bag of toys, Morgan's diapers, and fixed a gallon of Kool-Aid, and put it all by the back door, the hollow wooden door in the back kitchen wall. The one I had seen but never gone near.

"Is it safe for the children to play outside today?"

Montgomery nodded slowly. He had watched me work, asking no questions. Patient and tolerant. And suspicious.

"No snakes? No ponds?" I hadn't been outside since we arrived. Hadn't even looked out a window.

"The yard's fenced. Miles checked it out for you. Even put a swing out back."

I remembered the three kinds of peppers in the refrigerator. Miles had always loved peppers. I knew now that he had prepared this house, cleaned it, stocked it, turned it into a successful cage. His tire tracks had marked the stepping stones at the front door. The DeLandes stuck together. I shivered.

I smoothed sunscreen onto the girls and Morgan at the back door, opened it, and stepped out onto a small, screened utility porch. There was a rusted washing machine, several mops, a clutter of gardening tools. Nothing sharp.

The swing was a thick rope with a board seat, tied high in

a white oak. The grass was freshly mowed. A clothesline, newly strung, was just off the porch. Miles must have expected us to stay awhile.

I hugged the girls, put Morgan's hand into Dessie's, and knelt down to them. I met the girls' eyes the way I do when I'm going to tell them something important. They'll hate that look when they get older. I could see them already, rolling their teenaged eyes and heaving big dramatic sighs. The mental picture made me smile.

"Girls, I want you to stay outside all day till I tell you to come in. No matter what, you hear? If it rains, you sit on the porch and play games. And keep an eye on Morgan. But don't come inside till I tell you. Understand?"

"What happens if we have to go tee-tee?"

Trust Shalene to point up the flaw in any plan. And to be strictly practical. I went back inside and raided the bathroom for a roll of toilet paper, added it to the supplies I piled on the porch floor.

"We're leaving soon, aren't we?" Dessie whispered.

I smiled slowly and nodded once. Dessie grinned and took Morgan's hand again, leading him to the edge of the porch, down the single step and to the swing. I closed the hollow wooden door and turned around.

Montgomery was in the front room, sitting in a swivel rocker, his bare feet stretched out and crossed at the ankle. Waiting for me. Watching me.

I'd had little to choose from in my limited wardrobe, little to put on to make a statement, but I had done what I could. I had on one of Montgomery's old work T-shirts, the kind he wore when he worked in the five-car garage—his classic-car surgery department—out back in Moisson. White, threadbare, and thin, pulled taut across my breasts. I had removed the rib wrap. No bra. And loose shorts, too long, rolled up on my thighs. Bare feet. Little makeup. Hair down. I looked like a child. A teenager. But then, he liked them young, didn't he?

I walked over to him, watching his face, stopped at his

bare feet. Straddled his feet with mine, my bare toes moving slightly along his skin. "You said you wanted to know why. Who."

He nodded, something coming into his eyes. Like a victim of torture waiting for the next blow. Pain. Damn him for loving me.

"Glorianna DesOrmeaux."

A thousand thoughts crossed Montgomery's face, some remaining long enough that I could read them. Guilt. Shock. Relief. A hint of laughter. A small "so what" frown. And when an expression finally settled on his face, it wasn't real. It was a sham. False regret. False shame.

"She has a child," I said. "Two years old." I told him all about her. What she looked like, what the child looked like, where they lived. I told him about the financial arrangement he had made with her mother. Then renegotiated with her when she came of age.

When he still said nothing, something broke inside of me. Something precious, something valuable, something I had once treasured. It just cracked, seeming to make a sound as it broke, like the sound of my ribs beneath his fists. And I screamed.

I screamed at him about trust and fidelity and disease and vows. I screamed about pain and heartache and Paris. I screamed all the things I had felt when I looked at the pictures of my husband kissing Glorianna. I screamed all the feelings I had not reacted to that night. All the hurtful emotions and pain I had pushed away because my girls' pain was greater than my own. Theirs the biggest horror. The biggest betrayal.

I stormed around the house when he still said nothing. I threw dishes at him, the lightweight plastic things that could do no harm. I turned over the kitchen table. And finally had the satisfaction of seeing the false expressions leave his face, to be replaced with something else. Something I had not expected to see. Admiration.

I emptied the kitchen cabinets, throwing cans of food his

way. Each time my missile came, he moved to one side or the other and he never was hit. The DeLande grace. A dancer would envy it. Or a fencer. And all the while the admiration grew in his gaze.

When the cabinets were empty, I started in on the furniture. Tears fell now in earnest. In anger. And I broke a chair. Overturned the couch.

A small part of me stood aside watching the rest of me explode. A small calm, calculating center that critiqued my performance and watched Montgomery's reactions. His face, the way he moved, his body. A small part that suggested refinements in my aim or choice of chair to break. A cold and unfeeling part. Determined.

I knocked over the fans while they were still running, shorting out one in a shower of sparks. I broke a pane from a window. Demolished the coffee table that held the girls' clean clothes. And then I attacked him. Tried to claw his face. Slapped him. I bit him when he caught my arms and kissed me. Drew blood. And he laughed, deep and guttural. A victorious laugh, filled with need and sexual desire. I threw him off of me and across the room. Screaming at him.

Of my real reason for leaving, I said nothing. I knew better. I knew somehow that Montgomery wouldn't let me tell him about his molesting the girls. *I knew.*

Suddenly I quieted, standing sweat-streaked in the center of the ruined living room, my chest heaving with each painful breath, and my face mottled and swollen with tears and bruises. My shoulder was an agony, a hot, stabbing pain that ripped down my arm, settled in my fingers.

And I waited. Waited to see what he would do.

Montgomery came to me across the broken furniture, moving like a cat stalking prey. He stopped in front of me. Slowly he raised his hand and cradled my face, kissed my lips tenderly. Whispered that he was sorry. Begged my forgiveness. Promised to put her away.

And he meant it, every word. I could see it in his eyes. He would have given up the world for me in that moment.

Because he wanted the new woman I had just become. He wanted the fire and the anger. The violence.

Sexual tension flared between us, hot in his eyes, and he took me on the floor, amid the broken furniture and cans of food and dishes, the leg of a chair digging into the small of my back. And again immediately after, on the bed. And a third time in the small bathroom, my body sitting balanced on the small pedestal sink.

He was insatiable. And I made sure he stayed that way. I made love to him all morning and half the afternoon, not even stopping to eat. I made love to him till he was sated and relaxed and we both were raw. I made love to him till he was no longer on his guard.

As the sun set, I walked out on the back porch, called in my sunburned children. Bathed them. Fixed a huge meal in dishes I scavenged from the living room floor. And I put the children to bed. Then I bathed Montgomery, massaging him in the tub, his back and neck and shoulders the way he liked, and put him to bed as well. I took a quick bath myself and followed him to the darkened bedroom.

My husband was asleep. Snoring softly. His mouth slightly open. His face was scruffy with a four-day beard. He looked innocent and vulnerable.

I stared at his face, lit dimly with light and shadow. Raised my arm up high. Over my head. Brought it down and hit him. Hard, in the back of the skull with the wet brick I had just removed from the toilet tank.

He grunted, and I hit him again. He didn't move.

"Oh God," I whispered. "Oh God. Oh God. Oh God." I backed away. "Oh God. Oh God Oh God Oh God Oh God Oh God."

Switching on the light, I lifted the handcuffs Montgomery had left out on the bureau, the key beside them. Pulling both arms up above his head, I cuffed his wrists to the bed frame, wrapping the short chain around the thick wooden post and clicking it shut.

"Oh God Oh God Oh God Oh God . . ." I threw the key through the open doorway to the living room floor. I had no breath. Bile rose in my throat. Hot acid.

Montgomery's head was bleeding where I had hit him. Not bad, but bleeding still, the one small trickle in the matted dark red curls, bright red against the auburn.

"Oh God." I remembered his eyes as he looked at Shalene, my hand on her bottom. And I shuddered. "Oh God." I tossed the sheet up over his naked body. Gagged. Swallowed hard.

Grabbing the suitcase, I tossed clothes into it, pulling on a split skirt and white shirt, and slip-on Keds. I went through Montgomery's clothes until I found the car keys and the 9mm. The clip was gone. It wasn't among his clothes.

I dragged the suitcase into the living room, tossing in the girls' clothes and toys, searching among the scattered ruins of the living room furniture for panties, shorts, socks, coloring books. I could have left it all. There was nothing here that couldn't be replaced. But it seemed obscene somehow, to leave anything behind for Montgomery.

A hot sweat started beneath my arms and ran down my back. Trickling steadily. An annoying tickle unrelieved by the cool of the air conditioner. "Oh God. Oh God."

I tossed in toiletries from the bathroom. Stopped suddenly and ran back to Montgomery. He was still out cold, but breathing evenly. The bleeding had stopped. I almost touched him. Jerked back my hand. I picked up the brick, ran with it to the bathroom. Rinsed it thoroughly in the sink and replaced it in the toilet tank. Letting the water run, I washed my hands till they were clean and the drain trap under the sink was washed free of blood.

Very Freudian, that. Spill someone's blood, then spend the rest of your life trying to get clean again.

He wasn't dead, I reminded myself. *He wasn't.*

I carried the suitcase back to the Land-Rover, almost throwing it into the back. Making several trips, I carried out blankets, pillows, crackers and the opened jar of peanut butter, and the girls' dolls. It was pitch black. No stars or moon overhead. The sky jacketed in steel gray clouds.

Back inside, I found a sturdy, dull butter knife and crawled around the living room floor on my hands and knees. I was looking for a phone jack, knowing there had to be one. Somewhere. I finally found it, in the kitchen, tucked behind the corner of the refrigerator beside one of Montgomery's primed mousetraps.

With the butter knife, I pried away the old-fashioned cover and pulled loose the tiny wires. Yellow, red, green, and black. I ripped them loose.

My muttered prayers died away. Now there was only the sound of my breathing, rough and coarse and uneven, loud over the noise of the air conditioner.

I found a second phone jack behind the bed where Montgomery lay. Shoving the bed aside with a tear of strained muscles and tendons, I ripped it apart too.

And then it occurred to me. I ran out the back door of the little house. In the stygian darkness, enhanced only by ambient light from the back utility porch, I found the incoming phone line. Using a short weeding hoe I found on the back porch, its edge dulled by years of use, I ripped the line from the house, leaving it lying like my dead rattler, one end limp on the black ground.

I packed the sleeping children into the Land-Rover, securing Morgan with pillows and seat belts into the front seat. The girls curled in among the blankets and pillows and watched me sleepily.

Making a neat three-point turn in the front yard, I heard the four-leaf clover stepping stones crack and grind under the tires. I pulled down the long, winding drive, the two ruts lit by the high-beam headlights. Scrub oak and sweet gum pulled at the truck body with sharp, resentful fingers from the side.

A light rain fell, spattering on the windshield with big, slow droplets that ran down in thick tracks like tears. The drive was two miles long. Tree frogs were so loud in the night, I could hear them over the motor and air conditioner, inside the closed cab.

The sweat continued to pour, heavy and slick with fear. I was shaking. But I could drive.

When we reached the blacktopped road and the track widened, I glanced at the gas gauge. Almost on empty. Idling the Rover, I pulled my purse to me and flicked on the courtesy light. No cash. Only checks and old credit cards, ones I had used back in Moisson.

I fingered the cards, thinking. Paper trails aside, the cards were dangerous to use. Not only could Montgomery follow my trail, but he could also cancel my cards. May have already. And if I tried to use them after they were canceled, I could end up in jail for trying to pass a bad card. And from jail back to Montgomery's arms.

I could imagine his face when he found me this time. To break that thought, I turned to the girls. Shalene was asleep. Dessie was staring at me.

"You got us away." She smiled.

"Well, not just yet, actually." I shook Shalene. She ignored me. She could sleep through a freight train running into the house. *Me sha,* I need to borrow some money. Wake up, *ma petit du souk,"* I murmured in Cajun. Then I shook her harder. "Mama needs some money. Do you have any?"

"How much?" she mumbled sleepily.

"Twenty? Thirty, if you have it."

She sighed and fumbled at her waist for the money belt given to her so long ago by Miles Justin. She came wide-awake when it wasn't there. Black eyes vast in the partial dark of the Land-Rover, she looked around, a bit wild-eyed, startled. "My doll," she screamed. "My doll!"

I was surprised. Not that she was shocked at being suddenly in the Land-Rover instead of in her bed, but that she was so horrified. "She's on the floor at your feet, *me sha.*"

She dove for the doll. Dessie watched it all with contented eyes.

Shalene flipped up the doll's skirts, exposing the soft padded body. The money belt was strapped to the doll's middle.

"Now I see why you were so determined to bring the doll," I murmured. She flashed me a conspiratorial smile and opened the belt. It was stuffed with green. I gaped. "How much do you have there?" It looked like a fortune.

Her shoulders went up in a high, innocent shrug. "Don' know. Unc'e Miles said it was more than two hunner', but my fancy gave me more. For my t'ousseau."

I swallowed back a laugh. Shalene couldn't have any idea what a trousseau was. Could she?

"Could I borrow fifty, then?"

She considered as the Land-Rover idled away the meager gas supply.

"Two dollars int'est." She held up two fingers.

I nodded. "Done. When we get back to New Orleans."

She nodded and leaned forward to shake my hand. Shalene. My little deal maker. Her hand was frail and small in my grasp. She passed me the money belt and watched anxiously as I counted out fifty dollars. From the back of the wallet, I pulled a crisp one-hundred-dollar bill.

"Where did you get this?"

"Unc'e Miles. It's a hunner'-dollar bill."

"Yes, I know." Feeling rather faint, I reinserted the bill, passed back the money belt, and eased the Land-Rover forward and right. It was the only turn I could remember from our arrival.

We got gas from a little crossroads store. Two pumps out front, bars on the windows, clapboard facade missing several exterior boards, no sign. The place was closed, a pimply-faced boy getting into his beat-up pickup truck to drive away, but I put a ten-dollar bill in his greasy fist. He smiled, unlocked the door, and turned the pump back on, moving faster for the cash than for any teary-eyed sob story I might have given. Money talked. He even pumped the gas and gave me directions to the nearest town.

But he looked several times at my face, blackened eyes wild and frightened. When I got back into the Rover, I pulled down the vanity mirror and applied heavy makeup.

Two hours later, near midnight, we found St. Genevieve and stopped again at a small Cajun diner and bar. I woke the girls, who trooped in behind me. We bought a map, a dozen boudin balls—highly spiced rice and pork—fried onion rings and colas for the girls, Pampers for Morgan, and a thermos of coffee for me. Even though the gas tank still showed almost full, I topped it off. My fifty bucks was gone.

Back in the car, I munched onion rings as I searched for St. Genevieve on the map. I was farther north than I had expected, and there were only just so many ways we could head south from this part of the state. To avoid possible detection in the event that Montgomery got loose sooner than I expected, we turned north, then east, until we hit Natchez, Mississippi. In a pouring rain, we took 61 toward territory I recognized.

We played games and sang songs until sleep reclaimed the girls. Then there was only silence and darkness and the far-off sound of thunder. And the thoughts that turned to fear as the hours passed.

I knew the DeLandes. And I knew Montgomery. I knew he'd never forgive what I'd just done. He might have wanted the woman of ice and fire who accused him of adultery and broke up furniture—the woman I'd never been before. But he'd never forgive the woman who deceived him. Who hit him with a brick and left him to walk his way out of a backcountry house in the middle of godforsaken nowhere.

I couldn't stop watching for headlights in the rearview. I couldn't stop thinking about Eve Tramonte. And Ammie. And bloody clothes piled in my bath. Why had I never done anything about Ammie? . . . Why had I just let her die? . . .

We made Baton Rouge close to four A.M., and took a room in a Holiday Inn. I gave the innkeeper cash up front, enough to hold the room until four P.M.

I was desperately tired, worn-out from days of no sleep, inadequate rest, and unending pain. I had pulled my shoulder and strained my broken ribs breaking furniture and moving Montgomery's bed to break the phone jack. I locked the room door, chained it, dumped all the kids onto one bed, and fell into the other one myself, instantly asleep.

I slept through breakfast and lunch, the "Barney" show, "The Flintstones," "Super Mario Brothers," and "Oprah." I slept so hard, I didn't even roll over, waking up late, bleary-eyed and stiff.

The hotel tub wasn't deep enough to ease my aches and pains, but I felt better just sitting in the hot water. I knew better than to get the water too hot. Hot tubs were harmful to unborn babies, and I had been careful so far to keep the temperature of my baths at a reasonable level. Not today. There wasn't enough water to satisfy me, so I made up for the lack with extra heat. And it was wonderful.

We made New Orleans just after six P.M. Four days after the hurricane. For once the Crescent City didn't welcome me. Rather, I felt eyes on me at every corner and a danger more cloying than the heat.

After a stop at Avis, a stop at the bank to pay back Shalene her principal and interest, I stopped at a gun store to replace my clip and ammunition. I drove around the French Quarter as the sun set, the 9mm on the floor beside my seat, Morgan strapped in with his pillows. The makeshift baby seat was probably more comfortable than his car seat. The girls, however, became restless and cranky with the driving, demanding supper.

Several stops later, I pulled up at a pay phone and studied the streets. There were the usual homeless men, smelling of wine and marijuana, sleeping in doorways, knees curled to their chests. The usual revelers, still standing, still carousing, and also smelling of beer and liquor. I put my finger on the safety of the 9mm and tucked it up under my T-shirt as I got out of the Rover. New Orleans isn't the safest place in the world to be at dark, and the French Quarter even less so for an unescorted woman and three children.

I inserted a quarter and dialed the number from memory. Adrian Paul answered on the third ring. I could hear voices and the clink of china and silver in the background. Soft classical music. A party?

"Adrian Paul? It's Collie."

"Good God, girl." The background sounds diminished, as if he had cupped his hand over the phone. "I've . . . We've all been worried sick. Where are you?"

"Where are you?" I countered. It didn't sound like a home, somehow, the ambience of the background noise. It sounded big and open and spacious. Hollow.

"At a company party. I had my calls forwarded here. Sonja and Philippe are here as well."

"I'm in trouble." It surged over me then. A wave of fear. An awful paralyzing fear. What would Montgomery do? Tears coursed down my face, a torrent, and I turned so the girls couldn't see from their place inside the truck. I couldn't breathe. "Oh God. I hurt Montgomery."

There was a short silence. "Where are you?" He was concerned. I could picture his face, calm eyes narrowed with worry.

"I need . . . I need you to leave." My breath heaved. "Leave the party."

"Of course."

"I need you to drive to the place where Shalene adopted JP."

"You mean—"

"No!" I shouted. "No places. No names. I'm scared, damn it. No names."

"Collie—"

"Drive to that place and stand by the pay phone. Make sure you're not followed. Hear me? Make sure." I sounded hysterical, loud and panicked.

A couple passed by at a distance, avoiding the crazy lady and her weeping one-sided quarrel. A man, alone, stopped. Listening. Watching. I lowered my voice but kept my eyes on him, my hand on the gun butt beneath my shirt. He drank from a bottle in a brown paper bag.

"And tell Sonja to leave at the same time. You remember the place where the k'doon lady was?" I asked, using Shalene's own personal code.

"Yes." His voice had changed, lowered, deepened. It sounded clipped and stiff.

"There's a phone a block or so away. One of those short ones you can just drive right up to. Tell her to wait. She won't have to get out of the car. Tell her I'll call." I stopped, took a deep breath that hurt my ribs, and tried to slow down my words.

"Oh God. I need to make a deposition. Under videotape. With a doctor present. Can you set it up? For tonight? For now?"

"Yes."

"But no phone calls from a line a DeLande could trace or tape, like the one we're on now. Pay phones only."

"When do you want me at . . . ah, the place you named?"

"How soon can you get there?"

"Ten minutes. Maybe five."

I paused. That meant he was here, nearby, in the Quarter. "Make sure you're not followed. I think I've said too much already."

"I will."

"Is . . ." I sniffed and wiped my nose. "Is JP okay?" I asked in a small voice.

"He's fine." A smile coated his voice. "The eye of the storm passed over the house not long after you left. Philippe came and got him. He 'bout choked your cat to death, though." He paused. "We've been worried, Collie."

Some of the weight eased off my shoulders, but its absence left me with an intense pain between my ribs. Pain and pressure and burning heat. "Yeah. Well. I'll call you in ten minutes. Make sure—"

"That I'm not followed. I know."

The phone clicked down, my shaking hands barely finding the phone carriage in the dark. I climbed back into the Land-Rover, locked the doors, double-checked the safety on the gun, and put it on the floor. Leaning forward, I rested my arms across the steering wheel, my head on my arms, breathing deeply. The girls were arguing in the backseat.

"Girls, if you get real quiet, I'll try to see that you get to see JP tonight." They quieted instantly. "You might even get to stay the night with him. But be quiet. Okay? Read a book to each other."

"It's too dark to read, Mama," Shalene said, pointing out the obvious, a little irritation in her voice.

"There's probably a small light just to the right, over your head," I said, without lifting my head. "Flip the little switch."

The courtesy light illuminated the cab a bit. I rose up, started the Rover, and drove away. The drunk with his bottle was nowhere to be seen.

I found another pay phone on St. Louis, better-lighted than the last one, just outside a tavern filled with high-class drunks. I called the pay phone in Van's, the restaurant where Shalene had adopted JP. Adrian Paul picked up instantly.

"Collie?" He sounded out of breath.

"Were you followed?"

"Not unless someone saw me slip out the back door of Petunias, run through the courtyard and out the front door of . . . Oh, it doesn't matter." He paused and puffed. "It doesn't matter. I pulled off the jacket to my tux and left it with Sonja. Rolled up my sleeves. I looked like a waiter running to work." He laughed, that wonderful, deep, secure laugh that made me hire him as my attorney in the first place.

"Do you see an Avis rental car? Look around. I told them

to circle the block till they were flagged down in front of Van's. The driver is supposed to have his driver's-side window down. His arm hanging out and a handkerchief in his hand. It's a tan four-door—"

"I see it," he interrupted.

"Flag it down."

"He sees me," Adrian Paul said after a moment.

I felt weak suddenly, and clutched the heavy wrought-iron casing holding the street-side phone, the metal still warm from the day's sun. Perhaps the children would be all right now. Perhaps they would be safe.

"Get in. The Avis man will get out. Drive to the Trade Center and wait for us there. We'll meet you."

"Okay. About the deposition. Philippe went to a pay phone on Bourbon, around the corner from Petunias. He's handling the details."

"Fine." I hung up the phone and again drove the Rover, circling around the French Quarter, moving in the general direction of the Trade Center, to the next pay phone. I had the route all mapped out, using one of those maps the city sells to the tourists that shows all the one-way streets, public parking, and landmarks. I had marked each pay phone with a tiny star, and numbers to the pay phones were jotted on the margins.

At the next pay phone, I called Sonja, who should have been there by now. She answered before I even heard it ring. "Where the hell are you? Are you all right?"

I laughed, the sound more sob than chuckle. I'd always been that way, even as a child. Relatively steady throughout a crisis, then falling to pieces when the trauma was over or when an adult appeared on the scene to take over. The day Sonja was bitten by the snakes, I had cried all the way to Daddy's clinic while Sonja lay gasping in the oily sludge of Old Man Frieu's leaky johnboat. She hadn't been out of danger, but someone else was in charge and Sonja was going to survive.

And it looked suddenly like I might survive long enough to get my children to safety. "I'm fine. Sort of."

"What the hell does that mean?"

I could hear a truck go by on Sonja's end. It badly needed a muffler. "I'll let you see me tonight and you can judge for yourself, if we can work everything out. Have there been people watching the house?"

"Yeah. Two cars around the clock, parked at either end of the block. Philippe says there's another one on the street behind us, so we can't sneak out the back way and take a cab. They folla' us everywhere we go, the slimy li'l turds." She was talking very fast, her words taking on a stronger Cajun accent as she spoke, sounding more like the Sonja I had grown up with.

"Were you followed when you left Petunias?"

"They tried," she said, sounding a bit smug. "But Philippe paid a couple of homeless men to block the street as I drove off. I'm not sure, but I think one of the men, ah, relieved himself on the hood of the car that pulled out after me. The other one was hanging into the passenger window yellin' for the guys inside to take pity and give a poor man money for a meal. I hope neither one got shot."

There was a sharp silence following her words. The kind of silence that only people who are closer than family can bear. The kind of silence that makes strangers uncomfortable and yet seems satisfying to friends. Sonja had once called me her soul mate.

I took a deep breath. "I hurt Montgomery." She said nothing, but I could almost feel her listening. Feel her waiting for me to continue. "I hit him over the head with a brick from a toilet tank." She laughed, a short sputtering sound, disbelieving. "Twice." She laughed again, but this time the sound was cold and hard. "I knocked him cold. And I chained him to a bed with handcuffs and then I ripped out the phone lines and left him."

For a moment she said nothing. "Serves the bastard

right." She almost growled the words, a snarl, then instantly her voice changed. "When?" It was Sonja the lawyer talking now, but I wondered at the growl. The intensity of it. The harshness of it. The near violence.

"Twenty-four hours ago, more or less."

"His thugs showed up this morning, 'bout nine."

"So either Montgomery got loose and got away, or he . . . died . . . and a DeLande found him."

Again Sonja said nothing, but I got the impression that she was hoping he had died. It was strange, the things one could perceive out of another's silence.

"Sonja. Why do you hate Montgomery so much?" I asked softly. And I heard her intake of breath. "He said something to me. About . . . about your pretty thighs. He asked me what you had told me about him. Like you knew something I didn't."

The silence was different now. Thicker and denser, the kind of silence one experiences when a low-lying fog, heavy and white, envelops you, cutting you off from the rest of the world.

"I'll tell you later." Her voice was low. Dead-sounding.

"Tonight, Wolfie. Tonight."

"Where do I meet you?" I had the feeling that she was changing the subject, even though she didn't refuse my request.

"Get on I 10, heading to Slidell. Once you're sure you aren't followed, take an exit and get back on, heading toward Baton Rouge. I'll be at the airport. You remember where that friend of yours went into labor?"

"You mean that gift shop where Leza's water broke all over that forty-thousand-dollar Oriental rug? I remember."

"Meet me there." The area I described to Sonja had exits to all parts of the airport. "I'll be taking you to the hotel I'm staying in tonight." I smiled slightly. "And, Sonja, you'd best take off all that glitter you're probably wearing. The neighborhood won't be to your liking."

"A dump?"

"Very."

"I'll change in the car."

"Be careful, Wolfie."

I could feel her smile. "You too."

It was a short drive to the Trade Center. I spotted Adrian Paul immediately. He was parked beneath a streetlamp, the handkerchief tied to the top of the radio antenna, as a signal, I suppose. As the Avis was the only car around, the gesture wasn't really necessary.

I pulled up slowly, my window down, meeting his eyes. A silence stretched quietly between us as he searched my battered face. It wasn't the same kind of silence I had shared with Sonja, a speaking, giving silence of old friends. But it was remarkably easy and peaceful. I was desperately glad to see someone familiar.

Without asking his permission, I transferred the children to the Avis, putting Morgan into the child seat I had requested. Adrian Paul just stood, watching. Not helping. At first because he didn't understand what I was doing, or why. And then because he did. He watched silently, as if he could see each pain I was experiencing at that moment. The ribs, the shoulder, both aching as I bent and lifted. The bruised face. The less apparent but even more real pain of putting my children into his car. The symbolism of the final farewell.

I kissed each child, promised them that Adrian Paul would take care of them for a few days, and shut the door. I hefted the half-empty suitcase and set it on the ground at the trunk. Adrian Paul unlocked the trunk and put the suitcase inside. My own things were on the floor of the Land-Rover beside the gun, in two grocery bags.

Had I thought of everything? If not, I likely wouldn't know it until it was too late.

"The car is a rental," I said needlessly, fighting back tears. "I paid for it with my credit card. That means Montgomery can trace the transaction. But it should be good for a few hours yet. Will you take them . . . home with you . . .

tonight? And then see that Sonja takes them somewhere that Montgomery can't get them? You and she might have to . . . take over my affairs for me. That is, if I'm not back in a couple of weeks." He said nothing, his dark eyes intense on my face. "That power of attorney you recommended needs to be signed. I want you and Sonja to handle things for me if . . . if I don't come back."

I could see the tension in his shoulders, his face, in his entire body. I could see the emotions changing, evolving, glittering in his dark eyes. Yet, for a long moment, he didn't move at all. He didn't speak. I could smell the Mississippi, dank and damp. The slight scent of cigar smoke and whiskey that clung to him. Finally he moved closer. I backed away, resting against the warm hood of the Rover, crossed my arms, cradling the injured one.

Adrian Paul placed his right hand on the roof of the Rover, close by my face, and gently, with his left, touched the swollen place on my lip. The bruised hollows beneath my eyes. Still he said nothing.

"I was wrong. A DeLande does beat a woman. Very efficiently, I might add." I tried to smile.

"Have you seen a doctor?"

"No. And I don't need one, except for the videotape. If this was as bad as it looks, I'd be dead by now. So there's no internal bleeding. I just need time to get better. But I want it all in the deposition. Videotaped. So all the bruises show."

"And then?" But I could see that he already suspected.

"And then I'm going to Montgomery."

"You don't have to do this." His breath exploded. "There are—"

"Yeah. Legal ways. Or I could run." I leaned closer to him. So close that I could see the fine lines in his face, smell beneath the cigar and whiskey the rich, earthy scent of him, strong after his run through the French Quarter. So close he couldn't miss my words or misunderstand my meaning.

"I have never run from anything. Or anyone. Not even Montgomery. And I have no intention of starting now. I've thought it all through. I thought it through while he beat me. I thought it through while he bathed me. Fed me. And then beat me again. I thought it through when he used me. It's called rape, you know."

He closed his eyes, his hand sliding around my head to my nape.

"It's slow and methodical and painful. Just like the beatings were. And you have a lot of time to think while you're experiencing it, that is, if you don't just shut down your mind entirely and simply exist, simply survive, close it all out till it's finally over."

He wiped the tear away from my face. I hadn't realized that I was crying.

"And I understood, when all my thinking was done, that I had to face him. With the truth. The truth about what he did to the girls. To me. We have to settle this, my husband and I. We have to bring it all out in the open. Face it. Look at it. And I know that I might not survive that kind of confrontation." Strangely casual, those last words. Not like life and death.

I looked into Adrian Paul's eyes. Black and glittering in the cold white light of the streetlamp. So close we might have kissed. Yet the tension between us held nothing of the sexual. Not as I understood the term.

"You should have your attorney with you." He smiled, and again touched my split lip. "Or your counselor. Or an army."

I shook my head. "I'm not going to do anything stupid. I want to live. I'm going to try to find a way to make Montgomery let me leave him."

After a moment he said, "You'll need these." He turned away, opening the Avis door and handing me a folder he took off the floor. It looked familiar, parts of it, as I thumbed through the pages.

"The part at the front is a transcription of a conversation Ann Nezio-Angerstein had with a woman who claimed to be a DeLande. Montgomery's sister. She checked out when I verified the information she gave. Ann brought it to you the day Max died. You left it on the floor in Sonja's den, where you slept all day. Did you ever read it?"

I shook my head. "No."

"I suggest that you do. And the rest of it as well. I suggest that you read every word before you talk to Montgomery."

"All right." I tossed the folder through the open window of the Land-Rover onto the front seat. I gave him the name of my hotel, the place where I was staying that night. The room number. He lifted his brows when I told him how to get there. It really was a bad neighborhood. "If you want to be there for the deposition——"

"I'll be there."

"I want the children safe."

"I called the security company—from a pay phone," he said before I could interrupt, "and requested the two guards be sent to my house tonight. We'll keep all the children together, somewhere safe and under guard, until we get this thing settled."

I nodded.

"I'll be there in an hour or so. Is there some kind of special knock when I get there so you'll know it's me? You know, like a signal." He tapped out "two bits" on the hood of the Rover, grinning, trying to make me smile back. "I don't want to get shot through the door."

I tried for a smile. Failed. "Sure. Why not?"

We left it like that. Too much unsaid. Too much left hanging. He'd be at the hotel; I knew he'd try to dissuade me again. But I was glad he'd be there.

I met Sonja in the airport, scarcely recognizing her in the old loose jeans and the oversize man's dress shirt, heavily starched and rolled up to the elbows. Her hair was up under a Mets baseball cap, tiny finger curls dangling below it as if she had worn her hair up to the party and simply hidden an elegant coiffure beneath the cap. She looked like a teenager. And the expression on her face when she saw me, all bruised and raccoon-eyed, proved she could hardly recognize me as well.

"Good-God-Mother-Mary-full-of-grace-what-in-hell-happened-to-you?" she said, the syllables running together like a long single word, no space between.

I shrugged. "Montgomery." It seemed explanation enough. "Come on."

I led her back through the terminal, down another, then back up again in case she had picked up a tail. Last, I led her to the Land-Rover. Only when we were safe behind the locked car doors did I speak again. Only when I had checked the 9mm—which I had left behind, fearing to take it inside—and placed it on my lap could I find any words.

We hugged. We laughed a bit. I drove. A circular route back to the sleazy old hotel, careful to lose any tail Sonja might have unwittingly led to the airport.

I talked as I drove, telling her everything. Everything Montgomery had done. Everything he had said. Everything I had said and done, including the breaking of the furniture and the demolishing of the house. She was impressed. Said it sounded more like her than me, and I guess she was right. I told her everything I had led Montgomery to believe . . . and the way I had left him.

She asked precise questions occasionally, clarifying points here and there. I suppose I was rehearsing for the deposition. I suppose she was nosy. But it helped.

I talked for an hour as we waited. Waited for Adrian Paul to get my children to safety. Waited for him to tell Philippe —safely—the location of my hotel. Waited for them all to arrive. Finally I was all talked out. So we sat silently, the TV lighting the room with a snowy no-picture. Fuzzy black-and-white images of Gene Kelly danced into an even more snowy background.

I waited for her to talk then. To tell me what Montgomery had done to her to make her hate him so. To explain the secret that she and Montgomery shared that made her so bitter against him. The secret from which I had always been excluded. But not one word would Sonja say about the reason for her animosity against Montgomery. And before I could talk her into it, the first of our visitors arrived.

Crowded into the tiny room, sitting or lounging on the worn-out bed, or tilted back in one of the aluminum-pipe chairs that flanked a chipped Formica table, was my legal support group. Philippe, still proper and upright, a bit stuffy perhaps, but elegant in his tux, and Sonja, looking like a lost waif in dressed-down play clothes. A doctor, smelling of Scotch, but appearing sober. A stenographer, looking bewildered, her hair sticking out on one side as if she had been dragged from bed, her head on a pillow, and mysteriously transferred here without her comb or her lipstick. Her machine was opened out on the Formica table; it was a small portable computer with printer. Compact and modern. Ann Nezio-Angerstein stood to one side with a video camera.

Adrian Paul was the last to arrive, rapping out a complicated series of rhythms on the door to gain admittance. I smiled at him when he stuck his head in the door, appreciating the easy way he brought a bit of lightness to the moment. He smiled back.

And then the deposition began. I told my story, speaking slowly so the stenographer would be able to keep up as she copied down each word and the videotape captured each image, each bruise. I told everything again, showed everything. Every bruise, every bite, every faint cut. Every broken bone.

The doctor checked me out, listening to my heart, taking my blood pressure, my pulse, probing and pushing on the cracked ribs, warning me about pleurisy, and infection, and possible future arthritis. I listened with half an ear, and pulled my shirt back closed as soon as he was done. I didn't like having been exposed in this room full of people. But it was necessary. These were my witnesses.

The stenographer spell-checked her work, printed off the copies, and witnessed the deposition. She was a notary public as well, it seemed. One of those multitalented, multiskilled office workers whom lawyers seem to snatch up.

Only when I drove away did I suddenly recognize her in my memory. Bonnie. Dressed down, drab and tacky to fit the decor of my rented room. The clothes really do make the woman, it seemed.

They expected me to spend the night in the hotel. After all, why would I lie? But instead, I drove away in the Land-Rover just after the last of them left.

I felt a bit like a mother bird, startled on her nest in the grass. Flying away to draw the aim of a hunter. Anything to protect her young. And I still did not know why Sonja hated Montgomery. She never told me what he had done, even though I asked her about it again, this time right in front of Philippe. Even though he urged her to tell. She had, in fact, crossed her arms across her chest and stuck out her lower lip, so like a teenager that Philippe and I both laughed.

But on the driver's seat of the Land-Rover, when I got inside, was a letter, sealed in a faded envelope. It was addressed to me, using my maiden name, and childhood mailing address at mama's in Moisson. All in Sonja's old, bold cursive. The stamp in the upper right-hand corner was old as well, the amount too small to cover today's postage. Ominous that, the old letter, never mailed. Like old secrets, hurtful and dirty and sad.

I was in Moisson before I found the courage to open the envelope and read the letter. It was dated two weeks before my marriage.

CHAPTER

12

Dear Collie,

I guess you've been wondering why I've been so different, so quiet, lately. I didn't mean to be. I tried to stay the same, for your sake and for the sake of our friendship. But if you're going to marry Montgomery, really marry him and live with him and have babies by him, then you need to know. Even if you don't believe me. Even if you tell Montgomery or ask him about what I'm writing and he denies it or says it was all my fault. Philippe says I have to tell you.

She had underlined the words *really, babies,* and *have,* with a different-colored pen. The letter was written in purple ink on lavender paper, but the underlines were black.

I never thanked you for Philippe, by the way. If it hadn't been for you and your mother and all those trips to New Orleans when we were growing up, I'd have never met him. Do you remember the day we met?

Sonja was avoiding the issue. Or was she?

I had come to New Orleans late that year, the year we turned eighteen. I rode down on the Greyhound bus, joining you at the Ponchartrain on St. Charles Avenue, as usual. And the Rousseaus were at a party in the old banquet room. We went in together, you and I and your mama, and literally ran into Philippe.

I remembered. Sonja had been strange for days, worried about something. Working it out in her mind. Only the night before, she had told me about the LeBleu heritage. The "tainted" blood and *plaçage*. But Philippe changed all that—the silence and the strangeness and the preoccupation.

She was engaged to Philippe before the end of the week. Engaged to a man five years older than she and still in law school. Tulane. A man who shared her history of so-called tainted blood, but had lots of money and lots of prestige and a place in society. Because even in New Orleans, if you have enough money and political power, your bloodlines don't count. Or at least not as much.

Well, anyway, you know what happened after that and how things were so wonderful and all.

Sonja had moved in with Philippe's mother, who had taken Sonja under her wing, so to speak, and seen to it that she was properly chaperoned for the six weeks it took to prepare for and execute the wedding.

Sonja's own family hadn't participated in the wedding. Hadn't even shown up. But then, they had planned on her to move to New York and marry well, putting aside the stigma of her past heritage. Everyone in Moisson knew that.

But I never told you why I came late to New Orleans that year. You know my family had always planned big

*things for me. New York and all. At least that's what
they had told me. But the week before my eighteenth
birthday, they told me the truth. It wasn't what we had
thought all those years. It wasn't what they had said.*

*And this is the hard part, Collie. The part that
Philippe says I have to tell you, but I don't know how.
So I'll just blurt it all out like I always do and hope you
believe me.*

*My father had signed a contract with Montgomery.
You remember the day that Montgomery came to
Moisson, driving that old car and stopping to ask for
directions? Well, he liked what he saw that day and
decided to stay. What I'm trying to say is, Montgomery
liked me.*

That black underlining again. Montgomery liked *me.*
Liked Sonja. My heart rate sped up a bit.

*He signed a contract with my daddy for my virginity.
For a fucking fortune, if you'll pardon my obscene pun.*

My heart stopped. Slowly I crumpled the letter. Set it
aside. I couldn't read any more. Not right now. Not this.

I was sore in every muscle, sitting on the side of the
whirlpool tub. My own whirlpool tub in my own house in
Moisson. The tub was nearly full now. Bubbles scarcely a
half inch thick on top of the water. I turned off the spigots,
reached for my wineglass, and sipped. Stripped. Climbed in.
Flipped on the jets.

Water and suds bubbled and churned around me. Drawing out the tension and the soreness and the pain. The wine
eased the burning and soreness in my chest. I sat for an hour
as the water pampered me, washing with the single bar of
soap I had found in the shower stall. I didn't think once
about Sonja and her damned letter.

It was oatmeal soap, handmade by a Frenchwoman in the

southwestern part of the state. It took her months to make it, her process leaving the soap so clean and pure that I could have washed my hair with it. And had. I had used it on my face and body always.

This was my last bar; I had left it in the shower when I moved from Moisson. I would need to place another order soon.

I shaved my legs and scrubbed my heels with a pumice stone and softened my cuticles and washed my hair. I got myself really clean. That Freudian stuff again.

But finally I couldn't sit there anymore, ignoring the letter. Blocking out the refrain that skittered into my mind every so often as I soaked.

He signed a contract with my daddy for my virginity.

So I got out, dried off, and went to the kitchen, taking with me the letter, the wine, my 9mm, and a robe. Padding barefoot through the empty and silent house. I opened out a TV tray, fixed myself a small snack from the supplies I had picked up in New Orleans, and then unfolded the crumpled letter. The paper was stiff and crinkly, sounding like Rice Krispies cereal in milk as I smoothed it out. My eyes fell on the line where I had stopped.

> *Four days before you left for New Orleans that year, my daddy called. Remember?*

I remembered. And ground my teeth.

> *He said I was sick and couldn't come that year. That I had the flu. Montgomery was there, listening. So was I. And then Daddy gave me to Montgomery.*
>
> *I won't tell you about that night, you hear? Not ever. So don't ask. I told Philippe. I won't ever speak of it again. I can't. Montgomery kept me till my eighteenth birthday. Four days.*
>
> *The day after I turned eighteen, he offered me a*

contract. The DeLande version of plaçage. *I'd have been rich in ten years. Real rich. And free from the contract. Ten years of an arrangement with your husband, while you were living with him. You were already engaged, remember.*

I did. Too well. And I remembered blabbering about it to Sonja for hours on end on that trip, when she finally joined us. No wonder she hadn't told me.

I got away from Montgomery, walked to the bank and got my savings, and then walked to the bus stop. And met Philippe.

It wasn't all my fault, Collie. And I'm sorry. I hope we can still be friends. And I hope you won't marry Montgomery.

Love always,
Wolfie

She had never mailed the letter.

I slept that night in my old bed in the house I had once lived in with Montgomery. A good life. Full and satisfying and complete. A lie.

The mattress felt good against my back, the expensive bed and silk sheets. Clean and smooth and unwrinkled. I think that's why I could sleep there. Someone—Rosalita most likely—had put on fresh sheets. No one had slept on them. Montgomery hadn't slept on them.

I had arrived in town after dusk and found the house much as I had left it. Or almost so. The yard was mowed. The garden untidy. The mailbox was so full, it was overflowing. No bills. Those went to the office to be dealt with by LadyLia. But magazines and catalogs and letters and junk. Most of it went into the garbage.

There had been a notice from Moisson Public Utilities wired to the front door handle with a long yellow bread tie.

The power would be cut off in two days. Nonpayment. Montgomery must have told LadyLia not to pay it. Strange.

An oversight? Or Montgomery proving a point? I had two days to enjoy the artificially cool air, hot baths, and hot food. I had no intention of paying the bill. But I did go ahead and fill the five-gallon containers with water. Our hurricane supplies. My first morning back, I got out the Coleman stove and the propane tanks and canteens and candles and then everything in the freezer.

Everything moldering in the fridge, I threw out. No point in having to smell the stench of rotting meat and veggies. There wasn't much left in the freezer anyway. Gumbo vegetables. Catfish. A ham bone for soup come fall. A pound of calf's liver, which I ate for the iron. I didn't have my pregnancy vitamins. Had left them behind in the hurricane.

There was nothing fresh in the house. Rosalita again. Perhaps cleaning out the kitchen on her last day. It had been weeks ago, I could tell. Dust hung over everything, fairly thick. I wondered if Montgomery had fired her.

The furniture had been moved around some. The gun cabinet put in the master bedroom. All the furniture was in there. Even the girls' old bed. Weird. As if Montgomery had lived in there surrounded by the few tangibles I had left him.

I checked the guns. Made sure that my shotguns were loaded. The house had been empty awhile. I didn't want to be startled in the night by a thief who had been watching the place. Or by Montgomery's hired thugs intent on harming me. Boss's orders, you know.

I checked the hunting rifle. There was plenty of ammunition. I could feed myself at least, even if I had to hunt.

There were a few fresh things in the garden, but not much. I wouldn't starve. I'd survive.

Until Montgomery came. Then what? I pushed the thought away.

That afternoon the power company truck pulled up in the yard and cut the power. I had just finished a long, leisurely bath, shaved my legs again, painted my nails, all twenty of them. Washed my hair. Then, suddenly, no power. No water.

I'd somehow lost a day. I wondered if I had slept through an entire day when I first came here. Possible. But at least I was clean.

I ate leftovers, cold, and lived by candlelight. Went to bed early. There wasn't much else to do. Over the course of the next three days, I read all the papers left for me by Ann Nezio-Angerstein. (I had stopped calling her Ann Hyphen, even to myself.)

The papers were grisly, some of them. Ann had earned her money, every penny. I would gladly have seen her drawn and quartered for doing such a fine job.

I couldn't read much at a time. A couple pages, then out to the garden. A couple more, then out to the dock by the bayou, to sit awhile in the heat, watching lizards sun themselves and turtles sitting just under the surface, long necks extended above the water, looking like a small stump or twig. Spiders hung limply on the still air; those, I killed with the flat of my hoe. I hated spiders. Then I'd go back inside and read a bit more.

Soon it was no longer cool inside, the air-conditioned air burned away by the Louisiana sun. I opened the windows on the back of the house and stayed outdoors more.

I was getting fat. The strap of the holster for the 9mm was too snug across my belly. But I kept it with me all the time. Could I shoot a thug, if Montgomery sent them after me?

Don't think about it. Don't. Just wait. It'll come to me in its own time. It'll come.

I started back praying then, during the long, lonely days of heat and sun. Even saying my Rosary as I walked about the property. The peace that finally settled on me was a gentle one. Not very deep. Not very spiritual. But it sufficed. Even with all I learned reading my investigator's reports.

Montgomery had signed a financial agreement with my father when we became engaged. A flat fee for the engagement. A flat fee for the marriage. An annual stipend for as long as the marriage lasted. No wonder mama felt betrayed when I left Montgomery. The money was a small fortune.

I took a walk after reading that one, exercising a body I had ignored for months. Walking hard, not thinking much. Maybe grieving a bit for the mother I had never known. Then back to the back porch, my little covered patio, out of the sun, to read another report.

Ann had indeed uncovered a DeLande sister, one of the ones people whispered about. The talk had always been about the number of illegitimate pregnancies and money and how most of them seemed to take off as soon as they turned eighteen, if not sooner.

Ann called her Miss X, and interviewed her in the Old Absinthe House Bar in the Quarter. I read the first page of the interview with Miss X and stopped, set the page down, and closed my eyes. After a moment, I got up, pulled on my worn Keds, and went to the dock.

With me, I took the raw meaty ham bone. There had been enough ice in the freezer to last a few days in the cooler, so I could keep a few things uncooked. I tied the ham bone with twine and let it over the side of the dock.

It was just the kind of meal to attract crabs. While the bait attracted my dinner, I rinsed out my fishing net, softening the stiff strands, using the handle to clean out the spiders and webs nesting in the crab bucket.

Sitting on the rough boards of the dock, I waited. But when I closed my eyes, all I could see was the page I had read.

ANN: Tell me about life in the DeLande household while you were growing up. [Note: Subject chain-smokes and drinks straight Scotch. See attached bar bill.]

X: When I was twelve, my mother, the Grande Fucking Dame, gave me to my brother. It's a DeLande tradition, you know, in that household.

As soon as your first period comes, you are given as a present to one of the bitch's sons to play with and train. You get locked up in a room with him. You share his food, his bed, his sexual needs. And believe me, sexual needs come first with a DeLande.

Brother dear teaches you about your own body, how to give it pleasure. How to give pleasure back.

On my thirteenth birthday, I was taken off the pill. On my fifteenth birthday, I left home in the middle of the night, taking nothing with me but my money and my jewelry. I even left my son.

ANN: Who was the father of your son?

X: Montgomery. He was about twenty at the time.

The twine moved ever so slightly where it disappeared into the black surface of the water, sending faint ripples across the still water. Again. Crabs attacking the meaty bone. Either that or a small catfish or gar.

I pushed to my feet, took the one-handled net—the kind fishermen use to scoop up the catch—and the bucket to the edge of the dock. Very slowly I pulled the twine up through the water, dipping my net into the water beside the ham bone as it rose. The moment the bait touched the light, still some twelve inches below the surface, I captured it in the net and quickly hauled it to the surface. Three blue crabs, one of them a monster, clung to the bait, trapped in the net.

Greedy little creatures, were crabs. Even at the threat of their own lives, they wouldn't let go of supper.

Walking back to the house along the damp, narrow path, I heard the refrain over and over again as though I were sitting in the Absinthe House Bar, listening to Ann's interview. I could almost see Miss X smoking, blowing smoke out through her nose, drinking in the smoke with the Scotch, speaking out smoke with each word.

Who was the father of your son?
Montgomery. He was about twenty at the time.

I made gumbo that night, my first full day without power, cooking on the patio, on my little two-burner Coleman stove. First I boiled and shelled the crabs, using Montgomery's precious automotive tools to crack the hard shells and remove the meat. Saving all the meat, I tossed all the shells and inedible body parts over the fence. It would attract scavengers, but so what?

I made a roux with bacon fat and flour, a dark, thick roux, heavy and rich. Darker than my usual recipe. I added spices, vegetables, and let it simmer. On the other burner, I sautéed onions, garlic, and peppers until they were dark, added them to the roux, then boiled water and rice.

Real good gumbo has to cook awhile at low temperatures before the meat is added, so I left it simmering, the rice cooling, and made myself some instant tea. It was tepid and bitter, but anything wet was refreshing.

I already missed the showers and baths that I had lost when the power went out. The heat was oppressive, unrelieved by the breeze that blew along the bayou out back, and I was "pert' near rank," as Mama might have said, mocking the white trash that lived nearby. Sponge baths simply didn't do the trick in this heat.

Propping up my feet on the patio lounge, I went back to the interview, my lukewarm tea on the warm concrete beside me, gumbo fumes blowing across me. The interview with Miss X went on for two pages, giving me a perspective of the DeLandes I never had before.

It was like opening a window on an old abandoned house and peeking inside. The rot and decay and dampness everywhere, corruption like a malignancy so widespread that there was no cure. The brief look answered so many questions. And raised so many more. The most compelling . . . Why?

Why had the Grande Dame given her daughters to their brothers for "training in the sexual arts," as Miss X phrased it one time? Why did she want the children who came from the incestuous unions of her children? Even the ones who were not quite "right," like Miss X's son. He was mildly retarded and born with an extra nipple low down on his chest. The doctor who cared for him had insisted that a birth accident had caused the retardation. A few seconds too long without oxygen during his passage through the birth canal with the cord wrapped around his neck. But then, the doctor didn't know about the incest.

Miss X had refused to answer some of Ann's questions. Like where she lived, how she made a living, when was the last time she'd seen another DeLande. Important questions all. "And the subject has since disappeared, having moved from her last known address, forwarding address unknown."

In her summary, Ann stated, "I believe the subject to be mentally unstable, secretive, vindictive, vengeful, angry, and mildly psychotic. But I believe she was telling the truth as she understood it."

I put down the report, added the meat to the gumbo, stirring in the crab pieces with a long-handled spoon I found in the back of an otherwise empty kitchen drawer.

Montgomery had another child, this one by his own sister. How many others were hidden around the state? And how had I lived with the man for so many years without knowing him at all?

Who was this man I married, this man who knew a woman's body so well that he could make even torture bearable because of the pleasure to follow? Who was this man who had seduced and raped his own baby sister?

I tasted the gumbo. It was marvelous, hot and spicy. Ready for the filé. I took my new bottle of the bitter herb, measured off a portion in the palm of my hand, and tossed it into the gumbo, stirring instantly. After a moment, I tasted it, bubbling hot and sharp on the tongue, and added a pinch more filé. Capping the herb bottle and setting the pot lid in place over the gumbo, I went back to the reports.

Ann had somehow finagled an interview with Priscilla, Andreu's first wife, the woman who lived in a form of religious seclusion near Des Allemands. It had been a short discussion, no more than ten minutes, and Priscilla had refused to say very much about her reasons for leaving her husband. As Ann had not been allowed to tape the interview, the conversation was summarized in her report.

I was the reason for the breakup of her marriage.

> Subject claims each DeLande wife was married young and trained in sexual practices by her husband. Each wife was expected to make herself available to any brother who desired her sexually. The process was informally called "sharing," and was begun six weeks following the birth of her second child, if not before.
>
> When Nicole Dazincourt married Montgomery, he moved her into a private residence instead of the DeLande Estate house. So far as any DeLande wife knows, Montgomery has never forced her to adhere to the family tradition. Subject decided she did not have to follow the traditional methods if Nicole did not have to follow them. She refused Richard some time after the birth of Nicole's second child. Richard punished her, and then raped her. He did it in front of subject's husband, with his full consent.
>
> When she could, subject left. She was granted a divorce with no contest because she left her children to be raised by the Grande Dame. The children are now of age.

I put the report down, fighting a sudden feeling of nausea so strong that I barely made it to the edge of the patio. I lost my tea. The sick feeling didn't dissipate quickly, perhaps because I didn't have Sonja around to put cool towels on my neck and cluck over me. But eventually the smell of the gumbo cooking on the little stove brought me around. And when the spell passed, I ate my supper. Gumbo and gummy white rice and a glass of wine.

Using some of my precious water, I sponged off some of the day's sticky sweat and heat, and went to bed before the sun set. For several hours I slept long and hard on the silk sheets, in the almost cool house.

But by two or so in the morning, the heat had built up in the room; the air was stuffy and damp, reminding me of the little house near St. Genevieve. My prison. Rising, I opened more windows on the back of the house for ventilation. The breeze blew in cool, damp air and the smell of approaching rain. Smiling, I went back to my sweaty sheets. The sound of raindrops drowned out the sound of crickets and tree frogs. Again I slept.

In the morning I rearranged the furniture, exercising my damaged shoulder. I put the girls' old bed into the family room. I put out TV trays—two out on the patio, one in the family room, one by the front door, one by my bedside, the shotgun on the floor beside its legs. The card table and chairs went in the breakfast room, the single hurricane lamp I placed on the table by the front door, and I positioned candles about.

At night I could move around the house using only four candles. One in the bedroom, one in the family room, one in the kitchen, one to take outside when I needed to relieve myself.

I didn't bother to count the days that followed. The hair grew out on my legs and beneath my arms. The polish chipped away from all my nails, the nails themselves becoming ragged. I ran out of clothes, washing what I had several times and leaving them to dry on the patio furniture.

Once, a boat puttered up the bayou, the motor cut to silence as it neared my dock. For ten minutes I waited for an attack, breathless, wondering if it was thugs, or Montgomery, or simple common thieves. Then the motor roared to life again and puttered away. Half an hour passed before I found the courage to slip down the path to the bayou, my twenty-gauge to my shoulder.

On the dock was a cooler. Expecting snakes or something from a horror movie, I knocked off the cooler lid, the shotgun pointed inside. It was a slab of fresh alligator meat on ice. A skinning knife stuck up through the meat. Old Man Frieu's knife, the one Miles left him so many years ago, stuck through a stack of hundred-dollar bills. I had no idea how the old man knew I was here, but the alligator steaks made great eating grilled.

I ran out of canned and dried food almost entirely, and shot a rabbit one night for supper as it was feeding in my overgrown garden. I ate fish I caught off the dock, from the bayou's black water, crabs, a few crawfish I netted in the shallow bay. I dug around in the weeds for carrots, small summer squash, greens and snap beans, flicking off the competing bugs. I drank a single glass of wine every day.

I walked a lot. I went nowhere I could not walk, and I saw no one except for the mailman once a day, and one time, the boy who cut the grass. I watched him from a window as he gassed up his mower and sheared off the too tall blades of grass.

I wore the Glock 9mm everywhere, strapped to my expanding belly beneath my clothes. Taking it off only when I sponged off the stink of heat at the end of the day and when I slept.

The Land-Rover, I pulled into the garage with Montgomery's toys. Profaning sacred ground to put a modern vehicle into the sanctuary of classics, but anyone who drove by the narrow drive would be no wiser about my presence here.

And I read the damning reports. All of them. About the monster I married.

When I dreamed, it was nightmares, and running, and

being caught from behind by burning hands. I'd wake up, strangling back a cry. Or I'd be the snake, burning on the garbage can lid in the blistering heat, writhing and coiling and helpless.

As each hot, miserable day drifted into the next and my body began to heal, I finally let myself remember the days in the little house with Montgomery after the storm. Let myself remember the words he muttered as he drove, as he beat me, as he watched me with too bright eyes. Words I don't think he knew he muttered. Words I didn't understand at the time, which seemed only the empty digressions of his drunken and rambling mind.

"I should have listened," he had muttered. "Put you in the big house with her." Or at another time, ". . . trained you right. Should have. Should have . . . The girls too. Should have." Or, "Should have listened . . . Too much freedom. Should have listened." "Put the girls there soon. Have to. Put them with her." "She knows. She knows. Kill the bitch if I have to." "Won't share, though. Can't share. Kill her if I have to."

The mumbling had gone on, half-heard, for the first part of my punishment, when Montgomery was too drunk to hear himself. It was a separate and distinct line of speech from his constant "Tell me. Tell me the truth." And I hadn't understood.

Montgomery had been thinking that I would have to be killed. Montgomery was planning to give my children to the Grande Dame to raise. He would have killed me if I had fought him. But I had come around. In a glorious fashion. Breaking furniture, screaming, giving him the one reason he could accept for my leaving. Jealousy. Not wanting to share him with Glorianna.

There was no chance now that Montgomery would let me leave. I had lied to Adrian Paul when I told him my reasons for coming here. I knew there would be no divorce. No second chance. And I thought of the mother bird flying up beneath the feet of the hunter, drawing his aim away from her nest.

It took him a week to find me, I suppose, though I had lost track of time in the monotony of my daily life. I heard the car coming for two miles, long after dusk, as I was pouring water out from my nightly sponge bath, the stream hitting the ground at the end of the patio. I stopped, cutting off the splash of water in midstream. Set down the bowl. Stretched my healing shoulders, and dried my hands on the towel beside me. The movement pulled at the holster I had strapped back around my waist after my bath.

I looked back at the house, lit by candles, a soft glow at several windows. I entered, thinking not at all, and lit the hurricane lamp at the front door. Its warm glow was cheery and bright in the near empty front room.

I opened a bottle of wine, Montgomery's favorite, the best white, and poured it into two glasses, splashing the pale yellow liquid into crystal. One I kept. The other I placed on the small TV tray holding the hurricane lamp beside the front door. I leaned against the wall in the shadows of the front room and waited.

The classic car he drove was an Auburn. A new part of his collection or a loaner from one of his brothers. He parked in the front yard, executing a three-point turn so he faced out toward the drive. Cut the motor. Got out. Shut the door. Opened the trunk. He walked toward the front of the house.

Slowly he came through the front door, the lamp making a hollow of his face. He still hadn't shaved, but his beard was neatly trimmed and shaped and shining with sweat in the heat. He was well dressed, elegant and casual. The epitome of *GQ* style. His eyes were hard and cold, his mouth a thin line.

The door closed behind him. He took the wineglass in his hand and sipped, just as if it were the end of an ordinary day instead of the end of our life together. I wondered about the open trunk, the yawning mouth black in the night.

We sipped our hot wine and stared at each other across the room, Montgomery in his tasteful attire, me in the T-shirt I slept in, bare-legged and barefooted. Tree frogs were background music, a stirring cacophony. Unable to stand the silence a moment longer, I started talking.

I told him what our babies had said. I told him everything I had learned from the detective. Everything I pieced together from memory, evidence old and new. Every filthy thing he had ever done. From the time his mama had given him his twelve-year-old sister to *play with and teach,* to the awful things he had done to his babies. He just stood there, the lamp flickering over his hands as they twirled the wineglass by its stem.

Patiently he listened, as if he was giving me a chance to empty out all my words. He sipped once as I talked, his movements elegant and refined, his manner polished. Till I finished my little spiel with the only part I hadn't rehearsed in the days of solitude and heat. I told him I was divorcing him. That if he contested it, the truth would come out in court. All of the truth.

He smiled then, a stranger's smile in his bearded face. Slow and sensual and so very cold. "I have our children, you know," he said casually. "I have four men surrounding the house they are in. I've watched them play in the yard. I've watched them undress at night through the windows."

He sipped. A cold fire started in the pit of my stomach, spreading outward. I put the wine on the TV tray beside me, hit the wooden rim. Spilled the wine. The glass cracked and broke, shards shimmering in the rolling wine.

"They really are beautiful, those pretty little girls." He sipped, his lips molding to the glass, his throat moving in the lamplight. So sensuous. "I've promised Dessie to Richard, as soon as you are gone." Montgomery smiled. "He really likes blondes, you know."

Slowly he put down his wine, on the TV tray beside the lamp. Took a step. His smile grew hard. He smoothed the palm of one hand over the knuckles of the other. It was a caress of his own flesh, as cold as the blue glitter of his eyes.

"I'm sorry, Nicole. But the Grande Dame was right about you. You really must go." And he rushed me.

He seemed to move in slow motion. A dancer underwater. His face unchanging as he came at me. A frozen mask.

It's strange how calm I was. Peaceful almost. I didn't even have to think about it. My reflexes were lightning-fast.

I pulled the 9mm and fired. Twice.

The bullets hit him, one in the upper chest, too high to stop him, one in the face below his left cheek, the reports loud in the empty house, the echoes going on and on.

He didn't go down. Crashed into me like a demon. Spurting blood, but not slowed.

We struggled on the floor, his blood giving neither of us purchase on the slick wood. He hit. He bit. I clawed. Lost the gun. Pushed away from him. Ran to the bedroom.

It was dark in the back of the house. No candle lit yet. I rolled across the bed, fell to the floor. Fumbled frantically for the shotgun. Touched it in the blackness beside the bed, the metal cool in the incredible heat.

I lifted the twenty-gauge. Braced it against my shoulder. Fired it as he filled the doorway.

Still he didn't fall, but backpedaled into the main room. I followed, slipping in his blood. Moving from the darkness down the hallway toward the lamplight. Racked the second round into the chamber. Following Montgomery. He stumbled once. Again as he reached the front door.

Finally he slipped in his own blood and fell, bouncing against the floor, blood still spurting into the air, across the room. Then slowing, pooling under him.

I stood over Montgomery, the shotgun pointed at his face, his mask changing, softening. I watched the life drain out of him. And only when he was long dead and the weapon hung heavy in my arms did I step away.

* * *

I found the Auburn in the darkness of the front yard. The living silence of the bayou and swamp, the usual clicks and chirps and croaks and roars, were drowned in white noise, the ringing of my ears, damaged by the gun blast. I opened the front door, slid onto the seat, the leather cool against my blood-soaked skin. With shaking hands I searched the blackness of the front seat for the portable phone I knew would be there. Found the small leather-covered carrying case with shaking fingers.

In the dark of the front yard, sitting in the Auburn, blood drying on my skin, I called Adrian Paul in New Orleans. He answered on the third ring. The wonderful laugh. "Hello."

"The place where my babies are," I blurted. Then sucked a deep breath of air. "Montgomery says there are four men there, surroundin' the place." I was screaming suddenly. "Four men. They're goin' to take my babies. Adrian Paul, do you hear me? They're goin' to take my babies! Adrian Paul? Adrian Paul!"

He came back on the line, and I realized he had been speaking to someone on his end.

"Adrian P—"

"Collie."

"Adrian Paul, did you hear me?" I sobbed. "He's got four men. Four men. Four men. He's goin' to take my babies." I slipped from the seat to the ground beside the Auburn, sobbing, cradling the phone on my lap like my child. Crickets started chirping in the oleanders near where I sat. "He's goin' to take my babies," I cried. "He's goin' to take my babies." I rolled to the ground, my face pressed into the soil.

"Collie." He was shouting. Adrian Paul shouting? "Collie!"

I put the phone back to my ear. "Adrian?"

"The children are all here with me. You understand? Here with me. And the guards we hired have gathered them into the bathroom for safety and called the police on the other line. The children are safe. Dessie and Shalene and Morgan are safe. So is JP."

"You don't have to shout," I whispered. I was glad I was lying down. They taught us in nursing school that you couldn't pass out if you were lying down. I took a deep breath.

"I killed Montgomery."

CHAPTER

13

I couldn't force myself to go back inside. Couldn't force myself to get up off the ground beside the Auburn. I lay in the dark, the sounds of the night growing louder as my ears adjusted back to normal. The sounds of the gun blasts echoed in my memory again and again.

I killed my husband.
I killed my husband.
I killed my husband.

Mosquitoes buzzed around me, attracted by the smell of fresh blood and sweat. I pulled the loose, stretchy fabric around my curled-up knees for what protection it offered. It was a long shirt, just for sleeping, and covered my bare backside too. The mosquitoes bit through my T-shirt.

Impossible as it seemed, I think I must have slept, because it was no time at all before the yard was filled with headlights and exhaust fumes and flashing blue lights and angry voices.

Adrian Paul had said he would handle everything. So where was he? It would take him hours to get here from New

Orleans. The cops milled around and shouted. I could hear them from inside the house.

Terry Bertrand stood over me, silent, his police-issue weapon drawn and pointed at me in the darkness. The only sounds were the night's chorus of insects and cops' voices.

". . . blew the fuck outta him . . ."

". . . murder weapon?"

". . . twenty-gauge . . . been fired . . . one round . . ."

Terry left me alone at first. Pulling me to my feet only when a female officer arrived on the scene.

They asked me a thousand questions while the sheriff looked on silently. I didn't answer. I don't think I could answer.

I killed my husband.

But my babies were safe.

I was charged in connection with the death of my husband. First degree because he had been unarmed. Because I was wearing a weapon. Because it looked like I had invited my husband over, tried to seduce him, served him wine, and then blew him away. Seduce him. In my old T-shirt. With unshaven legs. In a house without air conditioning or running water. Right.

I was allowed to dress, handcuffed, and taken to jail. Fingerprinted, photographed, stripped and searched intimately, then allowed to dress once more.

At last I was left alone, placed in a tiny holding room for two hours because Moisson Parish doesn't have cells for female prisoners and because I had refused to talk to the police. I sat on the old, scarred plastic chair, rubbing my hands together, peeling the blood from my body. Smearing it where the blood and sweat couldn't dry on my oily skin. I really needed a shower.

I kept touching myself. Pulling my fingers through my blood-caked hair. Crying.

I was alive.

Montgomery was dead.

My babies were safe.

Finally Adrian Paul entered the room, met my eyes, and stopped, shocked. I guess I was really a mess. He was followed by Philippe and another Rousseau brother. Seeing them all three together, there was no doubt. This then was the famous Gabriel Alain Rousseau, the Rousseau Firm's criminal counsel. He didn't even introduce himself. He just started talking. I stared at Adrian Paul while Gabriel asked questions, his voice crisp and to the point. Adrian Paul stared back.

"Mrs. DeLande."

I flinched visibly.

"Have you talked to the police?"

I shook my head. "No." And tears started to fall again, dripping bloody splotches on the clean clothes I wore. The bloody T-shirt I had worn to kill Montgomery was now evidence. "I haven't said a word," I whispered, "since I talked to Adrian Paul."

"I understand you were injured after being kidnapped by your husband. By a beating delivered at his hands just over a week ago."

Adrian Paul was dressed in a soft, white cotton shirt, open at the neck, and dark slacks. His too long hair was ruffled. I nodded. *Only a week?*

"Are you in any pain?"

I laughed then, choking on the tears that ran down my face. The shaking started, hard, fierce quakes. So violent my teeth chattered. And the world grew dark at the edges, closing in till there was only a pinprick of light framing Adrian Paul's face. And then blackness.

When I woke up, Gabriel had taken control, using my pregnancy and the beating to get me special treatment. They couldn't keep me in jail with the men, so over the sheriff's objections, arrangements were made for a hotel and a twenty-four-hour guard until bail could be set.

I got my shower while a deputy sat outside my room. I was seen by a doctor, and given fresh clothes. I was allowed to sleep. Strangely enough, there were no dreams that first night.

Eventually Gabriel found a judge who let me live in New Orleans till the trial.

It was an arrangement that saved the parish money and headaches. It gave me time to heal away from the press and the stares and the whispers of Moisson. Time to see the counselor, Dr. Abear. Time to tell my children that I had killed their father. Time to get them counseling to deal with his death and the concept of me as his killer. Time to talk to Father Michael, my priest. Time to live quietly with my children and search for some kind of peace amid my exhaustion.

And so months went by, sliding past as calmly as the still black waters of the bayou.

Five months after I shot Montgomery to death, I had my baby in Mercy Hospital in New Orleans, Sonja by my side, cussin' and yellin' and tellin' me if I didn't damn well push again, she would damn well beat my butt, she didn't damn well care how damn tired I was. The sister helping with the delivery smothered a grin.

A week after the delivery, two checks arrived in the mail. One hundred thousand dollars for my new son, Jason Dazincourt DeLande. The same amount for me. Courtesy of the Grande Dame.

I had killed my husband, but it seemed the DeLande traditions continued no matter what, in the form of the birth money. I set up a trust fund for Jason, and used my own for my defense. The irony was lost on no one, I imagine. Not even on the Grande Dame.

The trial had been delayed. Then delayed again. Once by Gabriel, several times by the prosecution. There were valid reasons each time for the delay they requested, but Adrian Paul said they were really trying to keep me from appearing in court in an advanced stage of pregnancy, claiming I killed my husband to protect my children and in defense of my life. The sympathy factor of a defendant in maternity clothes was more than the prosecution could bear.

Although I no longer needed Adrian Paul as a divorce attorney, he was assisting Gabriel in the preparation of my defense. *Pro bono,* of course, thanks to Sonja and Shalene. We had become friends, this dark-eyed Rousseau man and I, though I realized he wanted more. He was patient. And friends were in short supply in the months before the trial.

Back in Moisson, the rumors flew and mutated and expanded, deformed by each small bit of truth released by "confidential police sources" to the press. I always thought the confidential source was Terry Bertrand, but there was no way to prove it. My family had deserted me, my church had condemned me, and my old high school chums, the ones from Our Lady, were cheering on the gossipmongers.

The local press crucified me. Labeled me a murderer, hinted at adultery and all manner of evil doings by me. The bigger papers, those based in New Orleans, Lafayette, and Baton Rouge, took a more liberal slant, backed by the calls of every women's group in the country. They got wind, somehow, of the deposition I gave when I got back from the little house near St. Genevieve. The women's groups began cries of spouse abuse, kidnapping, and domestic violence. Their concerns were tossed about on the front pages, mixed with details of my crime. To this day, I think it was Sonja who told them about the videotape, though she denied it.

But at home I was a murderer. And it was at home that I would be tried.

I stayed away from Moisson, living quietly with my four children in the minuscule cottage behind Sonja's. The wet late autumn and the wet early winter came and went. So did Christmas, with a deluge of gifts from Uncle Miles, as usual, although he didn't come for the holidays as he once had.

I did little in those months except sleep, read trashy novels, and talk to my defense attorneys. Time passed in a fog; I was disconnected from the reality around me. Disassociated from the outside world, my life was solely my children, the Rousseaus, and Snaps.

Sonja and I never talked about the night Montgomery died. We never talked about the letter she had written me. Never lanced the wounds of what Montgomery had done to her. Perhaps we never will. Even between the closest of friends there are always secrets, mysteries, hidden places to be avoided in conversation. But the reality of the letter and of my husband's murder didn't become an obstacle or barrier between us. We were closer than ever.

The week before the trial, Ann Nezio-Angerstein, who could probably retire in style with what I had paid her the last ten months, finally tracked down Miss X again. Miss X, the DeLande sister who claimed she had given birth to Montgomery's child when she was fifteen. She was discovered sleeping in a doorway in Saint Louis Cathedral in the French Quarter. She was drunk. So drunk she had to be hospitalized for detox before she could testify. So drunk the trial might be over before she was sober and in her right mind. Even if she got sober, there was no guarantee that she would be willing to speak out against her family.

Priscilla, however, had agreed to testify. And it would help, her testimony about the DeLande life-style, a life-style from which I was trying to protect my children when I killed Montgomery . . . according to my attorney of record. Her testimony would help, but we really needed Miss X, sober and willing.

So I made decisions about my children's future, giving them over to Sonja and Adrian Paul in the event that I was convicted. And why shouldn't I be convicted? I had, after all, killed my husband. And I killed him over and over again in my dreams, watching him fall, watching him fall, watching him fall and die, in the shadowy slow motion of memory and nightmare.

I spent my last days with my children, nursing my new son, reading to Morgan, who had decided to talk at last, sharing my honest concerns with Dessie and Shalene, who needed the truth from me as much as they needed reassurance. Besides, they deserved to know the options. Not that they worried. Shalene stood in the center of our small front room and gave strict orders to Adrian Paul to keep me out of jail. Gravely, his eyes searching me out in the shadows of the room, he agreed.

The trial was scheduled for the last week in February, the chilly, dreary part of year when nothing grows, nothing blooms, and the rains fall in a steady sheet from dark, oily skies. Time seemed suspended, hanging in still air.

I moved back into the house in Moisson for the trial, Sonja and the boys and I. The girls stayed in New Orleans, living with Uncle Philippe and attending school, coming to Moisson twice, when Gabriel thought their appearance might do me the most good. He felt that they would have a positive impact on the jury, sitting behind me demure and pretty in little white dresses, like first Communion dresses.

The first day of court, I rode with Adrian Paul and Gabriel to the courthouse, entering behind the building to avoid the press, out early to get a quote. The courthouse sat on a square, facing the common grounds which were circled by a road, enclosing a green garden and a bronze Confederate war hero on a horse. There were entrances to the square from the four corners, and public buildings between, including the police department, the county building, and the city building. They were all majestic, erected in the years just before the Civil War when Moisson was growing fast and money was plentiful and the future bright. Built with slave labor and slave sweat.

The entrances to the square were blocked off today, and would remain blocked for the duration of the trial. The square was for the press, the raucous women's groups marching to show support, and the curious.

I was dressed conservatively, in a floral print dress of muted shades and a light jacket, matching shoes. I looked ladylike and feminine, and totally vulnerable. Not like a woman who had killed her husband in cold blood, as the prosecution insisted. I was shaking, and couldn't eat, the gnawing pain of my ulcer flaring hot and sharp after the coffee I drank for breakfast. I thought the months of Maalox had healed me. What medication had healed, stress made sick again, I suppose.

I nearly passed out climbing the back stairs to the courthouse. Adrian Paul took my arm, his face close to mine. He smiled. I couldn't smile back.

The jury selection was slow and tedious, as nearly everyone in Moisson Parish knew either me or my family, or the DeLandes. And the few who had no connection to us had all read the papers, seen the news, and heard the gossip. Gabriel moved for a change of venue, claiming that I could not get a fair trial in Moisson Parish.

Judge Albares, a Frenchman with a Spanish name and a southern accent, as is common in the Basin, denied the move as expected, and jury selection continued. After two weeks, I had run out of new outfits to wear to court. Since the birth of my son, I was too large for most of my clothes, and would now have to start wearing the same garments over and over. Finally, however, I had a jury of twelve with two alternates. Seven men, five women, evenly divided among French, black, and Anglo. And the trial started.

I think I slept through the trial. Oh, not with my eyes closed and sweet dreams, but with glazed eyes and a fractured consciousness. Everything in the courtroom seemed filtered over, softened at the edges. Sometimes at the end of a day of police testimony about the bloody murder scene, complete with photographs and bloodstained exhibits, all I could remember was the sound of rain pelting the tall windows, or the sight of the DeLande Bench, as I silently called it.

They were all there, every day, the DeLande contingent. Andreu, the Eldest, gray at the temples, bright green eyes stern and forbidding. Richard, cold-eyed and staring. Marcus, blocking the aisle with his wheelchair. Miles Justin, elegant and serene in a three-piece suit, charcoal cowboy boots peeking out beneath. They surrounded their mother, the Grande Dame, coldly beautiful, with a faint smile on her lips as if she was amused by the proceedings.

Had she really seduced all her sons? I thought as I watched her. Her smile seemed to grow sensual and seductive beneath my gaze. *Had they in turn really seduced their sisters?*

The trial, by the end of the second day of testimony, wasn't going well. The most damning testimony came from the first officer at the scene, a rookie, who described the scene of my house in vivid detail, from the candles and lamp left burning, to the two glasses of wine, to the blood-soaked floors. His description of me as uncooperative and covered with blood didn't help.

The homicide investigator who followed his testimony didn't help either. He explained with great relish that I had kept a loaded gun beside my bed at all times, and one on my person. And that I shot Montgomery with both, "for sho' she did dat," his Cajun accent strong in the hollow room, echoing off the twenty-foot ceiling and plastered walls. He explained that I was wearing the holster for the 9mm when searched by the police. That I refused to answer any questions put to me.

That "she seem' calm and unemotional followin' the murder—"

"Objection."

"Sustained. Accused is to be considered innocent until proven guilty."

Yeah. Right.

And when the pathologist who performed the autopsy finished his report, even I could see the presumption of guilt settle on the faces of the jurors. I was guilty of planning and carrying out the cold-blooded murder of my husband.

Gabriel, however, seemed immune to the jurors' reactions, the hard faces and eyes they leveled at me the day the prosecution rolled up their case and sat down, satisfied that they had me cold. He merely smiled, confident in the lineup of witnesses he intended to put on the stand when it came time to present my defense. And I must admit, even I was stunned at the variety of people who were willing to take the stand for me. Or rather, against Montgomery.

First, with the judge's permission, Gabriel introduced Priscilla. I turned around and watched the DeLande Bench as her name was called. "Priscilla DeLande, for the defense."

Andreu was startled, turning in his seat to see the wife who had fled so long before. He hadn't seen her in years, I knew, and he feasted his eyes on her, devouring her as she walked up the aisle. His eyes filled with tears and need as she passed him without looking his way. *He still loved her.* The realization was a shock.

Marcus laughed outright, his eyes on the Eldest as if enjoying his elder brother's discomfort. Richard, however, was angry; his eyes scorched me where I sat, burning me up in a dark tide of fury. Of them all, he seemed to understand what I was going to do. Expose the DeLande secret. Show it to the world. The Grande Dame narrowed her eyes and lifted a brow at me. Her expression was unreadable.

Miles Justin, the family Peacemaker, the family rebel, smiled at me, his face faintly amused. Our eyes held a moment and then he lifted his hand, touched the brim of an imaginary hat. The cattle baron greeting the schoolmarm. *Ma'am,* his lips moved silently.

I almost laughed, bit my lips together instead, and turned my eyes to the front of the courtroom, watching as Priscilla was handed to the witness stand. She was dressed in a blue suit, sky blue on a sunny day, crepe with matching shoes and stockings and a tiny blue bag.

She was beautiful, this runaway wife. Eyes the same color as the suit, hair like clouds floating above, platinum, and all natural. Soft and luxurious, full, falling down over her shoulders. Skin like white satin, belying her forty years. She was petite, and shaking so badly, she looked as if she might fall from the witness chair.

The prosecution was totally unprepared for the testimony she brought. Speaking so softly she could scarcely be heard, she had to be prompted to speak up so the jury could hear her tale. She told her story.

She told how she married the debonair Eldest, the charming Andreu. Bore him two children. And then was, for all practical purposes, abandoned in the DeLande household. Ignored. Shunned by the husband who had professed to love her. Later, when her loneliness grew to almost unbearable heights, she was seduced by Marcus. And bore him a child.

Only then was the life-style explained to her. Only then was she told what was expected of a DeLande wife. The sexual freedom that became a sexual bondage.

Andreu came back to her for an entire year after she gave birth to Marcus's son. The reunion was wonderful, passionate, intense. Until it was Montgomery's turn. "I had a child by him as well. And I was then turned back over to Andreu."

I shook in my seat, hands clasped tightly on the table in front of me, knuckles white. Her eyes met mine and she smiled.

"And then Montgomery brought home his new wife."

"Is she in the courtroom today?"

Lift of platinum brows, twitch of lips, sudden relaxing of the petite frame. She almost laughed. "Yes. Nicole Dazincourt DeLande, the defendant. She turned my world upside down. We didn't even know she existed until Montgomery presented her. She hadn't been *approved,* you see. The rest of us had been presented as prospective brides, looked over by the Grande Dame before marriage. And we were married, each and every one of us, on the DeLande Estate, under the watchful eyes of the matriarch." Voice sarcastic. Lips no longer amused.

"We lived in the main house, all of us wives, under the

DeLande rules. But she, she lived in Moisson, in her own home with her own babies, and she didn't have to share the attentions of the brothers. She didn't have to know that her husband was sleeping with his brother's wife this month. She was the exception, while we slept with whoever wanted us.

"And when Richard demanded my . . . *attentions,* I refused. If she didn't have to live like that, why should I." It wasn't a question. It was defiance. "I hated Richard," she whispered, her eyes glued to Andreu's. "I hated him."

Every eye was intent on her face. Even the reporters who had been taking notes fast and furiously, eyes wide and half-focused with the story, paused, pens in the air.

"I learned then that a female doesn't say no. Not ever. Andreu took me to a private room in a private wing and locked me in. And drank brandy and watched while Richard 'punished' me . . . and raped me." Her voice was dry, a bare whisper in the silent room. Slight echo as the sibilant words bounced off the high ceiling.

Gabriel passed her a glass of water, watched her drink, smiled at her to continue. The prosecution interrupted the quiet moment.

"Your Honor. What does this all have to do with the issue at hand? It is a fascinating account, of course—if true—but it has no real relation to the case before the court."

"Your Honor. My client is trying to prove her contention the she was protecting herself and her children when she shot and killed her husband. She was trying to protect them all from an unnatural life-style and a life of perversion, and did indeed act from self-defense in the death of Montgomery DeLande."

"I'll allow it."

Gabriel turned back to Priscilla. "Go on, please."

"I got away. There are ways to leave the compound if you can find them. And I found a place to hide, a sanctuary. I live with the sisters in a . . . convent of sorts. I'd rather not say where, Your Honor. I value my privacy. But . . ." She opened her little blue bag and passed him a slip of paper. "Here's where I live now. I work in the nursery, taking care of babies until they're adopted."

Judge Albares nodded, handed back the note, and shook his head. "Let the record show that the witness lives in religious seclusion in the state of Louisiana."

"Thank you, Your Honor." She turned back to the jury, speaking quickly as if she wanted to get it all over with and go home to the safety and prayers and hymns of the nuns. "It took several years, but I managed to convince Andreu that I wanted a divorce, and he agreed and I am. Single."

"And your children," Gabriel said. "What about them?"

Priscilla's eyes suddenly flushed with tears. "They're still at the DeLande Estate, I suppose. I wish I could get them out. I don't want them raised like . . . like I know they have been raised. I shouldn't have left them. I should have taken them with me." Tears fell, and Priscilla turned again to the little blue bag, pulling out a tissue and wiping her eyes.

"What would you do differently now than you did then, when you left?" Gabriel asked, his leg swinging slowly. He was sitting on the edge of the defense table, bending forward slightly, his arms braced on his legs.

"Differently?" She sat up straighter in her chair. "What would I do differently. . . ." Emotions crossed her face, indistinct, shadowy. "I'd kill the son of a bitch I married," she said softly. Her eyes sought out Andreu's again. "I'd kill him just like Nicole did Montgomery and I'd take my children and I'd live somewhere else where they would be safe."

Her face twisted. "The law isn't big enough to protect anyone against the DeLandes. They have their own rules. Their own laws. Half the state's lawmakers and law enforcement officials were elected with DeLande influence and DeLande money. The law can't protect you from the DeLandes. You have to protect yourself. And I'd kill Andreu and run." She looked down at the tissue in her hand. "If I could do it all over, I'd kill him and take my chances in a courtroom. At least then my children would be safe."

The prosecution requested a recess to have time to consider the witness's testimony, and court was adjourned for the day. The jurors looked from Priscilla to me and back again as they were led from the courtroom, their faces uncertain, speculative. It was the first positive sign.

I think I began to wake up on that day. The long months of hollow emptiness, of barely controlled dread, of fear and trepidation and bad dreams, seemed to come to an end as Priscilla stepped off the witness stand. She paused as she passed the defense table, met my eyes, and smiled.

"I hope you get your children back," I whispered.

"I intend to," she whispered with a smile.

The next day, the prosecutor had assistance. The assistant district attorney himself, smiling and jocular and just a bit worried as he took his place as advice to counsel.

Word had it that the DeLandes had offered—had insisted —that they be allowed to provide legal assistance for the junior prosecutor. They wanted to bring in some big-name attorney from New Orleans, pay his way, make sure the "murderer on trial gets what she deserves." The judge and prosecutor's office both declined.

The same informant passed along the news that the DeLandes were not accustomed to the state of Louisiana ignoring their wishes. But then there had never been a public display of their dirty linen. There had never before been so much inside dirt on the powerful family. The state of Louisiana was enjoying itself immensely. The papers were all filled with conflicting claims, and reporters were being flown in from everywhere as hints of scandal were admitted in court.

So the assistant DA joined in the fray, to make sure all the t's were crossed and all the i's were dotted, and so no one could say that the state hadn't done its job. There was great speculation suddenly that the accused was an avenging angel. And that a once hostile jury might just acquit her.

The DeLandes took up an extra aisle in court from then on. The older sisters and the wives appeared each day, wearing pearls and jewels and designer clothes, even, one day, a fur. All to show the world that, contrary to some testimony, being a DeLande wasn't bad at all.

For the rest of the week, my defense concentrated on the reports of expert witnesses. Dr. Tacoma Talley appeared, to defend her contention that Dessie had been molested. Dr. Abear—Anita Hebert—appeared as well, to explain the long- and short-term effects of sexual child abuse on children in general and on my children in particular. And to consider, for the prosecution, the effects on my children of "their father being murdered in cold blood by their mother."

"Objection, Your Honor."

"I'll rephrase the question, Your Honor."

Gabriel even called the deputy who had tried to serve papers on Montgomery to testify as to the violence of my husband. The jurors liked that. So did the press.

On Friday Gabriel put Glorianna DesOrmeaux on the stand. He informed the jury, who were by now thoroughly intrigued, titillated, or offended, as was their personal inclination, that Miss DesOrmeaux was a hostile witness, and that his "treatment of her would perhaps be harsh. But you good folk will understand, won't you?"

Judge Albares reprimanded Gabriel for addressing the jury directly. But it was couched in the mildest of terms and pretty much ignored by all.

And then Gabriel proceeded to grill the poor girl about her financial, emotional, and sexual relationship with Montgomery. She was presented with Montgomery's copy of the original contract with her mother. She was presented with the financial contract that went into effect upon her reaching her majority. This one covered her home, her income, and the insurance that came to her upon Montgomery's death. She was grilled about the trip to Paris, and her subsequent relationship with Richard.

Richard's wife, Pamela, got up and walked out at that point. Pam obviously didn't know about the form of *plaçage* practiced by the DeLande men. She was followed shortly by Janine, Andreu's wife. Apparently Janine was surprised to learn about the woman living next door to Glorianna. Andreu's mistress.

Adrian Paul, sitting by my side, stifled a grin and clasped my hand under the table at the commotion the women made leaving the courtroom. The reporters loved it, half of them following the angry wives. Gabriel seemed pleased as well, though only when he turned back to the defense table, and not where the judge or jury could see his amused face.

We all celebrated that night. And the best was yet to come. Miss X had agreed to testify when court resumed on Monday.

Surfeited with good food and good wine, I slept well that night, and the two nights that followed. Really slept. No dreams. No nightmares. No waking in the dark of night in a cold sweat. Just sleep. Lots of sleep.

I woke clearheaded and feeling strong on Monday morning. I dressed in a favorite suit, a peach and cream confection that I hadn't been able to get into for some months, thanks to Jason. It fit perfectly, and I looked very pretty with my hair up and pearls in my ears. My wedding ring on my finger.

The doctor who examined me on the night of my deposition was the first witness called that morning. He was one of those debonair, elderly physicians who can look like the kindly frontier medical practitioner one moment and the Oxford-trained physician the next. He was genial, eloquent, open, and sincere. Also believable. He should have been. He was costing me an arm and a leg.

Although the prosecution tried to stop it, the videotape of my examination was allowed as evidence. For my privacy's sake, however, the courtroom was cleared of spectators and press, and the tape was run for the jury only. Every black eye, bruise, bite mark, broken rib, and handcuff abrasion was viewed by the wildly entertained jury. And one lone reporter who managed to sneak back into the courtroom and watch.

Adrian Paul held my hand beneath the table for a long moment before I eased it away. I wasn't ready yet for that. For the look in his eyes and the touch of his hand. But I knew it wouldn't be long before I would have to acknowledge what was growing between us.

That afternoon, with a crowded courtroom and rain pouring down the windows, Gabriel called his last witness. Bella Cecile DeLande.

The DeLande contingent blanched, turned positively white, then green around the gills, as my Mama would have said, had she still been speaking to me. I know because I was watching. They tried to get her testimony stopped, and did manage a recess so the prosecution could consider the impact of the new witness. The recess sent us home early, and I smiled all the way home in Adrian Paul's car.

The next morning, when we all stood in honor of the judge, the DeLande Bench was conspicuously empty. Only Andreu and Miles Justin remained. Andreu cold and calculating in his Italian suit, Miles amused and relaxed, his denim-clad legs stretched out before him. His arms were crossed, and the omnipresent cowboy hat rested on the bench beside him.

I suppose he thought he had done his duty for the good DeLande name by wearing a suit up to this time. And now that the name was about to be smeared in the mud, it was time to return to normal. Work shirt and jeans, hat and boots.

He seemed pleased, eyes feasting on his sister, occasional-

ly glinting my way with . . . what? Amusement certainly.
Miles was always amused. But also with . . . delight? Respect? Admiration?

I faced the witness box. Bella Cecile, Miss X, was a
pale-skinned beauty, but then, all the DeLandes are beautiful. She had blue eyes like Montgomery, but her hair was
darker, almost black with red highlights and silver strands
running though it. She was slender to the point of emaciation, but she knew how to dress to show off her body. In
white. Not pure white, but that shade called winter white. A
soft and woolly sweater, high on her neck. Loose white
slacks that moved almost with a life of their own as she
walked. Even white stockings and shoes, the season be
damned. And she topped it off with an unconstructed blazer
in what looked like a cashmere and silk weave in the rare
dark shade of oxblood that set off her short-bobbed hair.

Poised as if she had never been a drunk in a cathedral
doorway, she gave her name, age, and occupation. Which
was part-time call girl. "It's what I'm best trained for, you
see," she said, with a twist of her lips and a long look at the
DeLande Bench.

"Why is that?" Gabriel asked, his voice quiet, curious.
Sad.

"Because my mother—the Grande Dame DeLande, just
to be precise—gave me to my brother when I was twelve
years old. His toy. His pupil." She smiled and looked at the
jury, appearing suddenly as the open-eyed child, innocently
about to spill the family secrets. Bella Cecile had a mobile
face, expressive and open, almost liquid in its elasticity, a
perfect mirror of her inner self. Mercurial and capricious,
changing from amused self-pity to a delight in shocking her
listeners. She scanned the courtroom a moment as if pausing for effect, one corner of her mouth quirked up.

"You cannot imagine what it does to a twelve-year-old
child to be taken out of the girls' room and put into your
brother's bed to learn about sex."

There was a pause as the words sank in. Then gasps from the spectators and jury. One woman clutched her chest in shock. Faces were tight. Angry.

"Montgomery DeLande was, however, an excellent teacher. By far the best lover I've ever had."

One juror stood up, then remembering himself, sat down again.

Bella looked down, laced her fingers, suddenly pensive. I had never seen anyone so inconstant and changing and yet so mesmerizing. In just the few seconds since she took the stand, she had us in the palm of her hand.

"The concept of a girls' room was mostly a euphemism, you understand. Once my father died, all the youngest children slept with the Grande Dame." She smiled slightly. "The Grande Dame has a huge bed covered with silk and Italian lace and draped with gauze, and it's like a fairyland. Every girl's dream of a grown-up bedroom." Bella sounded wistful. She reached up to touch her hair and then stopped, letting her hand fall away. The courtroom was silent. Holding its collective breath.

"My mother had always been rather cold toward us girls as we were growing up. Saving her hugs and kisses and motherly smiles for the boys, my brothers. And when she suddenly changed and moved us into her bed . . . well, it was heaven. And for the first time, she started touching us. It was all innocent at first, but it quickly progressed from hugs and kisses to other things. I realize now she was touching us in ways the court might categorize as . . . unacceptable or . . . inappropriate." Her voice was suddenly wry and soft, and the jurors were leaning forward, straining to hear.

"And as soon as she thought we were ready, she gave us to our brothers. One by one."

The prosecutor struggled to his feet, moving in a disjointed manner, almost as if his legs had gone to sleep beneath the table and he didn't know it until he was halfway up. "Objection, Your Honor. This line of questioning, this horrific and twisted story, has no bearing on this case." The prosecutor was red-faced and tight-lipped, his eyes on Bella.

Gabriel stood in the same moment, speaking on top of the prosecutor's last words. "Your Honor, my client is on trial for her life, and anything, any circumstances that might have driven her to pick up a weapon in defense of her life and her children, must be permitted—"

"I'll decide what must and must not be permitted in this courtroom, Mr. Rousseau. For now, I'll permit this line of questioning, but don't push it too far, Counselor."

"Thank you, Your Honor."

"I didn't even know it was wrong until I saw my son and how . . . abnormal he was. The doctor tried to blame it on a birth accident. The cord was wrapped around the baby's neck as he pushed through the birth canal. He went without oxygen for a while. But I knew it was mostly because of Montgomery and me." She smiled, her lips moving slowly as she watched the jurors. "I left when I got pregnant again." Her words were spaced and distinct. "They don't have any idea where the second child is. And they never will."

"They who?" Gabriel asked.

Her features twisted with anger, her face slightly flushed. "The DeLandes, of course. My *family.*"

"Are you saying it was common practice for the girl children to be given to their brothers? As . . . as some sort of . . . plaything?" Gabriel sounded horrified, as if he hadn't heard her story several times before. The consummate attorney. The consummate actor.

"Of course." Bella smiled, widely this time, flashing white teeth. She leaned forward, resting her arms on the railing that surrounded the witness stand on three sides. She appeared to be about to pass along a confidence. A secret. "They are assigned to teach us all about sex and how to have babies. All about our bodies and how to find pleasure. How to give pleasure. Montgomery had virtual and complete control over my body for three years. It was wonderful and it was horrible, and if *she* hadn't killed him, maybe I would have myself one day."

Bella sat back. "I certainly understand Nicole's decision to protect her children from all that. Growing up in a family bordello rather warps one." She smiled again, now the tough-talking street-wise kid who has seen it all and done even more. "Sex twice a day quickly becomes the norm, and it seldom matters which brother demands attention."

She knew she was shocking everyone in the courtroom. She was working at it. She was enjoying it. The instability, the almost manic emotional swings, were all a sham. An act. Bella Cecile wasn't a woman on the emotional edge, about to lose control. She was punishing her family. She was enjoying her moment of power, her control over the DeLandes. If she had had an automatic weapon or a bomb, she would have killed them all and us with them with no hesitation. As it was, she used words as her weapons.

"Why? Why would a mother do such terrible things to her family?" Gabriel asked, laying his arm conversationally across the top of the witness stand. He looked like a kindly neighbor talking over the backyard fence.

"To the Grande Dame, sex is a responsibility. A duty. And a punishment all rolled up into one. A religion almost." Bella's voice came quickly now, almost gasping. "She talks about love and sex all the time. Love and sex are totally . . . interchangeable . . . to her. But she doesn't love us. Not at all. She hates us. All her girl children. Utterly and completely. A mother would *have* to hate her children to give them to one another. Wouldn't she?"

The prosecutor looked down at his folded hands. The assistant district attorney did the same. Then they put their heads together, whispering softly.

"My sister Jessica went to Andreu. He had first choice. She had four children by him by the time I left home. Marie Lisette went to Richard. She ran away and hid her baby too. But then, none of the sisters liked Richard very much. He liked to hurt us."

"Objection, Your Honor. I see no valid purpose to this ... this monologue. It isn't even a line of questioning."

"I'll allow it, but get to the point, Counselor."

"Anna Linette went to Marcus. I understand that Andreu's oldest legitimate girl was promised to Miles Justin, but that he refused. Of course, that's only hearsay."

Bella looked out over the silent packed courtroom and focused on Miles. "He really should reconsider. Better him than Richard for a teacher. And no one says he has to use her."

I looked back and caught an expression on Miles's face I had never seen before. Anger. Fierce unreasoning anger. He was staring at Andreu, his body at once both relaxed and taut, as if he were poised for attack. As I watched, his eyes blazed, his fingers curled into the wooden back of the bench in front of him, formed claws, and dug in.

Andreu ignored him, concentrating on the girl in front of the courtroom. She laughed, watching the scene.

"I'd say the Eldest is pissed at me, Miles, begging your pardon, Your Honor."

I looked at my hands clenched in my lap. I was twisting the ring on my finger. The wedding ring I still wore, wisteria vines twining around my finger, around my life, smothering me. I pulled it off. Stuck it in my pocket. I knew I'd never wear it again.

"There's no way to protect yourself against them, the mighty DeLandes. Marie Lisette went to the officials about the abuse. Explained what went on at the DeLande Estate. And you know what? They found her. Locked her up in a private hospital. She stayed there for three years until they finally let her go. The rest of us learned our lessons and kept quiet. The law isn't big enough or strong enough to protect anyone from DeLande power."

"Do you think the abuse is still going on? Do you think that children are still being abused on the DeLande Estate?" Gabriel was very intense, as if his heart were bleeding for a family of children abused for so many years.

"I don't know." Bella looked down at her hands, twisting together in her lap. "If I had to guess—"

"Objection, Your Honor. I must say again that this line of questioning by the defense is gratuitous and bears no visible impact on the case in question. The defendant never lived on the DeLande Estate, and therefore nothing that might have happened in another part of the state has a bearing on this accusation of murder in the first degree."

"On the contrary, Your Honor. My client is trying to prove that she was protecting herself and her children from a terrible fate when she shot her husband." Gabriel was tense, his hands in fists at his sides.

"Your Honor—"

The gavel came down twice. "Gentlemen. Approach the bench."

The conversation was short and sweet. The defense rested. And we went home for the day.

Closing arguments on the morning after changed the tide again for me. The prosecutor reminded the jury that no one has the right to take the law into her own hands and kill another human being. Then he reminded the jury that I had rearranged the furniture, lit candles, poured wine. That I was wearing a gun holster when searched by the police. That I had given my husband a glass of wine, and then shot him. Once in the chest, once in the face.

Then, coldly, while my husband bled all over the house, went and got a shotgun that I kept beside the bed and shot him again. And stood and watched him bleed to death, my feet in the blood that poured out of him. The evidence was incontrovertible. Nicolette Dazincourt DeLande was a murderess.

Gabriel closed with a recapitulation of the DeLande life-style, a mother's protective instincts, my kidnapping and beating, Montgomery's propensity for violence as proven in his attack on the deputy.

And then I was taken away. I wasn't allowed to return

home to my children while I waited for the verdict. I was kept in a small holding cell below the courthouse by day and only allowed to go home at night. The first two days of deliberations were bearable. But after the third, I was exhausted, so stressed I stopped giving milk and Jason had to be put on formula. Until then I had been using a breast pump, and storing my milk in the refrigerator each day.

My son cried and fussed and refused the ugly-tasting stuff until hunger wore him out and he finally took the formula. But his eyes that night locked on mine and promised retribution. I had a feeling he'd be a handful of rebellion and trouble someday just to get me back. A true DeLande.

The thought that I might not get to see my children again, except for visiting days, was terrifying. How long would I get for first-degree murder? Life without parole? Thirty-five years? Twenty? I fought depression and waited, hour by hour, in my dark, dank cell with nothing to do but watch the mildew grow down over the walls, water trickle down the brick, and rust stains spread on the sink.

The courthouse had been built in the middle part of the last century, using building techniques typical of the time. The foundation walls, which partially made up my cell, were eight to ten feet thick—hence no windows—composed of bricks that had never seen the inside of a kiln. Porous and rough, they absorbed the water in the soil, the air, and falling from the sky. Because the water table in this part of the country was only inches below the surface, the bricks were always wet. In the rainy season, better known as winter, the water wicked up through this porous material, climbing the walls, literally, and soaking into the plaster walls above. The courtroom had been known to "weep" in the past as the water rose. I was certain it would weep for me soon.

Even though I wasn't below ground, I may as well have been. The walls were wet, the brick floor was wet, the toilet seat was stained and corroded with fifty years of filth. And above me, a jury of my peers decided my fate. Peers. Did that mean that all twelve and two alternates had been mothers, had seen their children sexually assaulted? Had shot their husbands to protect them? No. I had no peers. And I knew it.

Meanwhile, my girls were living at Sonja's, forgetting their mama and all I did to protect them. Or so it seemed to me. Even when they were here in Moisson, in the house where they were raised and Montgomery was killed, even when I went to see them at the end of a day in court, they seemed distant. Cool. As if they were preparing for the day when I wouldn't come home anymore at night.

Two cells down, my defense attorneys, Gabriel and Adrian Paul, were talking strategy. The *what ifs*, should I be convicted. I indulged in a fit of self-pity, tears pooling in my ears as steadily as water ran down the walls. I was a mess and I didn't care. *I was going to jail.*

The door opened down the corridor. It was five P.M., Friday. Time to adjourn for the week. I heard soft voices, footsteps moving toward me. Adrian Paul entered my cell, sat on the bunk where I lay staring at the ceiling and feeling sorry for myself. He took my hands.

"Well."

I almost said "Deep subject," that tired old play on words. Instead I looked at him. He was incredibly handsome, this man who had stood by me, neglecting his practice for weeks. Dark-eyed, his skin appearing even more dusky in the poor light of my cell's single overhead bulb. And he was worried. Well, so was I.

"The jury's back."

It took a moment for the meaning to sink in. "The jury's back?" I whispered.

"And they have a decision. Wash your face and put on some makeup. We have five minutes."

I was shaking so badly, I couldn't put on my lipstick; Adrian Paul, watching from the cell door, came over and took the tube, lining my lips for me in the soft pink I had been wearing for the trial. I brushed out my hair, leaving it down, so I would have something to hide behind should I hear the word "guilty."

"Coward."

"I beg your pardon," Adrian Paul said, surprised.

I smiled, forcing the corners of my mouth up. "I was calling myself names." I took a deep breath, smoothing the wrinkles out of my suit skirt, then picking up my jacket and tossing it over my shoulders. "I'm ready."

He put his arms around me, stopping my forward motion. I froze. "You are many things, Collie. But not a coward."

It had been months since a man had held me. Months. I inhaled the fine musky scent of him, a rich smell, just a hint spicy. I let him hold me against him a moment, feeling the strength, the solid compact body so hard against mine. Without looking up, I stepped away and followed him from my cell.

The guard manacled my wrists in front of me, his eyes downcast and apologetic as he did. It was the same guard, the same look every time. *I'm sorry. Just doing my job.* But this time he paused, met my eyes briefly, and unlocked the handcuffs, hooked them to his belt. "G'luck, ma'am," he said, his voice a heavy Cajun accent. I suddenly couldn't remember his name, though he was the same guard who had watched over me throughout my trial. I looked at the name badge.

"Thank you, Officer Deshazo."

He led the way, my hands feeling odd hanging at my sides for once, from the first-floor holding cells in the bowels of the courthouse, to the second floor, where business was done. Almost as if through underground passages, we passed through a maze of wet and weeping, moss-covered brick hallways, lit intermittently by flickering fluorescent tubes, to the surface of light and human activity. Our feet clicked cleanly against marble tile until we entered the courtroom proper and the noise of the jurors, spectators, and press drowned out the sound.

It was raining again, the water pouring slowly down the twelve-foot-tall windows. The air was chill and damp, and I shivered. Tried to wake up from this miserable dream where I was about to be condemned to a wet cell in the dark for the rest of my life. *I had no choice,* I wanted to scream. *Montgomery gave me no choice.* Yes, I had murdered my husband. To protect my children.

Adrian Paul had my hand clasped in his. I let him hold it; the warmth cut through the cold of my skin like a hot metal glove. The jury entered and sat. Then Judge Albares. Adrian Paul had to help me to my feet. My trembling intensified, and I nearly fell as the strength left my legs. I managed to sit, landing on my chair with a thud of neck-jarring pain.

Suddenly Montgomery stood before me smiling that elegant risqué smile that so stirred my senses as a young girl. Blue eyes hot with desire, he traced my face with his fingertips.

Adrian Paul pushed the hair from my face, his eyes concerned. I swallowed. I didn't even hear the words, those awful legal words, that fell from Judge Albares's mouth, asking the jurors for the verdict. *My verdict.* So formal, those words, the syllables that would lead to my condemnation.

"We have, Your Honor."

I swallowed, fighting nausea and the burning pain I had been living with for so long. My ulcer. My verdict. I fought back an almost uncontrollable desire to giggle. My image of Montgomery smiled again. I turned away from him.

The foreman of the jury delivered the verdict to the judge, who silently perused the official words. His lips pursed and his brows quivered a moment, before he folded the paper and handed it to the clerk of court. The woman unfolded the verdict and read it through silently once and then aloud.

"We, the jury in the case of the State versus Nicolette

DeLande, in the charge of murder in the first degree, find the defendant . . . not guilty."

A roar started behind me. Within me. Pandemonium. *Not guilty.*

"Is this your verdict?" the clerk of court asked the jury. The reply was lost in the roar of sound.

Adrian Paul pulled me to my feet, his arms around me. He kissed my numb cheeks. My cold lips. *Not guilty.*

I looked back. The DeLande Bench was empty. *Not guilty.*

Adrian Paul pulled me down the crowded aisles toward the front doors of the Moisson District Courthouse, the eighteen-foot-tall doors opening slowly, majestically, before us. *Not guilty.*

A wet breeze hit my face, stirred in my hair hanging loose about my shoulders. Sunlight ahead. Sunlight? I thought it was raining. The foyer tiles were wet, tracked with mud and littered along the walls with umbrellas. Sunlight ahead. Definitely sunlight. *Not guilty?*

Not guilty.

Two deputies leaned into the outer doors of the courthouse, the massive heavy doors over a hundred years old, constructed to withstand the uprising of angry slaves, or the onslaught of pirates, or the attack of Yankees. And they opened for me. *Not guilty.*

Sunlight blinded me a moment, and I closed my eyes against the brightness. A brightness that lifted me from the dark corner where I had hidden myself since I killed my husband. I looked around, trying to focus through the too bright sunlight. Even his ghost was gone.

Not guilty! I am Free!

The sunlight was soft against my skin. Untouched by winter. Yes. It was March now. Early spring. The sun flickered gently as the clouds that had dropped all the rain passed idly across its surface. Adrian Paul led me toward the top of the steps. A podium was set up there, situated in the center of the white stone steps. I took a deep breath, stunned by the faint scent of spring roses and honeysuckle . . . and wisteria. Surely it was too soon in the season for anything to bloom.

A mourning dove cried its grief on the spring breeze, scarcely heard above the raucous crowd gathered in the square. The women's groups shouted victory. The irritation of the town, which had lost a wealthy and generous son, was equally vocal. The stiff silence and disapproving stares of the elder churchwomen who felt I should have simply put up with it, the beatings and the abuse. Even their silence was loud. They still refused to believe that Montgomery had touched his babies. *Is my mother in that group?*

I stood at the top of the courthouse stairs, eyes closed suddenly, ignoring the flood of spectators around me, ignoring the sound of reporters shouting inane questions at me, microphones thrust into my face. *How the hell do I know how I feel, you silly twit? I'm numb.* And I'm free!

Slowly I opened my eyes, resting my body gently against Adrian Paul, allowing him, finally, to support me as he desired to do from the first moment we met. Surprising thought, that. But true. Even through his grief and in spite of my troubles, he has desired to support me. To help me. To love me. Silly thought. Time for all that later. Much time. All the time in the world. He tightened his arm around my waist.

The courthouse square was ugly in the middle of early spring and milling with people. Some angry, some cheering. Bounded on four sides by archaic buildings not updated since electricity was first wired in. The blocked-off streets coming in from the corners, the city spreading out around it like a star of expanding spines and angles and patches of green against the ugly buildings. The statue of the conquered rebel rising above the crowd of heads. A favorite roost of pigeons who had defecated on the Confederate soldier's shoulders and head and horse for a hundred years. Ugly. Beautiful. *I am free!*

The roaring of the crowd deepened as I stood there for

them to look at. A rumble in the near distance like the sound of thunder. Bodies jostling against me. Adrian Paul steady and warm at my side.

The deputies closed in around me, a phalanx of protection. Sirens wailed in the distance.

A sudden splatter of rain from the almost cloudless sky. No one noticed. Nothing odd about rain from a clear sky in these parts.

The square was almost packed, the jury having worked through lunch. The bailiff, gossiping with the reporters, had more than hinted to them that the verdict was imminent. Long before word reached my counsel or me. I smiled finally, and the crowd screamed approval.

Adrian Paul hugged me. *I am free!*

Ahead of me, just beyond the barricade, in the edge of the milling crowd, rested a dark green '58 Chevy, familiar. A classic. I focused on it, the sparkling paint, the sun-touched chrome, glinting silver in the brightness. The car was empty.

Leaning against the closed driver's door was a man. Indolent, his arms crossed over his chest, his feet crossed at the ankles, he stared at me, piercing green eyes visible, even across the distance. Andreu. The Eldest.

I stiffened and stepped away from Adrian Paul, who hadn't picked out the single man in the swelling crowd. It was a message, meant just for me. They had known I would notice the classic car.

And even before I looked, I knew. Yet I forced my head to turn. To my right, behind the barricade, was Richard, his nondescript eyes slitted against the light, gnashing through the momentary freedom I had felt. Like his brother, he stood against the door of an antique Chevy, arms and ankles crossed.

I shuddered. I wished I were stronger. That I could resist the pull, the weight of the eyes I sensed. But I was not. Slowly I turned to my left. And across the last barricade was Miles Justin, standing just like his brothers against his own '52 Ford roadster, casual in his denim and snakeskin boots.

Miles. The one brother whom I had trusted, staring at me, impaling me with eyes dark as his mother's, tossing sparks as he met my own over the heads of the barely controlled mob.

Slowly he lifted one arm, grasped the crown of the charcoal gray cowboy hat he wore, and lifted it. The breeze caught the fine hair beneath, fluffing the strands. The smell of roses strengthened, and the scent of wisteria.

I am not free.

It isn't over. Not yet.

CHAPTER

14

~~~

I turned to Adrian Paul, took his upper arm in my fingers, and shook it slightly. He met my eyes, laughing, the wonderful sound lost in the blare of human voices. Gabriel was speaking into an array of microphones, something about the "basic human right to protect our children." When Adrian Paul bent, his face blocked out my other attorney completely. Breath warm against my ear, he asked, "Do you want to make a statement?"

"No. Just get me out of here." And suddenly I saw a memory of Ammie the day she stopped in Moisson to tell me she was leaving Marcus and to confess her destination. She had lied. She had no intention of going to Daingerfield, Texas. She hadn't even gone west. Her claim was a red herring. A lie to throw them off, lead them astray. I knew it with an unwavering certainty. Yet the brothers had found her anyway.

The image of a plan opened out in my mind, complete and full-blown, all of its parts firmly integrated. The unabridged version. It was like a flower opening, the petals peeling back, exposing the heart and soul of the plan in time-lapse photography. It shook me, that this thing, this thought, had come from inside me.

A laugh escaped my lips, lost in the noise. The images were so detailed, it was more of a memory than an idea, as if some part of my mind had long ago recognized the danger and the necessity and had been working on the problem for months.

Adrian Paul and the deputies had forced their way back inside the courthouse and to the right, bypassing the main courtroom, taking the back stairs down to the leaky bowels of the old building. I thought I had escaped all this. . . . But I had escaped nothing. Mildew smothered the walls, its smell choking. We passed offices. Poorly lit. Damp. I hadn't realized that parish employees had shared my interment, and I wondered what heinous crime they had committed to be given office space down here. Adrian Paul pulled me along, his hand holding mine.

Sunlight again, even more brilliant after the darkness. I was still blind when a deputy put his hand on the top of my head and guided me into a car. Adrian Paul's BMW roared to life, sounding for an instant like the crowd out front.

Reporters ran around the side of the building, followed by the cameramen, and then we were off, moving away from the reporters and the gawkers and the smell of the ancient courthouse. Hidden and protected by the tinted windows. Safe.

The illusion made me laugh, and Adrian Paul laughed with me, his voice sounding free and young. The conquering hero. My own laughter was angry and derisive. He didn't seem to notice.

"Where to?"

"My house," I said softly.

"How do you feel, lady?"

I didn't answer, my mind filled with lists of supplies I would need, a vision of the place where I was going. My face was tight, my eyes dry. Adrian Paul squeezed my hand as if he understood.

The drive to the house was mostly silent, Adrian Paul making occasional comments, yet he seemed content with my lack of response. The buildings fell away, the bayou raced along beside the car, elephant ear and lily pads lining the banks and the water's surface.

My house came into view, the grass cut, the woodwork freshly painted, the FOR SALE sign prominently displayed out front. The asking price was low. Even in a modern society, few people wanted to buy a house in which someone had died violently. Ghosts, you know.

A news van was parked out front, two people milling around outside it, one in a long navy dress and jacket, primping in a compact mirror. She snapped the gold lid shut when she saw the car and started to run toward the drive. Adrian Paul ignored her and pulled in.

"We need to talk, Collie. About Montgomery's estate and his will. It can go through probate now, unless the DeLandes contest it." He paused, slowing to avoid bumping the blond reporter and the cameraman. She was shouting questions into the reflective surface of the closed windows, as the cameraman recorded his own reflection in the glass. I couldn't make out her words. BMWs were built to keep the outside world outside. "You're going to be a very wealthy woman."

Blood money. But I didn't say it.

"You need to be thinking about the future."

I am. *I'm thinking about the DeLandes coming to kill me and take away my children.* But I didn't say that either.

Adrian Paul pulled around back, into the garage. Montgomery's sacrosanct garage. The classics were all parked at one end, the elaborate chrome bumpers only inches apart. Someone would have to crawl across the hoods to get in the cars. Desecration. But I'd needed room for the Land-Rover and Sonja's Volvo. And now the BMW. There was room. Barely. The garage door lowered behind us, cutting out the light and blocking the reporter. She stayed outside. Must be new at the job.

If I survived all this, I'd have to sell the cars. The classics. Time for such thoughts later. We got out of the BMW, my eyes adjusting to the gloom. I looked around. There were things I would need here, including the portable phone. Montgomery had two, so there should be a second one here someplace. The police had the one I used the night he died. They had the guns too. But I had others.

I bent over the garage worktable, conscious of Adrian Paul's eyes, watching. Went around to the back and rummaged in the darkness. There were no windows in the classic car surgery. Sunlight could rot the leather upholstery and damage the fabric of rag tops. I didn't want the artificial lights. The phone was in a corner on the bottom shelf. My eyes had adjusted to the dark and I began scouting for other supplies.

"Collie? What are you doing?"

"I need some things. And I know about the will. And the estate. And the life insurance money that will come to me now. It'll wait." I stopped and considered, picking out his face in the gray light. "You still have power of attorney for me, don't you?"

"Of course, but—"

"Well, you start proceedings, okay? I . . . I need to be away from legal . . . things for a while." I stopped. I'd stacked a battery-powered lantern, extra battery, canteen, thermos, tent, hammock, bedroll, and a small tool kit I could carry in my pocket beside the phone. The girls had given Montgomery the tool kit for Father's Day one year. I wondered if it was before the abuse began or after.

"If . . . If something happened to me . . . are the children still protected under the papers I signed before Montgomery died? The ones giving you and Sonja custody?"

"Collie? What the hell is going on here?"

"Are—they—still—in—effect?" I repeated, separating each word.

He ran a hand through his hair. It looked soft and feathery, and I wanted to touch it. "Yes. They are."

"Good." I turned back to my searching.

"You're going to get grease on your suit." His voice sounded odd. I didn't bother to analyze the emotion in it.

I grinned up at him. "There's no grease in here. Not anywhere. This is the surgery, the place where valuable classics are diagnosed and treated. It's clean enough to roll around in naked." I was quoting Montgomery. Once, in an amorous mood, we had rolled around on the floor naked just to prove his point. No grease was on our skin after the experience.

"Where are you going?"

I didn't answer at first, adding a box of shells, number three buckshot for my other twenty-gauge shotgun. And a box of ammunition for my other 9mm, the pretty Swiss-made SIG Sauer with pearl-handled grips Montgomery had given me on our fourth anniversary. It had been a terribly romantic anniversary night. Champagne, paté, imported crackers and cheese and fruit, and the gun. A box of shells emptied all over me on the hotel bed. We had made love in the mess, imprints of bullets and goose liver smeared into my skin. I was glad they hadn't been my sheets.

"Collie." His voice deepened. It held a note I'd never heard before. Not just worry, or friendship. Something more.

"Don't ask, Adrian. Please don't ask," I whispered. I left my pile of things and we walked out the door and to the house. The blond reporter was nowhere to be seen.

That night I spent with my children, and Sonja and her children, and Adrian Paul and JP and Philippe. It was a rowdy time, playing games and popping corn, eating it on the carpet that covered the bloodstained wood flooring where Montgomery had died. Back and forth I would wander through the house, touching things, gathering things, writing a note or two, and then hiding them. Adrian Paul watched as I roamed around the house, his eyes hooded, brooding. Waiting.

When I left Moisson, I had left all my winter clothes in

storage. They had been delivered by EZY White Cleaners and Garment Storage some months before. I had all that I needed. Boots, long johns, khaki army coat. Outerwear both waterproof and warm. But with the early spring, I might not need . . . No. Take it all. No telling about the weather this time of year.

I managed to pack a bag in the loud and boisterous part of the night. And a bit of food as well. Exhausted, I went to bed early, falling onto my silk sheets, staring at the dark ceiling, the Hunter fan turning slowly above me. It cast deep shadows as the blades cut the night. Sleep was far away. Slowly the house quieted around me as the Rousseaus and my bunch fell to sleep. Time seemed to slip past like a fog, insubstantial and tenuous.

Slowly my door opened to the darker shadow of the hallway. I didn't turn my head. I suppose I knew he would come. Lifting my hand, I waited. Adrian Paul walked silently into the room, his body still clothed, his eyes lost in the gloom. Moving slowly, he removed his clothes and slipped into the bed beside me. Gathered me in his arms. Only then did I realize how cold I was, as his body burned mine in the night.

That loving left me shaken. There was no technique, no instant and thorough understanding of what would bring me pleasure, no demands. Just an aching tenderness so fulfilling, it encompassed me, blanking out my fears, soothing my ragged emotions, comforting me. I learned the difference that night, between passion and need. Passion could be assuaged by the body. Need never could.

I slept for an hour then, held in his arms. Smiling in the darkness. He snored.

And then I left.

Moving without sound, I dressed, taped my notes to the back door, carried my bags outside to the garage, and loaded the Land-Rover. Tent, sleeping bag, a roll of mosquito netting. A snake hook and a handful of cloth sacks. A small shovel, a regular hammer, a rubber hammer, ten gallons of gas, four empty five-gallon cans for water. The cooler. The other things I had found that day. The guns.

The only thing I took that surprised me was the rosary Montgomery had left hanging in the shop, slipping it over my head to nestle between my breasts. It was cold and moist from the months in the shop, the silver chain warming slowly against my skin. The stone that comprised the beads and the crucifix remained cold far longer.

Breathing heavily, I realized that I'd never get all this into the flat-bottomed boat. Flipping the garage door switch, I climbed into the Rover, gunned its motor as the door rose.

I maneuvered the Land-Rover out of the garage and to the street as lights came on inside the house. In the rearview I saw Adrian Paul, dressed only in dark slacks, standing on the front porch.

"Collie! No!"

I ignored the anguish, the pain in his voice, and drove off into the night.

I checked my watch. Four A.M. Chaisson and Castalano's should be open. Fancy name for a bait-and-hunting shop that was little more than a one-room shack with bars on the windows, public toilet in the back, and about $150,000 worth of fishing tackle, hunting rifles, shotguns, ammunition, bait, and handguns. Out back was a target range so Chaisson and Castalano's customers could try out their prospective purchases. They did a thriving business, even in winter.

I'd seen Chaisson's house once. A three-hundred-thousand-dollar monster brick structure on the safe side of the levee, built up high with a five-foot brick fence around it, perfect to pack sandbags against in the event the levees showed strain in flood season.

I pulled up to the store just as the morning crew arrived. I was third in line. The morning crew consisted of Castalano herself and her twelve-year-old daughter. Both females were short, stocky, and dark-eyed. They could have been the same person a few years apart. I was reminded of the first time I saw Adrian Paul and JP together. And pushed the thought away.

I loaded my cooler with twenty pounds of ice, filled the canisters with water, and went inside. I added army rations to my list of necessities, and mosquito repellent, which I had forgotten. A few other things. Coffee. How could I have forgotten that? Also a campfire-style drip coffeepot. Dried fruit. A propane tank for the stove. Tablets to purify water. Aspirin. Two small kettles. Rice. Mixed gumbo seasonings. Vegetable oil.

When I reached the register, Castalano eyed my purchases, then me. "The DeLandes hav' account. You keep it open, yes?"

Deciding quickly, I said yes.

"Bills out on fifteenth of month. Balance due de twenty-fifth. Any later, you talk to Chaisson." It was a good threat. Chaisson wasn't someone I would want to owe money.

I nodded. "I'll need a flat-bottom johnboat to trailer after mine. And I need mine out of storage."

"You know how to use one? Is tricky to pull a trailer on de bayou."

I nodded again.

"'Specially b'fo' the sun comes."

I grinned, finally understanding. It would be a big total, and I might have an account, but I wasn't Montgomery with all his money. The smile was wide and felt strange on my face. I don't think I had smiled often in the past year or so. "I'll pay for the boat. And the other things." I handed her my Gold Card. The one I'd gotten in my own name with my own credit during the months I waited for trial. I may have been charged with a felony, but my net worth spoke for itself.

Castalano rang up all my purchases, totaled them, and handed me the credit slip to sign. "I'll hol' it till the fifteenth, den sen' it in if you don' come back and pay it off."

I nodded, then stopped. "Castalano? Send it in now. I may not be back around on the fifteenth after all."

She grunted, looked around. We were alone for the moment. "Dey comin' after you, girl? Dem DeLandes?"

Shock shivered through me. *She knew.* "Yes. I think so." My voice came out breathy and weak.

"You got enough ammo?"

I laughed. Anyone else would have said, "Go to the police." "Hire guards." "Don't be stupid, you're only a woman." Not Castalano. I had a feeling I had missed knowing someone special all these years.

"I don't know. Hope so."

"Wha' you usin'?"

"Number three buckshot."

"Twen'y-gauge?"

"Yes. And a nine-millimeter."

"Hollowpoin's?"

I shook my head. "No."

Castalano measured me a moment, looking me over from head to toe. Then she bent over and disappeared behind the counter, her mammoth butt rounded up beside the cash register. When she rose up, she placed a box of shells on the countertop. "Starburs' rounds. Once one a dese penetrates, it splinters and spreads out." Her hands, pressed together, bent back at the wrists. Then her fingers spread out, opening like a flower blossoming. "Rips you open."

I nodded, visualizing the damage inside a human body.

"Dey got vests?"

"Vests?"

"Kevlar. Bulletproof."

"I don't . . . know."

"If dey do, shoot de lower abdomen or head. A starburs' will stop dem. Even if you hit a extremity, it prob'bly stop dem. Tear arm or leg up, yes."

I closed my eyes, taking a deep breath.

"You got a vest?"

"No."

"Come on. I got one should fit you in de back."

In back? I thought this place was one room.

When I reached the back wall, Castalano unlocked a door more than half hidden by a display of life vests. She stepped into a long, narrow closet, about ten feet long and three feet wide to either side, the walls hung with weapons, the narrow shelves stacked with ammunition. A stockroom of sorts. I didn't look too close at the collection, however. I had a feeling that not everything in here was strictly legal.

"Take off you' jacket."

I complied, and Castalano strapped a Kevlar vest to my torso, Velcro bindings adjusting the fit. The rosary was crushed against my skin. "You' Gold Card good for all dis?"

"Yes, but just list it under merchandise. I don't want them to be able to tell what I bought."

"Yeah, okay." She flipped her short black hair out of her eyes. "You got binoculars?"

"No. I forgot." I wondered what else I had forgotten.

"Here." She thrust a black case at me, then added a large waterproof knapsack and waterproof pouch. "For you' gun if de rain come."

The light went off, the locks clicked shut, and I followed her to the register. We were still alone. Her daughter was outside, talking to some boys in hunting fatigues. I zipped my jacket up over the vest, slipping the binocular strap over my shoulder. The vest was lightweight and nonbinding, but still claustrophobic. I could feel it around my ribs.

My total was outrageous, but my Gold Card balance was zero. The bill would be drafted from my account. I'd never even have to look at it again.

Castalano walked to the dock while I pulled the Land-Rover around the store and down a slight incline right to the dock. The black water of Grand Lake sat silently on the other side of the wood boards.

The proprietor of the largest boat storage facility in Moisson Parish pulled a file box and riffled the cards, then gunned a forklift on and pulled my fourteen-foot aluminum flat-bottomed boat out of the stacks of fancy fishing boats and ski boats and pleasure boats, and drove outside to the water. With a delicate touch, she set it into the lake in the yellow glare of a sodium vapor light.

It was the same boat Miles Justin had bought so many years ago. His gift to me.

It was one of only a few flat-bottomed boats she stored. Most people kept boats at their own docks, those who used them these days. With the levees and better roads, boat travel wasn't a necessity for most homeowners.

Before sunrise, we had loaded my supplies on the fourteen-foot johnboat, and the shallow-draft flat-bottomed trailer boat. From a storage chest, Castalano served up two oars and a long pole, for poling the boat through tricky shallow water. Two life vests, bright orange, were stored in the aluminum storage shelves, the side pockets that ran along the sides of the boat.

"I service' de Mercury pas' fall. Shou' be okay." She tossed in a couple of oil cans, gassed up the boat, and secured the trailer boat to the back of mine. Her movements were spare and economical. She talked as she worked.

"I don' recommen' no faster dan ten mile hour wid de trailer boat. Maybe less. De trailer won' plane out b'hind you much easy wit'out more power dan dis old Merc is got. If I'd a know you was goin' to haul, I'd a put on a power prop for you."

"It's all right. I'm not in a hurry now."

"No," she said thoughtfully. "Once you hit de Basin, no one goin' fin' you 'less you wan' be found." The question hung unspoken on the air between us. I sighed. The sour smell of the Basin filled my nose. Fish, dead things rotting along the shore, mold and rotten trees, exhaust and oil.

"I brought a phone. Once I get situated, I'll call."

Castalano pulled a card from her shirt pocket and tucked it into my jacket pocket. "Do tha' thing then."

I hadn't meant that I'd call *her,* but what the heck. Straddling the backseat, I inserted the key into the steering handle and dropped the prop into the water. Pumped the bulb at the gas gauge a half dozen times and turned the key. The old Mercury thirty-horsepower motor bellowed into the night, sending a cloud of gas and oil exhaust out over the water.

"Wait a minute," Castalano shouted. She left the yellow glare of the security light and reappeared carrying a handful of hats. She tossed them to me the few feet I had drifted from the dock. "On de house," she shouted.

I laughed at her generosity, noting the company logos on the hats. Probably cost her all of a dollar a hat. "What's your name?" I shouted back over the roar of the Mercury. "Your first name," I added, thinking she wasn't above answering simply Castalano.

She rolled her black eyes. "Calleux. But keep it unda' you' hat. My men cus'omers woul' never let me live it down."

I laughed again. *Calleux.* French for "callused." Or horny. Not the sexual horny, but she was right. The men in Moisson would never let her live down the play on words.

I put one of her hats on my head, turned the accelerator on the steering handle, and puttered out of the sodium vapor lights and into the darkness. When I was fifty feet out, I flipped a switch, lighting the red and green bow lights, and gave the motor just a bit of gas.

Just before I passed around the bend in the bayou, I looked back. Castalano was still on the dock, following my progress with her eyes, but she wasn't alone. Old Man Frieu was with her, his short, stocky body easily identifiable in the night. Castalano was pointing at me out over the water. The old man was scratching his stomach. I turned my face to the lake.

And vanished into the blackness of the Basin, the motor so loud, it drowned out all other sound.

People still lived back here in the Basin, in isolated small groups or even more isolated solitary houses. The government had tried to move them out when the Basin was slated to become part of the Mississippi River's flood control, but not everyone left. Out of those who did, many returned.

Shacks rested on creosoted pilings, molded over and slick, mollusk shells and debris cemented to the wood. Mildew coated the underside of every house, and everywhere bare wood showed through. Tar and newspaper filled the cracks in the wood slats. Rusted tin roofs hovered above the small places, and out front, sinking docks were propped up with fresh two-by-fours dug into the muddy bottom. There's no place like home.

At ten miles per hour, I had a long trip ahead of me. Two days maybe. The sun came up and I slipped out of the khaki coat and Kevlar vest, lathered on sunscreen, braided my hair, and put the hat back on. I was heading east and north across the lake to Big Gator Bayou.

I'd take the trailer boat up the big bayou and turn onto the small unnamed bayou Old Man Frieu had shown me so long ago. I'd trailer in as far as I could go, then tie it off and motor on till I found the campsite I was looking for and unloaded. Then back to the trailer, transfer the supplies to the larger johnboat, and putter back to my campsite. If I was lucky and the rains held, I could sleep on dry ground two nights from now. *Dry* being a relative term, of course.

It grew warm as the morning progressed. Fifty. Then sixty degrees. I shed my work shirt, added more sunscreen, and ate dried fruit, drank plenty of water.

Animals still hibernating a week ago crawled out of burrows of mud, out from under fallen trees, out from the twisted, exposed roots of old cheniers, out of holes in rotten wood, and sunned themselves. A gentle rain fell as a cloud passed over, wetting down the snakes and turtles and alligators who were hungry for the sun.

Alligators were one of my main concerns, and I kept my shotgun handy beside me on the floor of the boat, wedged in by supplies. Although alligators weren't normally aggressive to motorized vehicles, I didn't want to run into the one big mother gator who didn't know the rules. I figured that a blast from my shotgun into water would scare off most anything. I just hoped that in case of emergency, I didn't forget and blast a hole in the bottom of the boat. It had been known to happen.

Egrets were hunting by ten. Snowy white and delicate on long, bony black legs, soft and fragile-looking, they fished in the shallow water along shore, reflected in the black water. A brown pelican stood on a four-foot-tall tree stump in a swampy place and spread his brown-gray wings to the sun, his big, flat-looking beak tucked close to his chest. Wild geese and ducks were sitting in still ponds, resting, wintering in the sun.

Around noon, I passed a family of nutria and shuddered. The man who brought the ugly beasts here from South America should have been shot. The nutria, whose pelt was politely referred to as Hudson Bay beaver in New York fur markets, was really a nine-pound cross between a beaver and water rat. It had webbed feet for swimming and razor-sharp incisors, and I'd heard tales about the not-so-rare nutria who swam over and climbed into a passing johnboat. I would shoot the bottom of my boat out for sure if one climbed in with me.

The motor droned on, the sound heavy and dull at this low speed. Occasionally a bird, startled by the noise, took flight out over the water.

A few of the lilies wore tight buds. They were imports, too, like the nutria, and just as much trouble. But most of the plants were closed up tight. Cattails, alligator grass, march elders, tallow trees, vines, and green water lilies that weren't really lilies. What were they? Purple water hyacinths. But nothing blooming. The occasional fisherman. We nodded and went back to our own business.

Toward midafternoon I slowed and made the turn in to Big Gator Bayou, watching beneath the water for the sunken shrimp boat blown here by a long-ago hurricane, tossed inland on high water and high winds and swamped. Literally. I saw it finally, half-hidden by the water lilies attached to the scum that coated its surface.

The smell began to change, from bayou to something a bit sour. Stagnant. Swamp in the distance.

I passed Old Man Frieu's summer shack, the one-room shanty papered with money and decorated with shotguns. The dock where Miles and I had confronted the Cajun and his shotgun, and where Miles and he had gambled for a thousand dollars, was almost underwater, one end completely submerged.

I turned in to the narrow bayou, slowing, finding the deeper branch to the right, easing my boat into the black water. Beside me, land frogs jumped from lily pad to lily pad, traversing the water without ever getting wet. A huge lizard or salamander, black on top and white beneath, dove to the water, landing with a splat. *Salamander sure. But a big mother salamander fo' sure,* I thought, quoting Old Man Frieu. Talking to Castalano had brought back the French voice with all its poetry and melodious tones.

I could hear Old Man Frieu's gravelly voice, his cadence as he told Miles and me about the bayou, and I realized I had been thinking in his accent for hours as I made this trip to the past.

Birds, nesting in the tops of oak and pecan and hickory, took flight at the sound of my motor. A dozen buzzards watched me from the dead limbs of a single tree, a cypress killed by salt.

It was peaceful and isolated, and if I made the slightest error, I could die here and my body would never be found. Well . . . that's what I was planning, wasn't it? To disappear into territory I knew better than any of them did. To leave a trail they could follow. Like the mother bird, drawing the hunter away from her nest.

I took a break in late afternoon as the sun began its decline into the swamp behind me and the air began to cool.

The water lilies had clogged the way ahead of me, and I knew I would have to row or pole the rest of the way in.

I hunted for and found dry ground—well, sort of dry—and beached the boats. Pulled the supplies I would need for the night. The hammock fit between two sturdy pecan trees, the mosquito netting draped over a branch above, hanging to the ground below it.

Using moss and the dry bark from a white willow, I built a fire, piling on bracken and fallen limbs. I would save the Coleman stove for rain. The fire smoked, but the smoke would keep away mosquitoes and predators.

I boiled water for coffee and took a steaming cup with me to the water. A cove was only a few feet beyond where I had beached the boats, and a fallen tree rested its whitened limbs in the pool.

Moving slowly and sipping coffee from a tin cup, I dropped four lines into the water, deep enough so the bait, a slice of wiener from my meager supplies, pierced through with a hook, rested just above the bottom. Tying off the lines in the limbs above, I figured I could fish and relax at the same time. The sun set in a stunning display of red and plum and fuchsia as my wiener bits attracted my meal and I waited for the red floaters to move. Half an hour later I had netted two small catfish and a crappie. A respectable supper.

Never very good at skinning catfish, nevertheless I skinned both and scaled and gutted the crappie before full dark settled over me. I heated the small skillet and fried up the fish with a little flour and cornmeal, eating in the dark. Then, sleepy beyond compare, I stuffed my bedroll into the hammock and fell into it, praying it wouldn't rain. If it did, I would regret not bothering to put up the tent.

The fire crackled and spat, night birds called, owls hooted, small night hunters splashed in the water. Yet it was the silence that kept me awake. The noisy silence of the bayou. And the memory of Adrian Paul's hands the night before. I had never been alone on the bayou at night before.

Always before I had had my brother, Logan, or Sonja or Montgomery. Or even my father, when I was very young and wanted to do everything Daddy did. But never alone. And so the memory of Adrian Paul's hands touching me beneath the silk sheets was comforting. My cheeks burned in the night, remembering.

Cold claimed my world, and as the temperature dropped, so did the silence, a true silence, like a cloak, covering everything, a blanket of quiet over my solitary world. The fire died and left me in blackness beneath the starry sky.

I was awake before morning, packed before the sun could burn off the low-lying fog that rested above the water like the ghost of a coiling snake along the black bayou. I pushed off before it was really safe enough to see, but I wasn't far from my goal now. I left the ten-foot trailer boat beached, tied and hidden in the leaves. I'd be back tonight. Sooner if the bayou wasn't completely blocked by lilies.

Using the Mercury motor, I made good time until the waterway grew smaller and the lilies denser, slowing as the watery pathway in front of me closed off in a smooth bed of living green. The growth ahead was undisturbed. I had no choice but to turn off the motor, lifting the small engine till the propeller was above the choking beauty of the lilies.

The rest of the way was hard going by oar and pole, and it was past noon by the time I reached the campsite. I don't think it had been used since that time Old Man Frieu and Miles Justin and I had camped here one year to watch the alligators mate.

The cleared place was smaller than I remembered. But dry. And the lean-to roof was still in one piece covering rusted metal beds. World War II army surplus. So well constructed that the beds had survived God only knew how many seasons out in the elements.

I dumped out my supplies and poled back down through the water lilies. I'd left a trail the width of my boat through crushed leaves, stems, and twisted roots. A blind man could have followed me, as the old saying goes. When the DeLandes came, there would be no doubt that they had found me. And they would come. I would make certain.

Even though I was exhausted, the second trip was easier. I could motor most of the way without fear that the water lilies would choke out the Mercury. Still, it was dusk before I got the tent set up, the campsite arranged, the hammock hung from two trees in the shade, firewood gathered and a fire started.

The foul-smelling fish heads I had saved from the night before were perfect temptation for crabs. A net, a bucket, a ball of twine, rotten meat, and boiled rice. What a recipe for gumbo. I left water boiling in two small kettles, one with rice, one for the crabs, and went back to the water. Ten minutes later, I had enough crab for dinner. Easy pickin's, a cotton-pickin' saying. I smiled at my whimsy.

I had no crab implements, but I made do with pliers and a small hammer. In my skillet I burned a little grease, added flour and darkened the roux, dumped in a bag of dried vegetables, and soon had dinner. It was the first time I had ever made gumbo with broccoli and cauliflower and no onion, but Mama wasn't here to complain. I hadn't eaten all day, so I thought it was wonderful.

I made fresh coffee and took a sponge bath before turning in. The coffee satisfied. The bath didn't. I had heated bayou water to a boil, let it simmer for half an hour, then washed myself with Joy dishwashing liquid. I had forgotten soap. I did the dishes in the same water. Like I said, Mama wasn't here to complain.

The sun came late the next day. Long before it rose, I had freshened the fire, made coffee, and collected enough Spanish moss to pad my bed. No more sleeping on hard ground. I prayed that there were no spiders or spider eggs in the moss, knowing that it was a favored nesting ground for all sorts of insects.

I collected more firewood from the fog-shrouded ground. Deadfall, enough for a week, which I stacked beneath the lean-to, on the metal beds to keep them off the wet ground. If it rained, at least my firewood would be dry. I had the stove, of course.

I cleaned my weapons and transferred gas to the tank of the flat-bottomed boat. I loaded my other equipment into the boat and banked the coals in a pit of rocks for later.

I was feeling pretty smug, but it was colder today, the sky dappled with blue amid the clouds. The clouds began to smother out the blue sky as the day progressed. I developed the feeling that my conceit was about to be rained out.

Using both horsepower and arm power, I poled and motored to the island Old Man Frieu had shown us once, Miles Justin and me. I was going snake hunting.

According to the old man, this island had more cottonmouth water moccasins per square foot than anyplace on earth. It was bounded on three sides by bayou, on one side by a swamp, one so thick, it looked like black and green slime and crawling death. Stumps sticking up everywhere. Nothing alive.

Maybe the island had more cottonmouths than anyplace on earth, but in the cool weather, it took me six hours to find four. And I wouldn't have found those if the sun hadn't finally come out for an hour. Okay, so technically it was winter. But it was warm for winter. You'd think all the snakes would come up for air and a little sunshine.

Contrary to popular fears, no snake is really dangerous unless you step on it. Even then, about fifty percent of the time that a snake strikes out of fear, it is a dry bite. A voluntary decision on the part of the snake not to inject venom. It's the other fifty percent of the time that you have to worry. And you can't ask the snake ahead of time which it's to be, a dry bite or a wet bite.

This time of year, catching snakes was easy. All I needed was a snake hook, a cloth bag, and a string to seal the bag. My snake hook was an old golf club handle with a bent piece of steel welded to the end. Capturing a snake consisted of opening the cloth bag several feet from where a snake lay, sunning himself in the weak sunshine. Then all I had to do was lift the snake with my hook and drop him in the bag. Easy.

The only hard part was forcing myself to reach for the bag and twist the mouth shut.

The sacked snakes didn't care much for the trip back to camp. Bouncing and jostling on the bottom of a johnboat while imprisoned in a bag isn't my idea of a good time either. By the time my campsite came into view, my snakes were pretty riled, squirming and wriggling in their bags like crazy.

There was just enough ice left in the cooler to finish off the hunt. I dumped out the cold water and set all four snake bags on top of the ice. Two minutes later, my cottonmouths were dormant. Carefully I opened the bags and transferred all four snakes to the largest bag and sealed the top. I hung the bag in the shade, from a low-hanging limb.

The snake limb was safely away from camp, of course. I didn't want to bump into it in the middle of the night while going to the latrine. The latrine was another tree, downwind from camp. The shovel sat beside that tree, its tip buried in the ground, handy and convenient.

With the remaining hours of daylight, I explored, caught my supper, and hid the johnboat down the island a ways. It was a simple matter to cover it with bracken and the leafy lower limbs of a live oak. I was still enjoying fish, and had fried crappie with lots of black pepper that night. I even opened a treat I had picked up from Montgomery's shop. A bottle of aged single-malt whiskey. I wasn't much of a whiskey drinker, but it did seem to complement the crappie.

That night, with a tin cup of whiskey in one hand and a tin cup of coffee on a makeshift table, I pulled out Montgomery's second portable phone and called Castalano at home. I needed the sound of a human voice. And not one that would make me cry.

"'Ello."

"Calleux."

"I knew I shouldn'ta' give you dat name." But she sounded pleased to hear from me.

"The world still out there?"

"Most a it. And most a it is lookin' fo' you, girl."

"Oh yeah?"

"Yeah. You know a pretty boy? Dark hair, black eyes, Frenchy-lookin'?"

She could have been talking about most of the parish, but I took a chance, sipping the whiskey. "Adrian Paul Rousseau?"

"De very one. He' pretty pissed at you, girl. And so's his wife."

"Wife?" The whiskey sloshed in the tin cup, spilling on my hand.

"Mus' be. I never knew a man yet could put up wid a mouth like dat, 'less 'e was married to it."

I grinned out over the black night. Sonja. "Dark hair? Short? Designer clothes?"

"Don' you forget her mouth."

"She's his sister-in-law."

"Yeah, well, anyway. They come by yest'day. Spotted de Rover from de street. Wanted me to follow you in and bring you back."

I laughed, watching a bat swoop at my campfire and flit away.

"They don' know much 'bout bayou country, eh?"

"Very little," I admitted.

"I tol' dem you had de phone. Figur' you call dem soon enough. Dey stayin' at you' ol' place till dey hear from you. Which I hope is soon."

"Why's that, Calleux?"

"Look. You got to call me a name, call me Cacahuete. Is what de boys call me down to de sto'."

"Okay, Peanut."

"But no Caca."

"I promise," I said, laughing. God, how I had missed the sound of another human voice.

"Anyway. Dey mus' a call' a dozen time' t'day. Lookin' fo' you. Askin' fo' you. Then the police come by. De sheriff."

"Terry Bertrand?"

"Yes'm. Dat hem."

Terry Bertrand was still sheriff, but for how long was uncertain. The state boys were looking into his role in my kidnapping back in the hurricane. I hadn't pressed charges, but the state boys didn't take kindly to cops stepping over the line. They were pursuing the matter on their own.

"He was here. Unofficial, you unnerstan'. Askin' questions. I tol' hem de same as I tell de others. You done gone into de Basin. Dat's all."

"Yeah. Well. Anyone else?"

"'Fraid so. A DeLande. De one wears de hat—"

"Miles Justin."

"—and boots. He was drunk. Well, don' know 'bout drunk, but he was drinkin'. And he was plen'y upset, I tell you."

"What did he say?"

"Say he was comin' aft' you, but you got away."

"I'll call him later."

"I figure' you do dat. He stayin' at de Ol' Fishin' Hole Hotel nex' to Loreauville."

"That dump?"

I could practically see her shrug. "You wan' de number?"

"Please."

She gave me the phone number and the room number, and we said our good-byes. But before I called Miles, I called home. I thought maybe I could take it now. Talk to them, hear them, without crying. I was wrong. The tears started when the receiver left the cradle.

"Collie?"

Not even a hello. "Wolfie."

"Where the hell are you?" She sounded afraid. Not like my old friend at all. She hadn't even cussed me.

"In the Basin."

"Why?" She was crying, which made it harder for me to control my own tears.

"So the DeLandes can find me, Wolfie. On my own terms. So no one else gets hurt."

"You silly, stupid ass. I'd have taken care of you. You've got money now. Adrian Paul told me how much." That was a breach of lawyer-client privilege, but I wasn't exactly in a position to sue over it. "You could hire a friggin' army for that much." She sniffed.

"And be looking over my shoulder for the rest of my life. Eventually they would find me. And then they would get the kids. I can't let that happen."

"The Department of Social Services is looking into the DeLandes. Pretty soon—"

"Pretty soon it'll all blow over," I interrupted. I couldn't let her talk me back. I knew I was making the right decision. *I knew it.* "Pretty soon another scandal will hit the press, and then the officials who've been eating out of DeLande pockets will quietly shove the case under the carpet, or lose it, or . . . This is the only way, Wolfie."

"Adrian Paul is here," she said in a small voice. "He wants—"

"No." I hadn't meant to shout. "Just tell him . . . tell him thank you. He'll know what for. And I'll see you all soon. I gotta go, Wolfie."

I cut the connection, then broke down and cried. I cried all the whiskey out of my system, and all the fear. Well, most of it. It was an hour before I had myself under control enough to call the Fishing Hole Hotel and ask for room 127. Pretty fancy for a joint that has only twelve rooms. But they do offer clean sheets, HBO, and Playboy for one low price: $19.95 in season. Fishing season, that is. It's $15.95 out of season. The hookers think it's right reasonable. Or so I hear.

Miles answered on the first ring, the TV blaring in the background. "Hello."

"Miles."

The TV was instantly muted. "Collie?"

"Speaking." I was so polite. The nuns would have been proud.

"Where are you?"

"Waiting for you. Who all's coming for dinner? I was planning on fried catfish, but you'll have to bring the potatoes and a salad. And the hush puppies." I was rambling, but I was nervous. "I'm fresh out of greens and low on flour and cornmeal. No beer either."

"I'll keep that in mind." I could hear the wry laughter in his voice. Why did he have to be one of them?

"What's the Eldest got planned for me, Miles? The same thing you boys did to Ammie?" He sucked in a deep breath. "Or more along the line of what you watched happen to Eve Tramonte?" I said softly. He didn't respond. "Are you planning on helping?"

"I'll be there. I'm sorry, Collie." And he did sound sorry. For a DeLande.

"You remember the place Old Man Frieu took us once, to see the alligators mate?"

"I remember."

"Think you can find it again?"

"Yes." His voice was so soft and sad, it would tear your heart out. Except that might be what he was planning to do to me anyway.

"I'll be waiting." I clicked off the phone and stuffed it in its carrying case. Even if they left at daybreak, it would take them all day to get here. It would be morning after next before I would see them. Plenty of time to have a good cry.

CHAPTER

15

The temperature finally made the low seventies that afternoon, just before the bottom fell out. Do Yankees use that term, I wonder, for a deluge, or big trouble? Well, my big trouble started with rain. Lots of rain. Even under the lean-to I couldn't keep a fire going. And no self-respecting fish would be feeding in this downpour. The black surface of the bayou turned white with the splash of the heavy rain. It was army ration time.

But first, I had a shower. The rain was fairly warm and steady, and rinsed the dishwashing liquid out of my hair and off my body quite well. I stood in the rain for fifteen minutes before I finally slipped naked into my tent and shivered until I was dry. I don't care how warm the low seventies feels in the middle of winter, it's too cold for an outside shower.

Just before sunset, with the temperature dropping, the sky blew clear. It was then that I smelled smoke. Someone's cook fire. The DeLandes. I stood up in my tent, clean and damp and not quite prepared for them. They were early. Just as suddenly as the smoke blew in, it blew away, leaving the air rain-swept and fresh.

I had expected them in the morning. But they didn't have to trailer supplies. And they probably rented a boat for the ride in. How long had they been there? Since before the rain? Would they chance moving on the bayou at night when the water and the sky above are the same shade of midnight black?

A DeLande would chance anything.

I looked down at my hands. They were shaking again, and it had nothing to do with the cold. I took the big old lantern, the one Montgomery used when he hunted elk with Terry Bertrand . . . or was it moose? . . . and wrapped it in my damp, dark, filthy slacks to hide the light. Tucked it into my sleeping bag on its bed of moss. I added some of my supplies. The two kettles, more dirty clothes, the phone. Feeling all the while like a kid pulling a prank at summer camp. Stuffing my bedroll so the counselor would think I was sleeping instead of skinny-dipping with the boys in the lake.

Carefully I set the sack of cottonmouths on the open sleeping bag as well. Untied the mouth of the sack and dropped the slow-moving things onto the cold bed.

They were lethargic, ready to hibernate. Cold from the rain and the falling temperature. I laid the flap of the sleeping bag over them slowly, cutting out the faint light. I turned out the lantern. When I turned it back on, the bag would warm from the heat of the lantern. The snakes would migrate to the warmth. Become active and restless.

Under the lean-to I started the stove and made a pot of coffee. A full pot. I drank the coffee black, sitting on the shore where I could be clearly seen, watching an egret fish in the shallows. I wished for cream and sugar, and hot beignets. I made a second pot of coffee and filled the thermos, and a third pot to sip on until full dark settled upon me. I wondered what had happened to my ulcer. All these days on little but coffee and fish, and not a twinge.

Army rations heated were only slightly better than army rations cold. But I ate. Sitting before the little stove, glad of the warmth, I made a spectacle of myself for any DeLande who might be watching. I combed out my still damp hair, dried it in the heat of the stove, and braided it again. One long French braid down the back of my neck, starting high on my crown. Then I pinned it up. My hair had grown out during the last year. It nearly touched my waist now, even braided. The whole time I sat, I drank coffee.

After dark, I rearranged the campsite like I wanted it. Trying to stay out of the dim stove light, I put some supplies where they wouldn't be discovered in a cursory search. The snake hook went in the lower branch of a chenier near shore, so I could retrieve my snakes later. One five-gallon container of water, I lugged from the boat, where the canisters had all remained during my days on the island. I hid it in the dark behind the lean-to. Other necessities, I scattered around in the darkened campsite.

Turning off the stove, wishing I could take it with me into the tent, I zipped the flap shut. In the dark of the tent, I dressed more warmly, gathered my supplies and weapons, turned on the lantern in the sleeping bag, and slipped out the back of the tent. I hated to cut through a perfectly good tent, but going out the front way was out of the question.

Moving as silently as I could, I walked through the black night toward the swamp at the far side of the island. A dead fish odor carried on the breeze, sour and rank. There was a tree I wanted, an old chenier, bent and twisted like a full-sized version of one of Mama's bonsai.

On the day I had gone exploring, I had found the old oak, climbed it, and chose the broad limb on which I could sit comfortably to watch my campsite. In the early night there was no moon, and I didn't dare use a flashlight in case someone was watching the island. After what seemed like hours, I found the old oak in spite of the lack of moonlight. Tripped and fell smack into it actually, but it was right where it was supposed to be. I secured my supplies in the limbs and climbed up beside them, settling myself for the wait.

It was a long one, well after midnight before I heard anything, and then only the faint slap of oar against water. I'd never learned the trick of that, rowing silently.

The mosquitoes were bad, the warm weather of the last week hatching out thousands from wherever mosquitoes lay eggs in the fall. Mosquito repellent worked pretty well, but I forgot to put it along the back of my neck up high, where my braid left more bare skin exposed than usual. I suffered several bites in the tender area before I remembered to put on some of the sticky white cream.

Bats dove and flitted. An owl's heavy wings beat the air. Crickets and tree frogs filled the night with a chorus of sound. Time ceased to have meaning.

My legs went to sleep twice. But my heart, stimulated by too much caffeine, kept the rest of me awake. The moon rose low on the horizon, casting shadows through the treetops, ghostly shadows on the ground.

The scream shattered the night. Horrified and terrified, full of pain, the sound of someone whose nightmares had just become reality. My heart pounded. A hot sweat broke out on my skin. The howling went on and on. I couldn't see my watch. Couldn't see anything. Even with the binoculars.

Minutes passed as the screams continued, agonized and wounded. Was I in the right tree? Was I looking in the right direction? The screams suddenly grew softer, panting, more frantic. A desperate sound in the night. A gurgle.

"Collie?" Miles's voice, shouting. Odd sound to it. Amusement. And something else.

"Nicole!" Richard, angry. "Nicole, I know you're out there. I know it. I can smell you, bitch."

Bats, startled by the screams, swooped through the trees.

"I watched you in the rain, bitch, strutting that little body. We all did."

My face burned. I unzipped the khaki jacket. The panting sound became grunts, labored.

"Andreu liked it so much, he claimed the Eldest's right to

have you first. You hear me?" His voice resounded through the trees, echoing off down the bayou. Eerie and wailing. Then silence. Only the grunting coming from the campsite, the sounds echoing off the trees, seeming to come from everywhere and from nowhere.

The moon was bright, and I could see a faint mist through the trees, rising from the black water. The grunts slowed into a faint wheeze, then stopped.

"He wanted you first. All my sisters liked Andreu. Just like they liked Montgomery. Said they were good. The best." He laughed, the sound sliding into the mist. "Could always make 'em come, you know. But they're both dead now, Nicole."

I bit my lip, pulled the 9mm. Held it with shaking hands, in the dark, sweating with fear.

"You killed both of them. Andreu . . ." He paused, then chuckled again, the sound hanging in the tree limbs around me like bats at rest. "Andreu hated snakes, Nicole. One of your toys, all warmed up in your sleeping bag, got him in the throat. You know what a cottonmouth can do to a man's breathing when it takes him in the throat, Nicole? He turns red and swells up instantly with a pain like acid eating away at him inside."

Richard laughed again. He sounded truly amused, as if it were all a marvelous joke, this deadly summer camp prank I had envisioned earlier. "And then his breathing passages begin to swell shut, Nicole. And he screams with the pain until the poison suffocates him. And he dies.

"But you forgot one thing, Nicole. Andreu's being dead makes me the Eldest. Did you forget that? Or did you ever know what that meant?"

He waited, almost as if we were having a quiet conversation, and it was my time to speak. I was cold suddenly and shivered in the tree.

A night breeze filtered through the limbs of the chenier. The bayou seemed to sigh. The mist lifted and settled as if with the movement of its chest. The smell of the earth was musky, the soil rich and damp. The water a faint delicate scent underlying it all.

"The Eldest makes all the decisions. In business, and in the family. He gets first choice of all the sisters and nieces and even the little boys. I'm not picky, Nicole. I'll fuck anything. You hear me?" His voice rose on the last words and carried down through the night. There was anger now in his voice. Fury. Not like Montgomery's contained and deliberate rage. Richard's anger was blazing. Uncontrolled.

"You hear me? When I finish with you, I'm going back to Moisson and take your children. They'll be mine, Nicole, because no one will be able to find them. You hear me?"

I swallowed in the silence, my hands gripping the gun. The breeze died. An owl hooted in the distance, the sound haunting and serene.

"I already got little Dessie ready for it. And I'll use her till she wishes she was dead."

Tears started then. Tears of anger, and impotence, and fear.

"You hear me?" he screamed. The sound of his words bounced off trees, off the water.

There was a light then. A flare of fire, too quick, too intense, to be anything but gasoline. I holstered the SIG and raised the binoculars to my eyes, focused on the campsite through the trees. They had set all my firewood aflame under the lean-to. They had dumped a bucket of gasoline over my partially dry wood and set a match to it. It blazed up high, even setting alight the lean-to that had protected it. The wood burned merrily, looking falsely welcoming and cheery in the distance.

I could see Andreu in the firelight, spread-eagle on the ground, face up to the night sky, his head thrown back, his chest bare and bloody, as if he had clawed himself before he died. Both hands were buried in the wet soil, outstretched to his sides, gripping the earth.

The flames danced in the night, throwing shadows that

brought the trees alive. Two forms moved in my campsite, elegant, refined. That uncanny smoothness of movement every DeLande possessed. That dignity and grace that made even the most mundane gesture a dance. In anger, it was a savage dance. They were burning my campsite.

They torched my tent. I hadn't expected that somehow. What had I expected? That they would see the snakes, get scared? Run back to the Grande Dame with their tails between their legs?

Richard was now the Eldest.

I dropped the binoculars on their strap, to hang around my neck, pulled my khaki jacket closer, and tucked my cold hands into the sleeves. I waited. Near dawn, Richard cried out again.

"Nicole! Listen to me, bitch!"

It was the blackest part of night, the dark just before the sky faded gray. The moon was far down on the horizon, a mist thick and heavy, with a slow wind movement along the treetops. I could see it billow around me. I stretched on my branch, trying to find a comfortable position, feeling the prickles and electric pain of human limbs waking from a too long sleep. My muscles were numb from poor circulation.

Almost irreverently I realized that Richard was the only DeLande I had ever heard use profanity . . . with the rare exception of the few words Montgomery had used as he beat me. I don't know why I found that amusing, but I chuckled. The sound carried on the still air. Ghostly laughter.

"You got nothing left, bitch. You won't find it so funny when you get thirsty. Or hungry. We found the water can you left in the dark behind the tent. It showed up real fine in the light of your burning supplies."

"My water," I whispered, laying my head against the rough bark. "No." Dumb. And where had I put the water purification tablets? . . . In the tent, of course. Which was now ashes. "Oh God." Very dumb.

I heard a motor start, followed by three shots, then the purr of a powerful engine down the bayou. I prayed the engine would foul in the water lily roots, but God wasn't listening to me today. The motor, echoing in the darkness, magnified by the fog, sped up, moving into the distance.

Why had they left? I had expected them to take the snakebite victim back to civilization for help, a trip that would have taken an entire day. A day during which I could prepare for phase two of my plan, which involved a direct confrontation with my brothers-in-law. But Andreu had died . . . so why leave? My clear, easy-to-follow plan was suddenly less clear.

I crawled from the tree, falling the last few feet and landing hard, my thigh bruised by roots. My face hit the dirt. I was lying down anyway, so I rested, shed a few tears that had been building up in the night, my breath loud in the white/black mist and dark. If a DeLande was waiting on the island to take me, he'd have no trouble finding me. Just follow the sound of the whining right to my feet. But I was alone. Just me and the bugs and the bats and the nutria and the spiders.

I cried until my nose ran and my voice gave out and I was weak as a baby. It was a perfectly delightful cry. I was snotty, exhausted, and had a headache. A ten as far as cries go. I had never cried much in my lifetime, but since getting pregnant with Jason, and since leaving Montgomery, I seemed to cry all the time.

I got up, pulled my supplies out of the chenier, and looked them over. I drank some of my hot coffee, took some aspirin, and ate a quick energy ration bar—cardboard with sugar on it. Left over from the Middle East war. Even the hungry Iraqis hadn't wanted it. Vile stuff.

My campsite was ruined. Still smoking. Everything either burned or broken, including my little stove. I managed to save a charred ball of twine, my fishing net, which could be mended with the twine, my rod and reel, and some hard plastic lures from the tackle box. The soft, squiggly, worm-looking ones favored by bass were melted.

I avoided the rough place in front of my burned-out tent.

The ground was raw and scraped, scored with superficial scratches and grooves, as if someone had clawed the earth with his hands as he died. *Was Andreu really dead? It should have been Richard.*

The thought surprised me, and I stood in the dawn light staring into the mist. I suppose, somewhere in the recesses of my mind, I had thought Richard would die by the snakes. It was his body I kept picturing, writhing on the ground and dying. And where was the remorse? The agony I should have felt at killing another human being? I piled my supplies together and walked down to the bayou, drinking the last of my coffee from the thermos.

I don't think my daddy would approve the uses to which I had put his training. The education he had provided. So far, I'd shot one man and poisoned another with snakebite. Both had died because of skills taught me by him. I'd have to send Daddy a thank-you note. If I survived this.

My johnboat, hidden in the limbs I had thought would protect it from sight, was full of water, sunk to the black bottom of the bayou in about two feet of water. It sank because it had three holes in it. The bullets had passed first through the water canisters, then through the aluminum boat bottom.

I stood watching the boat on the bayou bottom as if it might heal itself and float. It didn't. The light brightened around me.

I had no backup plan to handle the loss of my boat.

I wasn't coming up with any dynamic replacement plans either. My mind was blank.

Little tendrils of dread seemed to thread their way into my soul, freezing my ability to think. To plan. The image I had once seen as clearly as a flower opening was suddenly dead and wilted.

I waded into the water, salvaging the long pole, the oars, and the life vests. My shoes and feet were wet, but I had plenty of coals to dry them over, thanks to the DeLandes. *Always look on the bright side.* That was Mama's advice. I wondered what bright side she had looked on when her father was molesting her. Or if she just looked on the bright side because the dark side was too unbearable to face.

I packed up my supplies and used an oar to poke through the smoldering tent. I found the black melted mess of the phone and the warped plates of the Kevlar vest. Money down the drain. It was almost amusing.

I found the water purification tablets. They were a bit scorched, but they were all I had, so I stuck them in my shirt pocket. The jar of tablets was warm against my skin, and transferred the warmth to the rosary where it lay between my breasts. I had forgotten about it.

I found three of the snakes. Dead. I hoped the one that got Andreu had gotten away. A reprieve for good behavior. I added a dented kettle to the pile and surveyed my heap of supplies. There was too much. And not nearly enough. At least I had taken all the army ration packs to the chenier with me in the night. They didn't know I had them.

I left the oars and the pole, but took my snake hook, the weapons, fishing equipment, and the rations, stringing what I could to the snake hook and to the life jacket. I was still standing in the campsite trying to decide what I really needed to take and where to go, now that I didn't have transportation, when I heard the boat. Powerful thrumming down the bayou, the sound carried for miles on the fog.

They were back. I turned and ran from the campsite, carrying everything I had over my shoulders. Pick a direction. Any direction.

I stopped, breathing in deep. Trying to force the panic from my mind. Then I struck out for snake island. Snakes were my friends, right? And they hated DeLandes.

I ran as long as I could before the stitch in my side forced me to slow down. I walked as long as I could before I was forced to stop and lighten the load. I left the kettle, the shotgun, the binoculars, the fishing rod, and my cold weather clothes except for the khaki jacket, tying them all in a tree, high off the ground. I couldn't figure out why I had taken the kettle anyway. Panic.

Sweat was pouring down my body. Fear. I stank with it. Heaving breaths, I tied the scorched twine with shaking fingers, the bark tearing at my knuckles. And then I heard it. The dog. Baying behind me.

I dropped forward, resting my hands on my knees, fighting the darkness at the edges of my vision. "Dogs," I gasped. "Okay, Mama. Only one dog. The bright side. Right." My voice was hoarse from crying, then running, breathing in the early morning air. I stood up and moved on, pounds lighter, but less protected. If it rained, I'd be soaked. If it turned off cold again, like it should, I'd freeze. If I needed the shotgun, too damn bad. "Of course, I'll be lucky to live out the day. How's that for the bright side, Mama?"

I hadn't spoken to my mama in some nine months. And here I was talking to her just because I was going to die. I wished I still had the damn phone. I'd call her. Ask her how to handle this little inconvenience. Find out if simply being strong would work. I laughed beneath my breath, feeling a little light-headed. A little crazy. The stitch had returned, a hot pincher of pain in my side. And then I ran out of island.

Every bit of so-called dry land in the Basin is an island, especially in the rainy season. Winter. Now. Swamp or bayou surrounds every square inch of earth. I had been running in squelchy, wet soil for some time, not even noticing the way the mud sucked and pulled with each step. The way the water-soaked ground was harder and harder to traverse. Until it was suddenly gone. No more land. Just black water and lily pads and an alligator sunning itself— himself?—on the far shore.

Where had all the mist and darkness gone? My plaint sounded like a sixties flower-child song.

I had filled the thermos and the canteen with bayou water before I left the campsite and dropped half of one of the water tablets in each. The directions had been burned off the bottle, and I didn't know how long to wait, or if there was too little water in the thermos to handle the tablet. One tablet might have been good for a gallon.

I drank the whole thermos, so thirsty I didn't even notice the taste, if it was nasty or not. I just dipped up more water in the empty thermos, added another half tablet, and screwed on the lid. I suppose I could have left the thermos with the shotgun, but the canteen cover was damp around the seams. I thought it might be leaking. Even though the thermos was bulky, I carried it along.

I checked the pearl-handled 9mm and the starburst rounds. I had two full clips loaded with starbursts, each holding nine rounds. I had left the regular shells with the shotgun. If I couldn't do what I had to do with eighteen rounds . . . What was I going to do anyway?

Kill the DeLandes.

The thought rocked me. I had never allowed the actual words in my mind. "Coward," I whispered.

I wrapped the SIG and the extra clip in the waterproof bag provided by Castalano, floated the life vest on the still water, added the knapsack filled with ration packets, the thermos, the khaki jacket, the snake hook, and the handgun. Everything was secured with the straps of the life vest so nothing could fall off. Miraculously, the unwieldy bundle floated. Last thing, I pulled down my pants and urinated in several places along the shore, then secured my pants and slipped into the water.

The dog was noticeably closer. I could have relieved myself in the water, but every country girl knows that hunting dogs can't track if their noses get confused. The impact of urine was always confusing. Maybe it would buy me a little time.

The bayou had no noticeable current, but I moved south, in the direction I thought was downstream. Only feet from shore, my boots sank in mud, tangling in the limbs of dead trees. Oh well. I had never gotten them dry anyway.

I made good time, sliding around the bend in the bayou before I remembered the gator. I looked back; the water behind me was still. No alligator. I crossed the water to the other side, wetting myself to the shoulders on the way across, and stepped on the shore, my hand against my side. The stitch was still there. A tight ache, a rare spasm.

The sky was the blue of Montgomery's eyes when he was angry. The sun blinded, leaving a bright yellow orb against my eyelids when I closed them. Half the day was gone. And the dog was closer. I could hear men's voices, diffused by the trees, their words lost in the distance.

A sudden cramp caught me, spreading out from the stitch in my side, engulfing me in spasms of pain. I fell to my knees, curling into a fetal ball. Whoever heard of hunting with just one dog? Must be a damn good one. If I survived this, I'd end up cussin' as bad as Sonja did. Maybe worse. The spasm eased. Finally disappeared entirely.

I dragged myself to my knees, still gasping, stripped off my wet work shirt, and tied it around my waist. My T-shirt was wet, and clung to me like a transparent second skin, the rosary and my nipples clearly visible beneath.

Wrapping everything in the knapsack, tying the sleeves of the khaki coat to it, and hooking the canteen over my shoulder with the snake hook, I set out. Which way? Away from the dog, of course. Some decisions in life are so simple.

I moved along the bank of the bayou, stepping carefully, watching for snakes and gators sunning themselves. This was snake island. I needed a tree. A chenier, ancient and weathered. A big mother tree, to quote Old Man Frieu.

Much later, the dog was closer. I imagined I could hear his breathing, snuffling and blowing. But the men's voices seemed no more distinct. Perhaps my mind was going. Seemed likely. My feet were steaming and raw in the wet boots. My breath was a bellows. The cramp in my side had stretched and moved down into my bowels, a constant hot pain. My back and legs were so tired, I couldn't bear to go another step, yet I pushed on, leading the dog and men past a half dozen snakes, sunning themselves. Maybe a DeLande would step on one and die.

I crossed another bayou, moving along the shoreline, drank more water, urinated on the ground, and moved back across again. I should have been an Indian. Actually, there was some Indian in Daddy's lineage. Of course, Mama had been devastated to learn of the fact. Yes. My mind was going.

And then I saw my tree. A gnarled old oak, its limbs twisted gracefully out over the water and far back onto shore. Easy climbing. I urinated again, drank all my water, even that in the canteen. It was half-empty. Definitely leaking. I made more. I couldn't tell if the water tablets were working or not. My abdomen was twisted in knots and aching, but whether from bad water or too much exercise, I couldn't tell. I did know my hips were aching.

I climbed the tree, my supplies slung over my shoulder, trying to remember what it was about hip joints and pregnancy. Something about the joints in the entire pelvic region getting soft so the baby could spread out the bones when it passed through the birth canal. Something like that. God in his infinite wisdom didn't plan on a woman running for her life through bayou country and climbing trees two months or so after delivering a baby.

I climbed the bark-covered trunk, pulling myself up on branches, my wet boots more a hindrance than a help till I got to a fat limb. I climbed all around the circumference of the tree, finally choosing a place about twenty feet off the ground. It was a massive limb, stretching out over the water, actually touching the branches of a smaller tree on the other side. It was a good thing I had stopped. The land and water converged just ahead, forming a thick, slimy mush. Swamp. Impassable.

The bayou spread out, the bottom came up, the water stilled completely. Thick green slime coated the surface of the water. Algae. Cypress trunks rose out of the slime, stunted and twisted. Oak and hickory grew up in places where the water wasn't quite as deep. All were heavy with moss. Hundreds upon hundreds of the ubiquitous mosquitoes buzzed low on the water. Cypress knobs, the rounded remains of old dead trees, protruded above the water.

It was Old Man Frieu's swamp, the several-miles-wide sour mire I had passed on my way in days ago. I had come miles back along my pathway, but this time overland. Not in a boat. No wonder I had blisters all over my feet.

I moved out over the water to a fork in the limb and sat, wrapping my legs around the limb. I unslung the knapsack and ate a lovely meal. Chicken Cordon Bleu. Cardboard with melted cardboard cheese and shredded cardboard rice. This stuff didn't reconstitute well without heat. Just add water and feast on crap.

Really. Mama would wash out my mouth with soap. Except that there was no soap. I began to dry out as the dog and men grew closer. I stank, smelling myself even above the smell of the swamp behind me.

It was a beautiful day for a romp through the swamp. Low eighties, cloudless, soft breeze. Springtime. If I weren't so exhausted, I might have enjoyed it. Stretching out on the limb, my face to the sky, I fingered the stitch in my side. It was really a bad one.

I closed my eyes, breathing shallowly. The dog was closer. Soon. Soon. I tried not to think about Miles.

A featherlight touch on my face. On my hand. I sat up, gripping the limb with my legs. Thrashing my arms. Slapping my face. Trying not to scream.

Spiders. Oh God. Spiders. There was one inside my T-shirt. Crunched it with my fingers. Black spider blood staining the dirty cloth. I slapped and slapped.

The heat had called them out of sleep. Or they just hatched this big. One got caught in the fold of my elbow and bit in with fangs, its legs braced on my skin. I caught it up in my fingers and threw it out over the water. Lost my balance. Fell. Silently to the water.

I didn't scream. I even kept my mouth closed. But the splash resounded out over the water, through the trees.

The water was deep here. No bottom. I fought the pull of the depths with waterlogged boots. Heavy. My head broke the surface. Went under. I saw a spider crawling through the water. Drowning. *Die, you ugly thing. Die.*

I broke the surface again. I could hear the dog. So close. No time to make it back to the tree. I struck out, swimming with my arms only, letting my feet hang heavy until they hit bottom.

I swam until I was knee-deep in water, close to shore. I tried to stand, my feet sinking to my knees in mud. I made it to shore. To firm ground.

I could hear the dog. Hear Richard. Cursing. Shouting. So close.

No time for the tree, for the weapon waiting above. I could see them move through the trees on the shoreline.

No place to run but the swamp. They wouldn't expect that, would they? That I'd go into the swamp. I could go in a little way, lose them, and backtrack. Circle around for the gun.

I looked at the sun, glinting so peacefully through the lace of the tangled tree limbs above, picked up my heavy feet, and ran.

I ran till the earth got squishy. Then vanished beneath slime. And still I ran. Splashing through the muck, sometimes knee-deep, sometimes deeper. Once I slipped, fell, and went facedown in the sludge, filling my mouth with the awful stuff.

I gagged and spat. The rosary swung on its chain, beating the air, then my chest, with slow, lazy thumps.

The stench was unbearable. I passed something dead lying half under the water. Nutria were feeding on the carcass.

I looked back. Stopped. Breath so painful, it was like flames searing my lungs with each labored breath.

I had left a trail. Wide and broken. They wouldn't even

need the dog to follow me. And there would be no going back for the gun. The slime hadn't closed together behind me. My passage was marked with a wide black strip, mud swirling on the surface.

I glanced at the sun and changed direction, hoping I was now moving toward the old man's cabin, back toward the bayou. And the shotguns Frieu had hanging on the walls.

I could hear them, just behind me. To either side. But no dog. Wonder what they did with the dog.

I started running again. Ran till I had no more breath left and sobbed with each step. My mouth was parched, and my exposed skin covered with sweat and mosquitoes. My skin was stinging with a hundred lash marks. My hands were bleeding. Attracting more mosquitoes. Probably other hungry things as well.

I was forced to breathe with my mouth closed to keep the cloud of stinging pests out of my lungs. I fell. Stumbled to my feet. Rested my hand on a cypress knee. The rounded wood was warm and slick beneath my sweaty fingers.

My heart thudded in my ears, my breath so loud, I couldn't hear my pursuers anymore. It was getting dark. Oh God. Not night in a swamp. Tree frogs started their grinding sound. An alligator roared.

A huge spider, the size of my hand, lifted a leg beside my thumb, questing. I crushed it under my palm. "Bastard," I whispered.

The shot took me through the left side. I felt the burning even before I heard the blast. Fell to my knees. Driven forward by the force of the shot.

I looked down in the sudden gloom. Clean hit. In and out, back to front. High in the lower left quadrant, at the waistline. Too low for kidney. But maybe the spleen? A loop of intestine?

My mind was crystal-clear in that moment. No emotion. No fear. Just logic. Clear, precise thinking as if my mind were illuminated by bright white light.

How long did I have? How long could I survive with a hole in my side? Keep moving. The cabin was just ahead. Wasn't it?

I splashed forward. Moving slowly. Fighting to stay on my feet.

Richard laughed. "Nicole. You look a bloody mess, girl."

A copse of trees ahead. Maybe a half dozen. High ground? A place to sit? A cramp stopped me for a long, breathless moment. Another step. Another.

"I'm going to enjoy taking you, Nicole. Even with you all filthy and bleeding. And when I'm through, I'm going to string you up for the alligators."

I could hear him splashing toward me on one side. The sound of slower steps from the other side.

"Then, when I'm through, I'm going to go back, have a long, hot shower—" he drew out the words, making it sound wonderful, something to go through hell for "—and drink a gallon of cold ice water."

I brushed the tears from my eyes. Took another step. The ground was sloping upward. It was getting dark fast. Night comes swiftly in the swamp. Daylight one moment. Dark the next. Dry land. Only a few feet ahead.

"And then I'm going to go get Dessie. Fresh meat. You hear that, Miles? Maybe you'll change your mind, boy, when you see little Dessie. Miles don't like them young," he shouted, his voice aimed at me, "but he likes blondes."

Another step. Another. Blood running black down my side into the black water.

"Don't you, boy? I'll dress her up so she looks older. Then you'll take her. Right, boy? Hear that, Nicole? Fresh meat."

I sobbed, trying to hold in the sound. Just another step. Just one more.

A shotgun racked to my left. Movement to my right.

"Nicooooole," his voice rang out, singsong. "We got you." So close. Just behind me now, to the left. Laughing.

Movement in the gloom, immediately ahead. I looked up.

Startled. Into tiny eyes, like black beads in the night. Old Man Frieu, standing on dry ground in the copse of trees.

"Ge' down, gir'." Whispered.

I dropped into the water.

The blast was shattering. So close it burned my face with its heat. Took the sound of the swamp with it.

Richard screaming over the white noise of damaged ears. The sound of splashing. I turned, looked into a black hole the size of my fist. It was low down, at his waist. Blood, blacker than my own, blacker than the night, bubbled out. Splashed on the black water.

The sound of a shotgun racking again. "You move, bo', you die too."

Richard fell back into the water, screaming.

Miles lifted his hands above his head, his hunting rifle held high, balanced in both open palms. "It's a new gun. Don't want to ruin it," he said softly. His voice carried out over Richard's screams, his thrashing in the muck. Over the gasps and strangled cries. Amused. Elegant. A bit wry. A DeLande at his best.

Carefully he placed the rifle on dry ground, at the feet of Old Man Frieu. Raised his hands in the air again. Backed away a step. The barrel of the shotgun pointing at his midsection.

"You don't have to kill me, you know," he said, sounding playful, conversational. Hell, elated. As if this were a jolly good frolic, what, old boy?

Cramps lanced through me, doubling me over in the water. I couldn't breathe.

"Why's dat?"

"Because I don't want to hurt her. And because as soon as Richard dies, I'll become the Eldest. Except for Marcus, of course. But then he's half-dead anyway, so he doesn't count. And as Eldest, I choose to let Collie live. That's why."

So simple. So frivolous. So candid, as we all watched Richard squirm in the black water. Grunting like a dying animal. No words. Just the low, breathy grunting. An animal. Like Andreu. The air was filled with the scent of feces suddenly.

Miles chuckled softly. "My word on it, old man. My word."

"The word of a DeLande. It never mean' nothin'."

"The word of this DeLande does." The tone implacable. I couldn't see his face in the night. But I had a feeling Old Man Frieu could. And that he was remembering a stack of hundred-dollar bills, stuck through with a skinning knife. A wager paid.

Moments passed as Richard's breathing sped up. And my pain worsened. I'd never be able to stand. I was going to die here with Richard. Suddenly I smiled. Dessie was safe from Richard.

"What you smilin' 'bout, girl."

I ignored Old Man Frieu's question and looked at Miles, focusing on his dark form in the twilight. "Your word," I said. Just a whisper really, the sound snaking out over the still swamp. I had no breath for more. "Your word you'll leave us alone. You'll all leave us alone, including the Grande Dame."

A flash of teeth in the gloom as Miles smiled.

"The Grande Dame has no real power, Collie. No financial muscle. Not now. The Eldest has the most power. The most control of the family's finances. And every time a brother dies, his voting power—his proxy—passes to the Eldest. A peculiar arrangement, I agree, but then, we *are* the DeLandes. I *am* the DeLande, now."

So calm. He could have been in a boardroom talking to shareholders. I laughed, though no sound came from my mouth. A frenetic gasping sound only. *I was going to survive.* I wasn't going to die alone in the swamp with enemies at my heels and a dog on my trail.

"I . . . I want it in writing . . . when we get back. That you'll leave me and mine alone. My children. My life. And my finances," I added. Why not? It was something a DeLande could understand.

"Certainly. If you'll agree to sign over your proxies to me. Those not covered by the DeLande family contract. You can have the money. I just want the control. And first option on Montgomery's classic cars."

"Done." Whispered. No voice left. No breath left.

"Do you have a boat, old man? Will you float us out of here? I need a bath. Oh. And would you do me a favor and turn that shotgun away? Those things can be dangerous."

I laughed into the water finally, a soft gurgle of agony, clutching my body with pain. Oh God. There was nothing like a DeLande for unabashed arrogance.

Richard stopped struggling and lay still. The water closed up over his face.

Miles Justin lifted me in his arms, his face only inches from mine. I nearly screamed with pain. Waves of it. A burning agony. A rhythm of pain to the beat of my heart. He held me still for a moment, as if he sensed that even the slightest movement on his part would send me over the edge.

"You'll live, by the way."

I couldn't respond. I fought to catch my breath.

He started walking, following Old Man Frieu overland, placing his feet carefully on the mushy ground. "I put the shot in the one place I was sure you could live through."

"You?"

He chuckled under his breath, the vibration feeling almost good against my chest. The rosary was warm between us. The stench of the swamp fell away. I smelled honeysuckle, sweet on the air. "I'm a much better shot than Richard is . . . was. He said shoot. So I did. He might have done some real damage, had I refused and he shot you instead."

Before I could think of a reply, Miles Justin, the Eldest, placed me on the seat of a johnboat, then settled in beside me, taking me in his arms to cushion my body for the ride. The little two-cycle engine roared to life, filling the air with fumes. The swamp fell away, black water opened up before us. Black sky above. A quarter moon. Stars.

"It's okay, Collie," he whispered in my ear. "You're safe now. And so are your children."

EPILOGUE

Survival is a curious thing, a peculiar entity comprised of equal parts guilt, astonishment, a poignant bewilderment, shock, and wonder. I touch my hands, pressing on the little hurt where the IV slips beneath the skin, tracing the shapes and outlines of the bruises up my arms, smoothing the bulk of the bandages across my abdomen.

I am amazed at the life still beating and breathing within me, and oddly enough, a little sad, as if there are now two parts of me inside this body. One that watches, one that responds. One that observes, one that feels. It is disconcerting, this duality of nature. But I tell myself I will conquer it in time.

The nurses gave me a mirror today, so I could wash my face, comb my hair, apply a bit of lipstick, in honor of my first visit by the girls. I stared at myself for a long time in the little oval glass. I was still staring, my mouth pulled down in a faint frown, when Dessie and Shalene came in, bringing with them the smell of fried onion rings, plastic rain slickers, and the damp ozone scent of storm.

Putting away the mirror in the little drawer of the rolling

bedside table, I smiled and hugged them as tightly as the surgical staples, tape, and layers of gauze allowed. I said all the right things, mouthed all the proper phrases, and watched with surprise and awe and growing delight as they talked and teased and picked at each other. I don't know what they said. The content didn't seem to matter. It was only the fact of their safety and their happiness that had any significance at all.

Still . . . how will *I* adapt to the reality that I killed my husband? That I loved a man, respected a man, and lived with a man whom I didn't know at all.

His death at my hands hangs heavy around me. I breathe the knowledge of his death. I feel it cold on my skin like his cooling blood. And even now, I shiver at the memory of his body falling. Falling, and dying.

And yet I remember Montgomery on the first day I saw him, his blue eyes and lanky frame captivating every young girl for miles around. God knows I would have given my soul to have him look at me once. I almost did. I may have.

My sister's murder is the central fact of my life, and I live with it every day, like a blind man lives in the dark...

GLORIA

This extraordinary accomplished first novel will put the name Mark Coovelis firmly on the literary map. Echoing the atmosphere and powerful noir style of James M. Cain, GLORIA tells the absolutely riveting story of a man driven to penetrate the lies and secrets surrounding his beloved younger sister's death. And, in a spirit of modernism reminiscent of the work of Paul Auster, Mr. Coovelis reminds us that, in investigating the wrongdoing of others, we're often lured back into the treachery of our own hearts.

A Novel by
Mark Coovelis

"Stan Washburn brings wit and humanity to this taut narrative of the police pursuit of a serial rapist. Washburn shows assurance and a maturity unusual in first novels and admirable in any book."
—Richard North Patterson, author of <u>Degree of Guilt</u>

Blending unrelenting psychological suspense and a compasssionate, hauntingly realistic portrait of police investigation, *INTENT TO HARM* moves as swiftly and strikes as unpredicably as the terrifying assailant at its dark and mesmerizing heart—a savage serial rapist. What the novels of Thomas Harris have done for the inner workings of the FBI and the war of wits with the criminal mind, Stan Washburn now does with a police procedural that transcends the ordinary and transfixes its readers.

INTENT TO HARM

A NOVEL BY STAN WASHBURN

POCKET BOOKS

Available in hardcover from Pocket Books

966-01